SUZANNAH ROWNTREE

The House of Mourning

Watchers of Outremer, Book Five

In memory of Mariupol
a city containing 500,000 living images of God
yet none treated you as holy

Author's Note

This book depicts rape, but not explicitly. It also depicts religiously justified violence in the context of the medieval crusades, as well as war, violence, forced pregnancy, traumatic pregnancy, abuse of a pregnant woman, and references to pregnancy loss. I have done my best to communicate the truth of history in a way that is both accurate and sensitive, but if this kind of content may be triggering for you, please be aware and stay safe.

Prologue.

Jerusalem, 1185

The navel of the world lay within a tomb, within a church, within the holiest city in the world. Here at the centre of everything, Marta Bessarion stood in the narrow, hushed streets of Jerusalem with tears streaming down her face. The great fact, she thought, was that the tomb had been occupied, and was now empty. Christ was alive.

Christ was alive, but the Leper King was dead.

Marta had last seen Baldwin a week ago, having been summoned to his bedside for the first time in months. Of course, Lord Balian had told her the king was seriously ill; for some time, the great lords of the kingdom had gathered in Jerusalem debating terms of succession and *bailliship*. Part of her had been dreading the summons; a greater part had refused to believe it could really happen. Baldwin could not *die*. Not when he was still so very young. Not when the kingdom needed him like this; not when he had squandered himself so prodigally to rule—chairing meetings of the High Court, adjudicating bitter grievances among the barons, carried like a standard at the head of his army.

Not when she had entered the crumbling edifice of his spirit once already to drag him back from the brink of death.

At first, when she was admitted to the king's solar, Marta had felt a stab of hope. As always, open sores crawled across Baldwin's face and body; his eyes and nose were sunken cavities and his withered legs would never ride or walk again. Yet he sat propped up on his couch awaiting her in a fresh, crisp tunic made of rich blue silk that she had dyed and woven herself, patterned with threads of gold; and when she was announced he turned his head on the pillows, and what there was of his face creased in a smile.

"Baldwin," she said once the chamberlain had bowed himself out—it was her privilege to use the king's name without honorifics. "I've been misled. They told me you were…"

She stopped, realising that her voice did not sound as steady as it ought to. In the silence, Baldwin's breath came in heavy, rasping gasps.

"I don't want to die," he said in the end. "I thought—for such a long time—that I just wanted to rest. But I can't. I have work to do. White Watcher, please—if there's anything you can do…"

Marta had dared to touch him only once before; now she caught the bandaged hand reaching blindly towards her and leaned towards him until her forehead gently touched his. She closed her eyes, remembering how often she had heard people say that God loved the Leper King, that while he lived, the kingdom would be strong.

In the same moment, another memory stirred—a quavering old voice prophesying that his death would herald destruction. *After the Leper King, the fire.*

Please, was all she could think to pray. *Please, Sir God, we need him.*

This close, she smelled a faint perfume of balsam mingled with aloes and myrrh: the ointment with which the king was embalmed while yet living by his attendants from the Order of St Lazarus. More strongly she smelled the scent of decaying flesh, felt the quick fluttering beat of his heart and the laborious bellows-work of his lungs. She found herself counting them: *three, four, five,* but nothing changed. At length, softly, resignedly, he spoke.

"It's all right, Marta," he said between breaths. "You shouldn't—risk your life for me."

She let go of him, disappointed and angry with herself for not being able to do anything. "There's a gifted Watcher, a Healer, at the Hospital," she said. "Benjamin of Borca."

"Yes. I know."

"I wish I could *do* something."

"I know," he repeated. "There's one thing—you can do for me." Another rasping breath. "Protect them all when I am gone."

It was no more than she had already determined to do; all the home and family she knew was in this kingdom. "With my life, Baldwin. You can rely on that."

"Your life," he replied sadly. "It may take that—in the end. It did mine." He took another breath, no easier than the others, and managed another smile. "I want to give you something—but I don't know what. Virgin warrior saint—very difficult to impress."

She must have sighed, because he was certainly laughing at her. People compared her to Saint Marina of Antioch, to Saint Catherine of Alexandria, virgins who had died to protect their chastity. Marta could never help but feel that she was expected to follow suit.

Baldwin said, "Isn't it a grim reputation—to have to live up to? Trust me, I know. Ask something of me, Marta. Anything within my power to give."

That day, his death had still seemed impossible.

Now, Marta stood in the packed Jerusalem streets to watch the king's bier on its last journey. She had not known there were so many people in Jerusalem—lords and merchants, burgesses and craftsmen, slaves and peasants, and pilgrims from every nation under heaven. Some wailed, some quietly sobbed, but more simply stood in silence, as though aghast. Although the April day was unseasonably clear and sunny, it felt to Marta as though some thick darkness had come between herself and the sun.

The bier passed, preceded by the kingdom's clergymen and great nobles, followed by the Leper King's family. The chief mourner rode a white mule, a stiff and distant figure like a little doll: Baldwin the Fifth, now sole king at eight years old. His mother followed behind him, pale-skinned, dark-haired, leaning heavily upon a waiting-woman: Countess Sibylla, sister of the Leper King and the woman who should have been queen had the nobles not taken such a disliking to her husband. Others followed: the late king's young half-sister, Isabella; his stepmother, the Greek queen dowager, Maria Comnena.

Nearby, Marta overheard a woman asking, "What about the White

Watcher? Where is Marta the Knight?"

Fostered by Maria and Lord Balian of Ibelin, and rumoured to be close to the Leper King himself, Marta might indeed have taken her own place behind the bier. Lord Balian had certainly suggested it. Instead, she had hidden behind a thick black veil and tucked herself into a high doorstep overlooking the Street of the Patriarch where she might see without being seen. Her face was too well-known now to pass unnoticed, and today it was too ravaged by grief to risk being remarked upon.

After the ladies of the king's family came a great crowd of poor folk in the sturdy, dark-coloured new robes they had been given for the occasion, many going haltingly for lack of limbs that had been claimed by Saracen raids or Frankish justice, yet mourning lustily in pleasurable anticipation of the food and payment they would receive for the sake of charity afterwards. Then the procession turned onto the Street of Palms, where it would vanish within the holy darkness of the Holy Sepulchre, where the kings of Jerusalem were buried very close to Calvary, not far from the empty tomb itself. There was room for a great many people within the church, and Marta did not doubt that space would be made for herself. It would be a comfort to attend even the Latin liturgy, but again, she did not want to be seen. Her grief was her own. Tomorrow, perhaps, or next week, she would begin to do as Baldwin had asked her and look after his kingdom. Today she could only mourn.

She drifted with the crowd anyway as it closed on the heels of the mourners. Thinking again of the empty tomb so close to Baldwin's, Marta felt a stab of distress that the day was yet so far off when all tombs would empty and he would at last know the pleasure of a body not racked with agony and dying by inches. She did not wish to go in, but perhaps she would stand outside the Sepulchre to watch and listen and remember, repeating the liturgy in the comforting Greek of her childhood.

The thought was arrested by a touch on her arm. At first Marta supposed it was only some jostling in the crowd, but then the grasp firmed and she turned to see a weathered old woman, so ancient that the hands grasping her walking-stick were as gnarled and dark as the smooth-worn stick itself.

She squinted up at Marta through flyaway wisps of silver hair and spoke crisply despite the gaps in her teeth. "Run to the Temple, Marta Bessarion. Run and do not stop."

Marta's hand flew to the black veil that covered her face. How had the old crone recognised her in this crowd?

"Run!" the woman insisted, and something in the commanding voice shook loose a memory. She had seen this woman before: it was she who had appeared five years ago, when Marta was new to the kingdom, to prophesy fire after the Leper King's death. She was a Watcher—a Messenger, as Marta's own mother had been.

All the hair prickled on Marta's scalp and down her back, as though someone from an upper window had upturned a bucket of cold water down her neck. She turned, yanking at her skirts of grey linen and shortening them to the knee with a few quick practised tucks into her belt. Then she ran.

The Temple complex stood at the highest point of the city, on a broad platform green with fruit orchards and kitchen gardens. Marta was breathing hard by the time she mounted the steps of the Beautiful Gate and paused, snatching off her veil to see more clearly. At the centre of the platform to her left was a paved courtyard where the Temple of the Lord stood, a great, domed, octagonal church built in the Greek style, though with an odd lack of images. At the south end of the platform, to her right, a low but massive building squatted, lined with arches: the headquarters of the Knights Templar.

At first, she sensed nothing out of the ordinary, apart from the utter hush on the air: a bell tolled from the Temple, slow and mournful, and although there must be watchmen and servants on duty in the complex, no other sound could be heard. Today Jerusalem was struck speechless with grief. Even the mourning bells seemed unutterably far away.

Something white moved through the gardens ahead of her with a shimmer like desert heat. Marta's throat went dry and she shivered. Two years unrolled and she was back in Arabia, bathed in fire, while a seraph branded her forehead. She touched the place, smooth and unmarked now.

When she started forward again it was with eagerness; she forgot her shortness of breath.

Passing the very lemon-tree where Miles of Plancy had once kissed her, Marta turned the corner of the Temple courtyard and looked down towards the Golden Gate on the city's east wall, set within its small gatehouse. What she saw there drove all other conjecture from her mind.

A seraph waited at the gate, a white-hot dragon bright as a star. In that fierce light, all else seemed faded and lifeless by comparison: the sky was milky pale, and even the cypress trees were faded, blue as smoke. Marta swallowed hard and hurried closer, not wanting to keep the creature waiting. When she came as near as she could stand, however, she found that the seraph seemed to be speaking, and not to her: its head was lowered, its burning intelligent eyes fixed on some point in the air.

Marta stopped, waiting her turn while the air around her shimmered like glass. The grass beneath the great seraph's feet was burning cleanly, clearly, and disappearing without smoke or flame. She felt something like a vibration in the air, a thrum in her lungs, a vice that gripped her temples. She knew instinctively they were voices inaccessible to her ears. Perhaps if she heard the voices clearly, she, too, might burn to ash. The whole garden blazed with light and heat, all focused upon her, and all unbearable: she stood amidst fierce intelligences, the merest sight of which would annihilate her. Just as she was about to crumple from the burden of so much attention, the seraph bowed its head gracefully, as though bidding farewell to someone. It turned to her, and Marta sank to one knee.

"My lord," she whispered. "Will you kiss me again?"

The answer was in no voice that any onlooker might have heard. *You must use your own good judgement now, Marta Bessarion.*

Somehow, she still managed to feel heat rise in her cheeks. "Yes, my lord."

You will need it, the seraph told her. *This kingdom dares to call upon the Name of God, and its judgement is at hand. What you have been warned of is coming.*

Marta put a hand to her heart as it stuttered for a moment, leaving her out of breath. She felt as though the ground had dropped away from beneath her feet. "Is it true then? Are you leaving us?"

I have been the guardian of this kingdom long enough.

"Don't go," she choked. First Baldwin, and now the seraph. "How can I do this on my own?"

You will never be alone.

Again, she felt the press of those invisible others.

"But will you come back? Is there no mercy?"

Mercy for whom, daughter? For those who sit at ease in this kingdom, or for the captives toiling without hope, on the roads, in the workshops?

Marta put a hand over her mouth. She could not seem to say anything right today. "Tell me, then, what I should do."

You shall triumph over your enemy. Not by your spear, Marta Bessarion, but by your sword.

The creature bowed its head one more time in farewell and turned away, towards the gate. Marta stared at the scorched white dust where it had stood; knuckled the tears from her eyes, and glanced up to see where the creature had gone. It had already vanished. After a moment, a cool breeze soothed her hot skin.

Marta drew a deep breath. "I will triumph," she repeated softly. She would keep the kingdom standing, prevent another disaster like the one that had happened at Oliveta.

She got up slowly, but as she went down again into the city, she felt hollowed-out inside, like a bowl scraped clean in a famine.

Ask something of me, Baldwin had prompted her days ago. But the truth was, there was nothing he could give her.

She had everything she needed, except him.

"Give me your tears, Baldwin," she had whispered. "I am going to have to care for the kingdom without you, and I—I do not know how."

Chapter I.

Galilee, September 1186

A fly, glinting like steel in the sun, settled on the lip of Marta's water-bottle. She flicked it away and swallowed the last lukewarm dregs before returning the bottle to its place at her saddle-horn. If she didn't find a spring soon she would need to descend from the hills: between the late summer heat and the burden both she and her horse bore in armour, trappings, and equipment, it would be too easy for both of them to overheat and faint.

Not that water was easy to find, even in the lowlands. Last winter had been unusually dry. People were saying that the rain had stopped with the death of the Leper King, eighteen months before. Marta knew the drought was not her fault, but all the same she felt responsible.

Tugging her white hood forward to block the sun, she gently urged her horse—Pomers, the destrier Baldwin had given her when he could no longer ride—north along the sheep-path skirting the shoulders of the hills. To her left the ground was hilly and broken, perfect for concealing bandits. To her right the mountains of Gilboa descended sharply to a broad plain bordering the Jordan River; a road ran along it like a white ribbon, angled towards the distant whitewashed houses and dark cypresses of Bethsan. In the distance, Marta watched the caravan of travellers inching its way along that road—pilgrims making the journey from the holy sites clustered around Jerusalem to those in Galilee around Lake Tiberias, before taking ship at Acre for their homes in Alexandria, Constantinople or France. It was a small group—not large enough to merit a Templar escort, but still ripe pickings for the local bandits. From her vantage point in the hills, Marta kept pace with the distant travellers, having shadowed them ever since they had left Nablus at dawn.

The White Watcher was on the wing.

She crested a rise in the ground and found herself looking into a deep valley cutting between the tawny hills. There, near the road but screened from it by a tumble of honey-coloured rock and a tangle of low dark scrub, were the ruffians she sought—no doubt the usual motley collection of renegades of any religion, dressed in gaudy stolen finery and armed with a shoddy array of clubs, spears, slings, and knives. Last night in Nablus, the tale of their latest exploit had been the talk of the town. A local peasant had lost his entire herd of sheep to the marauders. Following the year's drought, crops had been bad and with the lords exacting half the harvest, as ever, some in the countryside were going hungry. The milk, cheese, and wool provided by his sheep must have been the only thing standing between this man's family and starvation. Overcome by despair, he had hanged himself.

From her vantage point, Marta assessed the terrain, picked out the best path into the valley, and let Pomers take the slope at his own careful pace. She used the time to buckle her helmet over her mail coif, unsling the Bessarion Lance from its place across her shoulders, and check that her crossbow was loaded and wound.

By the time the bandits' own lookout caught sight of the approaching pilgrims and signalled his fellows with a shrill whistle, Marta and Pomers had the even gravel of a dry watercourse underfoot. Urging the horse to a gallop, Marta thundered through the thin belt of trees that concealed her from the lurking robbers.

They heard her coming. Marta burst upon them as they were already turning, shouting, scrambling to their feet from the rocky outcrop overlooking the road. One of them loosed an arrow, which skipped harmlessly from her armour. Reversing her spear so that she was using the iron-shod butt-end, Marta cracked the pate of a burly man who came at her with a cudgel, tripped a knife-wielding boy who grabbed for her bridle, then spurred Pomers after a woman in a striped tunic who started to her feet and rushed towards the road. A rake of the spurs, a quick swipe of the Lance, and the female bandit was sprawled on the ground. Marta threw Pomers into a quick, skidding stop and laid the damascened point of the Bessarion Lance gently to the fallen woman's sternum.

"Consider yourself my prisoner, Hind bint Bashar," Marta announced between breaths. She raised her voice, throwing a glance towards the rest of the half-dozen bandits, who stood scattered among the rocks staring at her and their leader in frozen surprise. "The rest of you go home. Dawud, I'll be calling on your mother in the morning."

With a scuffle, the others dropped from the rocks and vanished into the valley. Abandoned, Hind spat on the ground. "Kill me now. I'd rather be eaten by ravens in this godforsaken wadi than hanged in Nablus square."

Marta sighed. Hunting bandits was no challenge and endless trouble. Untrained and poorly armed, they were easily intimidated by an armed knight. The trouble came after, when you tried to sort out what to *do* with them. Some were stupid youngsters, like Dawud, minds addled with the promise of easy money, in need of little more than a stern talking-to by a parent or village headman. But there were cold-blooded thieves and killers who did not care who they destroyed, fanatics who believed themselves striking a blow for some holy cause, and worst of all, people who had endured horrors and did not know how to live afterwards.

"I won't do that," she told Hind. "I have to take you back to Nablus, but Lord Balian is a reasonable judge. I'm sure there must have been a reason why you killed your husband. Our law forbids a man to treat his wife with hatred or cruelty."

"I've killed others since," Hind muttered, which was undeniably true; but she seemed resigned, for she got up and handed over her sword without further argument.

It was at this moment that the pilgrim caravan came in view: a dozen or so travellers by foot and mule, a merchant's ox-cart heaped with grain sacks, and a guide—a sunburnt Greek from Tiberias who was loudly telling the story of how, over there, King Saul was defeated upon that very mountain and slew himself for shame, and over here, Saint Joseph was cast into a pit by his brothers.

"Also on your left," he added smoothly as the small caravan drew level with Marta and her prisoner, "we have the famous White Watcher herself, Marta Bessarion! In truth, friends, this is that same Marta the Knight who, at the siege of Kerak, challenged Saladin, the king of Egypt and Syria, to single combat. Now, as always, she roams the hills of Galilee and Judaea, protecting poor pilgrims like ourselves from the depredations of bandits. Did I not promise you we would be well guarded? See that lance she carries? Why, that is the self-same Holy Lance carried by Emperor Heraclius himself in his wars against the Persians, blessed by none other than the Pope at Rome and carrying such a virtue that the wielder can never be defeated in battle!"

Marta gritted her teeth. "Angelos, you should hire your own guards if you mean to set up as a guide. He's talking nonsense," she added to the wide-eyed, whispering travellers. Latins, most of them; had they been Greeks or Nubians or Slavs, the Lance would undoubtedly have been blessed by St John Chrysostom, or St Michael, or St Cyril. "I didn't fight Saladin when I escaped Kerak."

"Is it true that you have the strength of ten men because you're a clean maid?" a perspiring matron asked from atop a mule.

Marta was famous now, and she hated it; hated everyone knowing her name, recognising her plain white shield and loudly discussing the state of her maidenhead. She certainly did not like the entire kingdom gossiping about the miraculous power of her spear; someone might try to take it from her as Miles of Plancy had done. The dust of the road mingled with the sweat on the woman's face and mount, making her look nearly as grimy as Marta did herself. For once, an answer rose easily to her lips.

"Not quite. At present you can see that I'm a very foul and dusty maid." She reached out and caught Hind, who seemed to be thinking of bolting for the wadi. "If you won't behave, madame, I'll be compelled to bind you. Come, Angelos, I'll see you as far as Bethsan. I'll need to water my horse there before turning back."

With Hind's wrists strapped to the cart and the bandit leader herself being watched by plenty of eager eyes, Marta escaped to the front of the column to speak to Angelos in their own native Greek.

"I meant it, Angelos. Hire guards, and don't promise people safety on my account. I can't always be watching over this road."

"I know," he said with an airy shrug, "but you are here today, and that is the main thing. One must work while there is light. You know, don't you, that world ends this autumn?"

Marta stared at him. For a moment, she wanted to laugh. Yet she had been waiting for something to happen ever since Baldwin's death. "Are you serious?"

"You haven't heard? All the learned men and astronomers, Christian and Saracen, have been discussing nothing else these past thirty years. In September at Embertide, all five planets will gather in the house of Libra. It is a great marvel that has never occurred before, but Libra is an airy sign, as all men know. The exact significance is not known; but it is *said* to presage a great storm of wind, which shall destroy all life on the earth. People are digging shelters, stocking caves with food and water. I have prepared one in these very hills."

Oh, Marta thought in some relief, *that old story*. "I don't know, Angelos. To my memory there is nothing in Holy Writ concerning such an end to the world."

"You sound like a Latin," Angelos said, offended. "It is very ignorant and superstitious to cite Holy Writ against men of great knowledge and learning."

"Forgive me." Marta was unwilling to debate; she had never been much of a scholar, and after more than seven years living among the Franks, she did sometimes wonder whether she was becoming too much like them. "I thought you might have news from Damascus, from the merchants travelling through Tiberias to Acre."

"Ah! There's another portent," Angelos said solemnly. "Saladin is in Damascus even now, recovering from his illness and marrying his sons to the daughters of strong amirs. He celebrates his recovery with a solemn vow to devote himself entirely to the destruction of the Franks and the conquest of Jerusalem, no matter the cost in lives and money. He has even settled his quarrel with Mosul."

Was this it, the calamity she had been awaiting all these months? Marta nearly hoped that it was. A threat like this was something she could understand. Something she could charge with the Bessarion Lance and overcome.

"Was there any news," she said, "of a man named al-Aziz?"

"The sorcerer? Oh yes." Angelos nodded vigorously. "It's thanks to his arts that the sultan recovered his health at all, when he was on the brink of death."

Al-Aziz Khalil commanded demons of pestilence, Marta remembered. What odds Khalil had himself engineered the very illness that had brought the sultan down?

"Why the silence?" Angelos prompted, grinning at her. "So long as the kingdom has the White Watcher, it has nothing to fear from men. Eh? Just be sure to come to my cave at Embertide. Those of us who survive the wind will want you and your lance on our side."

* * *

Sweat dripped into Marta's eyes and she blinked it back, too busy to use the back of her wrist.

She sidled, bent from the hips with sword and buckler held low in front of her, wrists crossed to keep both hands sheltered behind the small round shield. Opposite, her assailant kept pace in the circle, before suddenly blurring into motion. His black shadow danced across the sand as he snagged her blade with his own, forced it down, and followed the momentum with his own buckler. Disengaging his sword, he lashed for her neck.

Both Marta's hands were trapped beneath his buckler, but she moved fast. As her shield hand dropped suddenly, Marta instantly reversed her grip on her sword and brought the pommel sharply up under his guard, striking him beneath the breastbone. The stroke aimed at her throat went wide. He doubled over with a grunt. Marta danced back to disengage, but she must have struck harder than she had intended. Her opponent staggered back a few steps and fell to the ground.

Marta had already crossed her wrists again and resumed her stance, always moving, always ready. "Resting, Ernoul?"

His face was red, either from exertion or from embarrassment. "My knee is paining me," he wheezed. "Otherwise, I would have won that bout."

"I'm sure you would," Marta said quickly, coming off guard and throwing a glance around the sand-covered courtyard. Hacked pells stood to one side, their battered sides testifying to the frequent sword-practice of the knights and squires of the Nablus palace. In the shadows of the portico, Persi's vividly dyed yellow dress made a splash of colour that contrasted gloriously with her midnight-dark skin. She waved at Marta when their eyes met, and Marta sighed, stripping off her gloves. No doubt it was past time to stop.

She had been working Lord Balian's new squire hard these past few days, ever since her journey to Bethsan. *Not by your spear, but by your sword.* If Saladin and his sorcerer were planning a new raid into the kingdom, Marta meant to be ready for them. She had never been as formidable with the sword, always preferring the insuperable advantage afforded to her by the enchanted Bessarion Lance. Now, she offered a hand to Ernoul and said, "My reach is shorter, and I don't hit so hard as you. But I think I'm becoming more skilful."

Ernoul—a young Frank about her own age, with dark eyes and curly black hair that suggested Greek or Syriac blood in his ancestry—took her buckler and wooden practice sword with a frown. After a moment, as they walked towards Persi, he said, "It isn't natural, a woman roaming like a knight-errant."

Marta smiled. "Lord Balian allows it."

"Maybe he shouldn't. For your own safety. It's dangerous, Marta. You could get killed, or hurt, or captured—and you know what the Saracens do to their captives, especially women."

"It can't be any worse than what the Franks do to their captives," Persi said with a sniff. There was someone with her—a young Syrian with a dark beard, in neat and crisp white cotton tunic and trousers beneath a meticulously embroidered red vest. Michael Zakar, the Acre weaver whose workshop produced many of the woven fabrics Marta and Persi designed. These days Michael made frequent trips to Nablus, exchanging finished bolts of cloth for new patterns. Persi had been delighted to find a business partner who treated his weavers as well as Michael did, but Marta had seen at once that weaving was not the only partnership the young Syrian had in mind.

More than two years since the two had first met, however, there was still no apparent movement on that front. Marta assessed the pair thoughtfully. Both were wearing unusually fine clothes and Persi, she knew, had spent a great deal of time yesterday with Amataxos the Abyssinian—the only other woman in Nablus with such tightly curling masses of hair—having it all freshly woven into tiny, sleek braids. All that effort, and now Persi stood with her back to Michael, her arms folded defensively across her chest.

Persi narrowed her eyes at Ernoul and added, "Besides, plenty of women have been taken captive who never set a foot astray, but remained meek and demure in their own homes."

Women like Persi herself, who had been a slave when Marta met her, but liked to keep that information to herself now that she was free and a weaver renowned throughout the kingdom. "It's all right, Persi." Marta untucked her gown, smoothing down the grey, dusty folds over the pair of light cotton trousers she wore beneath. "I know this is a dangerous occupation; that's why I have been training so hard."

Ernoul grunted and disappeared into the armoury. There had been an icon of the Virgin hung above the doorway once, but it had been torn down and hacked apart a year or two back, when Saladin had raided across the Jordan and briefly occupied the town. Since then, the house had never quite felt like home; it was a little scarred, a little unsafe.

"He's embarrassed," Persi said, watching Ernoul go. "He's trying to impress you, and you knock him on his rump."

"Impress me?"

"Don't be dense," Persi told her. At that, Marta could not help glancing at Michael Zakar, who screwed up his nose in a wry smile. Evidently, they shared the same thought. Unaware of their exchange, Persi went on: "Isn't it obvious? He fancies you, but he daren't say anything because you're the famous White Watcher, saintly and inviolable. Saint Margaret of Antioch grant *me* the same reputation; heaven knows I could do with it."

She turned abruptly and disappeared into the house, leaving Marta staring after her, mystified. "Is something wrong?" she asked Michael.

He waited until Persi's footsteps had faded somewhat before replying. "That's what I wanted to ask you about." Tucking under his arm the wallet in which he kept his new set of patterns, Michael paced towards the stables where his mule was waiting to begin the journey north. As Marta fell into step beside him, he threw another glance over his shoulder, towards the house. "I asked Persi to marry me again, today," he said quietly. "She turned me down. I don't want to bother her again, but…"

Marta bit her lip. "Again? You've asked her before?"

"You didn't hear of the first time? It must have been—oh, a full two years ago at least." Michael frowned. "Oh, Lord. Maybe I've made a mistake. I thought Persi shared everything with you."

So did I, Marta thought. "Did she say why?"

"No." Michael buckled the wallet to his mule and looked at Marta across the animal's saddle, a pained crease between his eyebrows. "I thought maybe you…" He stopped.

"I can't imagine why she might have turned you down," Marta assured him. "She's wearing her favourite dress today. She spent half of yesterday having her hair done. She's always talking about you—Michael says this, Michael does that, I'll ask Michael when he comes. I could swear…" She bit her lip. "I was looking forward to a wedding."

"So was I," he said with a bleak smile.

"I'll talk to her," Marta offered. "Heaven knows I've been holding my tongue the better part of two years."

"It's a kind thought." But Michael did not move on, and the crease between his brows deepened a little. After a moment, with an effort, he said, "Persi told me, once, that she had been a slave. I've known many former slaves, Marta, and…"

"What?" Marta asked, when he did not go on. The implication of his words troubled her. "Didn't she tell you I was a slave, too? No one troubled us; no one came into the workshop but the old woman who oversaw it."

Michael sighed. "It's not something I can or should press her on." Taking the mule's bridle with a resolute gesture, he started towards the palace gate and the caravan that was gathering in the square beyond. "For now, I'm happy to be whatever Persi needs me to be. Perhaps it was selfish of me to ask, but it's enough to know that that was her favourite dress. Do you understand?"

"Not entirely." In truth, she felt even more mystified than she had when Persi had first left them. She touched Michael's arm gently. "But I do understand that you love her better than you love yourself, and for that, you can always count me a friend."

He gave her a bittersweet smile and shook her hand before venturing out the wicket to join the camels, donkeys, horses, guards, merchants, and pilgrims gathering to form the caravan to Acre. Marta turned from the gate, frowning. Perhaps it was time she asked Persi about Michael. Perhaps Persi had been waiting to be asked. Marta knew what it was like to wish to broach a subject, but not to know how to begin.

She had not moved far from the wicket gate when hurried hoofbeats approached it and it began to shake beneath a frantic knocking.

"Open up!" a voice called in the Frankish tongue. "Word from Tiberias! Count Raymond and his household seek lodging!"

Chapter II.

Sibylla hated herself. When the news had come of her son's illness, her first thought was as cold as ice: *At last, you are to be queen.*

Perhaps the thought was her own. Or perhaps it came from the one who lurked at her shoulder, invisible, whispering poison into her mind. Sibylla could hardly tell anymore which was which.

Now, she stood like a carved image at the foot of her son's bed in the palace at Acre, looking at the flushed, feverish cheeks and listening to the weak coughing. The child was a pitiable sight, almost lost in the shadows of the great canopied bed. Never strong, he now seemed thin, fragile, and dull. He had barely looked up when she came in.

She had been welcomed to the palace by William of Montferrat. As the father of Sibylla's late first husband, the battered old count had of course been summoned to his grandson's bedside.

"Leaving so soon?" she had asked him.

"I'm no nursemaid," Montferrat had growled, yanking on his gloves. "I'll only be in the way." Then he was gone.

He had not stopped to ask whether she thought herself any better suited to the task.

"My lord king," Sibylla said, bowing before the bed, the picture of a dutiful vassal before her liege. "I am sorry to see you so ill."

The boy king touched his lips with his tongue. "Everything hurts, mama."

Beside Sibylla, her husband—young Baldwin's stepfather—squeezed her hand comfortingly before going to sit beside the child. "I know it hurts, comrade." Guy put a gentle hand on the boy's forehead. "They're mixing you a draught to make it go away, but it's nasty stuff. Mama and I wanted to see you first."

Sibylla stood paralysed, prey to disobedient thoughts. *He is going to die,* she thought. *Just as the Leper King died.* She could not remember what it was like to have a king who was not dying. When her father was alive, King Amalric, she was at her lessons in the convent at Bethany. What would it be like when she was queen and Guy was king?

Difficult. It would be horribly difficult. After all, the barons had denied her the crown because they could not bear to be ruled by her husband.

Guy held out a hand to her, beckoning. Her son's eyes had drifted shut. The doctors meant to drug him with hemlock to take away the pain. Without a miracle, he would die. Now was her last chance to bid him goodbye, this son she had carried with great pains for nine months, this last of the male line of Jerusalem, this rival who had supplanted her on the throne.

Sibylla opened her mouth, but no words came. "I can't," she told Guy suddenly, and fled the room.

He caught up with her at the antechamber window, where she had thrown open the alabaster-paned window to gulp great breaths of outside air. It was a warm day and the multifarious stink of the city nearly choked her: street food and livestock, hearth fires and sewage, tanners and perfumers. Sibylla slammed the window shut and turned so that her back was against it, and put her hand against Guy's chest before he could gather her up in his arms.

"Don't," she whispered, afraid to be overheard by the attendants clustered around the king's door. "I am no natural mother, Guy. I cannot feel *anything* I ought to."

He lifted her hand to his lips. "I've spent my whole life feeling things I shouldn't, Sibylla, beginning with my love for you. I will not reproach you for this."

"All I can think is that I am about to become queen, and there is so much, Guy, so much that will need to be done..."

"I know." His eyes were soft, the way they always were when they looked at her, and Sibylla's throat closed up, thinking how little she deserved his devotion. "I'll sit with the boy. Come back when you're ready."

Sibylla watched him return to the king's room. She had always been wary of her son, unable to avoid seeing him as a rival. Beyond that, he had never been physically strong, and she had lost so many children to miscarriage or childhood illness. It made no rational sense to become attached to someone who might hurt you later. Guy she could rely on; he was a grown man, hale and strong, and she had chosen him carefully, having tested his loyalty.

Somehow, Guy was able to forget that her son was his rival, or that their daughters were raised only to be married far away for some political advantage. He was a better mother to young Baldwin than she ever had been, and could comfort and distract the boy better than she ever could.

Sibylla could not do that, but she could still fight for him.

This antechamber was too crowded, too near the sickroom. Sibylla stalked into the loggia and downstairs, seeking a room that would be empty and private. She found it in the audience hall, paved with coloured marble and painted with frescoes. An empty throne was set just to one side and slightly below the stand bearing a copy of the Gospels, tacit acknowledgement that the kingdom belonged to no mortal king.

She stopped, tracing the carved ivory covers with her fingers. Scenes from the life of Jerusalem's ancient king, Saint David, adorned the book. In the foliate borders between the tiny carvings, studded with gems, the virtues battled the vices. Sibylla had no particular reason to believe it might help, but she begged the saint to pray for her as she called upon her tormentor.

"Lilith. Show yourself."

A voice spoke behind her. "You needn't call so loudly, descendant of mud. I'm never far from your side."

Sibylla turned, pressing a hand to her leaping heart. Lilith lolled on the throne, part bird, part woman, part shadow. The demon's arms dripped black feathers; her feet were claws, and her face was shadowed by something that might have been either a beak or a visor.

Sibylla felt sick, almost dizzy.

At first, Lilith had appeared only in Sibylla's dreams. That changed after Sibylla had sent Guy to attack a Bedouin tribe wintering at the Leper King's demesne at Darum. It had been a petty thing to do, intended not so much to teach her brother a lesson for trying to force her to divorce the only man in the kingdom she really trusted, as to ensure that her followers could not defect to her brother without facing consequences for their attack on his property and allies. It had been a cold, pragmatic decision; but Lilith had accepted it as a blood sacrifice, binding the two of them together.

Lilith had not shown herself often in the past two and a half years. She had no need to. Always Sibylla knew that her evil angel watched everything she did, prompting bizarre, destructive and obsessive thoughts, or targeting friends and allies with pestilential arrows.

She ought to have done something long before this.

"My son is dying," she said, not quite bold enough to look the demon in the eye. "Is this your doing?"

"You wished to rule, did you not? The brat stands in your way. Soon, he will be gone."

Sibylla looked away, flattening her hand against the cool ivory of the bound Gospels, wishing that they brought her any strength or wisdom. "And all the miscarriages I have had? Were those your doing, also?"

"It wasn't as though you wanted them, was it?"

"Wanted them?" In her indignation, Sibylla forgot caution. "Of course I *wanted* them. Would I have suffered through so many months of sickness if I did not? A royal house is not built without children."

"Ah, yes." Lilith shook with low, nightmarish laughter. "I know what you wanted them for. Pawns and pets. Heirs and spares, arrow grist and marriage alliances. To you they were never really living souls at all."

"And they were to you?"

"Of course they were," said Lilith. "Why else should I find them such delectable morsels?"

Sibylla put a hand against her mouth. For a moment it was all she could do to breathe. Then she straightened and said, "Leave my son alone."

"Why?" Lilith shrugged. "He's a poor, sickly thing, and you are young enough yet to bear stronger heirs. Besides, you will have my help. Together we could create an immortal. Ah! That thought intrigues you."

"You are wrong," Sibylla said through numb lips. "Such a thing is impossible. Impious. I want my own son to live. Ask of me anything, only spare his life."

"I don't understand the creature," Lilith said fretfully, as though to herself. "To secure the throne, you'll go to war against your own brother, barter your daughters into the beds of strangers, and send your boys to war before they've grown their first beards, but you won't let your son die peacefully in his bed? Don't you *want* to be a queen? Saladin gathers strength in Damascus, the skies predict disaster, and no rain falls. Your son is a child, the *bailli* is a knave and a fool, but you are a shrewd and able lady."

The *bailli.* With Guy resented by the nobles as an upstart newcomer who had somehow managed to win the hand of the heiress, the Leper King had not dared to install Guy as the regent of the kingdom after his death, even though he was the new king's stepfather. Instead, the *bailliship* had gone to the count of Tripoli, Sibylla's cousin Raymond—who had already made at least one attempt to snatch the throne.

Sibylla's mouth tightened. "This kingdom requires stability. If the king dies, my accession will not go undisputed. Tripoli will do what he can to seize the throne."

"That's not the half of it," Lilith told her. "The one you call queen dowager has already laid her plans to make her own daughter queen in your place."

Sibylla's younger half-sister, Isabella, was nearer the throne than their cousin Tripoli. Those who did not trust the iron-grey count, or worried that he, too, had no male heirs, might find the younger princess a better candidate.

"That will never happen," Sibylla said crisply. "Isabella's husband is a fool and will never challenge me for the throne. I arranged her marriage for this express reason. Even if Humphrey was mad enough to do so, his stepfather Chatillon has proven himself one of my most loyal supporters. He'll nip any rebellion in the bud."

Lilith laughed again, low and gloating. "You've given this a great deal of thought for someone who wishes only for stability." Sibylla opened her mouth, but Lilith went on. "Do you forget my power? I lurk unseen in the council chambers of your enemies, child of flesh. Believe me when I say that Chatillon knows he can wield more power as the king's stepfather than as his loyal servant. He has already met with the queen dowager to plan Isabella's succession."

Was it true—had Chatillon really betrayed them? Sibylla pressed her lips together. "All the more reason to keep my son alive. *Please.* Shall I fall on my knees?"

"But I can make you strong," Lilith purred, getting up off the throne and brushing an inviting hand over the smooth, polished wood of the arm. "Haven't you noticed that you've been less ill these past two years? I can make you strong politically, too. I can tell you what your enemies whisper in secret. I can make you queen."

Sibylla touched her tongue to her lips, unable to help projecting move and countermove, feint and stratagem. If young Baldwin died and Chatillon had betrayed them, she and Guy would need to move quickly. Who among the nobles could she truly count upon? Her maternal uncle, Joscelin, of course. The Master of the Temple had a grudge against Tripoli, and might be useful. But that was all.

Of course, Lilith might be lying to her. "Why are you doing this?" she challenged the demon. "Why would you help me?"

"Because it amuses me." Lilith smiled. "I am darkness. I am chaos. I feed on blood and gain from war. It is said in this kingdom that if Guy of Lusignan becomes king it will be the destruction of the realm—which would be a thing of great profit for *me.*"

Sibylla stared at the creature, stunned by her audacity. "Never."

"Well, really." Lilith snorted. "What did you expect me to say—that I was filled with reverence for the holy city and wished to defend it? I've been devouring lives in Jerusalem for thousands of years. Canaanites, Jews, Assyrians, Babylonians, Greeks, Romans—oh, you Franks are not the first to believe themselves divinely appointed to rule here, and you certainly will not be the last."

If Lilith did not mind *whom* she fed upon, then surely Sibylla need not feed her *Frankish* lives—

"So you see," Lilith added, "that I will be satisfied only when you are queen; and for that your son must die."

"Leave me," Sibylla shrieked, terrified of what she might say otherwise. "I won't take your help. I won't—"

The door to the throne room burst open, admitting her waiting-woman, Alix, and the sergeant who had been on duty in the courtyard. Sibylla caught herself mid-shout. They must have followed her to the door when she came in, ready to answer should she require anything.

"My lady," Alix gasped. "We heard a commotion—"

When Sibylla glanced at the throne, Lilith had vanished. A tide of fire rushed up her face. If she was to claim her birthright, she could not be found ranting at thin air in her own throne room.

With an effort, she composed herself. "I am going to the chapel," she muttered, "to pray for the life of my son."

But first, she returned to the bedchamber where little Baldwin now lay asleep in the circle of Guy's arm. She came near and looked down on the boy. Except for the flush given by the fever, he was pale as wax beneath his freckles. His hair was dark, like Sibylla's, and there was a scar on his cheek from where he had fallen and cut himself during a game. She had not been there when it happened.

"Did he take his draught?"

Guy nodded. "I'm sorry. He was in pain, and…"

"You did right," Sibylla said hastily. There was a hard lump in her throat; it was difficult to speak around it. "My mother was taken from me when I was only three years old. My aunts were busy ruling the convent and saw me only at my lessons. It's no wonder I don't know how one is supposed to be a mother. I never had the chance to learn."

Guy's eyes were full of pity. How different he was to her! "Your father must have been a good man," she said.

"He left us when I was ten years old. He came here on pilgrimage, was captured by the Turks, and died in captivity." Guy swallowed. "I don't know how to be a father either. But at least I can be *here.*"

Again, he held out an inviting hand, but Sibylla almost recoiled. If the boy could feel his stepfather's presence, Sibylla knew it would give him more comfort than her own would. "Send for me in the chapel if anything changes."

Sometime between midnight and Vigils, Guy came himself. His face was haggard and lined with grief, and with something else—the sudden dazed consciousness of a coming storm.

Her son, Baldwin of Montferrat, the fifth of that name to be king in Jerusalem, was dead.

Guilty, cursed, Sibylla went to the audience hall, shut the doors behind her, and summoned Lilith. The demon appeared with a catlike smile. "I knew you'd call me back," she said.

"You will make me queen," Sibylla told her. "But not in exchange for Frankish lives, nor for the lives of any of my subjects or children. I will give you my enemies to feed upon."

Lilith looked intrigued. "And if I refuse this generous offer?"

Sibylla hesitated a moment. If she had any weapon to use against Lilith, she would have employed it years ago. But the kingdom still had something close to a genuine saint, if a fraction of the stories were true—and Sibylla had reason to believe that Marta Bessarion was truly incorruptible.

"Then I'll set the White Watcher on you."

There was a long silence. Lilith's eyes narrowed. Then she seemed to come to a decision.

"There's no time to lose," she said. "Tripoli plans to summon the High Court to Nablus, to have himself elected king while you bury your son. We must forestall him."

Chapter III.

"Speed," said the count of Tripoli, "is nine-tenths of the succession."

As usual during the last long, exhausting days of the Samaritan summer, a pavilion had been pitched on the flat roof of the Nablus palace. Fountains played at each corner of the roof, and aromatic lemon trees in tubs helped to capture the moisture, further cooling the dry night air. Freshly bathed in a shapeless undergown of linen, Marta kept to the shadows, not willing to make a spectacle of herself. But in the pavilion, now that the servants and children had been sent away, the great Watchers of the kingdom clustered beneath the flickering light of the alabaster lanterns, making their dispositions for the succession now that the child king was dead.

"But what of the funeral? And the Court?" asked Lord Balian of Ibelin, perplexed. Tall as a Fleming and dark as a Syrian, Marta's foster father was always the sort of man to put personal loyalties ahead of politics. "Baldwin of Montferrat was our anointed king. It's our duty to pay our last respects."

"Guy of Lusignan wants the kingdom," Tripoli said. Iron-grey hair and eyes, and sharp, aquiline features gave the Leper King's cousin the appearance of a great bird of prey. He remained on his feet, pacing the rooftop with restless energy. "The man is a fool, with no notion of how to rule a kingdom. No notion of how we do things here in the east. If one must speak of *duty*, what of our duty to the kingdom? Leave the mourning to women and monks."

"To Sibylla and her supporters, you mean," Queen Maria said quietly. Niece to a former emperor of Constantinople, the queen dowager wore silk dyed with imperial purple; her neck was weighted with pearls and gold. Her second marriage to Lord Balian had made him the lord of Nablus and a great man in the kingdom, but Maria never allowed anyone to forget she had once been a queen. "With Sibylla in Jerusalem, what's to prevent her holding her own court and having herself declared queen while we waste our time in Nablus?"

"She would not dare," said Baldwin of Ramla with a growl. His thick brows made a shadowed bar of his eyes. "Tripoli is *bailli;* she cannot hold valid court without him." Lord Balian's elder brother was a battered warrior of none too gentle a reputation, at least where his peasants were concerned. Marta gathered that he had some implacable grudge against the Countess Sibylla and her husband.

"Besides, they must hold the funeral before they are able to elect a king," Tripoli said.

"If that's so," Lord Balian put in, "then why can we not hold court in Jerusalem, *after* the funeral, together? Meeting in Nablus, without them…it will look as though we are trying to outmanoeuvre them."

Persi sat beside Marta, quietly eating dried figs. Now she leaned towards her and whispered, "Who's going to tell Balian that that's precisely what is happening?"

"Surely not," Marta whispered back. "This is a Watchers' Council, not a meeting of the High Court."

Persi shrugged. "These days, what's the difference? No one here is devoting themselves to good deeds and piety. Listen to them."

"Calm yourself, Balian. It won't look that way," Tripoli was saying. "If anyone asks, we are only responding to aggression. Sibylla's men are already repossessing the lands I was given when I became *bailli.*"

Persi sniffed. "All *that* means is that Countess Sibylla got wind of Tripoli's intentions."

Marta stared at her. Persi had been in a mood ever since Michael Zakar's visit—but did she really believe this to be no more than a cynical power grab? "We're Watchers, Persi, sworn to see justice done. How can we allow someone like Countess Sibylla to become queen? Didn't you warn me yourself that she carried a demon's mark?"

"Just because the countess has a demon, doesn't mean Tripoli has an angel," Persi said darkly.

"You see?" Tripoli continued. "Countess Sibylla and her supporters are already seeking to throw me out of the kingdom. But I am yet *bailli*. I've summoned all the lords of the kingdom here, to Nablus."

"To do what?" Lord Balian made the very objection that sprang to Marta's mind. "The Leper King made us swear that if young Baldwin died before attaining his majority, we should consult with the great lords of the West before choosing between Sibylla and Isabella."

Ramla made a disgusted sound. "Don't be foolish, Balian. We *tried* to get help from the West, remember? The Patriarch himself went around France, hat in hand, begging for money and troops and a great lord to come out and act as *bailli*. No one answered. Not even the king of England, and he was own cousin to our King Amalric."

"The Leper King was a youth of keen intelligence and rare piety," said the queen more gently, "but his plans were not always practical. Jerusalem cannot go without a king for so long. The question is whether that king will be Latin or Saracen."

There was a momentary silence. Marta had told her foster-parents what she had heard from Angelos in the mountains of Gilboa. They were not surprised: their own agents in Damascus had warned that Saladin was preparing for war.

"But then," Balian said heavily, "the choice is between Sibylla and Isabella, or more to the point, between Guy of Lusignan and Humphrey of Toron. And *that* choice is clear, surely."

"I've sworn Guy will never be my king," Ramla said, with a scowl.

"Countess Sibylla is prudent and able," Balian argued. "She will be difficult to circumvent, and when all's said and done, Humphrey is a youth with little experience of war. Could we not make some agreement with Sibylla, to limit Guy's authority? Such things have been done before."

"Sibylla will take that as an insult," Queen Maria said. "No, either both of them must be accepted, or both must be dislodged. I have already spoken to Reynald of Chatillon, if you recall. He has already consented to help us."

There had been a faint scuffle among the four princes of Galilee, who had arrived with their stepfather. Now the third of them, Raoul, said, "All right, then *I'll* say it. Why not our esteemed stepfather Tripoli? Why should *he* not be king?"

This time, the silence was not a resounding but a dead one. From the expressions on the faces of Lord Balian and his wife and brother, even Marta could see that this suggestion was not a welcome one.

"That may be a step too far for Sibylla's party," Balian said at last, gently. "In any case it would only be a temporary solution. You have no heirs of your own body, Raymond."

"Through no fault of our mother's," Raoul was heard to say, and received a cuff from his brother Hugh. "Hullo! Here's someone else!"

In the outer palace courtyard, hoofbeats and men's voices could be heard echoing from the stones. Marta got up and leaned over the parapet.

"It's the lord of Caesarea," she called to Balian as she returned to her place. That started the gathering discussing who else they might expect to see at Nablus in the next day or so: the master of the Hospital, one of the military Orders whose brother knights protected pilgrims travelling across the kingdom? Reginald of Sidon? Reynald of Chatillon?

"Not Aimery of Lusignan, of course; he will stick by his brother, as Joscelin of Courtenay will by his niece. And the Templars are firmly in Guy and Sibylla's pocket. But what about William of Montferrat?"

"Oh, he'll attend the king's funeral, of course. He only came to the kingdom because his grandson had become king."

Footsteps trod the external stairs leading up from the loggia, and Walter of Caesarea stepped into the lamplight. "My lords," he greeted them, still tugging at his riding-gloves. "I came as soon as I received your summons. Ah, and this is my clerk. A trustworthy man. Jehan of Cacho."

The name of the village was familiar to Marta: it was the place where she and Persi had met, enslaved in a textile workshop in the first few, terrifying days of Marta's coming to this time. She had spent all that time locked into the stuffy workshop with two dozen or so women, weaving. During that time, she had never laid eyes on the small, wiry, grey-haired man who now stood bowing before Tripoli and Lord Balian.

But Persi, beside her, had gone suddenly very still: the soft sound of her breathing stopped altogether for a terribly long time.

"Persi?" Marta asked, thinking at once of the mysterious Watcher's Gift which sometimes gave her friend such devastating insight into the hearts of others. "Have you Perceived something?"

Persi got up slowly. "Not at all; I just remembered something I must do in the weaving room," she said, but there was a tone in her voice Marta had never heard there before. Persi vanished down the steps into the loggia.

The great lords exchanged greetings and Caesarea sat down to drink wine, loudly agreeing that Guy of Lusignan could not be permitted to become king. Unnoticed by the gathering, Marta tiptoed to the parapet of the inner courtyard and leaned over. The screens and awnings that protected the private courtyard and its garden from the worst of the summer heat had been folded up for the night, allowing Marta a glimpse of Persi's yellow gown as she quickened to a run in the loggia. She did not turn in at their chamber door—nor, flying down the stair leading to the courtyard, did she go towards the cool dark room, half recessed in the ground, which they had converted from a storeroom into the headquarters of their weaving enterprise. Instead, Persi vanished into the shadows of the mulberry tree growing at the centre of the courtyard.

Marta hesitated only a moment. There was nothing happening on the rooftop but the sort of anxious talk that went over and over things no one could do anything about—certainly not Marta, who preferred to leave politics to those who understood it. But Persi had been behaving oddly all day, and Marta knew her well enough by now to realise that something had happened to upset her friend.

The mulberry tree had long, weeping branches and gnarled roots rubbed smooth by the feet of those who sought privacy in its shadow. Bordered on three sides by low hedges of sweet-smelling rosemary and on the fourth by a rectangular cistern, it was the perfect place to hide if you wanted to be alone. Marta slipped in to find Persi huddled by the cistern, holding her breath as though, by remaining still, she could escape discovery.

"Persi, it's me."

Persi breathed, and her hand dipped into the water, sending ripples through the pool. "I'm all right," she said brusquely, although Marta had not asked.

Marta sat beside her on the little bench-seat, where they had a view, between the cistern and the trailing branches of the mulberry tree, of the lights in the house with its graceful round arches in honey-coloured stone. But when she put a hand on her friend's shoulder, Persi flinched.

"Don't," she said in a voice that choked to a stop before she could say anything more.

Marta clasped her hands in her lap. "All right," she said in a small voice, not understanding anything. Then Persi began to weep in awful, racking, muffled sobs.

"Is it about Michael?" she asked presently.

"No!" Persi buried her face in her updrawn knees. "Not M-michael. It's that—that man. I didn't hear his name. The one from Cacho."

"Lord Walter's clerk?" Marta asked, perplexed.

Persi took a deep, shaking breath and her voice hardened to oak and stone, an impenetrable wall. "It was that man who bought me in Cairo, Marta, when they were selling me for a fine weaver. There were six of us, and he took us north by ship to Acre, then south to Cacho." She was silent for so long, Marta thought she would not continue. At last, more hesitantly, she said: "During the journey, every night by turn, he'd take one of us to his bed."

Everything Marta might have been about to say dried up in her throat. "Persi," was all she managed.

There was a faint sound of men's voices from the rooftop above. It sounded as though the council was breaking up for the evening. In the garden, some small animal rustled in the undergrowth and was still again.

Persi took a shuddering breath. "You're the only person I've ever told."

"Do…do you think Lord Walter knows?"

"Maybe he does. Maybe he doesn't. Maybe if I told him, he'd laugh in my face. Everyone knows what happens to captives." There was another silence. "He was careful to cover his tracks. Pregnant slaves are worth less, you know, because of the chance we may die in childbirth. Before he delivered us to the workshop, he made each of us drink some awful medicine. It worked. It brought on our menses within a few days. At least if one of us had been found with child it might have proven what sort of man he was." She laughed bitterly. "Do you know that I can't pass an apothecary without wondering which of them makes forbidden drugs in secret so that powerful men can cover up their crimes?"

Persi had always been particularly bitter about their experience as slaves, but Marta could never have imagined *this*. She shivered, realising for the first time how much she had taken for granted. "Persi, I'm so sorry." She swallowed. "Is that why you won't marry Michael?"

"I can't tell him this," Persi said, in a voice of utter finality.

Marta remembered Michael Zakar leaning towards her, saying earnestly, *I've known many former slaves, Marta.* "Maybe you don't need to."

"You don't understand," she said, still in that hard voice. "I can't conceal this if I marry. I nearly screamed just now when *you* touched me; what do you think will happen if I let Michael touch me?"

Marta opened her mouth and then closed it again. She could think of nothing to say. She felt numb, horrified. There were footsteps on the stair as the lords descended from the roof and dispersed to their rooms or lodgings in the town.

Persi got up. "My head hurts," she said dully. "I'm going to bed."

"The servants!" Marta said suddenly. "They must be warned! Someone must tell Lord Balian!"

"No! No, Marta, please!"

"But—"

"Not tonight. Please. Let me think about this. The house is full enough to keep everyone honest; they'll put him in his lord's room, and there's no evil he can do there."

There was a pleading note in Persi's voice, and Marta swallowed her next words, along with the urge to get up, take the Bessarion Lance, march up to Jehan of Cacho and ram three feet of Damascus steel and oiled wood straight through his guts.

And then stand there, and watch him squirm.

If she still bore the seraph's kiss, her forehead would no doubt be burning now. Still, how else could she ensure that what happened to Persi could never happen to anyone else?

"All right," she whispered. "I won't breathe a word. Lock your door. I'll knock two short and two long when I come to bed."

Persi touched her shoulder briefly. Then she left the shadows of the mulberry tree and ran up the darkened stairs near the children's rooms, where the lanterns had been put out so as not to wake them.

Marta sat beneath the mulberry tree, adrift on stormy water. She had never imagined—why had she never imagined? Michael had seen it. Persi herself had told her, so often. *You don't really know what it was like at that workshop, Marta—Marta, I worry so much about you riding out as a knight-errant; what if you got captured?*

The hairs prickled on the back of her neck: Marta had the sudden feeling that she was being watched. She turned, half expecting to see the wretch himself. She saw nothing but the silhouette of the mulberry's trunk, and its leaves outlined against the glow of lanterns from the house.

"Who's there?" she called sharply.

"Marta?" Lord Balian said from within the portico, too distant to have been an intruder. Marta did not reply, instead searching the shadows. There came a faint rustle from amidst the rosemary hedge. For a moment she saw a pale blur pouring like liquid across the ground; then it was lost in the shadows. A snake, a pale viper. She should warn the servants that a desert serpent had somehow found its way into the garden, lest one of the children should fall afoul of it. Then she sighed, seeing that the thing bore certain unsubtle allegorical interpretations, for which she did not have the patience tonight. She got up and brushed between drooping branches, and found Lord Balian on the pavement beyond with a hound at his heels.

"I was looking for you," he said with a quick smile. "Do you mind?"

He gestured towards the bench beneath the mulberry. Marta followed him like an automaton, afraid to open her mouth lest her thoughts spill out.

He sat, and the dog put its head in his lap for a scratch behind the ears. "What do you think of this matter? Something must be done, but what?"

Marta stared at him.

"Concerning the succession," he prompted.

"Oh." She must gather her scattered wits. "I don't know, my lord. None of this is what Bal—the Leper King wanted."

"The queen is right, though," Lord Balian pointed out. "The Leper King's will is impracticable. We all knew that at the time, though it was the one arrangement to which we could all agree. It was scarcely important, after all. We thought the young king would *live*."

"You still swore to it." Marta spoke bluntly, but there was no other way to say it.

"You'd hold us to our oaths, then, and let Countess Sibylla and her husband seize the throne while we keep a promise to a dead man?"

Countess Sibylla. Dread coiled in her gut. Marta had no reason to love the Leper King's ruthless sister, who had stolen the Bessarion Lance, kidnapped Persi, corrupted Miles of Plancy, and nearly killed herself—to say nothing of doing her best to embroil the kingdom in war.

"Understand me, Marta," Lord Balian added. "You yourself taught me that one cannot act by half measures if one wishes to do some good in this world. What am I to do? I failed once already when I allowed them to take Isabella from us and marry her to Humphrey of Toron. I cannot fail again."

Marta thought wearily of Hind, now awaiting trial in the Nablus lockup; of Persi's confession; of Isabella's innocent chatter the night before her marriage. She shook her head. "No one who abuses power deserves it, no matter how noble their blood."

"You will stand by the High Court's choice, then?"

So long as the High Court made a fair election, supported by all the barons, there was nothing Marta could do to challenge it. Nor, unless they chose Sibylla, would she wish to. "I'm nobody, my lord."

"That's not true, Marta the Knight, White Watcher of Jerusalem." Amusement shimmered in Balian's voice.

She let out a sigh. "Then I will stand by a fair and lawful election."

"Good." Lord Balian seemed relieved, and no wonder. Last time Marta had disagreed with the great Watchers of the kingdom on something like this, her escapades had cost him quite a number of grey hairs. Until now she had been standing in front of him, but now he patted the bench beside him. "Sit."

Marta did as she was asked. She did not like to leave Persi alone tonight, but she could hardly say so. Lord Balian was a comfortable, fatherly warmth at her side, and the dog pushed its nose beneath her hand, seeking attention.

"What do you say to Raoul of Tiberias?" he commented presently.

Marta bit her lip. *Not this again.* Lord Balian's efforts to get her decently married off had barely taken a pause during her brief betrothal to Miles of Plancy. "I say nothing to Raoul of Tiberias. Speak not until you are spoken to; that is the rule for a well-behaved demoiselle, is it not?"

He laughed, indulgent. "It is possible that Tripoli is soon to be greatly indebted to me. As I am indebted to you."

She was so weary, in every way. More than two years since Miles had betrayed her, she still did not have the strength to imagine loving anyone else. "I'm a Syrian, a weaver, a nobody. You think Tripoli would marry one of his stepsons to me for your sake?"

"Nonsense, Marta. Your modesty does you credit, but you have proven your nobility a hundred times over. By our Lady, they make songs about you. When you marry, you will go from this house as richly dowered as one of my own daughters. And Raoul is a pleasant youth."

Raoul had made her smile tonight with his brash words and mordant wit. She had no objections to him on personal grounds. But she had always wanted to make a pilgrimage to the tomb of Saint Thomas in furthest India, and that journey might happen in a great hurry if Raoul so much as looked her way.

She could not think of this tonight, so she said, "I doubt the Tiberias princes know of my existence. But Ernoul is painfully aware of it."

"Ernoul! The young cucumber," Lord Balian said with startled affection.

"Don't worry, Marta; he won't give you trouble. I doubt he has so great an opinion of himself as to aspire to your hand. A virgin knight with the strength of ten is a daunting proposition, especially when most of the kingdom depends upon your remaining a maid."

Marta forced a smile. Until now she had only been mildly irritated by her reputation; displeased that the entire kingdom compared her to a virgin saint. Tonight, with Persi's confession fresh in her mind, the thought was scalding. Did the kingdom also expect her to die a martyr sooner than marry? Did they think Persi ought to have died sooner than let herself be forced into that man's bed? Is that what Lord Balian would think if Persi went to him?

All she said was, "And Raoul is not to be put off by such considerations?"

"It's your birthday tomorrow." Balian's words were smooth and solemn, as though long rehearsed. "You'll be twenty-one, older than most women are when they marry. You've already done so much for us, Marta. There isn't a man in the kingdom who doesn't look up to you. If a young maid can defend the Sepulchre so valiantly, what excuse do the rest of us have? But sooner or later, it's natural for a woman to marry. Don't rule it out."

Marta did not meet his eyes. The prospect was scarcely more appealing than that of a saintly martyrdom. She knew what would be expected of her if she did marry: she must retire into a house, cover her hair, and attend to no affairs beyond those of her husband. Perhaps her experience with Miles had soured her, but as the years went by, she had asked herself more often what profit there was for *her* in such an arrangement.

Lord Balian had been permissive with her—too permissive, many had whispered, tutting over her weaving (a common, mercenary pursuit) or her knight-errantry (an unwomanly pastime). If she married a nobleman, she would need to persuade her husband to countenance both. If she remained unmarried—what then?

"Are you telling me I *must* marry?"

"Of course not," he said. "You are not like other women, Marta, and if you choose to live a life of celibacy in defence of the kingdom, it will be my privilege to support you with arms and horses, as hitherto." He drew her closer, pressing a kiss into her hair. "Only give it some thought, that's all I ask. Don't allow past disappointments to rob you of the life you want."

As Marta watched him go up the path towards the house, she acknowledged that it was true. Once, she would indeed have been willing to give up everything, even her weaving and her knight-errantry, for a life with Miles' love and Miles' children.

But that would never happen. Miles had proven himself a weaker man than she thought, unworthy of her respect, unworthy of her hand. Even after two years, a part of her still twisted painfully at the thought of him—the part that still wanted to see him though it gave her pain, the part that still hoped he would find his way back to her, broken and contrite.

A foolish thought. Marta pushed it aside, frowning up at the guest quarters. Ought she to say something tonight, to Queen Maria, or to the seneschal? Could she drop a word of warning without exposing Persi? No, she decided: for tonight all would be safe. Jehan of Cacho was too careful a man to take advantage of the servants in a house so full and busy.

Instead, she stole upstairs to the chamber she shared with Persi. When she knocked, Persi got up to let her in. There were so many things Marta wanted to say. That Persi was not to blame for what had happened to her. That she was still holy and pure, even if a miracle had not saved her the way it had Saint Marina and Saint Catherine—oh God, *why* had a miracle not saved Persi?

All she could manage was, "You *survived,* Persi. That's the main thing."

Persi gave her a weary look. "Not all of us did," she said heavily, and crawled back into bed.

Marta washed her feet and doused the lanterns. She would not have slept much that night, even if Persi had not woken periodically with bad dreams. She was much too busy lying awake, staring into the bed's canopy, pondering what vengeance might be taken on Jehan of Cacho.

Chapter IV.

The crowds of the day had departed, the doors had been locked for the night, and something altogether unusual had descended upon the Church of the Holy Sepulchre: *peace.*

The rustle of Sibylla's dress and the scuff of her embroidered slippers against the worn stone floor resounded softly beneath the soaring roof of the great vestibule. Not that the great basilica was empty, of course. A limited number of pilgrims remained within the church, praying under the watchful eyes of priests delegated to prevent any eating, drinking, or nodding off. Sacristans picked up rubbish, swept the floors and wiped reliquaries clean. Far above in the warm darkness, a dove cooed once and fell silent. Within the echoing choir, a small knot of noblemen gathered with their heads together, their voices insistent but indistinct.

Sibylla had always shied away from this place. An endless warren of chapels, holy places, and reliquaries, always crowded, always dirty, always stuffy, the Holy Sepulchre had been the scene of some of the worst moments of her life. The men of her family came here to be crowned; then they came back, always too soon, to be buried, as though the hourglass of their lives began to run when the crown was placed on their heads.

She wondered, when Guy was crowned here, how soon he would return, shrouded, on a bier.

Four tombs stood to her right. Godfrey of Bouillon and his brother, the first Baldwin, were tucked inside the entrance leading to the chapel of Adam, below Cavalry. Two more, her grandfather Fulk and great-grandfather Baldwin the Second, occupied a bay nearer the door. Beyond the Stone of Unction—a low rectangular altar worn smooth by the hands and tears of pilgrims, where it was said Christ's body had been prepared for its burial—four more tombs divided the vestibule from the echoing space beyond. Baldwin the Third, her uncle. Amalric, her father. Baldwin the Leper, her younger brother. And, beneath a slab of new marble marked off only with temporary screens of iron lacework, her son, Baldwin the Fifth.

Queen Melisende was not here; she was buried just outside the city, at the tomb of the Virgin, with her Armenian mother. Once, Sibylla had presumed she would end up beside them; Melisende and Morphia, more than any other members of her family, had given her the right to wear the crown and direct the affairs of the kingdom. And she had never liked the Holy Sepulchre. But the tombs of the kings had multiplied during her lifetime, and now so many small pieces of herself were buried here that it was difficult to think of lying anywhere else.

At her son's tomb she paused, laying a hand on the screen. Behind her, Guy put a hand on her shoulder. They had left their attendants outside the church—all but one. It was a special kind of torment, living at the mercy of someone who could never be sent away or shut out.

"Don't pretend you're mourning him *now*," Lilith mocked.

Perhaps Guy felt her stiffen, because he said, "Sweet love, you did your best."

Lilith was right, though—Sibylla's grief owed more to guilt than to any natural feelings. All her life she had prepared for the throne, and now her son had died for it.

Well, she thought. *The kingdom took my father, my brother, and my son. It can take me too. They will see that I can die as readily as them.*

"We'll build him a fine tomb," Guy told her, wiping the back of his hand across his eyes.

"The finest," Sibylla said defiantly.

She expected Lilith to scoff, but the taunt, when it came, caught her off guard. "Oh, he loved your son as his own. What would he say, if he knew why so many of his own sons had miscarried? Would he be so ready with his endearments then?"

Sibylla gritted her teeth: she had been in poor health her whole life, subject to mysterious pains, bouts of melancholy and debilitating pregnancies. Lilith's jibes were nothing she could not handle.

Above the tombs an arch soared overhead, bearing two balconies painted blue as heaven; beyond, in the echoing interior of the church, Patriarch Eraclius sent them a quizzical look. "The High Court is waiting for us," she murmured to Guy, "what's left of it."

He did not move, still staring at young Baldwin's grave with eyes suspiciously moist. "Do you ever wonder if we did the right thing?" he asked. "About Isabella, I mean. Taking her from her mother so young, and saddling her with Humphrey before she was of age?"

Sibylla opened her mouth. No words came out. Even Lilith said nothing. "You *encouraged* me to do it," she said at last. "What prompts this?"

Guy flushed. "I—well, it's just that I have daughters myself now, that's all. And now the queen dowager and her husband are hosting the other half of the High Court at Nablus, they say. Perhaps we went too far."

"Queen Maria has always been my enemy," Sibylla hissed, "and she would have opposed me regardless, as she did my mother, who was divorced for her sake. I did what I did because it was the only way to secure the throne, Guy. For *you* as well as for me. But by all means, indulge your maudlin regrets. I have work to do."

She shrugged him away and passed into the choir, nodding with quickly-forced graciousness to the men present as Guy hastened to catch her up. A worrisomely small number of people were in attendance: Guy's brother Aimery, the constable; Walter Durus, the marshal; her own uncle Joscelin of Courtenay, the seneschal; Eraclius, the Patriarch of Jerusalem; the Masters of the Temple and the Hospital, Guy, and some small number of lesser barons and rear-vassals, bishops and viscounts. But Reynald of Chatillon was here, the ruthless prince of Transjordan. She had half expected him to be in Nablus with the Watcher faction, rubbing his hands at the prospect of making his boneless stepson king. Reginald of Sidon, too, was here, a great landholder in the north, and one of the five most powerful lords in the kingdom. The other three were Caesarea, Tripoli, Chatillon, and, by right of marriage to herself, Guy. Which meant that, if Chatillon and Sidon stood firm, this meeting in Jerusalem, small as it was, held the greater power.

"My lords," she greeted them, "I thank you for answering my uncle's summons."

In the absence of a king, it was the *bailli's* task to convene a meeting of the High Court; but in absence of either of those, it was the task of the seneschal. By issuing his own summons to Jerusalem, Uncle Joscelin had implicitly declared Tripoli's *bailliship* over.

Sibylla barely listened to Joscelin's formal declaration of the opening of the Court; she was too nervous. Nobody else seemed to be listening either. They watched her and Guy like dogs baying where a fox has gone to earth.

"We have only one matter to discuss," Joscelin announced when the formalities were over. He bowed his head towards Sibylla.

"My lords," she said readily. How often had Sibylla rehearsed this moment? "I, the daughter of King Amalric, do lay claim to this kingdom by right of inheritance, and beg you for your advice and counsel in proving the same."

A quarter of an hour later, she realised blankly that what little confidence she had was entirely misplaced.

"What are you saying?" she demanded of Sidon, who had lost himself in some ominously convoluted line of reasoning. The man had been her stepfather, her mother Agnes of Courtenay's third husband—or fourth, depending on whom you asked. She had thought she could rely upon him. "Will you recognise my claim to the throne, or will you not?"

"He means," Chatillon said, thumping his heavy walking-stick against the pavement to punctuate his words, "that if you would be queen, my lady, you must part from your husband."

The blood must have fled Sibylla's cheeks; she felt as though she was watching herself from a long distance away. It seemed she had only just won the very same battle of wills with her brother, who had taken such a disliking to Guy. Her reply was quick and haughty. "I beg your pardon?

This again?"

"It isn't because of any *personal* objection to the count of Jaffa, my lady," Sidon said apologetically. "At least, not on my part. But look around you! Your choice of husband has always been…divisive. Now half the nobles in the kingdom are at Nablus, scheming to put the count of Tripoli on the throne, because they cannot stomach the thought of a Poitevin king."

To her horror, the Patriarch was nodding. "For the peace and stability of the kingdom, it would be desirable. Your sister is yet a child, my lady, and her husband is not much better. The count of Tripoli is childless and not fully trusted, either. A divorce would be a compromise acceptable to everyone."

Guy, beside her, said nothing. That was as she would have it: when she needed heads knocked together, he would be quick to do so. This was a battle he trusted her to fight—and she felt mortified that it was still necessary. Isabella was a child, Tripoli a self-important fool. Sibylla had everything: the blood, the training, the cunning and willpower to rule. And they threw Guy in her face as an obstacle? Were they fools? Who else could she marry? Practically everyone else in the kingdom was too closely related to her by blood.

No, Sibylla thought, it wasn't *Guy* they truly objected to. Guy had only ever carried out *her* orders. It was a time-honoured custom to blame a king's counsellors for his deeds—evidently Guy was to be scapegoated for her own policies. God knew he made an easy target: the younger son of an undistinguished family, a relative newcomer from the West. They could not bear that she, *she,* had gone behind their backs and made him her husband, a great lord of the kingdom, and the heir to the throne, in a single stroke.

The lords whispered the countess of Jaffa had made a fool of herself over a handsome face. They could not conceive that it was because Guy was the only man who had never betrayed her.

"Let me speak to my husband," she said in a low voice. "I'll give you my decision tomorrow."

"There's no time," Chatillon said. The dim lanterns of the Holy Sepulchre made an ugly map of his scarred, ravaged old face. He had been an obscure adventurer from the West once, too; he had gained his power first by marriage to the princess of Antioch, then to the heiress of Transjordan. Of all the barons in the kingdom, Chatillon ought to have stood by them. "Tripoli and his faction in Nablus will move quickly if we do not. We need a decision tonight, my lady."

She looked around the circle at the lords' faces—her brother-in-law Aimery's look of foreboding as he realised how the Lusignan fortunes were falling; Uncle Joscelin, rueful but nodding.

The Master of the Temple, Gerard of Ridefort, gave a shrug. "Anything to keep Tripoli off the throne."

None of them were willing to support Guy and risk war with the Watcher faction.

Lilith stood at her back, black wings spreading until it was impossible to tell what was shadow and what was demon. "Shall I eat them?" she whispered. "Shall I crush their skulls and drink their souls?"

Mutely, Sibylla shook her head. If she repaid them for their treachery, she would not even have half-hearted supporters. Desperation must have goaded her sluggish mind to action. The important thing, Sibylla thought, was to be crowned and anointed. That would mean something, even to the most hardened and ruthless opposition, for it meant consecration before God as queen. After that, few would have the temerity to drag the crown from her head. But for now?

For now, her hands were tied. If she would be queen, she must make some concession. Haste worked for her as well as against her; she did not want Chatillon to reconsider his choice to support her above Isabella and Humphrey.

"You cannot be such a simpleton," Lilith whispered. "Why is Chatillon helping you at all when he might be putting Isabella on the throne instead? I smell a hidden motive."

"I'll risk it," Sibylla said, so softly that none but herself and the creature behind her heard. She turned to Guy.

When he saw the look on her face, all the life went out of his eyes, and the faint, mocking smile with which he had been watching their opponents faded away. "Sibylla," he whispered.

She put out a hand and pushed herself away from him. His mouth opened in abject shock.

To the council she said, "I have heard your advice, my lords, and I will take it, since it is for the good of the kingdom. Guy of Lusignan will no longer be my husband."

"Swear it now; the formalities can be worked out later." Chatillon said.

Patriarch Eraclius nodded to one of his attendants. The altar stood at the far end of the choir from the aedicule; it was gorgeously carved of red porphyry, shining in that dim light with gems and marble inlay. As the attendant fetched the ornate copy of the Gospels from its stand, Guy found his voice at last.

"How dare you? Is nothing sacred to you? Not even the bond between man and wife?"

Sibylla's heart sank, but he was not looking at her. His scornful gaze raked the assembly. "Oh," he said thickly, stabbing a finger at Eraclius "I look forward to seeing how finely you'll shave canon law to justify the violence you do to us. But you were always a better politician than you were a churchman. Well, you shall see. If you think for a moment—"

"Stop it, Guy," Sibylla said, and he halted between words, still averting his eyes. She spoke very clearly, and with complete ruthlessness. "They do me no violence, *count*. I *choose* to leave you."

He looked at her, then, like a wounded animal.

If she could not convince him she was in earnest, she would never be able to save him—which meant that her best weapon was something he knew to be the truth.

"You have always known, my lord, precisely where you stand in my affections. My duty to the kingdom will always outweigh my duty to you, and I cannot be crowned if you are my husband. Now is the time to put away childish toys."

"Oh," Lilith whispered appreciatively, "you are *delicious*."

Sibylla turned back to the High Court. "I have but one condition to ask of you," she added. "I will forsake my husband, since you require it of me. But every heiress in the kingdom has the right to choose her own husband, even when she is required to marry for the protection of her fief. This is my right as a woman of this kingdom, and I will not forego it."

Sidon looked wary, doubtless tempted to point out that Sibylla's previous choice of husband was what had brought them to this difficulty in the first place; but Eraclius declared, "By law, no woman may be forced to marry without her consent. Otherwise, the marriage is invalid."

"Good." Sibylla put her hand on the Gospels. "In that case, I swear—"

"No," Guy whispered. She knew, even without looking, that the tears were running down his face. "Sibylla, please. You always said—"

"Must I have you removed?" she snapped, and to her great relief he was silenced. This was what she had come to: she was using him the way she had used so many others—as though he was no more than a pawn on her chessboard, to be sacrificed at will. "From this moment henceforth, I will forsake my husband, Guy of Lusignan, and I will put no obstacle in the way of the dissolution of my marriage to him. And this I do solemnly swear before God and the High Court of Jerusalem."

Guy drew a ragged breath and wheeled to go.

"Pray, Count Guy," she called after him, "send my woman Alix with all my household goods to the palace here in Jerusalem, for I will not be lying at your house tonight. And perhaps it would be best for you to withdraw to Ascalon."

He stopped, his back stiff. "Is that a command, my lady?"

"Have I taken your hands between mine? Have I received your fealty?" she asked. Only he and she knew that he had, on the morning long ago when she first asked him to marry her. The onlookers could not know that she spoke of love-fealty, not liege-fealty. She added: "It is but the advice of a friend."

"You will never be my *friend*," he said, his voice thick. Then he had gone.

Sibylla turned to face the council. "Are you satisfied, my lords?"

They nodded, grim-faced. "We'll send a messenger to Nablus at once," Uncle Joscelin volunteered. "And let us set the coronation for Saturday."

It was Wednesday evening now; tomorrow would be too soon, and Friday was, as ever, a fast day. Sibylla nodded. "Send word to me at the palace when you have your answer."

The meeting broken up, Sibylla found Chatillon at her elbow as she moved towards the door. "A word," he said, his breath tickling her ear. "In private."

At the same moment his grip fastened on her elbow, and she found herself whisked between the tombs of Godfrey and Baldwin into the small, dark chapel of Adam beneath the rock of Calvary. "Out," Chatillon said to a pair of nuns who knelt on the stone, praying. They departed hurriedly, with muttered reproaches.

The chapel was small and close and suffocatingly holy, and Chatillon stood between herself and the doorway. Yet she had only to raise her voice, and the others would hear and come. Sibylla tilted her chin to look him in the eye, and said, "You will not find me ungrateful for your support."

"I had damn well better not," he told her, casting a dispassionate eye over her, head to toe. "I could have had my stepson on the throne, but I've put you there instead. Such help doesn't come free of charge."

"Very well," she said, resigned. "What is it you want?"

"When you are crowned on Saturday, you will choose me as your husband."

Sibylla blinked at him. If it took a moment too long before she laughed, she hoped he would attribute it to disbelief, not to desperate calculation. "You cannot be serious. In all earnest, my lord—"

"I am not playing," Chatillon said grimly.

She shook her head, unwilling to dignify the proposal by taking it seriously. What! Exchange Guy, her own husband, for this brutal adventurer, old enough to be her father? "You are already married. The only standing you *have* in this kingdom comes by right of your wife."

"That need not stand in my way—any more than it stood in *your* way, my lady." He smiled mirthlessly and raised his hands. "Or perhaps I was mistaken. Perhaps Humphrey and Isabella would have a better notion of what is due their supporters."

It had been a very trying evening; Sibylla's patience, which had worn thin, snapped altogether. "You forget who I am," she said, icy with rage. "I am no puppet of yours. I am a descendent of Melisende and I will put you in fear of your life if you—"

Chatillon moved quicker than she would have imagined a man of his hard-lived years could. His hand went around her throat, crushing the breath from it. Sibylla staggered until her back hit the chapel's rough stone wall, well out of sight of the lords in the vestibule.

"You are no Melisende, my lady," he hissed. "You have never intervened to preserve the rights of your barons. Instead, you have insulted them again and again." His hand tightened, briefly. "And none of them will come to your aid as they did to hers. Best make what peace you can."

He released her then. Dizzy for lack of air and terror, it was all Sibylla could do for a moment to fill her lungs. As her vision cleared, Chatillon said with quiet finality, "You will choose me."

* * *

Sibylla had Miles of Plancy escort her to the royal palace. The big house was empty and echoing—it had not been in use since the death of the Leper King, for Sibylla's son had spent his brief reign at the newer palace in Acre under the care of his uncle Joscelin. Sibylla had the caretakers woken and ordered a bed made up in her old apartments. Then, while Plancy arranged for the guard to be strengthened from the garrison stationed in the citadel next door, Sibylla went to her old room, moving slowly. Nervous pains had begun shooting through her body and she felt sure that she would have a bad day or two.

Just as Lilith warned, she had fallen into Chatillon's trap. Well: it was no use repining. She had committed herself to the game, and must play it to the bitter end, using herself as ruthlessly as she did everyone else.

Her room no longer smelled or looked like her own. Only the shape of it, screened from the antechamber by a thin wall of carved wood, and the window were the same. Sibylla opened the window in hope of a breeze. Outside, the moon shone faintly, glimmering from the city's glazed windows and gilded domes. Six years ago, on nearly the last night she had spent in this room, Guy had climbed in at this very window to spend the night with her. He had no idea he was taking part in the culmination of a lengthy plot to arrange her own marriage to suit herself. How pleased with herself she'd been, the morning after, when one after another the traps she'd laid with such care had tripped, neatly arranging everything the way she'd wanted it!

How foolish she'd been, not to consider how she and Guy would be punished for daring to choose what *they* believed best for the kingdom. When Saladin had invaded Galilee at Bethsan, Guy had been appointed *bailli,* only to be set up for failure. He'd waited Saladin out, kept the army intact, and forced the sultan to withdraw across the Jordan without doing the kingdom irreparable damage. A shrewd passive defence; yet he had been blamed for not bringing Saladin to a decisive confrontation. Never mind that he could not have done so in any case. Knowing that a victory would have solidified Guy's standing in the kingdom, Tripoli and the Ibelins had categorically refused to follow him into battle.

And then the same faction—those meddling Watchers, who claimed Heaven's sanction for all they did to further their own political interests—had convinced her brother to arrange a divorce, regardless of what *she* wanted. Only the Leper King's change of heart had prevented her having to choose between losing her husband or going to war with her king.

Sibylla looked down at the onyx signet ring she wore on her thumb, wondering if she might solve the problem that way. Perhaps, if she sent the ring today—but no. It was a week's journey, more or less, to the stronghold of the Assassins at Masyaf. And she could scarcely afford to begin her divided reign by having one of her few supporters murdered, even if her involvement remained a secret.

The night was suffocatingly hot. She slammed the window.

The sound elicited a gasp from the other side of the wooden partition, and Sibylla swept through to find Alix there in the semi-darkness, her arms full of bags and boxes. "Ah," she said, "you're here. Put everything in my old room for now. Just where it normally is. Is that my writing-case?"

Sibylla had few possessions and liked to keep them rigidly organised. Alix, Sara and the tall serving-man who had driven them in a cart from Guy's house spent half an hour going back and forth between the courtyard and the bedroom, setting things up exactly the way they knew she liked them. Meanwhile Sibylla sat at the desk by the window and wrote a letter for the household at Ascalon, bidding her chamberlain to shut up the house and bring her daughters to Jerusalem. After that she hesitated, wondering whether she should write a second letter to Guy. At last, she decided against it.

"Sara," she said, as the attendant passed her, "where is your driver?"

"Here, my lady." The man, who had been rearranging furniture in Sibylla's bedroom, came to the door and stood in the shadows between rooms, waiting for his orders. Despite the heat of the night, he wore a hood pulled deep over his head, further obscuring his features.

"Wait outside a moment," Sibylla told the attendants. They withdrew unquestioningly, closing the door behind them. Sibylla lifted the letter. "Two errands for you, fellow. First, have this letter sent to my chamberlain at Ascalon. Second, a message, for the ears of the count of Jaffa only: tell him, as he is my man, to be at the Sepulchre for my coronation without fail."

The man in the shadows bowed. "Why don't you tell him yourself, my lady?"

"*Guy!*" She hadn't the strength to move; but she reached out her hands and before she could take another breath he was on his knees before her, his arms around her waist, his head pressed to her heart.

"Guy." She was weeping; she could not remember the last time that had happened. "You understand, then. You know what I must do."

He drew back, looking up at her with a flushed face closer to tears than to laughter. "Understand? Not in the least. You know that I'm a simple man, my lady. But I know that whatever you mean to do, you will need me by your side."

"Guy," she said helplessly.

"No, hush. You were right to remind me that I had sworn you my fealty." His arms tightened more firmly around her. "Let me speak plainly, since I may never be able to do so again. Two years ago, when the Leper King tried to part us, I know you must have thought of cutting me loose. Only a fool would have refused altogether to think of it, and you are no fool. You stayed true to me then, though it nearly destroyed you. I mean to stay true to you now. You may no longer want me as your husband, my love, but you'll always have me as your knight."

She kissed him, then, until both of them were a little breathless. "My love," she said, with a catch in her breath, "I will not confound your trust in me; but I will need you to be a little more distraught, at least in public."

"If that's what you want, you ought not to kiss me like this."

"Then I won't," she said with a laugh, pushing him away. "Be at the Sepulchre for my crowning, without fail. Now go. No one must know you were here."

"You're a fool," Lilith told her, when Guy was gone and she had eased herself into her lonely bed. "You'll gain nothing by this, and lose what few supporters you have."

"What other choice do I have?"

"Why won't you listen?" Lilith snarled. "Guy of Lusignan is your weakness. If it's power you want, you should marry Chatillon."

Chapter V.

Marta rose with the dawn, as soon as there was sufficient light coming in at the open windows to find her armour without lighting a taper and waking Persi. Still, she could not prevent the jingling of her mail habergeon as she collected it from the chest in the corner of the room.

Persi stirred. "Marta? What are you doing?"

"Thought I'd take the road before it gets too hot," she replied. "I haven't been out to Caesarea in a while."

Persi grunted and fell silent—to sleep, she hoped. There was nothing odd in her riding to Caesarea, of course. While residing in Nablus, Marta travelled the pilgrim roads regularly, seeing that they remained clear of local robbers or raiders from across the Jordan. Sometimes, too, travellers fell into difficulties of their own accord: the roads were sometimes precipitous, the expected wells dry. The hot summer sun could be unforgiving, especially to travellers unfamiliar with the local conditions. Today, it made a credible excuse.

Closing the door behind her, Marta circled the loggia as softly as she could. All the windows were open to make the most of the night's coolness, and the guests were still mostly abed, having sat up late the previous evening on the rooftop. Marta had taken care to note the apartment where Walter of Caesarea had been lodged with his attendants; it was a larger one than her own. Within, the lord let out a soft snore beneath a thin sheet on the bed; along the wall, his household men lay on narrow pallets, a row of half-clad, outflung limbs.

One of them was empty. Jehan of Cacho.

Marta felt again that prickle at the back of her neck, as though someone was watching her. She withdrew hurriedly from her place at Caesarea's window and scanned the house and courtyard. The windows of the house stared back at her, dark and eyeless. In the morning stillness, she heard the distant sound of Prime being sung in the Nablus church, and then the clop of horses' hooves from the direction of the stables.

From the private garden-courtyard, a covered passageway led beneath the house to the service courtyard, the training-ground and the stables. Slinging the Bessarion Lance across her shoulders, Marta hurried towards the sound of horsemen leaving the palace and found a yawning stable-hand closing the main gate.

"Hugh ibn Abdul," Marta greeted him. Despite his Frankish name, the young man was, like many of the peasants around Nablus, a Saracen. "Who was just leaving?"

"That was Sir Samuel, mademoiselle, escorting a man of Lord Walter's back to Caesarea."

Marta hid a triumphant smile. Fortune—or something like it—was on her side. "What a shame I didn't get up a bit sooner. Will you saddle Pomers for me?"

"As you will. Will you be taking a sergeant?"

Lord Balian liked her to ride out with attendants; sometimes, when she thought it necessary, she did. "Not today, Hugh," she said, and left it at that. She did not feel much like eating that morning, but she went to beg an orange and a bit of cheese in the kitchen, and by the time she had finished Pomers was ready.

Marta caught up with Jehan of Cacho and his escort just south of Sebaste, where the road ran atop hard, bare little hills, all white scree and stunted shrubs which provided grazing for sheep and goats. The day was getting hot again as it climbed towards midday; summer's last gasp before the rain set in next month. The travellers had been moving at a leisurely pace, sparing their horses.

"Sir Samuel," Marta greeted the young knight riding beside the clerk. "They told me you'd travelled this way."

Samuel Arrabi—a young knight from a Syrian family and the subject of some of Balian's efforts to have Marta respectably married—rubbed his dark beard, which was prickly with the heat, and asked, "Did Lord Balian send you?"

"No, but I wish I'd caught you before you left; I might have saved you a long, hot journey. I mean to go as far as Caesarea in any case." She hesitated, but Samuel did not take the bait. So she said, "You might as well go home. I can escort Lord Walter's man."

Samuel looked from her to Jehan of Cacho, and then to the hot sun, blazing in the sky. The clerk watched her with curiosity and a little awe: although Marta wore her helmet, with its faceplate to hide her from view, her voice revealed that she was a woman. He, like everyone else in the kingdom, must have heard of Marta the Knight.

"I'm sure the White Watcher will be ample protection," Cacho said.

That seemed to decide Samuel, who shrugged. "As you like it, mademoiselle. I'll not be sorry to escape this heat."

He turned his horse for home, and Marta nodded to the clerk before leading onward. As they rode, she studied Persi's attacker from behind the slits in her faceplated helm. It was shocking how ordinary the man appeared in the brilliant light of day. She might have passed him a hundred times on the road and never known—a thought that she found horribly unsettling. Although he wore a leather breastplate covered in lamellar plates and carried a sword, he was neither strongly built nor formidably armed, and his horse was a small but serviceable rouncey.

"Do you travel this road often?" Cacho asked her, all affability.

Marta did not answer: she knew that a blank faceplate and a stubborn silence could be unnerving to the one receiving it, and she did not care to converse with this man. Instead, in the privacy of her helmet, she frowned. What now? She had entertained some idea of challenging the man to a duel, but it would hardly be a fair fight, even if she limited herself to the sword. Her equipment was so far superior to his that any battle between them would be plain murder. That gave her pause—not because she believed he deserved life, but because she supposed the law would have objections. If the clerk failed to reach his destination it would be laid to her account as his escort.

Still, what Cacho had done to Persi he would surely do again if nothing was done; it was impossible not to do *something*.

Two hours' silent riding brought them to the edge of the hills, looking towards the coastal plain, dotted with villages, farms, and vineyards. On a low mound in the midst of the plain a small, squat castle could be seen: Cacho, the place where she had first awoken in this time, first wielded the Bessarion Lance. The plain had been green and cloudy that day, not scorched white by the summer sun, but the sight brought back bittersweet memories all the same.

Marta reined Pomers to a halt and reached for her water-bottle. Beside her, Jehan of Cacho did the same, and as he stretched out his arm, his sleeve pulled back and she saw the Watcher's Mark printed on his forearm. Her throat dried. For a moment there was only the hot sun, the smell of hot horses and sweat, the glinting clouds of flies surrounding them. The silence seemed almost sacred, inviolable, as though, if Marta opened her mouth, it would be she who had committed a crime, and not the man at her side.

Perhaps that was what gave him the courage to commit such outrages.

Marta removed her helmet, poured water down her throat, and pointed her mail gauntlet at the distant castle. "That's Cacho," she observed. "I lived there once, you know."

He seemed surprised. "Indeed? Then we are compatriots. I lived there myself until recently, serving the viscount as his agent."

"Compatriots? Hardly," Marta said derisively. "I lived there as a slave in a textile shop. I had none of the rights of a citizen."

There was a momentary silence, before he tutted gently and said, "There must have been a mistake. That is no place for a noble *demoiselle* like yourself."

A blandly conventional sentiment, but today it sounded to Marta as though he believed that someone of common birth could be abused with impunity. She turned a look upon him that wiped the smile from his face.

"It was not my enterprise," he added hastily. His mount shifted restlessly beneath his suddenly tense body. "I only served the lord of the place—"

Marta gripped the Bessarion Lance in her right hand and in one smooth movement swept it from her shoulders and into Jehan of Cacho's midriff, toppling him with a surprised *oof* from the saddle. No sooner had he landed on his back on the ground than she had the blade pressed into the brass plates over his breastbone.

"I know what you did to those women," she growled.

He ought to have been afraid of her. Instead, he was indignant. "I beg your pardon! Have I been accused of something?"

"You forced them into your bed."

He had the gall to laugh in her face. As though it was a conversation he had practised before the mirror. As though he believed it himself. "My dear *demoiselle,* you go too fast. I did not force them. Some women will do anything to try to win preferment. I may have succumbed to one or two of them in a moment of weakness, but I made sure they were Christians."

Her hands shook; she dug the blade harder into his sternum to steady them. *"What?"*

"I lay with no Saracens," he told her, unblushing. "That would have been against the law."

For a moment, Marta was speechless. "I'll tell Lord Balian," she said thickly. "You'll be thrown out of the Watchers."

"On what evidence? It will be my word against yours. And you aren't even accusing me on your own account. Why, if someone has been slandering me behind my back, it says little for your honour to be giving them credence."

He was calling Persi a liar—calling her honour into question. For a moment Marta again saw herself rising in the stirrups and skewering him on the Lance like a piece of meat. It would be a terrifyingly easy thing to do.

She blinked the sweat out of her eyes and whispered, "Or I could kill you where you lie."

"And be hanged for it," he said, with exaggerated patience. "A sad end that would be for the White Watcher. Now, won't you let me rise? I can see myself to Caesarea from here."

She had once had a seraph's kiss burning on her brow, showing her without a doubt what was right and what was wrong. Now, she was less certain. Cacho deserved death, but if she dealt it at spearpoint, without fair trial or clean combat, did that make her a murderer? Or, if she let him leave and he hurt more women, would *that* be on her soul?

She retracted the point of the Lance, allowing him to get up. "Watch yourself," she said. "You thought you were abusing poor slaves, that you'd bury us in that textile shop. But no mouth, no prison, no grave, remains shut forever."

He gathered up the reins of his horse, swung into the saddle, and then turned back, laughing at her. "Empty threats," he mocked. "With all your strength, there is nothing you can do to me."

With that, he rode away, down the hill, towards the distant castle and the workshop that, for all Marta knew, still held its prisoners.

* * *

Marta wanted to be alone, so she did not go home at once, instead striking across the hills to Sebaste and travelling north nearly as far as Nazareth before turning back to Nablus. The land was quiet, almost expectant. At evening the wind veered to the north and Marta came home on fresh, cold gusts that presaged the turn of the autumn and reminded her of Angelos' prophecy that the end of the world would happen at Embertide, next week.

The day's exertions had brought her no peace: she was still helplessly angry. Nablus buzzed with unfamiliar faces, and the palace was full of blazing torches and noble guests. In the stables, rubbing down Pomers and seeing that he got the best water and feed, she heard that the archbishop of Tyre had arrived, as had Isabella and her husband Humphrey of Toron. Even the servants gossiped, speaking words like *divorce* and *coronation* and *war*—words that would once have captured Marta's interest, but now only made her want to get away and hide. She kept her head down running for the bathhouse, but as she passed the workshop where she and Persi kept their looms, a hand reached out and caught her.

"Where have you been, Marta?" Persi hissed. "Lord Balian's been—" and then she cut off. "You look exhausted."

"Oh, Persi." She had been dry-eyed and furious all day; now, tears threatened to overwhelm her. "I should have listened to you. I tried to put the fear of God into that Jehan of Cacho, and he laughed in my face."

Persi looked as though she had been slapped, and Marta could have kicked herself. Persi had been through so much already; she did not need to bear the burden of Marta's grief as well as her own. "I'm sorry. I didn't—I didn't tell him about you."

Sighing, Persi drew her into the workroom, shutting the door behind them. She must have been blunting the edge of her own sorrow by working: lamps still burned to either side of her loom. Marta collapsed onto the weaving-bench and let her helm fall to the floor. "I thought I could frighten him," she added roughly, since Persi did not speak. "He is a Watcher, for God's sake—I ought at least to have defaced his Mark, but I was too angry to think of it. A Watcher! Watchers are the very people who are meant to *stop* such things happening. *He* probably thinks it's a license to do as he pleases."

"It's as I told you: the Bessarion Lance cannot cure all ills," Persi said wearily as the spate of Marta's words came to an end. "And now you know why I never spoke up. I spent all night asking myself if I should, for the sake of others, but who would listen to my complaint? I would only injure my own reputation, and no one would be the safer for it."

"There *has* to be a way. We *can't* let him get away with this."

Persi looked at her hands for a moment. "Do you know that some people think being baptised will wash me white?"

Marta blinked at her. "But you *have* been baptised."

"Of course I've been baptised; I'm Nubian. But that's difficult for some people to understand—especially if they've never seen one of my people before. They can't imagine that I'm not a pagan. That I'm like them. That I can be trusted." Persi sighed. "It's as I've always told you. Sometimes there's no way. Sometimes terrible things happen and all you can do is try to endure them."

Marta thought of Isabella, being married to Humphrey despite all that she could do; of Baldwin, dying little more than a year after she had pulled him back from the brink of death by a miracle even she did not fully understand. She thought of the seraph at the Golden Gate, departing the kingdom with a warning of what was to come.

"Can't you tell Michael?" she said in a small voice. Persi gave her a despairing look, but Marta hurried on blindly. "He loves you so much… You can't make that choice for him."

"Well, I can't make it for me either." Persi's voice rose almost to a shout. "So please, Marta, don't make this harder than it needs to be."

The words pierced her unruly thoughts. "I'm sorry," she whispered. What was she thinking? *She* was the only one who would be comforted by action; Persi would only be exposed. "I don't know what I'm saying. I think I have gone a little mad. I just want to *do* something."

Persi sighed, planting one hand on her hip and putting the other to her forehead. "It's enough if you only weep for me, Marta."

It was, by chance, precisely what she had said to Baldwin as he lay dying. Marta buried her face in her hands a moment. "I can do that," she said in a muffled voice. "Believe me, I can do that."

They were both still struggling to collect themselves when the door rattled against its latch. "Persi? Is Marta Bessarion in there?" The voice was Ernoul's.

"Oh," Persi said. "I ought to have told you. Lord Balian has been looking for you *everywhere.*"

"I'm coming," Marta called to the squire outside.

"He's in his cabinet," Ernoul told her, and then his footsteps stomped away.

"How do I look?" Marta asked, blotting her face on a kerchief.

"Ghastly," Persi told her. "But nothing that can't be solved by putting your head in the cistern as you pass it."

Marta followed this excellent advice, but she went upstairs to the loggia with a horrible worry at the pit of her stomach. She had beaten and threatened another lord's servant, before abandoning him on the road—as though she had become one of the very bandits she hunted. What if Cacho had returned to Nablus, or sent a message making a complaint? How would she justify her actions without exposing Persi?

But her worries were in vain. Lord Balian jumped up from his chair when she entered the cabinet. The others at the table—Tripoli, Caesarea, Humphrey, Queen Maria, a pair of Cistercians, and some others—fell silent as he began to speak. "Marta Bessarion, God be thanked. You must ride to Jerusalem at dawn on urgent business concerning the kingdom."

Chapter VI.

By the time the council meeting ended, Marta felt overwhelmed and not entirely sure she understood what was going on. Nothing pleased her about the morrow's venture: her first attempt to play at politics in the days of the Leper King had nearly resulted in disaster, and now she did not even have Miles of Plancy to counsel her.

After a quick visit to the bathhouse, Marta dressed hurriedly, bundled her armour and weapons beneath one arm, and ventured into the courtyard. A light still shone in the workshop, and Persi's loom was working: Marta had meant to spend all of tomorrow at the treadles herself, working on a commission for the princess of Armenian Cilicia. That work would need to wait now. "Don't be long, Persi," she said, putting her head in at the door. "I have an early start tomorrow."

She went upstairs to her room, which glowed with welcoming lamplight. The lintel above the door was scarred, chips of the pale limestone having been hacked away during the brief occupation two years before. Marta had no idea why.

She twisted the iron ring-handle and pulled her door open.

A breath of warmer air flowed through it. Uncomprehending, Marta stared into the paved courtyard of a house she had never seen. Where her bed should have been was an orange tree ringed by a reptilian mosaic. Where lamps should have hung from the ceiling were stars and the sliver of the waning moon. On the threshold stood a tall man in a black robe, his face a landscape of lamplight and shadows, young and bearded and remotely, terrifyingly handsome.

She knew him at once.

This man had slaughtered the people of Oliveta in a sorcerous rite. This man and his demons had attacked her as she fought her way out of besieged Kerak. This man wanted the Bessarion Lance and would stop at nothing to retrieve it.

Khalil ibn Hassan, called al-Aziz.

Actions were faster than words, and clearer. Marta recoiled a step, dropping everything but the Bessarion Lance. The next moment the weapon left her hand, hurled like a javelin, with all the breathtaking power the enchanted weapon gave her.

It flew through the sorcerer's shadowy form as though he had been made of smoke; she heard a sharp *crack* as it struck stone somewhere beyond him.

"Daughter of John Bessarion." The sound was distorted, like a voice heard through water. "I must speak with you: invite me into your abode."

"Never, by God," Marta shrieked. The Lance had failed her, and Khalil was upon her threshold. "You may not pass. Leave!"

To punctuate her words, she seized the door and hurled it shut with all her might. It slammed home. Suddenly doors were opening and closing up and down the loggia. People emerged from their rooms clutching swords and crossbows.

"What is it?" Queen Maria demanded. Even she had armed herself with a dagger. "What has happened?"

Marta was trembling. She could smell blood and fire; could hear screams and pleas for mercy as the people of Oliveta died.

Khalil ibn Hassan here, in Nablus—in her home.

Persi came running up the stairs half a step in front of Samuel Arrabi, and Lord Balian hurried towards them from the direction of his cabinet.

This was *her* home, and it was full of *her* people.

"Stay back," she told them. With a pounding heart she turned the latch and drew the door open. After a hesitant moment, Persi and the others crowded around her, staring in at an airy little room lit with lamps and lined with chests around the low bed at the centre, draped with filmy curtains to keep out the flies.

Directly opposite the door was a window set deep in the thick outer stone wall of the palace, a stone mullion dividing the arched casements. The Bessarion Lance had cut deeply into the lintel and still stood there. The courtyard, the sky, and the sorcerer had vanished as though they had never been there at all.

Numbly, Marta ventured into the room, laid hold on the horizontal lance and, with a grunt of effort, drew it from the cracked stone. There were gasps from some of the servants who had never seen the power of the Bessarion Lance before.

"I thought I saw something," she said lamely to the inquiring faces at the door, "but it was nothing. He wasn't really here."

"Who wasn't really here?" Lord Balian asked, pushing his way through the crowd just in time to hear the end of her explanation.

Persi and Queen Maria exchanged glances. "An old enemy," Persi said, effortlessly taking charge of the situation. "No one to worry about. I think Marta's very tired, that's all. Yes, my lord, I'll get her to take some rest." She slipped into the room and closed the door firmly in the watching faces. "Marta, what happened? Was it truly al-Aziz?"

Al-Aziz—a name, Marta knew, that might mean *The Beloved,* or else *The Mighty.* She thought she knew which meaning Khalil espoused, arrogant as he was. "I don't know," she said in a thin whisper, half afraid that the sorcerer might be listening. The house had always felt less safe since the occupation two years ago, but tonight it felt particularly vulnerable, as though the walls might at any moment dissolve and leave her unarmed and alone before her enemy. "The Lance went through him as though he was not even standing here."

"Then he wasn't truly here," Persi said with decision.

Marta bit her lip. Khalil *was* here; she was sure of it. "He spoke to me—asked me to invite him in. Persi, he could *see* me."

Persi looked so troubled that Marta reproached herself for worrying her friend again. "He went away when I told him to go," she added. "I don't have a Gift, but—"

"You don't need a special gift for your words to count." Persi shrugged, forcing a smile. "I should snuff the lamps in the workroom, but I'll be back directly."

Ill at ease though she was, Marta tried to suppress her worry: she had already demanded too much of Persi today, and after all they had slept here night after night without incident. With Persi gone, she tossed her armour onto the lid of its chest, but the Bessarion Lance she placed at the head of the bed, ready to hand.

In the lamplight, something twinkled on the coverlet—a dagger, carved and etched with vines and flowers. The hilt was made of ivory with a great carnelian captured in its pommel. The silver scabbard was etched with vines and flowers. She suddenly could not breathe. When she slid the well-oiled blade from its sheath, Greek letters twined together on the blade. Her monogram, *MB*.

She dropped the blade onto the bed as though it had turned in her hand and cut her. Her monogram. Her dagger. It was the gift her brother Lukas had given her for her fourteenth birthday, seven years ago. On the night of Oliveta, she had thrown it at Khalil in a futile attempt to kill him. She had long forgotten it even existed.

The fact that Khalil had kept the dagger all these centuries—even had a new scabbard made for it—was horribly disquieting. How had this gift come to be in her room? What did Khalil ibn Hassan want with her?

At Kerak three years ago, when Khalil had been with the besieging army, she'd allowed Miles of Plancy to persuade her to flee rather than go back to face the sorcerer in single combat. Perilous as the thing would have been, Marta wished heartily that she had done it anyway.

Persi's footsteps sounded in the loggia, hurrying towards her room. Marta slammed the dagger back into its sheath and swept it beneath her pillow.

Some battles could not be avoided; only deferred. She slept fitfully that night, plagued by bad dreams.

* * *

It was twelve miles from Nablus to Jerusalem on a road kept in good repair by chain gangs of Saracen prisoners. The trip could be done inside three hours at a steady walk, or two if the rider was in a hurry.

Marta was in a hurry, keeping her horse to a swift trot—not Pomers, who was tired from yesterday's knight-errantry, but a swift chestnut named Javelin, a brother of Arrow whom she had lost in Arabia. Today she wore the black robe of a nun and the all-enveloping black veil worn by well-born women out-of-doors. She had decided to leave heavy armour and the recognisable Bessarion Lance behind her in Nablus: she did not intend to advertise her presence within Jerusalem. And, since it was not safe for an ordinary woman to travel alone and unarmed, Marta had a sergeant with her—one of Tripoli's men, Miquel of Coliat.

Yesterday while she had been chasing down Persi's attacker, great events had occurred. First, a messenger had arrived to formally summon the High Court barons to Jerusalem for Countess Sibylla's coronation. Two Cistercian abbots from Tripoli's fiefdoms had been hastily sent to forbid the coronation until the oath to the Leper King had been kept, and counsel sought from the great kings across the sea. In Jerusalem, the Master of the Hospital had added his voice to this argument; but the other lords responded that if this was the best the Watcher faction could offer, they would proceed with the coronation. With that, Count Joscelin had ordered the gates of the city shut and barred. The Cistercians had only managed to get out of the city via a small postern in the north wall; they had ridden the twelve miles to Nablus in a great hurry with their news.

The ceremony was to be moved forward. Countess Sibylla was to be crowned without delay—today, Friday.

Unless Marta was able to stop her.

The sun came up in a welter of gold and rose, then slipped behind the grey clouds brought by last night's cool wind. Marta slowed her horse to a walk as she came within view of the city at last. Beyond the Valley of Ashes, the domes and towers of Jerusalem glittered with glass and gold, its cypresses marching like thin dark spears within its gardens. Stone terraces bulwarked the fine dust of the fields and orchards on the slopes surrounding the city. Almond and olive trees softened the aridity of the valley.

Friday was a fast day, yet far and faint on the morning air, the bells of the Holy Sepulchre were ringing, ringing, ringing.

Marta wondered whether Lord Balian and the others truly believed she would succeed where the great lords had not. Persi's words came back to her—*Sometimes terrible things happen and all you can do is try to endure them.* But sometimes there *were* things you could do, and Marta knew she had to try. After the things Countess Sibylla had attempted or done—to Isabella, to Baldwin, to the Bedouins at Darum, to Marta herself—she could not be rewarded with the crown of the kingdom. The countess of Jaffa had abused her power when it was small; what would she do when it was great?

Marta had sworn an oath to the Leper King to protect the kingdom—she could not stand by and do nothing now. If nothing else, she must somehow get the kingdom's seraph guardian to return before Khalil could finish whatever it was he planned, and a second Oliveta could happen here, in Jerusalem.

But oh, she missed Baldwin. If he had still been here, none of this would be happening.

"What now?" Miquel asked, dragging her attention back to the present. Marta cleared her throat, pointing towards the distant Saint Stephen's Gate on the city's northern wall.

"It's as we were warned—the gate is closed. I doubt that they'll allow even a nun and her attendant inside. But there's a postern we can use."

This was the same postern the Cistercians had used, in the Syrian quarter which connected the great church of the Madeleine within the city to its daughter monastery just outside the city wall. Marta had to beg an audience from the abbot, but when he learned that, besides being a Syrian herself, she was on a mission from Nablus, he had little hesitation in opening the door for them. Even the local Syrians did not entirely trust Countess Sibylla's foreign husband.

Beyond the dark little tunnel piercing the wall, Marta and Coliat re-emerged into mild morning air between the north gardens and the Syrian quarter around the church of the Madeleine. The bells tolling from the Holy Sepulchre must have attracted everyone in the city to one spot, emptying the streets: the echoing alleys reminded Marta uncomfortably of the Leper King's funeral.

"Quickly," she told her attendant. "They must already have begun. We must lose no time."

The stalls in the Street of Bad Cooking were shut up, and the Street of Palms was clogged by a vast overflow of people waiting in a strangled, expectant silence. Only one voice rose in the street, wailing and howling with none to pay it heed. "Woe! Woe!" the voice cried. "The heavens have spoken! The planets stand in conjunction to witness the wrath of God upon this crooked and perverse generation!"

Rather than fight her way through the crowd at the Holy Sepulchre's main entrance, Marta took the Street of the Sepulchre and entered by a small courtyard on the north, where the press of people was somewhat lessened. Within the church, however, half of Jerusalem seemed to have been packed into the warm darkness of the choir and the stacked balconies above. Marta used her elbows mercilessly to fight her way through the crowd, Miquel following her with muttered apologies beneath the hooded monk's robe he had donned at the monastery of the Madeleine. *"Pax vobiscum,"* she heard him murmur in her wake, "your pardon, good sirs."

The Holy Sepulchre had been built piecemeal, a complex of Greek and Syrian chapels and churches incorporated into one building by the Franks. At the west end was something rather like the round church Marta had known, built over the small aedicule that housed the empty tomb itself, with a high wooden dome painted with stars. But the rotunda had been extended, and now a great choir on massive pillars stretched all the way from the tomb to the high altar at the east of what had once been a separate basilica. From the shadow of the nearest pillar, not too far from the spot where Saint Mary Magdalene had encountered the risen Lord, Marta caught a glimpse of a white figure standing pale and stiff before the high altar, beside the empty, glittering throne.

Countess Sibylla looked slender as a reed and brittle as a pane of glass. Beneath the plain dalmatic she wore, with its wide sleeves and narrow bands of red and gold embroidery, she wore a silk gown in subtle, opalescent shades of white and grey. Marta knew the fabric; it was one of her own favourite designs. Above it, Sibylla's mouth was a thin slash of red in her pale face, the lips pressed tight with worry.

Marta's mouth went dry with sudden terror. What she had taken for shadows behind the countess was, after all, the looming shape of a woman, covered in black feathers, with claws for hands. Her pale face bore a disturbing resemblance to Sibylla's own, but Marta recognised her at once, together with the great bow clasped in one claw. A remembered chill that ran through her at the sight. It was Sibylla's demon. It was the feathered woman, whom Marta had encountered in Arabia and confronted in Kerak.

It was the creature which would rule Jerusalem once Sibylla was crowned.

Sibylla did not speak, but the Patriarch Eraclius ascended the steps beside her and turned to face the crowd, oblivious to the waiting fiend. Prince Reynald of Chatillon followed a step behind him. The prince of Transjordan had not donned festive silks or jewels today: as always, he wore a coat of mail and a plain leathern jerkin. There was a look of triumph in his scarred, brutal face as he faced the crowd.

"My lords," Chatillon announced in a booming voice that instantly hushed the crowd. "You know well that King Baldwin and his nephew are dead, and the kingdom is now without an heir or a governor. Give us leave to crown this lady, Sibylla, the daughter of King Amalric and the sister of King Baldwin, for she is the nearest heir."

Where was Count Guy? Marta wondered. She could not pick him out among the barons clustered around the dais, raising their hands and crying, "Give us the daughter of Amalric, for we love her above anyone else."

"Good people of Jerusalem, do you acclaim the lady as the true heir to the kingdom?" asked the Patriarch.

"No," Marta said, but a thousand throats within the church began to chant: "Yes! Yes! Yes!"

In the shadows, the feathered woman ran a red tongue over her lips. The waves of sound were taken up by those in the street outside, so loud that Marta felt almost dizzy with the thunderous acclamation. Three times the word was spoken, before silence fell.

One other figure did not raise a hand or join the shouting: a tiny, cloaked figure bent over a gnarled stick, silent in the shadow of the nearby pillar. For a moment Marta felt certain it was the old Watcher she had seen twice now, but then the crowd shifted, blotting the small woman from view.

"Where is the crown?" The Patriarch's soft voice echoed through the hushed church.

"Still in the treasury, my lord," someone said, pushing his way forward: a fair, blunt, heavyset man clad in black, whom Marta recognised as the Master of the Temple. Gerard of Ridefort was a rising man in the kingdom, who had once been snubbed by Tripoli and had never forgiven him. "I have brought the key, my lord, but not the crown. There are two locks upon the treasury, and the Master of the Hospital holds the other."

Ridefort bowed deeply, laying a heavy iron key in the Patriarch's hand.

"Does any man see the Master of the Hospital here?" Eraclius asked. There was a jostle among the lords, men turning their faces to find their neighbours. The Patriarch lifted his voice. "My lord Roger des Moulins! Come forth!"

No answer. A murmur of surprise and disappointment swept the church.

Marta gave a wordless exclamation of triumph. The Hospital stood with them; and so long as des Moulins held the key to the treasury, Countess Sibylla could not be crowned. Not even her demon could do anything about that.

She must waste no time here. Turning, Marta came face to face with Miquel of Coliat. "Stay here," she told him. "Watch what happens and be ready to report it." Quickly, she fought her way to the door and into the street of the Sepulchre.

She dared not run for fear of drawing attention to herself. But the Hospital stood just south of the Holy Sepulchre, a great complex fit to house not only the hospital building itself—a massive white two-storey building beautifully arcaded with many windows—but also churches, an almonry, orphanage, and school. There were also stables, armouries, and smithies to serve the knights of the Order, for the Hospital had a strong military arm dedicated, like the Templars, to the protection of the holy places and the pilgrims who visited them. Last of all were the conventual buildings to house the brothers, sisters, and knights, together with their servants and animals. The gate was open, and despite the coronation, the Hospital seemed nearly as busy as ever, its courtyard full of patients, beggars, doctors, apothecaries, and nurses.

Marta went directly to the conventual buildings: three stories of dormitories and cabinets surrounding a tiny courtyard in the most inaccessible corner of the complex. Five minutes later she strode into the Master's cabinet tearing her black veil from her head. Behind, shouts and running feet announced that the nun who a moment ago had been demanding an audience with the Master had given the sergeants the slip, dashed into the courtyard and then climbed, with a far from nun-like agility, up the grapevine and into the second-floor loggia.

Marta was now enjoying herself. She knew what she had to do, and she meant to do it with everything she had.

Between two pigeonholed racks of documents, the Master of the Hospital stood looking through a deep-set window into the courtyard. He was an older, greyer man than the Master of the Temple, and with a greater reputation for caution. One hand was hidden inside the folds of his black robe, near his heart. The other held his longsword, the tip resting lightly against the floor. When Marta burst through the half-open door, he turned resolutely to face her, but whatever he had meant to say, the sight of a woman silenced him.

Behind her, the running and shouting grew louder. Des Moulins' eyes flickered to the sergeants running from the far end of the loggia.

"Don't be alarmed!" Marta panted. "I'm a friend. I come from Lord Balian."

He stared at her without recognition. Maybe she ought to have brought the Bessarion Lance, after all, as her passport. "I'm not really a nun," she added apologetically.

He must have seen her climb from the courtyard. His eyebrows rose. "I never imagined you were. Lord Balian?"

"And Count Raymond of Tripoli. And the rest of the High Court—those at Nablus, I mean. My name is Marta Bessarion. Please—I was in the Holy Sepulchre just now, and—"

The two sergeants of the Order arrived on either side of her. "My lord," one of them panted, "we do apologise—"

"All's well," the Master ordered. "Leave us, but for heaven's sake don't let anyone else in without my express permission."

As suddenly as they had arrived, they saluted and withdrew, still breathing hard from their chase. The Master sheathed his sword.

"Well, mademoiselle?"

Marta twisted the black silk veil between her hands. "Do you know they've acclaimed the countess of Jaffa queen?"

"I heard."

"Of course." She sucked in another breath and went on, reciting the message she had been given. "The count of Tripoli and Lord Balian send greetings and bid you know they mean to keep their vows if it is possible to do so. Remember that Countess Sibylla cannot be lawfully elected queen by only half the High Court. They ask you to stand firm, to deny her the crown. The *bailli* is still the *bailli,* and so long as no heir is anointed and crowned, the Leper King's will can still be carried out."

"Countess Sibylla has been acclaimed, by the people as well as half the barons," the Master said, sending a frown out the window. "By now they will be anointing her. And how can I refuse a duly acclaimed and anointed queen her crown? I am the Master of the Hospital. Does Tripoli expect me to shed blood in the streets?"

"God forbid," Marta began, but before she could go on, another commotion began downstairs at the courtyard's entrance. One of the sergeants, even more harried, panted along the loggia.

"My lord, it's Sir Miles of Plancy, one of the countess of Jaffa's knights. He's alone."

"Well, then, send him up."

Marta's heart stuttered, and she hurriedly covered herself in her black veil. There was nowhere to hide, but she made herself as inconspicuous as she could, just inside the door. "Remember that only the High Court can compel you to give up that key," she told him.

"I do not need to be told my duty," the Master said, with some hauteur. Then Miles pushed his way through the open door and came to a halt upon seeing des Moulins' wary posture.

She had seen Miles only twice or thrice since they had last parted at a postern gate in Ascalon, when he had threatened to kill her but proven incapable of doing so. Now he was near enough to smell the clean, pleasant, familiar scent of his soap. Even through the cloudy barrier of her veil she saw that he was well, the sharp alien angles of his northerner's face hale and sunburnt, his hair bleached nearly white by the sun.

Over the thundering of her heart and the uproar of her thoughts, Marta barely heard him speak. "My lord," Miles said with a bow, "the Patriarch sends me for the second treasury key."

The Master kept his stiff posture, his right hand hanging open and tense by his side as though ready to grasp his sword-hilt. "I give the key up only by the counsel of the barons of the kingdom."

"They do counsel it."

"Some of them do, no doubt," des Moulins said. "But I will not give up the key until the High Court meets in full, together with the *bailli* appointed by the Leper King. I will have nothing to do with a faction that means to seize power."

Miles shrugged and bowed. "If this is your answer, I will convey it to the Patriarch."

As he turned, he threw Marta a look full of surprise and a little residual anger, but there was no recognition in it. She was glad he did not know her; she was cut to the heart that he did not know her. *Miles.* Her lips moved involuntarily behind her veil, but he did not see them.

As quickly as that, he was gone.

Marta watched him return down the loggia on the sergeant's heels. The Master took out a kerchief and blotted his forehead. "They will not accept this answer," he told her.

"No," Marta agreed. "You cannot stay here. We must get you and the key safely out of the city, to Nablus."

The bells of the Sepulchre had fallen silent, as though the whole city held its breath. The Master bit his lip.

"The gates are closed," he said, "and my first duty is to the Order as its Master..."

"The Order has good men and true, who can see to its affairs for a day or two," Marta said. "And I have an entrance to the city, which will open to let us out. For the kingdom, my lord. For the defence of the holy places and their inhabitants."

The Master was evidently reluctant, but he sent her a faint smile. "They could not have sent me a man? It will not look well, if the Pope comes to hear of my leaving the city alone with a woman."

It would not *be* well, if the kingdom was taken over by that feathered demon. "There's no one Lord Balian trusts like me," Marta told him stoutly. "And we cannot afford to draw attention with a full escort, but a couple of men and horses will not go amiss. How soon can you be ready?"

"Within half an hour."

"Is there any secret way out of the Hospital?"

"We might go through the kitchens, via the Street of Bad Cooking."

Marta nodded. "Give your orders, my lord, and I'll scout the street." She hesitated on the doorstep, remembering certain distasteful rumours. "Better to make it a quarter of an hour, if you can. Miles of Plancy won't be the last of their messengers, and if Prince Reynald should come, he won't hesitate to use violence."

"Mademoiselle, I hardly think—"

"He didn't hesitate to peg the Patriarch of Antioch out in the sun," Marta said. The Master's objections died away.

"I'll conceal myself, and order my men to hurry," he acknowledged. "When you are ready, go into the courtyard here and take off your veil. I'll be watching."

"Thank you," Marta said, with complete sincerity. Not many men of his rank would have taken such orders from a young maiden, no matter whom she represented.

She skipped downstairs and passed from the quiet cloistered garden into the busy service courtyard. Miles had gone; he would of course lose no time in reporting back to the countess at the Sepulchre. She wasted no time asking after him. Instead, she turned directly towards the kitchens, the black silk of her habit rippling like a thundercloud. A narrow, covered alley led between the ovens and the rear of the chicken market before terminating in a dark little postern. Marta raised the latch and slipped through into the shadowed street beyond.

She found herself in the three parallel lanes of the great Jerusalem marketplace, each lined with tiny shops and stalls and roofed with groin-vaulted stone. First was the Street of Herbs, the vegetable market. The middle was the Street of Bad Cooking, where for a small sum you could get skewered meat, stuffed olive leaves, or syrup-drenched pastries; it was filled everlastingly with the odour of stale oil that gave the street its name and reputation, poorly ventilated through openings in the vaulted roof. Beyond was the Covered Street itself, full of relics and textiles, tin jewellery and lamps, cloaks and boots.

But the shops were closed today, doors bolted and stalls folded up. That was unsettling: Marta would have preferred the market to be open and bustling, for then her departure with the Master might have been less noticeable. She hurried through the silent market towards the Holy Sepulchre. Not far from the market gates, the street was choked with people who waited restlessly, passing rumours to and fro. Marta plucked at the arm of a woman who had craned her neck to hear from someone further ahead.

"What news, madame?"

"It's the Patriarch and Prince Reynald," the woman said eagerly, "and they're going to look for the treasury key!"

Marta thanked the woman, backed into the market, and flew back towards the postern. There was no time to lose. Ready or unready, she must get the Master out of the Hospital at once.

After her brief foray into the daylight, the darkness of the covered street was nearly blinding. Once she nearly lost her footing on some rotten, slippery greenery. Then, just as her eyes accustomed themselves to the gloom, she identified the opening leading to the Hospital. She swung around the corner and collided with a tall, solid body.

His arms went around her with a grunt of effort, and a familiar voice said, "Ha! I have you."

Miles.

Chapter VII.

Marta's first impulse was to twist out of his grasp. But his arms had fastened around her like iron, and when she struggled her black veil was dragged awry. At that, she went stiff and still. The veil was all that prevented Miles recognising her. If he did, it was all over; she would die from sheer embarrassment.

Miles held her with a low chuckle that reverberated through her lungs. "Saints," he said, "it's actually a woman. I had thought it would be a sergeant in disguise."

Then she felt his body go as stiff and still as her own. The next instant he seized her by the arms and held her away from him. In the alleyway gloom she saw that he had men with him—four other shadows. She twisted her wrists, trying to break his grip via the hinge point at the thumb, but he only tightened his hold until she had to forbear with a gasp.

"I'll take her inside," Miles said. His eyes never left her veiled face. "You men, stay out here. I want a watchman at each entrance. If anyone leaves, follow them."

He hauled her through the unlatched door into the light of the Hospital service courtyard before stopping and turning her to face him.

Even without the faint smie that tugged his lips, the look on his face told her he had guessed. "Marta Bessarion. I should have known it was you."

"Let go of me," she protested. A moment ago, she had been terrified that he would tear off her veil. Now it felt like a barrier between him and her anger, and she yanked it impatiently from her head. How dare he gaze on her with such fondness?

"How did you get into the city?" he asked, releasing her. "What's your business with the Master?"

"Private," she snapped.

"I doubt Prince Reynald will agree," Miles said.

There was a silence. He might no longer be holding her, but without her spear, escaping would be a tricky business. And Chatillon was descending upon the Hospital.

Hope was not entirely gone. Even now, she might give Miles the slip and get the Master out of Jerusalem.

"Are you threatening me?" she challenged, backing away half a step.

He shook his head, no longer smiling. "Begging you to be reasonable. Not that you ever listen."

"The prince won't touch me." Marta lifted her chin. "Haven't you heard the songs, Miles? I'm Marta the Knight. I fought Saladin in single combat, wielding the lance of Emperor Heraclius himself."

"Chatillon will tear out your fingernails one by one, if he thinks it will serve him." Miles spoke in a low, even voice so utterly matter-of-fact that for a moment she really believed that he would stand by, wearing the same carefully blank expression he did now, and let Chantillon do it. "Hell, Marta! What does Balian think he's doing, sending you into danger like this?"

"Don't take the high ground," Marta snapped. "You were happy enough to see me in Arabia."

"I would have been happy to see *Humphrey* in Arabia, so long as he had a fast horse I could use."

There was a stir at the other end of the courtyard as a small band of armed men pushed through the main entrance. Prince Reynald was at their head, with the Master of the Temple at his right hand and Patriarch Eraclius at his left.

Marta tried a dash for the cloister, but Miles caught her again.

"You have to let me go," she hissed, battling his grip on her arm. "If you hand me over to them, you are no true knight."

"First tell me your business with the Master."

"Can't you guess? They can't crown Countess Sibylla. They made an oath to the Leper King. We have a *bailli*. This is a rebellion."

"So Balian sent you to offer the Master—what, exactly? in return for his support."

"A clean conscience!"

Miles made a sound of frustration in his throat. "See, Marta, this is the thing about you. You're so *damned* self-righteous. You do what you think is right, and get on your high horse and look down your nose at all the rest of us. Try treating us with respect sometime. Try imagining, even for an instant, that we're actually doing what we think is *right* for the kingdom." He shook her. "As for the Master's conscience, are you really such a simpleton as to believe he will help you for *that?* If he stands by Tripoli, it's only because Tripoli owes him money!"

Marta had nearly choked on her own words, but now she got them out. "Doing what is right for the kingdom? Your count and countess *attacked* the Bani Iaith, Miles! The very people who saved our lives in Arabia, after Baldwin had promised them his protection! Where were you when al-Na'im and his people were slaughtered?"

Miles made no answer; only his lips went white. He yanked Marta towards the centre of the courtyard. "My lords," he shouted. "I have a Watcher spy!"

Prince Reynald's face was dark with anger. "They say they cannot find des Moulins," he said to Marta. "Where have you hidden him?"

"I didn't hide him anywhere," she replied, bold in the consciousness of truth.

"That key," the Patriarch said to a worried-looking Hospitaller Marta recognised as the prior, "is the property of the kingdom. If it is missing, a search will need to be made."

"The Master gave orders…" the prior began.

"The Master is not to be found," put in Ridefort, the Master of the Temple. "Who is your second in command?"

Chatillon's gaze narrowed on Marta. "You're behind this," he breathed softly, as the dispute continued. Marta stiffened at the malice in his eyes:

until now she had not known the formidable prince of Kerak was aware of her existence. "Tell me where to find that key, or, by God, I'll have every tooth torn from your head."

His men flowed to surround her. Miles stood at her back, silent. Marta lifted her chin, too angry to be intimidated. "I cannot tell what I do not know."

"Take her," Chatillon ordered, turning on his heel. The prior, joined by a little knot of Hospitaller knights and priests, shouted objections as Chatillon headed into the cloister of the conventual building. Sergeants in the livery of Kerak shouldered them aside, dragging Marta after them.

She twisted in their grip, trying to catch a glimpse of Miles. He stood watching them drag her away, his face grimly shuttered. For the first time a breath of panic caught in her lungs. She had never really believed Chatillon would dare to touch her, nor that Miles, who had let her leave Ascalon rather than hand her over to Countess Sibylla, would do nothing to save her.

They marched her through the cloister and in at the first open door, an empty cell furnished with a low bed and a solid wooden stool. The door slammed, shutting her in with Chatillon and half a dozen grim armed men. They forced her onto the stool and strapped her wrists together with a thin cord, anchoring them and her ankles to the rung of the stool.

"Have you your pincers?" Chatillon asked one of the sergeants, who obligingly produced the tool—the sort used by barbers to remove bad teeth. He turned to Marta. "I am not playing, mademoiselle. The key."

Marta tested her restraints in vain. "How dare you offer me violence, you coward? Put a sword in my hand and I'll teach you the respect due to a lady."

Chatillon struck her across the face with a heavy, gloved hand. The whole world was swallowed in a fireburst of pain. Marta blinked up at him, furious to discover tears in her eyes; she did not want him to think she was afraid.

His breath was heavy in her ear. "If you want to be treated like a lady, you should act like one."

Marta dragged in a breath, remembering one last weapon. "If you hurt me, Lord Balian and Queen Maria will never help your stepson to a throne."

"If I wanted Humphrey on the throne, I'd be in Nablus, not in Jerusalem." Chatillon straightened. "Take out her front teeth. Both of them."

The door opened just as Chatillon's man grabbed her jaw. "That's enough," said an even voice.

Miles. She neither trusted nor liked him, but at that moment she could have thrown herself at his neck with relief.

Chatillon growled. "Don't interfere, boy. Continue."

Marta, jaw clamped shut, could only make a high-pitched keen of desperation as the sergeant dug fingers and thumb into the softness of her face, trying to force her mouth open.

Chatillon stiffened with a gasp, and Miles appeared behind him with a wicked-looking dagger angled beneath the older man's jaw.

"Don't mistake me for that poor devil of a bastard you used to own," Miles said in a voice smooth as silk. "I'm the left hand of the queen, and you—she hasn't even taken your hands in fealty yet. Tell your men to wait outside."

Chatillon flushed red—almost purple. "Outside," he growled, and the grip on Marta's face, which had relaxed in uncertainty, now fell away altogether.

Miles put his dagger away with a smile. "You too, my lord. Give me quarter of an hour alone with her. Believe me, she's stubborn as a mule; you'll get nowhere pulling teeth."

Chatillon scowled. "If we don't have the key by then, she won't be the only one to suffer for it, Plancy."

Nevertheless, he followed his men out, and Miles smiled as he closed the cell door, evidently in very good humour. "Perhaps I should thank you," he said, sitting on the bed and swivelling her stool so that her knees almost touched his. "I've been waiting *years* to say something like that to Chatillon."

Marta leaned away from him as far as she dared, her fingers already at work teasing apart the knots binding her. "You might as well not have bothered. I still don't know where the key is."

He gave her a melting look. "Saints, Marta, there are times when I'd wring your neck myself, but you *know* I couldn't stand back and let Chatillon torment you."

"I know nothing of the sort. You have betrayed me so often that I would be a fool to expect anything else."

Yet he *had* stepped in. If in the past she had laid plans that hinged upon Miles' treachery, she had also laid plans that hinged upon his willingness to spare her, and neither had been disappointed.

"The rose has thorns." He studied her face thoughtfully. Suddenly, he smiled and cupped her face in both hands. "Do you know what I think? I think the thorns are there to protect you. I think you are afraid of me, because you know I am your fate."

"You're my curse," she hissed.

"I know," he said, and kissed her.

It was not like the last time they had kissed, three years ago at a postern-gate at Ascalon when she had never intended to see him again, and he had tasted of salt and desperation. He kissed her now with gentle, unhurried mastery, as though he thought he had quarter of an hour to do as he liked with her.

She bit his lip spitefully, and he recoiled with a yelp of pain. "Ah, you *vixen.*"

"You know nothing about my fate," she said, wishing she had a hand free to wipe his kiss away.

"Perhaps, but I'll wager you know how to find the Master," he said, wiping blood from his lip. "Of course you know. He would not have parted from you without some prearranged rendezvous or signal. Tell me, Marta, for God's sake. Otherwise, I'll need to hand you back to Chatillon. You know I will do it."

She thought he might. She wished to heaven she still knew the boy who would have protected her freely, without asking anything in return. But he was gone; Sir Miles of Plancy had smothered him in his sleep, and in his place was only this man—smooth-tongued, ambitious, unscrupulous;

watching her for the slightest sign of weakness. Not quite able to bear his scrutiny, Marta took the offensive. "In that case, why the little display just now with Chatillon? Did you mean to impress me with what a great man you are? You used to be Chatillon's lapdog; now you are both lapdogs of the countess."

"As you are for Tripoli?" Miles looked scornful. "What has he done to gain such loyalty?"

"You can't really believe I would endure this for *Tripoli's* sake."

"But you *do*." Miles clenched his fists. "You're here at his behest. Yes, yes, maybe Lord Balian sent you, but it wasn't for the sake of *your* scruples. I'm sure you didn't walk into the Master's cabinet and say *My lord, Marta the Knight bids you do this and that*."

"The right thing doesn't stop being the right thing just because it's espoused by a man you dislike."

"Dislike? Is this what you think this is?"

"Whatever it is, it's beneath you."

"The count of Tripoli killed my father," Miles shouted.

Marta rocked back on her stool. "What?"

"My father, Miles of Plancy the elder," Miles said more softly. "King Amalric's seneschal. The Leper King's first *bailli,* when he came to the throne as a boy of thirteen. I was not much older myself when they set upon my father in the dusk, in the streets of Acre, and stabbed him to death. It was a clever murder and no one was ever caught or charged with it. But Tripoli wanted to rule the kingdom then, twelve years ago, just as much as he does now. The High Court didn't listen. Not until my father had been cleared out of the way."

"All this is suspicion, and not proof."

"What proof could possibly be brought against the most powerful man in the kingdom? Tripoli became *bailli* within a month of my father's death," Miles added, still in that soft, relentless voice. "No one else stood to profit so greatly. I know you're a simpleton, Marta, but I gave you credit for greater wit. Don't you remember how you and I met in Cacho, at the very time we were travelling with Tripoli to Jerusalem to compel Countess

Sibylla to marry Ramla? Your precious Leper King was so frightened he married his sister to the nearest eligible knight and spent the rest of his life regretting it. Or did you pay no attention to what happened at Bethsan when Saladin occupied it? Tripoli and Lord Balian first refused to follow that same knight—Count Guy—their *bailli,* into battle. And then they cried coward when he went home without giving battle, despite having seen Saladin off without losing a single life. Now, the same men seek to impose a king on us. Your Watchers are just as self-interested as anyone else in this kingdom, Marta. The only difference between them and Countess Sibylla is that at least *she* has the backbone to own her deeds, and does not seek to varnish them with an appearance of holiness."

Marta's face burned with anger—and with doubt. She had once been close to concluding the same thing herself; three years ago, when Lord Balian had almost persuaded the Leper King to arrange Countess Sibylla's divorce against her will. Miles had no way of knowing that she had doubts of her own about the rupture that had opened between the kingdom's factions.

"Have you finished?" she asked.

"Saints, Marta, why won't you listen? The Watchers are corrupt, and they're using *you* as their tool."

That made her laugh. "If I was Lord Balian's tool, I imagine he would have fewer grey hairs by now."

Miles stared at her a little longer, and again she had the feeling that he was looking for weakness, a crack that he could use to pry her open like a pistachio-nut. Moreover, she was horribly conscious that he had found it. If what he said was true—if she had been overlooking corruption among the Watchers, then where truly did her duty lie?

Miles stood. "For God's sake, Marta, tell me how I can find the Master of the Hospital. You don't know what Chatillon is like once he determines to break someone. He's pitiless, and it would be folly to martyr yourself for *Tripoli.*"

He touched his lip, which had swollen and darkened since she had bitten it. A thoughtless gesture, but it reminded Marta that the sort of man who took advantage of a bound woman deserved a split lip. And if Count Raymond of Tripoli chose to murder and manoeuvre his way into a crown, he did not deserve it; but that did not mean she had to support Countess Sibylla, who had chosen to do the same, and had a demon to boot.

"I recall you giving me much the same kind of advice some years ago, in Ascalon. I disregarded it then, and lived."

"You survived Ascalon because *I* saved you, at a price too terrible to speak," Miles spat. "I do not mean to save you again."

Still, for a moment he lingered as though he hoped she would speak—hoped she would beg. Marta remained silent, not out of courage but rage. She would die before she gave him that satisfaction.

With an angry grunt he threw the door open. Two of Chatillon's ruffians waited in the cloister beyond, and at the sight of them Marta's heart nearly failed her.

"Where's the count?" Miles asked them. One, the tooth extractor, jerked his head towards the loggia opposite them. As they watched, a door burst open and to the clamour of angry voices, the Master of the Hospital backed out of it until he was pressed up against the balustrade. Chatillon and the Master of the Temple followed him.

Miles wheeled, drawing his dagger. Marta flinched as he fell to his knees beside her, but he only cut at the cords securing her hands and feet. "Oh, God loves you, Marta Bessarion," he muttered. He pulled her free of the stool and marched her out among the hedges, herbs and flowers of the cloister garden.

Above, Chatillon had drawn his sword. "Give up the key, man," he told the Master coolly. "I can take it just as easily by force."

"I'll have you excommunicated," des Moulins gasped. "And you, Ridefort—"

But no one was to learn how the Master of the Hospital meant to threaten the Master of the Temple. "My lord master!" Miles shouted. "I believe this imitation nun is a friend of yours?"

The Master turned, and Marta saw his resolve crumble at the sight of her, a captive.

"Keep faith, my lord!" she cried.

"Give it up," Chatillon repeated. "There's no point in being stubborn. No help is coming to you."

"Then *take* it!" the Master cried. "And God grant you repent it not!"

His hand flashed out and the key flew from the loggia, end over end, and landed upon the gravel at Marta's feet. She resisted the childish impulse to grab for it: Miles had her wrist firmly in hand, and would easily have taken it from her. She let him swoop down and gather it up.

"Do you have the key?" the Patriarch asked, hastily crossing from the cloister where he had been waiting and watching.

"I have it," Miles said, wiping the key upon his tunic and offering it to the Patriarch with a flourish.

"And about time. Devil take it, it's nearly noon. You, Chatillon—go to the treasury and take a pair of crowns. I'll be waiting for you at the Holy Sepulchre."

Roger des Moulins slumped against the balustrade with his back to her, weariness and defeat in the line of his shoulders. Marta wanted to go up there and tell him it was all right, that the Watchers at Nablus would thank him for his loyalty; but she did not know that it *would* be all right, and she did not know that she wanted to speak on the Watchers' behalf.

Miles drew her arm tightly through his own.

"Come," he told her in cold triumph. "It's fitting that you should see the end of this."

Chapter VIII.

Marta put up no resistance: she had come to Jerusalem to do what she could and had failed. Like Miles, she thought it was fitting that she should see the end of the matter. Nor had she yet entirely despaired of finding some way to change that end.

Beckoning two of Chatillon's men to follow, Miles hurried her through the Street of the Patriarch in the wake of Eraclius and his attendants, entering the Holy Sepulchre by the door that led from the Patriarchate. The palace itself was new, built since Marta's time, but with the old service courtyard intact: with a sharp pang she recalled the last time she had been within these gates, collecting the True Cross and other relics for safe transfer to Constantinople ahead of the invasion.

Once inside the Sepulchre, the Patriarch moved through the restless crowd towards the altar, but Miles led her up by the stairs on the south to the great gallery running around the base of the dome. The watching crowd stretched and muttered for tedium, but still parted deferentially to let them through. Soon, they stood at one of the arched openings looking down onto the tomb and the altar beyond, where Countess Sibylla waited on her knees as though the passing hours had left her too weary to stand; her figure was pale as death in the gloom cast by the great feathered shadow. Of course, thought Marta, she could not take her seat upon the throne until the coronation regalia had been brought.

Miles did not relinquish his grip on her wrist, and the two sergeants in the livery of Kerak were like an armoured wall behind.

"Am I your prisoner?" Marta murmured. "Will you hand me over to your mistress as a traitor?"

A muscle flickered in his jaw. "Lord Balian and Tripoli must learn that their interference has consequences. But don't fear. If you do homage, I'm sure Queen Sibylla will let you go unharmed."

"Unharmed," Marta said very quietly, her eyes fixed on the people below. She was still angry with him—would die angry, she thought. For a moment, as he had ordered Chatillon and his men away from her, she had almost believed that the Miles she once loved had returned to her. When he appealed to her sense of justice, the world had trembled on its foundations. Just for a moment she had seen the thing through *his* eyes, how unjust Lord Balian and the count of Tripoli and the rest of the kingdom's great Watchers might seem to their enemies…but it was the coolest calculation, only spoken to shake her. "Unharmed, but shamed. Like you."

She sent him a sideways look to see how he reacted. The corners of his mouth were very tight, but otherwise he made no sign. After a moment he bent to murmur in her ear.

"You're still unmarried, they say. How old are you, Marta? Twenty, at least. So old, it will be a marvel if anyone wants you now. Not after the immodest way you've conducted yourself. Riding about in men's garments. Intruding upon affairs of state. Travelling about Arabia in the company of men, without a single female attendant. They say it's no wonder Lord Balian hasn't been able to get you off his hands. You should have taken me when you had the chance."

Marta's hands went white on the balustrade; if she had relinquished her grip she might have struck him. He leaned so close that even in the stifling church she could feel his breath warm against her cheek.

"Saints, Marta, I'd still take you, if you'd have me. I can't seem to imagine any future for myself without you in it."

In the midst of all her rage, her traitor heart struck her. She felt the same. She would die rather than admit it. If she thought it might help, she would tear out her own heart to escape it.

"That's a great misfortune for you, but I hardly see how it concerns me."

He went on, every soft word a blow: "I know you feel the same. One day you'll come to me humbled, and willing. I only pray you aren't irretrievably broken by the time that happens."

She turned on him with bared teeth. He could not love her, not if he could wish harm and humiliation upon her. Miles laughed, but he stepped away, relieving her of the oppression of his presence.

"Will you bite me again?" he invited. But there was a stir among the people below. Near the altar, the Patriarch straightened, and Countess Sibylla climbed to her feet again, looking suddenly less weary.

The crowd parted as the Master of the Temple and Reynald of Chatillon strode towards the altar ahead of two sergeants bearing a small, heavy casket between them. It was deposited on the steps and unlocked, and one by one, two crowns were lifted from it and passed to the Patriarch, who laid them on the altar. One was made a little smaller than the other—intended for the head of a woman—but otherwise they were identical, consisting of gem-encrusted golden panels joined by hinges and surmounted by Frankish fleurs-de-lys.

"There's no orb, no sword or ring," someone in the crowd muttered, as Countess Sibylla took her place on the throne. "This is not how King Baldwin was crowned."

Marta had never witnessed a coronation: the Leper King's had occurred before she came to the kingdom, and her own reticence had kept her away from that of his nephew. But something had been bothering her all morning, and suddenly she put a finger on it.

"There are two crowns," she murmured, "but where is Count Guy?"

Miles looked at her, startled. "You don't *know?* But we sent express word of it to Nablus."

She had missed something—whether because she had been preoccupied with Persi, or because they had intentionally kept something from her. "I haven't been much at Nablus this past day or two."

"Then you came here without the full truth." He pushed a hand through his hair in a gesture of frustration. "It was an attempt to find a compromise, something even your Watchers up at Nablus would agree to. We agreed it was best for the peace of the kingdom to bar Count Guy from the throne.

Even Countess Sibylla saw our point. She has agreed to divorce him and choose herself a new husband to act as king. Without Count Guy, surely there's no reason for Tripoli to—"

A bolt of lightning seemed to have rushed through her. It was the chance she had been waiting for. Marta seized his arm almost fiercely. "She said she would do so? She promised to divorce Guy? Miles, *she lied.*"

"Marta, for God's sake—"

"I know it," she hissed. "I know it the way *you* know that Tripoli killed your father. She spoke to me once, unguarded—"

Below, the Patriarch lifted the queen's crown. It flashed in a ray of incense-blued sunlight and began to descend upon Sibylla's head. Marta threw herself against the balustrade. "No! Stop!"

But her voice was lost in the roar of acclamation: *Vivat regina in prosperitate!*

Miles dragged her back from the edge, turning her to face him. His eyes flickered to Chatillon's two sergeants behind her. "Keep your voice down!"

"Miles." She had to make him understand. "She stabbed me rather than leave him. She said she would have them both: the crown and the count—"

Miles clapped a hand over her mouth, stifling her words. "For God's sake, Marta!"

Marta stared at him with wild suspicions flashing through her mind. Did Miles know Sibylla's plans? Was he trying to keep them a secret?

The sergeants must have thought so, too. One of them pushed forward, seizing Miles' hand. "Let her speak," he said. "Go on, mademoiselle."

Marta might have laughed, then, if she had had the time for it. It turned out that *Chatillon's* men would be the ones to help her stop Sibylla's coronation. "Ask him," she told them. "Ask him whether Countess Sibylla will give up her husband. He was there, that night she fled to Ascalon. He was the one who scraped me bleeding off the street."

Miles made no attempt to deny it. "Listen," he told the sergeants, "the queen was *promised* she could choose her own husband—"

The men turned. "Make way! Make way!" they shouted, and the people scrambled aside to clear a path to the steps. Cursing, Miles thrust her aside and raced after them.

Marta turned, gripping the stone rail, leaning out to search the crowd. Where was Count Guy?

* * *

The crown was heavier than Sibylla expected. Its weight seemed to constrict her aching temples unbearably, and for a moment, as the kingdom acclaimed her, she thought she would drown in sensation. The noise, the heat, the incense, the weight of the crown were overwhelming. Nervous pain radiated from head and neck and spine after so many hours, so many *years,* of holding herself upright and hoping, hoping, with feverish intensity for this very moment.

She blinked at the faces of the barons by the dais: Uncle Joscelin, Chatillon, and there beside Chatillon, precisely where she had made him promise to be, Guy. Guy, watching her with something like the look he had given her on the day of their wedding: stunned, awed, a little frightened, and wholly, entirely in love.

The church hushed as the Patriarch raised his hand. Sibylla dragged her attention away from the man she had promised to divorce as Eraclius cleared his throat and spoke in that clear, exquisitely modulated orator's voice that could be heard at every corner of the great basilica.

"Lady, you are a woman, and it is fitting that you should have a man by you to help you govern your kingdom." Eraclius reached out to the crown of kings where it rested, alone, on the altar. "You see that crown there. Now take it and give it to such a man as you choose to aid you in your task."

Some kind of disturbance seemed to be occurring further back in the church, in the galleries around the rotunda. Sibylla quelled the impulse to hurry. Likely it was nothing, and she could not afford to stumble now, when the thing was nearly done. She knew well how to keep her face smooth and expressionless; she held it before her now as sternly as a shield as she rose from her throne and lifted the crown from its place between the candles. Slowly—it was good pageantry—she turned, raising it in her hands until it caught the light.

The Patriarch sank to his knees before her, followed by his prelates and the barons. Then, like long grass bowing in the wind, the entire congregation bent the knee. Again, Eraclius spoke in that sonorous voice, in those rolling cadences:

"O God! King of all Kings, Lord of all Lords! Provide for yourself a man to rule your people and defend them from the enemies of your Cross!"

In all that church, Sibylla was nearly the only soul on her feet. She ought to have felt like a giantess, but she only felt like an archery target, exposed and vulnerable. Chatillon, beside Guy, watched her fiercely, his jaw flexing. She remembered the grip of his hand about her neck, the heat of his breath as he whispered his threats, but she kept any spark of hatred out of her eyes as the Amen echoed through the church.

Perhaps, a voice whispered in her mind as she descended the steps, perhaps she should choose him. Chatillon was a brute, but perhaps she needed a brute to teach her enemies their place. Sibylla need not fear him herself. She had no less wisdom and courage than her grandmother Melisende, who had tamed her own husband, the old count of Anjou, and taught him to go in fear of his life. And if wisdom and courage failed her, she still had Lilith.

Sibylla found that she had stopped before Chatillon. The two crowns were heavy on her head and hands. Kneeling though he was, the prince pinned her with a look that was both triumphant and grimly foreboding.

Do it, the voice whispered again. *The battle is only beginning. You know they will not accept Guy as king.*

From the rear of the church, the disturbance seemed to have reached the floor. Sibylla heard jostling, voices.

"Do it," Chatillon growled.

More commotion. Sibylla cast a glance towards the back of the choir, where a man in the livery of Kerak elbowed his way towards the altar. Behind him, another grappled with her own knight, Plancy. Understanding went through her like a flash of lightning. Somehow, Chatillon's men knew what she was about and Plancy was fighting to buy her time.

A chill swept over her; that voice in her head had never been her own. *Lilith.* Lilith wanted Chatillon, and not Guy, on the throne.

There was no time to think, only to act. Sibylla jerked her chin high.

"By the grace of the Holy Ghost," she began. And then it all flowed smoothly from her lips, the speech she had composed and rehearsed, agonising over every word, for it was all the chance she would ever have to explain herself:

"I, Sibylla, choose for myself as king and as my husband, Guy of Lusignan." With the words, she stepped past Chatillon, now suddenly slack and breathless with amazement. "For I know that he is a worthy man of upright character: with God's help he will rule his people well. And I know that while he lives I cannot, before God, have anyone else. For as the Scripture says, *Whom God has joined, let not man part.*"

She was dimly aware, as she finished the speech, that already people were reacting, protesting, cheering. At the last moment, when she lowered the crown to Guy's head, Chatillon swore and moved as though he meant to snatch the crown from her by force. Sibylla flinched, but the Master of the Temple took a quick step to her side and steadied her hands.

"For shame, Chatillon," he chastised, "we promised the lady most solemnly that she should have her choice."

Sibylla knew then, even as the crown settled on her husband's head, that they would be safe. She had sworn the divorce to placate the Watchers at Nablus, but the Watchers at Nablus had not relented. Since the attempted compromise had failed, only Chatillon would really object to her resumption of Guy. And she had judged her speech well, calling upon religion and love-fealty. Some would curse her for a lovesick fool; others would laud her as a virtuous wife.

Only then did she really look at Guy: he remained on his knees before her, eyes wide beneath the circle of his crown, dumbstruck with amazement. The dear fool!

"Take my hand," she urged him. He touched his heart in almost an inquiring gesture.

"Yes, you," she said through her tears, as the church echoed with acclamation. "Who else will love and serve me so well?"

He did as she asked and rose to his feet the king of Jerusalem.

* * *

There was nothing Marta could have done, she realised, listening to the shouts echoing through the church. Queen Sibylla had run her own rebellion within the rebellion. No one would oppose her, not even for putting Guy on the throne when she had promised not to.

Perhaps God would be merciful, Marta hoped. Perhaps Sibylla's faithfulness to Guy in the face of so much opposition was a sign of hope, that she had learned to prize something other than power. Or, perhaps she simply believed herself entitled to whatever she wanted, and would brook no curb on her desires.

Below, the Patriarch anointed the newly-crowned pair with oil. In the gallery, the crowd stirred as Miles came running back up the steps to the gallery with a bloody hand pressed against his nose.

"You lost," he greeted her drily, fishing a kerchief from his pocket. "Chatillon appears to have lost also, though God knows what game *he* was playing."

"He must have had a notion of marrying her," Marta said dizzily. "Why put Humphrey on the throne when he could take it himself?"

"Well, it's over. I'd pay dearly to see the look on Lord Balian's face when he hears the news." Miles dabbed at his nose and regarded her with a twisted smile. "For that matter, why are you still here? I thought you'd have taken the chance to run for it."

She should have run. Instead, she had lingered here, hoping to see him again, though the lightest brush with him brought her pain.

"Come." He reached for her hand. "We ought to go."

"Yes," said Marta. There was no point in arguing with him; it was like running her head against a wall. "Goodbye, Miles. I hope it all turns out to have been worthwhile."

She turned to the balustrade, putting her hands on the rail again with her hands reversed, fingers gripping the inside edge. Bright banners hung from each arched opening. She launched herself forward.

Miles shouted her name as she tumbled over the balustrade. Her fingers slipped free of the stone and for a sickening moment she plummeted feet-first; then her momentum brought her against the streaming banner and she caught it in her arms, slowing her descent until the fringes burned through her fingers and she dropped the last four or five feet to the floor.

Above, Miles hitched up his jaw and found his voice. "Seize that woman! Don't let her escape!"

But there was too much noise, too many bodies. Marta slid into the crowd, slipping from her nun's habit as she went to reveal the plain grey linen gown she wore beneath. Miquel waited where she had left him, leaning against a pillar.

"There's nothing else we can do," she told him. "Let's go."

As the postern of the Madeleine came within sight, Miquel spoke. "I don't suppose it matters terribly. They say the world is predicted to end on Wednesday."

In the space of two short years, the kingdom had exchanged the Leper King and his angel for Sibylla and her demon. In a sense, Marta thought, the end of their world *had* come.

Chapter IX.

"Married at Easter and crowned on a Friday." Back in Nablus, Queen Maria was the first to break the silence that fell in the wake of Marta's report. "It's clear that Sibylla derides all pious custom and gentle usage."

"I can scarcely believe Eraclius went through with it," Lord Balian put in, pulling his beard. "Allowing her to crown Guy of Lusignan, once she had sworn on the Gospels to divorce him!"

The weather had turned, and tonight they sat indoors in the queen's solar around a table filled with the remnants of supper. The furnaces had been lit when Marta came home, and a little warmth radiated from the hot-water pipes that ran below the marble floor. She felt almost suffocated by the brooding atmosphere of the room.

It was true then—they had known.

"Perhaps it was thought," she put in softly, "that once you had refused to meet their compromise, they might as well crown him."

No one paid any attention.

"I'll leave the kingdom," Ramla growled, knitting his thick brows. "I vowed that puppy would never be my king. He'll not have the satisfaction of seeing me break my word. I can find a welcome in Antioch any day."

"No." Tripoli spoke for the first time. His eyes had narrowed; in that moment, Marta thought, he looked as though he might indeed be the sort of man to quietly and ruthlessly remove a rival from his path. "For pity's sake, Ramla, this is no common kingdom, which may be abandoned at will. This is *Jerusalem*, to be protected with our lives for the sake of all Christendom."

"I have sworn on my sword," Ramla said stubbornly.

"King Amalric had a second daughter," Tripoli said.

Marta, like everyone else, looked to where Isabella sat beside Humphrey on the low divan, near the warmth of the floor. Only fourteen, she was still scarcely more than a child, with her mother's fair hair and large blue eyes. She had been amusing herself quietly with a book, and now reddened when she found herself the object of attention. Beside her, Humphrey—a tall, handsome youth with a scholar's stoop—cleared his throat uncomfortably, but said nothing.

"Once Isabella is crowned," Tripoli went on, "we shall go to Jerusalem and take it, for we have the support of the Master of the Hospital and many of the barons."

A leaden silence followed his words. "But that will mean war," said Marta blankly. She had only narrowly averted conflict two years ago when Countess Sibylla had been prepared to fight rather than divorce her husband. How could the Watchers throw away such a hard-won peace? "We could not afford to fight each other when the Leper King was alive and Saladin was at war with Mosul. How much less can we afford it now?"

"The Saracens will give us no trouble." Tripoli spoke to Lord Balian, not to her. "The truce I have made with Saladin will last until next Easter. Indeed, I am on such good terms with him that I think he would send troops to assist us if necessary."

Was the count mad? For a moment, Marta was bereft of speech. Did Tripoli really think the sultan, who scarcely allowed more than one or two years to pass without attempting to raid or besiege some part of the kingdom, and had now made a solemn vow to conquer it, would so readily help them to anything but an early grave?

But before she could summon the words—and the courage—to say so, Queen Maria said, "That won't be necessary."

She had gone to the door a moment ago at a servant's signal, and now came back to the lamplight with a tiny slip of paper unrolled between her fingers. "I have just received a pigeon from Jerusalem," she announced. "Prince Reynald of Chatillon writes that as Sibylla has acted against the express wishes of her supporters. He himself is coming north tomorrow, ready to support Isabella."

"Am I going to be queen?" Isabella half whispered, her eyes opening wide.

"You have been your sister's pawn long enough, I think," Queen Maria told her. To the assembly at large she added, "This settles it, surely."

"It's good enough for me," Ramla said, striking a meaty hand against his thigh.

"If Chatillon comes to us, Sidon will not be far behind," Walter of Caesarea added.

Lord Balian pulled at his beard one more time and nodded. "Since you are all agreed, I am with you." He looked up at Marta, who had not taken a seat—nor, indeed, had eaten or changed her clothing since returning from Jerusalem. "Marta?"

She hardly knew what she was meant to do anymore. If only she still bore the seraph's kiss, it would all be easy, but that was long gone. After what Miles had told her, she could not help seeing them all as he would: Tripoli's ambition, Queen Maria's resentment, even Lord Balian's unwillingness to stand up to his wife and brother.

"This is a matter for the High Court to decide, not me," she said. But the words seemed horribly like cowardice to her now.

Still, Lord Balian seemed content, and it was agreed to hold a coronation the next day, since haste was necessary. The meeting broke up. From the loggia, Marta watched Humphrey and Isabella walk away with their attendants to the house they had rented in the town. Neither of them spoke much: they seemed numb, and it occurred to Marta that nobody had asked either of them whether they cared to challenge Sibylla and seize the throne.

It had been a long, wearisome day. She ought to rest, but safety seemed as small and ephemeral a thing as the flickering circle of light from the lantern that hung above her head in the loggia. Darkness pressed close: Jehan of Cacho's ugly secrets, Saladin's vow, Sibylla's coup, Khalil's watching eyes that itched and itched on the back of her neck.

And now, Tripoli's ambition, and the look of mute terror on Isabella's face.

She felt horribly alone. Her father would have known what to do. Or her mother, a Messenger, would have given her a vision. Lukas would not have thought twice about beating Jehan of Cacho to a pulp. And Paulus and Elisa might not have been much comfort, but they would have been happy to cuddle her and listen to her stories.

None of them were here, in this time: she only had the family she had adopted for herself, and they were about to be dragged into a war. Marta bit her lip. Was it worth the bloodshed, to keep Sibylla off the throne?

There was only one way to answer that question. As soon as she had bathed, Marta set off into the town.

* * *

Humphrey and Isabella had taken a house in Nablus not far from the palace, among the wealthy houses around the city's main square. It was a charming place, which Marta had often admired from outside, catching glimpses of a sunny green courtyard with a fountain as she walked past to the perfumer's in the next street. Tonight it was blazing with torches as servants and sergeants hurried to and fro. The gate opened; as Marta recognised the Syrian sergeant guarding it, she could hardly repress a shudder. She was almost sure she had seen him before in Chatillon's livery.

"Tell Countess Isabella that Marta Bessarion is here to see her," Marta ordered.

Before the guard could do so, a door in the darkened loggia above flew open and Isabella leaned over the balustrade. "Who is that, Ittack? Is someone here?"

"It's me, my lady," Marta called up softly.

"Marta?" A hectic breath was drawn in. "What are you doing here?"

"It's been three years since I saw you," Marta reminded her former foster-sister with a laugh, "and six or seven since we had a proper talk. I won't stay long if you're busy."

"No, no, do come up!" In the loggia, Isabella kept pace with Marta as she found her way to the foot of the stairs. "Don't mind the servants; they've a terrible lot to do with the coronation tomorrow, and Prince Reynald expected any day. Marta, it *is* good fortune you came. Humphrey's gone to bed early and I have no one to help me pick my gown for tomorrow. There's Heva, but she keeps telling me I ought to wear the blue dotted, and I've worn it till it sickens me. It makes me feel like the Blessed Virgin."

Marta could not help but laugh. "Who would you rather feel like?"

"Like Queen Guinevere," Isabella said, putting her nose in the air as Marta reached the loggia and kissed her cheek.

"You've been reading French romances, I see," Marta teased her, reaching down to scratch the ears of a tiny greyhound that had followed its mistress into the loggia. She had often wondered what sort of person Isabella was growing into; it seemed she had lost none of her taste for love and intrigue. The years suddenly seemed to vanish: her old schoolfellow was the same as ever. "Now don't they say that Queen Guinevere betrayed her lord with a knight of his household? What does Humphrey say to that?"

"Oh, Marta! Humphrey was the one who *gave* me the book." Isabella drew Marta into a large, brightly-lit apartment that looked as though a windstorm had swept through it, for it was strewn with gowns, veils, gloves, shoes, books, jewels, and a small lute. The tiring-woman, Heva, whom Marta remembered from the hectic days at Kerak, stood in the midst of it all grimly packing the mess into two or three large chests.

"Go and get us some sherbet, Heva." Isabella flapped a hand, then scooped up the dog and kissed its nose. "Miles used to laugh at me for drinking the sweet stuff, but I do not love the taste of wine. Can you do my hair in the morning, Marta? You were always so much better at it than me."

"I will if you like." Marta touched her shoulder. "But...do you really want to be queen, Isabella?"

Isabella had been fluttering and chattering like a bird. Now, the look she gave Marta was almost frightened. "Well, I can't very well say *no*, can I?"

Marta felt sick. It was true: Isabella had never been permitted to say no to anything.

The young countess went on fluttering, harder than ever.

"You promised to help me choose my gown." Dropping the dog, she dove into one of the chests and pulled out an ocean of glimmering sky-blue silk with silver spots in clusters of three. "That's the one Heva wanted me to wear. Countess Stephanie had the fabric sent from Constantinople. But *I* like this." A crimson gown made of silk that walked the fine line with purple, a dazzling trick of fine blue threads among the red. Half in love, Marta reached out to touch it, but Isabella had already whisked it away, holding it to the lamplight. "Heva says it would be positively orgulous. I don't see why a queen *shouldn't* be orgulous."

"That reminds me. I have a gift for you." Marta held out the package she had made up in her own quarters before she came. Isabella gave a squeal of excitement as she unwrapped the raw silk into which Marta had folded a filmy white veil, its border sewn with delicate threads of silver.

"For me?" Isabella held it up to inspect the wonderful shimmer. "Marta, it's beautiful! Did you make it? I love it. I'll wear it tomorrow. I've never seen anything like it. Everyone in Kerak will be wearing one next."

"I wish you were not forced to live there," Marta murmured.

"Oh, I *know*. It's such a desert backwater," Isabella lamented. "Humphrey likes the silence; it's good for his studies. But it's so *hot*. I wish I was queen and could live in Jerusalem or Acre or where it pleased me."

"You *will* be queen, tomorrow."

"Oh!" Isabella laughed. "I had forgotten. Yes, that's so."

"Humphrey treats you well, then?"

"How can you ask such a thing, Marta? Of course Humphrey treats me well. He gives me lovely presents and doesn't mind what I say or whom I speak to." Isabella's face darkened. "Countess Stephanie says he spoils me. She says I will disgrace him and myself if I do not show more modesty. What an idea! I would do *anything* for Humphrey. I'd—I'd ride into Arabia to rescue him, as you did for Miles."

For the first time that evening, there was a note of genuine feeling in Isabella's voice. As though everything else had been a bubble of glass and it had suddenly cracked to reveal a steel knife inside. The silence stretched and frayed. Marta heard a sound from the next room: slow, heavy footsteps, like those of a man in full armour trying very hard not to be heard.

I would do anything for Humphrey.

Such as, for instance, distract the White Watcher with gowns and small talk while he fled Nablus.

"Why would men need to be in the stables at night, saddling horses, to prepare for a coronation in the morning?" Marta asked softly.

Isabella's eyes were wide and terrified.

"He's running away, isn't he?" Marta turned on her heel and wrenched open the door to the next room.

She was greeted by a jingle of mail and a reedy yelp of alarm as Humphrey turned from the chest from which he had just taken a sword and belt. He was certainly dressed for a journey, his helmet and cloak lying ready on the bed beside him. For a moment he stared at her with wide eyes and parted lips. Then Isabella threw her arms around Marta from behind and said, "Go, Humphrey, I'll hold her!"

"No, Isabella, st-stay back," Humphrey protested, pulling his sword free of the sheath and extending it in a trembling hand. "I'll take care of this."

But Isabella held her tightly. "Don't do this, Marta! Please!"

Marta had not moved a muscle. "It's all right, Isabella—"

"Stop lying!" Isabella fairly shouted. "It *won't* be all right. There's going to be a *war.* We're *tired* of doing horrible things for other people. Neither of us wants the crown, so there! If Sibylla wants it so much, she's welcome to it!"

Humphrey still had his sword raised, and his face was as pale as paper. Marta sighed. She was half his size and unarmed, but sometimes it felt as though her reputation was as *much* as five armed men.

"I don't have a weapon," Marta told them, patting the arm which Isabella still kept locked about her neck. At fourteen, Isabella was not yet fully grown, and Marta saw no reason to throw the girl off with violence. "I came only to talk."

Neither of them relaxed. "Isabella is r-right," Humphrey said. His stutter was worse than ever, but he forced the words past his trembling lips all the same. "T-tripoli is quite happy to throw us into a war. I may not have much experience of ruling, but even I can see what a piece of f-folly that is. I won't be a party to it, mademoiselle."

Marta had come here with one last sliver of hope, and now it was snuffed out. A great wave of exhaustion came over her and she said, very gently: "I know, my lord. That's why I would have sworn you my fealty. The last thing this kingdom needs is someone who *wants* to rule it. You're the only man I could think of who might put the kingdom first, and yourself second. Who might actually fill the Leper King's place."

Humphrey seemed utterly speechless. "Then there can be no k-kingdom, because I am no king. I wasn't raised to it. I'm just a d-dog at Chatillon's table, and if I do what he bids me this night, I'll *never* be free of him."

He had been so frightened of her, yet he stood his ground, this brave scholar whom they all derided as foolish and effeminate. They were both so impossibly brave.

Marta thought there might be tears in her eyes. "Then go to Jerusalem and be free of him."

Isabella's grip loosened. Humphrey blinked. "Y-you won't tell?"

"The night before your wedding, you made me a promise which, as far as I can tell, you have honourably kept. So long as you keep that promise, my lord, I am your true friend."

"What promise?" Isabella wanted to know.

"Humphrey will explain someday," Marta told her, feeling her face redden. It was Humphrey who had offered the promise, after all—that although he had no choice but to marry Isabella at Chatillon's orders, he would not consummate the marriage without her free consent. "You should ride with him, Isabella. Tripoli will crown *you* if he can't catch Humphrey."

She helped Isabella pack a few necessities and saw them off with a small escort of knights and one attendant for Isabella. By the time Marta returned home, the palace gate was closed; near the stables, however, a grapevine and some protruding masonry made it possible for one as small and agile as herself to climb over the wall. As Marta slipped through the covered passage which led from the service courtyard to the garden, she was surprised to find that, although she had failed in everything she had attempted today, she nevertheless felt at peace.

There would be no war, at least.

"Where have you been?" A whisper sliced the air as she reached her own door, making her jump. Queen Maria was sitting on the bench in the loggia, arms folded within a voluminous woollen shawl.

"My lady!"

The queen rose to her feet. "Persi asked if I knew your whereabouts. When you did not return from your bath, she worried."

Marta swallowed. "I was only seeing a friend in the town." *Strife.* Queen Maria was no fool. When Humphrey and Isabella were missing the next morning, she would instantly know Marta had had a hand in the matter. The truth, then: "Isabella, in fact. The young countess wished for advice in choosing a coronation gown."

The queen considered this. "I'm glad to hear that Isabella is taking the thing seriously." But something in her voice told Marta there was more. "You expressed yourself quite freely in council tonight."

"Yes, my lady."

"You may have made a name for yourself, Marta, and your word carries a great deal of weight with my lord. But do not forget upon whom you depend for position and patronage."

"No, my lady."

As Queen Maria left, Marta let out a long, soft breath. She would be in terrible trouble tomorrow morning.

Chapter X.

In fact, it took so long for anyone to notice Humphrey and Isabella's flight that by Terce, Marta could no longer bear to wait.

All that morning the servants had been going to and fro from the palace to the great basilica of Saint Joseph, decking the church in banners and green boughs. When Marta attempted to soothe her mind with a little weaving, a servant came running to say that Lord Balian wanted her. Marta went up to the cabinet expecting the crisis to break upon her, but Lord Balian only glanced up from his conversation with Tripoli and Caesarea to say, "Oh, Marta, will you trot around to the house of de Riveri and remind Humphrey that he was to be here by Terce?"

There was nothing to be gained by prevarication; Marta drew a breath and said, "Humphrey is in Jerusalem by now."

Lord Balian did not quite hear her. "I beg your pardon?"

"He and Isabella," Marta said, speaking slowly and clearly, "do not want to be crowned. So they have gone to Jerusalem to submit to Queen Sibylla."

* * *

"God help us, Marta," Persi said later, when Marta told her about it, "what happened then?"

"They had another council," Marta said wearily. She was becoming tired of councils, but she had not been able to escape this one.

"Was Tripoli very angry with you?"

Marta grimaced.

This is what comes of allowing a Syrian tirewoman into your councils, Balian, the count had spat. As it was the first time the count had condescended to recognise her existence, Marta supposed she ought to feel thankful. In fact, her gratitude was reserved entirely for the fact that Lord Balian could no longer attempt to arrange a marriage for her with one of Tripoli's stepsons.

"And then?" Persi asked. Her loom had fallen silent while she pressed both hands against her mouth, though whether she was horrified or trying to suppress laughter, Marta could not tell.

"They tried to decide what they would do next."

* * *

With Isabella gone, the next nearest heir to the throne was, of course, Tripoli himself, but that was impossible. Caesarea and the archbishop of Tyre had both absolutely refused to be party to Tripoli's coronation. Lord Balian had objected more tactfully, and Ramla had scowled beneath his forbidding black brows and said, "We might just as well crown Balian, if it comes to that."

"Balian has no claim to the throne," one of the stepsons had objected.

"Maybe not, but he's the kingdom's Prester, King Baldwin's stepfather, *and* the father of two strong sons. Can Tripoli say as much?"

"Ramla." Lord Balian had thrown up his hands. "You're romancing. For one thing, Presters aren't kings. If that were so it would have been my grandfather, Prester John, who became the first king of Jerusalem—not Godfrey."

Ramla had muttered something under his breath about any choice being better than Guy of Lusignan, but no one else had taken him at his word.

"I want to hear what Marta has to say for herself," Queen Maria had said then. She sat at Balian's right hand, white with fury.

Everyone had stared at her then, until Marta began to feel like a prisoner on trial. She folded her hands in front of her—her fingers were cold—and said, "It is not right to make anyone king by force."

* * *

Now, in the workshop, Persi raised incredulous eyebrows. "And what did they say to that?"

Marta shook her head. "They said I was too nice, objecting to Sibylla because she wishes to be queen, and to Humphrey and Isabella because they do not. Perhaps I ought to have told them about the demon."

"The thing is," said Persi, "they're *right*. It's as I've always said: if no one ever lorded it over others, there would be no kingdom. No kings, no peasants, no masters, no slaves."

Marta stared at her. "Then how would anyone find safety? Who would stop Saladin then?"

"I don't *know*," Persi said. "I've only got as far as Gregory of Nyssa did, all those centuries ago, when he asked, *If God does not enslave what is free, who is he that sets his own power above God's?* That's why I just go on living in this kingdom, Marta, and doing the best I can with what I have. Because I don't want to break this fragile peace for a good I can't even imagine." There was something like desperation in Persi's voice; but she softened as she looked at Marta. "All the same, I'm proud of you."

Marta looked up from the interlaced fingers she had been wringing together. "You are? You think I did the right thing?"

"Of course I do."

"Maybe Humphrey would have been the best choice. I don't know. I don't have a seraph's kiss anymore."

"Yes, you do. In *there*." Persi pointed at her breastbone.

"Oh, *that*. Everyone has that."

"Not everyone." Persi picked up her shuttle. "You haven't told me what the lords decided."

"There isn't much else to tell. All of them knew it was over. Tripoli demanded they should keep their oath to the Leper King, but Lord Balian and Caesarea agreed that with Saladin threatening the kingdom, the unity of the realm is of first importance. Even Queen Maria could see that." She fell silent, gnawing her lip in worry. The queen, as she had guessed, was none too happy with her, evidently having her heart set on Isabella's inheriting the throne.

Marta sighed. "Ramla vowed he would leave the kingdom sooner than submit, and Tripoli only looked black as thunder when they told him."

"Probably thinks Ramla's deserting him," Persi said with a decided nod. For a while there was no sound in the small room but the thump of the loom.

"It isn't going to work, you know," Marta said in a low voice.

"What isn't?"

"Lord Balian's attempt to bring peace." Persi sent her an alarmed look as Marta sank onto the bench of her own loom, positioned as it was so that she and Persi could talk easily as they worked. "I mean, it's only a feeling I have. I once met an old Messenger who prophesied some terrible trial by fire after the death of the Leper King. For a while, I hoped that fate might have been averted—but if there is no choice for the kingdom besides Sibylla…" Marta sighed. "I think a battle is coming. A battle for the whole kingdom."

Persi frowned. "Do you think we should follow Ramla's example? Leave the kingdom?"

Marta shook her head. "I'm not afraid," she said. And it was true. Councils and coronations, spies and assignations, sickened and wearied her. But a fight was a clean business, just a matter of lining up your spear with your enemies. She thought of the kingdom she loved, and she thought of Khalil ibn Hassan, who she knew would be her death if she could not first arrange to be his. "If it comes to a fight, I'm *ready*."

Chapter XI.

Sibylla did not expect Chatillon to let her defiance go unpunished. Nevertheless, when her chamberlain announced, on that first morning of her reign, that Prince Reynald had come to beg leave to depart Jerusalem, she agreed in the belief that surely he would not air his grievances during an official leave-taking.

She was wrong.

Sibylla received the prince in the audience hall of the palace, a great echoing room which looked east towards the Temple Mount. At this hour, it was full of clear golden light and noisy with colour. Golden stars glimmered from the blue ceiling, and frescoes above the waist-high marble wall panelling depicted scenes from the life of Saint David. Sibylla, who best loved plain whitewash, had always felt overwhelmed by this place, but it was better than using her brother's solar, which still reeked faintly of medicines, ointments and the sweet sickliness of corrupted flesh.

When Chatillon stalked into the audience-hall it became apparent that he meant more to take, than to beg, his leave. "I am going to Nablus," he announced with a scowl that raked not only Sibylla but her attendants with scorn.

"Indeed," Sibylla said without inflection. She had an idea what he would find at Nablus, but saw no particular reason to enlighten him. "You must convey our greetings to the barons there."

"I'll convey your treachery," he said, wasting no breath. "I don't need to remind you, my lady, on what terms you purchased my support. Or how I promised to reward double-dealing."

"As I'm sure I need not remind you that you swore public fealty to me yesterday afternoon," Sibylla replied. Her body was in a slow panic. When he left, she would start panting as though she had run a mile, but at present she appeared calm, detached, and entirely in command of herself. "Do you mean to break your sworn oath?"

"Yes," he shouted.

Miles of Plancy stepped in front of the prince as though to bar his way to her; a silent warning to moderate his speech. Sibylla forced a smile.

"Then you have taken leave of your senses," she told Chatillon. "You were not the only one to swear oaths yesterday. I could not divest myself of the crown now even if I wished to, and you will not do so without a war. As the lord of Transjordan, even you must see what folly that would be. Next time Saladin besieges you, where will you look for aid?"

"I will not be set at naught," Chatillon bellowed. "All the kingdom knows your sister is Amalric's true heir, and you're no more than an entitled bastard."

"My *lord,*" said Miles of Plancy, mildly. Well, she would sooner be protected by a hireling than by Guy, who would surely make an Aquitan romance of it, complete with flung gage and broken lances.

Moreover, although Chatillon was the first who had dared to say it to her face, Sibylla was painfully aware of certain irregularities in her father's first marriage. Of course, nobody had raised any objection to her brother's accession, though he was whispered to be a bastard and known to be a leper. No, the old scandal was only raked up now because Sibylla had become politically inconvenient.

Lilith flashed into view at her elbow and, for once, restored her equanimity with two words. "They're coming."

Sibylla smiled. "The true heir, as you call her, may have her own opinions on the matter of the succession."

"Isabella will do as Humphrey bids her," Chatillon growled. "And Humphrey will do as *I* bid him."

The doors to the audience hall opened. Her chamberlain, who had had his orders, bowed deeply.

"My lady, Lord Humphrey of Toron and his wife beg admittance."

"What?" Chatillon barked, wheeling to face the two young people as they entered the room.

It was indeed her sister Isabella and her husband: Lilith had prophesied truly. As Chatillon gaped at the errant pair, Sibylla felt the spirit's laughter in her own bones. Humphrey went as white as paper when he saw his stepfather, but he approached the throne anyway, resolutely not meeting Chatillon's murderous gaze.

"M-my lady," he stammered. "I have c-come to offer you my loyal greetings upon the occasion of your c-coronation."

Sibylla did not speak—she was enjoying herself too greatly, and she thought Humphrey deserved to sweat a little before receiving her welcome.

"From Nablus," Isabella added in a clear, high voice. Her cheeks had gone a little pink, and she gripped Humphrey's arm with both hands as though he was a wilting plant and she meant to prop him up. "We've come from Nablus, my lady, in a great hurry, and we only barely got away from Marta the Knight."

Marta Bessarion, Lord Balian's tame saint. Sibylla's lips curled incredulously. She still had a score to settle with the little Syrian who had got her claws into Baldwin, but even she was forced to admit that if the Bessarion was true to form, she had almost certainly sped the two defectors on their way and perhaps been stabbed for her trouble.

Chatillon had recovered his voice. "I'm going to beat you within an inch of your life," he said thickly.

Likely it would not be the first time. Humphrey flinched, looking like a whipped cur. "My lady," he appealed to Sibylla. "They would have made me king by force. Don't hold me to account for a thing I neither dreamed nor wished."

It was a good speech for a youth who had never been permitted to have his own will in anything. If Humphrey was finding his backbone, he might yet become a threat to her; but Sibylla could afford mercy now. In one stroke he had cut off all opposition at the knees.

"Sir Humphrey, you have done well in coming to me, and I will no longer be angry with you. See that you do homage to the king before the morning is out. As for you, Chatillon, it pleases me to have your son and his wife at court with me. You may return to Kerak at once and have their household goods sent to Jerusalem."

Chatillon's only response was an explosive curse and a precipitous departure. Letting out a deep breath, Sibylla relaxed into the stiff wooden embrace of her throne. As she had predicted, her heart rattled her bones as though it was trying to escape from her chest. She would be lucky not to be confined to her bed for the next few days. Chatillon had been right, after all: Sibylla was no Melisende, able to supervise every detail of government. Yet she was happier than Melisende, for unlike her grandmother, Sibylla was married to a man she trusted to rule in her stead.

If only the rest of the kingdom could be brought to see it.

Sibylla had Sara help her from the throne room, aching for the time that all this pother over the succession would be over and she might step back a little from the day-to-day business of state. But even when she had made it back to her chamber and collapsed into bed, rest evaded her. Lilith appeared in a sulky moult of black feathers.

"I told you we should have taken Chatillon. Such fun the three of us could have had together!"

"I did not make myself a queen because I wanted *fun*," Sibylla said.

"I'll yet teach you to relish the taste of blood," Lilith promised. "Still, I don't despair of Chatillon bringing me quite a lot of fun in due season. You know he'll be your enemy."

"But not forever," Sibylla murmured through the fog of her exhaustion. "He can't afford to be."

Lilith did not press the point, and Sibylla fell into a restless sleep from which she was by no means refreshed an hour later when the side of the bed dipped and she woke to find Guy with a hand on her hip.

"Already tired?" he murmured.

"Single combat with Chatillon in the throne room this morning," she answered. "He had an idea I was about to make him king." Guy gave her a look, and she smiled. "This time I did nothing to encourage the misconception, I give my oath."

"Are we winning?"

"We are winning. Where were you?"

"Out with Aimery, inspecting the citadel, taking possession of the keys, and God knows what else. I'm sorry I missed the battle."

"Don't be. You'll have your turn on the throne this afternoon, when the rest of the Watcher faction comes down from Nablus to swear homage."

She said it off-hand, simply for the joy of seeing the look of awe on his face, as though she was a juggler, or the man at the feast who balances on sword-points.

"How can you know that?"

She was not willing to confess her connection with Lilith, so she said only, "Humphrey and Isabella fled Nablus last night and came to do homage this morning. You'll need to see them at once."

"I will." Guy was overwhelmed. "What, *all* the Nablus barons are coming?"

"No, not all." Lilith's information had been clear. "Not Ramla; and possibly not Tripoli, either."

"Not Tripoli?" The wonder faded from his face. "But Tripoli is one of the greatest barons in the kingdom."

So was Chatillon. "They'll come around," she told him. "Neither Tripoli nor Chatillon can afford to go to war with us. Let them cool off and they will see it quite clearly."

But Guy looked at her with foreboding. "Not everyone's head is as cool as yours, my love."

Chapter XII.

That Wednesday, when the world was supposed to end, there was a conjunction in the house of Libra. Yet, the sky remained clear and the weather calm. That night, Marta sat with Lord Balian, Queen Maria and the people of their household in the loggia of their villa at Jerusalem, where they had gone within a few days of the coronation to do homage and swear fealty to the new king and queen. They warmed themselves at a brazier and listened to the minstrel sing of Roland's war with the Moors in Spain. Around midnight, when the end of the song came, Lord Balian stirred in his chair and said, "Well, my queen, shall we kill the fatted calf?" The queen said nothing, and no beast was killed. But within a few days it rained for the first time in more than a year, and after that no one talked of the world ending. Only Marta felt certain that it *was* ending, just not in the way the astrologers had predicted.

By October, the rain was steady and Queen Sibylla had departed Jerusalem for Acre, where she and the king intended to establish their household. Lord Balian and Queen Maria followed them, for the High Court had been summoned to meet at the cathedral of the Holy Cross—and Marta followed Lord Balian, because Persi did not want Michael Zakar to come to Nablus to exchange patterns for cloth as usual.

Queen Maria's house in Acre was not far from the royal palace at the city's centre. Marta ventured out that cool, wet morning sniffing appreciatively at the salt in the air. The honey-coloured walls and roofs of the city, splashed here and there with the vivid turquoise of a dome or broken by the skyward leap of a clock tower, sloped down towards the great harbour embraced by its long moles. North, the city had begun to spill past its wall. West, orchards and vineyards, sugar cane and wheat fields clothed the distant hills.

The largest and richest city in the kingdom, Acre never slept: always there were ships coming and going from the harbour, and caravans filing in and out of the marketplaces. It was not quite as beautiful a city as Jerusalem, for there were fewer gardens and a greater population, together with all their disputes, refuse, and smells. Merchants, pilgrims, tradespeople, beggars, burgesses, and craftsmen clogged the streets while princes and counts clattered up the hill to the palace at the head of armed households, their ladies carried in silken litters. Marta stood back as a pair of burly Hospitaller brothers hurried past carrying a man with a broken head and cut purse-strings; no doubt the victim of one of the city's plentiful criminal gangs. "I wish the lords across the sea would stop sending us their thieves and desperadoes," one burgess-woman grumbled, watching them pass. "The holy places do them no good and they do us much harm."

"And then *we* are blamed for failing to keep the peace," said her friend with disgust.

Marta could not help thinking of Jehan of Cacho. It was a bitter thing that not all malefactors roamed the streets after dark, nor attracted the whole world's censure.

The brothers of St John passed and Marta stiffened as she glimpsed Miles of Plancy on the opposite side of the street. Though he had no attendants to ward off the press of the crowd, the broad bands of golden embroidery on his fine woollen tunic, and the saffron-coloured lining of his cloak, loudly proclaimed his rank and cleared a little deferential space around him.

Marta, as ever, wore a plain tunic of soft dove grey, and since the day was overcast, she had left her black veil at home in favour of a simple rectangle of unbleached linen pinned over her hair and wrapped at the neck—nothing to draw attention, but nothing to hide behind, either. Miles recognised her at once, and the moment the street opened, he made straight towards her.

"I take it you're in town for the *parlement,*" he said, using the Frankish word signifying a meeting of the kingdom's High Court.

Marta shrugged, relieved that he had no harsher words for her. "Not really. I came to see a weaver."

"That's a shame," he said. "Something very interesting is about to happen, and I particularly wanted you to attend."

She did not trust his reasons, any more than she trusted the smirk with which he said the words. But curiosity had always been her weak point. "Well, I won't. You'll have to tell me about it."

"And ruin the surprise?" He raised an eyebrow, but the mutinous look on her face must have decided him. He bent down to whisper in her ear. "Now that Sibylla is Queen, I'm to receive a fief. What do you make of that?"

A fief of land, he meant, with peasants, and rents, and household knights attached to it; not the money-fief with which he had been forced to content himself thus far. Evidently, he meant to rub her nose in his triumph. Marta was not sure why Miles thought she would be affected by the thing at all.

She did her best to overlook the unmistakable gloating tone in his voice, to speak sincerely. "If anyone in the kingdom deserves such a thing, it's you."

"That's magnanimous of you!"

"Of course I'm glad to see you receive a thing *you* have always wanted and *I* have never begrudged you!"

"But you're dissatisfied."

Marta dragged a hand down her face, wishing she could shake him until his teeth rattled. Instead, very softly, she said, "How does it feel? You let me go because you thought you would never get preferment if you married a nobody of a Syrian. And now everyone in the kingdom knows my name. You betrayed me for nothing, and it's eating you hollow. All right. I'll come and see you get your fief. But not out of envy, Miles. I wouldn't know how to envy *you.*"

She turned her back before he could reply, and went down towards the harbour to Michael Zakar's textile workshop. The walk was not quite long enough to calm her frustration, and by the time she reached her destination she still wanted to hit something. The low building was, as ever, loud with the clacking of looms. In the message she received last night, Michael had directed her to knock on the door of the house upstairs if she arrived before Terce; she did as he asked, taking the external staircase from the alley. A young Syrian woman opened the door to her. Knowing that Michael was a bachelor, Marta wondered if she had mistaken her way.

"Good morning," she told the other woman. "Is this Michael Zakar's house?"

The girl's face lit up. "Oh! You must be Marta Bessarion. Come in! I've heard so much about you!"

Marta followed her inside and found a roomy apartment with a small hearth at one end and a sleeping-platform beneath a window at the other. The space between was cluttered with so many bedrolls, cushions, chests, pots, and cabinets, that it was clear Zakar did not, after all, live alone. The man himself sat cross-legged on the sleeping-platform with a desk across his knees, meticulously checking what appeared to be a book of accounts.

"Marta, welcome," he said, getting up. "Will you have anything to eat?"

Last night she had enjoyed a good dinner of spiced lamb, and noon was still some way off. "Thank you, but no." There was a disappointed sigh from somewhere behind her. Marta realised that a plate had been set upon the low table at the centre of the room, carrying dried figs, roasted almonds and soft cheese preserved in honey, with bread to serve it upon. "On second thought," she said politely, "is that cheese and honey?"

Michael smiled fondly at the young woman. "Marta, you've never met my sister Rahel."

Sister. Well, that was all right, and come to think of it, Michael had mentioned a sister. Then something struck her.

"Rahel Zakar?" Marta inquired. "That's a familiar name."

"Indeed?" Rahel blushed and glanced at her brother. "Perhaps you met mother before she died."

"It's an old family name," Michael put in. "The eldest daughter of the family has been named Rahel going all the way back to Rahel the Messenger, at the fall of Jerusalem."

Marta, who had just taken a mouthful of honey and cheese, barely managed not to choke on it. By the time she was able to swallow, she had marshalled her thoughts a little.

"I know—that is, I know *of* Rahel the Messenger," she said. "You can't mean to say that you are her descendants?"

"That's the story," Michael told her. "Her son, Paulus Zakar, was our ancestor."

"Paulus," Marta repeated mechanically. The last time she had seen her younger brother, he was a child, breaking Khalil's sigil in his attempt to drag himself to safety. At only six years of age, he had been trapped in the inferno of Oliveta along with the rest of them, wailing with terror as he watched Khalil's men slaughter the people of the town. Sometimes, when she closed her eyes, she could see his face, tear-stained and desperate, just out of reach and infinitely beyond her power to protect or comfort. Her throat closed, so that the words barely escaped. "Paulus; are you quite sure?"

She only saw Michael's nod; she did not hear a word he said.

Paulus, after all, had survived that inferno, married, fathered a family. Somehow, against the odds, her brother and his descendants had made a life for themselves. It might not look like the life she had enjoyed as the daughter of a Roman noble, but it was a *life.* Full of joys as well as sorrows, and a daughter named Rahel...

The thought washed over her like a cold wave on a summer's day: a shock that took her breath away and left her wanting to laugh and shout. She had family in this time. She was not alone, as she had always thought. Michael was her nephew—many generations removed, but her nephew.

He had stopped speaking and was staring at her in some concern. "Mademoiselle? Is something wrong?"

"Nothing is wrong," Marta said with an effort, pulling herself back to the present. "I thought that Rahel the Messenger was named Bessarion, though."

"Bessarion?" Michael frowned. Naturally, his thoughts went at once to the disaster at Oliveta, which generations of Watchers had come to blame on her father. "I never heard of Rahel Zakar having anything to do with *that* family."

"*Michael!*" Rahel hissed, shoving at her brother. "Pay attention! The Bessarions are *her* family—she's saying we're family!"

Michael blinked at her. "Oh! Oh, pardon!"

"It's all right," Marta said breathlessly. "It's only that Rahel the Messenger was my—my ancestor, too." Perhaps her mother had reverted to her maiden name to avoid being tainted by slander. Watchers had remarked upon Marta's sharing a name with the villain of Oliveta before; she had learned to bite her tongue sooner than flash up in her father's defence. Perhaps someday she would have the courage to tell Michael exactly where she had come from. "I never dreamed I might still have family here. If you don't mind my claiming the relationship?"

Both of them protested warmly. "Of course we don't mind," Michael said. "To think that we're cousins of Marta the Knight! We'll be the envy of the kingdom." He laughed. "If it wasn't so early I'd open a bottle of wine."

"That's all right," Rahel said cheekily. "We'll dine out on this for months."

At that she went downstairs to commence her own work at the looms, leaving Michael and Marta to transact their business. Marta had several bolts of cloth to collect, and two or three samples to inspect for dye colour and quality.

"You know the merchants from Damascus have been predicting a war," Michael said rather soberly once their normal business had been concluded, and he had locked away the gold Marta had paid him.

"I've heard something about it, yes."

"It'll be worse than anything else in our lifetime," Michael told her. "It's been centuries since Egypt and Syria were united under the same sultan. And Saladin can no longer afford to leave the Coast at peace."

"I suppose we have Prince Reynald to thank for that," Marta said bitterly. The prince claimed that his constant raids on passing caravans were intended to injure the sultan's reputation and sow discontent among Saracen merchants and pilgrims who could not rely upon the sultan for protection. Did Chatillon never imagine that such harassment, rather than dividing their enemies, might unite them in hatred of a common foe?

But Michael shook his head. "It isn't Chatillon's fault."

"I don't see that," she said acerbically.

"I don't mean to defend Prince Reynald," he said hastily. "Doubtless he is a man of blood. But for the sultan, this is a matter of religion, just as it was for Duke Godfrey ninety years ago when Jerusalem was taken. Some men go to war not for common, tangible things like a burned farm or a stolen caravan, but for an article of faith that says certain neighbours do not have the right to *be*, whether they be at peace or war." Michael stared at his hands, calloused where the threads ran through them. "I fear this is the sort of war we now face. To justify his wars against his co-religionists, Saladin requires a victory against us. If he can drive out the Christians from the holy places, he will secure his throne for generations."

"Drive us out!" Marta repeated. "Even he cannot expect such a victory."

"He's sworn himself to it all the same," Michael said simply.

All this confirmed what she had heard from Angelos some weeks ago, and others since—but Marta had scarcely given the idea any credit. "We're too strong for him," she said. "He may try, but he'll never succeed."

"I've given some thought to what I would do if Acre fell," Michael said gently. "At present my idea is to move the workshop to Tripoli, or even to Cyprus. If the worst should happen, Marta, you and Persi can always find a place with us for as long as you need it."

If the worst should happen, Marta thought, she would be dead on the battlefield. She meant to kill Khalil or die trying; she would not live to become a fugitive, and sooner than be made a slave again, she would seek an honourable death in battle. All the same, she was touched by his concern. "You're very kind. I'll give Persi your message."

Michael looked at his hands again as though wishing to hide whatever emotion crossed his face. Marta heard what his silence said: that Persi would not go with him if she could help it. Marta ground her teeth, wild with frustration. Where she had failed in bringing Jehan of Cacho to some measure of justice, Michael, with his subtler wits, might succeed. And though Persi might be unable to bring herself to speak to him, Marta would be telling him no more than he had already guessed.

"Jehan of Cacho," she blurted. Michael only looked confused. "A Frank in Walter of Caesarea's household. He was formerly the agent of the viceroy at Cacho; he used to buy weavers in Cairo, to stock the workshop there. *He's* the one Persi can't tell you about, and he's been walking in and out of Nablus as cool as you please. I tried to do something about him, but he only laughed at me and called Persi a liar, and said that no one—"

Michael had gone white—she supposed he must have been speechless. Now he choked. "Marta, stop. Stop talking. Just…" He took a long, deep breath and dragged both hands down his face. "Marta," he said again, in a voice of compressed emotion, *"you cannot be telling me this.* Certainly not against Persi's wishes."

"But she couldn't tell you herself, and there might be other victims—"

"Please tell me you didn't disclose all this to this Jehan of Cacho."

Marta's cheeks flamed. "Of course not."

Michael disappeared behind his hands again. "Thank God for that," he said in a muffled voice.

"I shouldn't have told you, only I thought you already guessed." Marta pressed her hands against her heated face. *Strife,* she thought, as the echoing silence went on. She could imagine, now, as she had been unable to a moment before the words were uttered, what Persi might say if she knew how Marta had betrayed her secret. *Strife,* she thought again. Knowing Michael, he was likely to consider Persi off limits now that he had gained this unfair advantage. "Michael, promise me you'll treat her no differently because you know—"

"What do you take me for?" he protested, looking up with reddened eyes.

Worse and worse. "I don't mean like that!"

She stopped before she could say anything to make things worse. For a long time, Michael only stared at her, looking savagely grieved. At length he got up and turned away from her.

"Jehan of Cacho, you say?"

"Yes. He'll do it again if he thinks he can get away with it." Marta bit her lip. "I'm every kind of fool in the world, Michael, but you're a man of business. Can't you ruin the man somehow?"

"Oh, I can think of a dozen ways to do it," Michael said, almost contemptuously. "Give me three days in his company and I'll learn what he fears. Three weeks, and he'll be ready to kill himself with his own hand.

Marta could not help a shudder. "Will you really do that?"

"I could," he said, still not turning to face her. "At this moment I could. But I'll let myself cool a little before I decide exactly what must be done."

"And you'll come to Nablus yourself, in the usual course of things? For Persi, I mean?"

"I need to think," Michael repeated doggedly. "You should go."

Marta did as he asked, feeling desperately ashamed. Persi's story was her own to tell, not Marta's. If something of the sort happened to her—and Marta was not naïve enough to assume it could not—she would never want Persi blurting it out to Miles. Or to anyone.

Remembering Miles, she sighed. She had promised to attend the *parlement*. The thought was hardly appealing, but she had no other pressing matters, and at least it would take her mind off Persi, and her own folly. It was an hour or two until Nones; time enough to find a place within the cathedral to conceal herself.

Chapter XIII.

"They're waiting for you, my lord and lady," the chancellor announced. In the vestry to the cathedral of the Holy Cross, Sibylla rose from her seat and held out her hand. Guy took it with a nervous laugh.

"What a mess you've gotten me into, my queen!"

Each of them knew this would not be an easy battle, but Sibylla was in no mood for her husband's anxieties. "You knew this day would come when you married me," she retorted. "Remember what I told you."

"I will," he said. As the doors swung open and they moved into the soaring vaulted church, filled with the expectant faces of barons, burgesses and onlookers, he added very softly, "It was a jest, my lady."

Two thrones of carved and polished wood had been set up on the dais to one side of the altar, and Guy seated Sibylla at one of them before ascending to the lectern. A complete hush fell over the cathedral, as though everyone was holding their breath: few of the Acre burgesses would have been in Jerusalem for the coronation, and half the barons had been in Nablus. Now they were waiting to see what sort of king Guy of Lusignan would be. If he faltered or misspoke, they would be quick to turn it against him.

As Lilith had predicted, Tripoli was not here, nor his four stepsons. But—"Ramla is here," Sibylla breathed.

Lilith appeared, lolling on Guy's throne beside her, invisible to the rest of the church. "Oh, yes," she said with a low chuckle. "You didn't think he would move on without making a scene?"

Guy cleared his throat, an explosive sound in the hush, and then recited his brief speech.

"My lords, you know by now that I have been crowned king in Jerusalem. I know that it is God who has granted me so great a favour, and none other. And therefore, although I cannot but be aware of my own unworthiness, I beg you not to hold me in any scorn, but to pay me homage and do fealty, the better to serve and counsel me as vassals should their lords."

That said, he stepped down from the lectern and met Sibylla's eyes as though looking for her approval. She bowed her head to him, knowing how important it was that she should be seen to support him. If Guy was tolerated, it was only by right of his marriage to Amalric's daughter.

Taking his place in his own throne—which Lilith vacated with a flutter of black wings and a mocking laugh—Guy addressed the chancellor in a clear voice. "Bishop Peter! Who has not yet done homage?"

The bishop consulted a wax tablet. "Baldwin of Ramla, my lord. And Count Raymond of Tripoli, who is your vassal by right of his marriage to the Princess of Galilee."

"Very well." Guy drew a deep breath. "Prince Reynald, will you summon Raymond of Tripoli to do homage?"

It was the day's first skirmish, and perhaps the most decisive one. Chatillon had, to Sibylla's surprise, answered the summons to Acre. She had half expected that he, like Tripoli, would withdraw to his fief in high displeasure. Nevertheless, he was here, arms folded and scarred face scornful.

"Until now Chatillon has been our supporter," Sibylla had said, as they laid their plans. "We must give him the opportunity to continue. We must make him feel secure. If you call upon his support it will show that whatever you know or suspect, you are willing to be reconciled."

"I'd rather declare the man felon and exile him from the kingdom," Guy had said with a flash of temper.

But both of them knew this was not the time to disrupt the kingdom further. Sibylla could not help breathing a sigh of relief when, at last, Chatillon pushed away from the pillar he had been leaning against and, stepping onto the dais, turned to face the crowd.

"Raymond of Tripoli, come forward to do homage for the fief of Galilee."

Custom dictated that a man should be formally summoned three times before being held to have defied his lord, but Ramla interrupted loudly: "He is not here. He is in Tiberias."

This was the day's second skirmish, and seemed unlikely to be resolved as easily as the first. For the benefit of the onlookers, Sibylla lifted an eyebrow and asked, "Was the count not informed of his duty to attend court?"

"Yes, my lady," the chancellor said with a sigh. "We sent by the hand of Ralph of Rochefort."

"Then he has defaulted, as a felon and rebel," Guy said. "We will debate his punishment soon. Chatillon, summon Baldwin of Ramla."

"Baldwin of Ibelin, come forward to do homage for the fief of Ramla," Chatillon said with an ironic bow towards the man he addressed, who stood four-square at the centre of the choir, with every eye in the church upon him.

Ramla folded his arms, glowering at Guy with implacable hatred.

"Baldwin of Ibelin, lord of Ramla, come forward to do homage," Chatillon repeated. Still, Ramla made no response.

"He means to keep his oath," Lilith whispered. Sibylla restrained herself from attempting to brush the demon away like a troublesome gnat. Of course Ramla meant to keep his oath. When he had made it, Sibylla had not counted him any great loss; but then, she could not have known how desperate she might be for supporters once she did take the throne. She hardened her heart. Ramla was a fool and she would waste no regrets on him.

Guy was not so ready to give in. "Come, my friend, give me your homage and fealty," he said when Chatillon's third summons received no reply. "Not for my own sake, but out of pity to Christendom and goodwill to these high-born men who are here."

Only then did Ramla unhook his thumbs from his belt and come forward, followed by the knights of his household. He stopped at the foot of the dais steps. The whole church seemed to hold its breath.

Ramla lifted his chin and spoke. "My father never did homage to yours.

Why should I do homage to you?"

From the back of the church, someone cheered, but was at once quelled with hisses and shouts of "Shame!"

Guy flushed to the forehead and said, "You must do homage, my lord, if you wish to hold your fief."

"I know the law of this kingdom," Ramla said scornfully. "I commend my fief to you until my son Thomas comes of age. Then, if you wish my friends to continue to be your friends, you will bestow Ramla upon him. I do not care to whom the boy swears fealty, but I have sworn to quit your kingdom within three days."

"Will he not stay and fight?" Lilith complained. "What a child!"

Sibylla did not move or speak. Ramla's defiance did not trouble her so much as Tripoli's. It was better that Ramla should leave the kingdom in a childish fit of pique than stay and make war.

Ramla turned to face the assembled barons, and Sibylla thought that his gaze lingered on his brother, Balian. "I despise you all," he declared, "for giving up your privileges and liberties to a usurper." Then he clicked his fingers and stalked down the nave towards the door. He was followed by the knights of his household, but then others began to leave also, rear-vassals and knights whom Sibylla had not imagined had any great objections to her or her husband. As the church emptied, one of them approached the dais.

"Sir, these are the names of the vassals who tender their fiefs again to the king and declare their intention to leave the kingdom, and not return."

Guy's face had gone slack and pale. Sibylla twitched the paper from the man's hand and then he, too, joined the exodus. She watched numbly, grasping in her thoughts for some explanation. Most of the kingdom's vassals and rear-vassals had already done homage and did not need to attend a *parlement* of the High Court. Ramla must have intentionally seeded the church with his own followers, meaning to convince all onlookers that the new king lacked popular support among his own barons.

It was nothing, Sibylla thought. Some few dozens of malcontents. But then, with the kingdom's full complement of knights numbering barely a thousand, how could dozens be spared?

"Where will they go?" Guy asked, staring at the void that had opened up, not only in the echoing nave but also the defences of the kingdom.

Lord Balian cleared his throat. "To Antioch, my lord, to take service with Prince Bohemond."

"Saint John, pray for us!"

"No doubt he does," Lord Balian replied smoothly.

"Ah," Lilith whispered, in Sibylla's ear. "You didn't know they would do that."

"Why didn't you tell me?" Sibylla pressed cold fingers to her lips, fiercely angry with herself for sitting silent and helpless while her hard-won kingdom frayed at the seams. She had been too complacent. She ought to have foreseen this—ought to have found some way of making Ramla stay, or at least his followers.

"Thrones and Powers, mortal, I can't be everywhere at once. You should have offered Ramla one of your daughters as a wife for his son."

"You should be quiet," Sibylla hissed behind her hand, "and then perhaps I would be able to *think*."

The last footsteps soon faded from the vestibule and the sun shone uninterrupted at the door. Guy seemed to have recovered his countenance. "I will not be defied," he said, straightening in his chair. "You have made me your king, and your king I will be. Chatillon, summon Miles of Plancy."

At the first summons, Plancy started forward, a smile tugging at his lips; he gave Chatillon a look of triumph as he kneeled before the king.

"You, Sir Miles, have done the queen and myself faithful service," Guy said, "particularly in the matter of the treasury key. Now we wish to reward you with a fief. I am giving you the village of Legione."

It was the final skirmish Sibylla had planned for this day, and as she suspected, the news sent a murmur through the remaining barons. Lord Balian started forward. "That village is part of Galilee, my lord. It is in the gift of the count of Tripoli."

"Tripoli has committed felony and treason," Guy growled. "As such, his land is in my gift now. Or does anyone here say that he has not?"

There was a numb silence in the church. All the barons who remained had paid their homage, even Balian of Ibelin and Walter of Caesarea.

Guy stood, extending a hand to Sibylla as a signal that the meeting was over. "We will take counsel, my lord Miles, for the recovery of your fief."

The vestry door closed behind them; but even through the solid walnut panels, Sibylla heard the hum of many agitated voices. She put up her hands and lifted the crown from her aching head. Her face must have betrayed her sense of foreboding, because Guy put a comforting arm about her waist.

"They must know who their queen is, Sibylla."

"And their king," she told him, but her smile did not sit well on her face. Sibylla had won herself the crown: now she wondered whether the cost might be more than the kingdom could safely afford to pay.

* * *

"You may have been crowned, my lord, but a king you will never be, until you've reduced Tripoli to obedience—or else to his grave."

It was the Master of the Temple, Gerard of Ridefort, who spoke with such bald honesty. Sibylla did not mind honesty. In the king's solar, a comfortable south-facing room that still smelled faintly of her dead brother, a small group of their most trusted supporters had assembled to take counsel—her uncle Joscelin, Guy's brother Aimery, the Master of the Temple.

In better days, there would have been another in attendance.

"I asked Chatillon whether he meant to be here tonight," Uncle Joscelin said. "He said he was more inclined to follow Tripoli's example than to devise his punishment."

Ridefort frowned. "What is that supposed to mean?"

"Chatillon was offended at my having crowned Guy without consulting him," Sibylla said. There was no point in making further explanations.

"By heaven, who else ought you to have crowned?" Ridefort asked in exasperation. "Tripoli would have defied you even had you offered to marry one of his stepsons. He's a Saracen at heart, and too proud to pay homage to anyone, unless it should be Saladin himself."

That was a ridiculous notion, but then, Ridefort had been venomously at odds with Tripoli for years, nursing some old insult to his honour. Sibylla had no high opinion of her cousin, but not even Tripoli would go to Saladin for protection. The sultan did not take Christians as vassals, and no one in Tripoli or Galilee would accept a Mahometan convert as their lord. "Tripoli will never do that," she said coolly. "Which means that he will capitulate. Our task is to make that sooner rather than later."

"Show him who is king," Ridefort said promptly. "Muster an army and besiege Tiberias. Bring Tripoli to heel, and Chatillon will also fall into line."

"You mean to begin a war?" Uncle Joscelin protested. "Can we afford that at present?"

"Can we afford not to?" Sibylla put in harshly. "How can we allow this state of affairs to continue, with six months of truce left and Saladin mustering an army in Damascus?"

"Galilee can raise a hundred knights," Aimery said—as the constable of the kingdom, it was his duty to command the army. "You can muster two hundred from your counties of Jaffa and Ascalon alone, my lord king. The numbers are in our favour. But without a quick victory, you'll risk devastating a border fief and decimating the fighting strength of the kingdom—what's left of it."

"Tripoli will capitulate," Sibylla repeated, but even as she said the words she doubted their truth. Had Tripoli meant to capitulate, he would surely have attended today's *parlement*. Evidently he had made up his mind to give them a battle, if they wanted one. Still, why should the fool not have a battle? He had been her rival all her life. It was he who had tried to force her into a marriage with Ramla. It was he who had driven a wedge between Guy and the Leper King. Had it not been for Humphrey and Isabella's blessed obstinacy, he would have done his best to topple her from her throne and put a pair of children there instead.

Sibylla did not want to frighten Tripoli; she wanted to crush him.

"Then it's decided," Guy was saying. "Send out the *arriere ban*, Aimery. We will muster at Nazareth."

"Decisive action," Ridefort said approvingly, "is just what you need to prove your authority, my lord."

The meeting broke up. Sibylla surfaced from vengeful dreams of Tripoli when Guy put a warm hand to her cheek.

"What is it?" she asked.

"Are you sure you're well?" Guy hesitated. "You aren't normally so reckless, Sibylla."

She stared at him with parted lips. Devil take it: he was right. She was normally more cautious than this; more in command of her emotions. "I'm tired," she said. "I need to rest."

Sibylla hurried to her own chamber and shut the door in the faces of her attendants. "Lilith," she whispered, and the demon stepped from behind her. Tonight, Lilith was almost human in appearance: only a cloak of iridescent black feathers hinted at her true nature. Nonetheless, Sibylla almost screamed at the sight of her. Pale skin, black hair, shadowed eyes, red lips—it was just like looking into a mirror.

A sudden, horrible thought occurred to Sibylla: that one day the demon would resemble her so well that Lilith could take her place, and no one be any the wiser.

"What is this?" Sibylla gestured to the demon's assumed shape, so like her own.

"Oh, this? Call it practice."

Sibylla swallowed, hard. "What, do you mean to supplant me?"

"It's tempting." Lilith shrugged. "What did you want?"

Sibylla stared at the demon. "You've been influencing me," she hissed. "You tried to make me crown Chatillon. Now you're trying to get me into a war with Tripoli."

"I wouldn't say that I've *tried*," Lilith said with a laugh. "I'd say that I've *succeeded*."

"And now you mean to take my place?"

"Why not? Possessing you would put me in command of the Enemy's own city, and no one would be any the wiser." Lilith ran a pointed, inhuman tongue across her lips. "Imagine being able to boast of *that.*"

Sibylla had never been a particularly devout woman, but she felt suddenly, appallingly sure that she was damned; that she was only beginning to experience the torments of Hell. "Leave me alone," she whispered.

"It'll be better if you don't fight," Lilith told her. "It's been so long since I've inhabited a body of flesh. I'm going to eat honey and milk. I'm going to drench myself in perfumes. I'm going to take that handsome dullard of yours to bed and make you a demigod for an heir—"

"You won't *touch* my husband." Sibylla sucked in a ragged breath. "And I don't want that kind of heir."

"You should really consider it, my sweet. The Saracens will have a demigod of their own before too much longer, and then you'll wish you had listened to me."

To fight so hard for a kingdom that was hers by right, just to become an empty shell for Lilith to inhabit—the thought was unbearable. In desperation, Sibylla went to the jewel-casket at the foot of her bed and threw it open, tossing aside rings, necklaces and circlets. The thing she searched for was not there. Brushing past Lilith again, she threw open the door, startling Alix and Sara from their embroidery.

"Have you seen my charm?" she asked them. "A silver hand, with an eye of blue glass in the palm?"

The ladies looked at each other as though they agreed with Guy that the queen was not herself today. "That little thing of silver gilt? You'll find it with your hairpins, my lady," Alix said.

Sibylla dug out the little trumpery thing, given her as a gift so many years ago to ward off the Poison Mother. The ladies eyed it dubiously.

"Have you tried speaking to the Watchers, my lady?" Sara asked.

"To Hell with the Watchers," Sibylla retorted, putting the charm on its thin leather thong around her neck, and concealing it in her bosom beneath the folds of her veil. For a moment she stood looking at herself in the mirror. Lilith had vanished, whether because of the charm or because of boredom she could not tell. The Watchers! Was that the best Sara could offer? Sibylla could never go to Prester Balian for help. Even if they were not enemies, that would be a humiliation too great for her to stomach. As for Marta Bessarion—well, Sibylla had stabbed the Syrian and nearly killed her, and then had tried to sell her and the Lance to the Saracens. Even if Sibylla could have swallowed her pride, there was no hope of help from the Watchers.

That left the charm. Sibylla touched it where it lay beneath the neckline of her plain silken gown. She would wear it, but she would not trust it. Even if Lilith never reappeared, Sibylla could never again believe that her thoughts were entirely her own.

She bowed her head, the pains that had haunted her all day now returning to rack her body as her agitation worsened. Damned? She was already in hell.

Chapter XIV.

November—one month later

Tiberias, that chilly November evening, was far from a welcoming prospect. As Marta and Pomers descended the rolling Galilean hills, the stronghold on the shores of Lake Tiberias glimmered with homely lights amid the descending twilight. Once she reached the town gate, however, all welcome proved to be an illusion. The walls had been fortified, with screens to fend of missiles and ditches to impede siege-towers. Red torches blazed from every tower, strong enough to illumine the shadowy figures of sentries patrolling the battlements. As for the great gate, that was locked tight. When Marta rapped on the door with the carnelian pommel of her dagger, for a long moment there was no answer: only feet running to and fro above, and low voices hurriedly conferring.

She knocked again, but all she received was an unfriendly shout from the gatehouse.

"Be off with you! No admittance after sunset!"

"But I'm a friend," Marta protested. "It's me, Marta Bessarion, a fosterling of Balian of Ibelin!"

"We know who you are," said a new voice, this one amused and lazy: Raoul of Tiberias. "You might as well open the wicket for her, Bertrand. She's from Lord Balian, and she doesn't take *no* for an answer."

Marta waited to be let inside before saying apologetically to the reluctant Bertrand, "As a matter of fact I've come to see Princess Eschiva. I have a delivery of cloth for her."

Four weeks ago, in the cathedral of the Holy Cross at Acre, Marta had watched from the shadows while Miles received his long-awaited fief—a Galilean village. In giving it to Miles, the king had effectively declared war on the count of Tripoli.

"I would expect nothing less of Guy," Lord Balian had protested when the *arriere ban* came to Nablus, summoning the knights of the kingdom to muster for war, "but has Queen Sibylla taken leave of her senses? The kingdom cannot afford a war *now,* of all times. They ought to negotiate, not fight. Why not offer a marriage between one of Sibylla's daughters and one of the Galilee stepsons?"

"Will you go to the muster?" Queen Maria had asked. The question had struck Marta with a sense of foreboding; during the Leper King's lifetime no one would have dreamed of defying the *arriere ban.*

"I'll go," Balian had said at once, "because there ought to be someone with the king who can appeal to him on Tripoli's behalf."

Even now, as Marta made her way through the rain-sodden streets towards the palace of Tiberias, Lord Balian was in Nazareth with the king, hoping to soften Guy's purpose. But with the kingdom on the brink of disaster, Marta had been unable to sit still and wait. Perhaps King Guy had responded in haste, but the longer she considered Tripoli's behaviour, the more she doubted his motives. If he really thought Sibylla an unworthy queen, he ought to leave the kingdom. His lands in Tripoli owed no allegiance to the crown of Jerusalem. To stay and fight when he had no allies and no hope of victory—that was an end Marta could sympathise with if it was truly done for the sake of conscience; but was it?

Was Tripoli so aggrieved that he meant to destroy the kingdom rather than let Guy and Sibylla rule it? It was this question that had brought her to Tiberias.

"I don't recall ordering any cloth from you," said the princess of Galilee when Marta was admitted to her private cabinet. Princess Eschiva was not a young woman, but tonight she seemed particularly weary, her severely handsome face scored with deep dragging lines. She was facing a siege, and her desk was littered with ledgers and accounts.

Her very weariness gave Marta hope. "Forgive me imposing upon you, my lady. I *have* brought you a bolt of siqlatin. As a gift." She laid the fabric on the princess' desk, smoothing out its rich, rust-red sheen. It would match beautifully with one of the princess' former commissions, and make a very fine undertunic or cloak lining.

The princess touched the fabric appreciatively, but then her eyes narrowed. "Did you come on some errand from Lord Balian, then?"

"No, my lady. I came on my own account." Marta sighed. "You know that King Guy is mustering an army at Nazareth to besiege you."

"It would be strange indeed if I did not."

"Well—Tiberias is yours, my lady, and a patrimony for your sons. They will not profit in any way from going to war with the king."

Princess Eschiva reddened slightly. "Count Raymond took up the command of my fief when he married me. By your leave, I'll debate the good of my fief with him."

"Forgive me for seeming to interfere," Marta said. "But surely a lord as great and experienced as Count Raymond of Tripoli ought not to risk the honour and fortunes of all Christendom so lightly."

Princess Eschiva stood. "Then trust that he has not."

It was a clear dismissal, but Marta did not move. "I wish that I could," she said bluntly. "Before he died, King Baldwin made me promise I would protect the kingdom. I cannot stand by and let this feud bring down ruin on all our heads. I wish to believe Count Raymond means well, my lady; that's why I am here at all. If you will not answer my questions, perhaps he will."

The princess' mouth tightened; but her shoulders rounded with defeat. Like everyone else in the kingdom, Eschiva must have known the tales of the White Watcher and her wonderful lance. "Very well. Wait in the antechamber here, and I will send the count to meet you when he returns from inspecting the wall."

Marta entered the antechamber, a room comfortably furnished with low seats near the heated floor. A stoppered glass jug of watered wine stood on a chest to one side lest guests become thirsty during their wait. She had scarcely set foot within than the door closed behind her and the lock clacked.

That was never a good sign. She glanced about the room and spotted a second door to her right, which must lead into the loggia. Marta tried the ring-latch, but that too had been locked from the outside. The only windows were narrow and looked into the loggia, where a couple of sergeants now took up their position on either side of the door.

Marta had the Lance slung over her shoulders and good sound armour on her back; it was rather charming the princess believed a few locks and sentries could stop her leaving any time she wished. At present, however, she had no intention of doing so. She had come to see Tripoli, and she would not leave until she had seen him.

In any case the wait was not a long one, and it ended with Tripoli himself entering the room flanked by two knights and followed by his wife. Marta bowed when he entered, but the count's welcome was not a warm one. "My wife tells me you have been making threats, mademoiselle."

"That was not my intention, my lord. I came to tell you that Lord Balian is going to try to make peace between you and the king. Please, for the good of the kingdom, accept what they offer."

The iron-grey count looked stubborn. "You may tell Balian that I will accept nothing less than the kingdom."

For a moment, Marta thought her ears had deceived her. Then, in her shock, she spoke more bluntly than was perhaps wise. "Even Lord Balian has now done homage to King Guy, and has joined the muster at Nazareth. How do you imagine you will make yourself king?"

"Worse men have done so," Tripoli said with a scowl. "Guy of Lusignan had no allies, either. Nor any family. Nor courage, nor even wisdom. All he had was broad shoulders and a pleasing face. What fools women are!"

Anyone who had spent five minutes in Queen Sibylla's presence, Marta thought, ought to know that she was no fool. In her own coldly rational way she was devoted to her husband: a rarity in noble matches. No doubt she felt she could trust him. Who was to say that marrying for love was not wiser, in the end, than marrying for practical reasons of trade or politics?

Before Marta could stop herself, she said, "And you, my lord, do not even have the pleasing face." One of the knights choked. Tripoli reddened. "I mean," she added hastily, "that not even the Watchers will take your part now. I would have done anything to prevent Sibylla becoming queen, but without hope of success, any rebellion will only harm the kingdom to no good purpose."

"I would have had *every* hope of success, had the Ibelins stood by me," Tripoli said. "As it is, let Guy come against me. I am ready for him."

"You will face the combined strength of the kingdom with a bare hundred knights?"

"That's no business of yours." Tripoli turned to leave.

Marta raised her voice. "And once you're king, what then? When Saladin sees that you and King Guy have destroyed each other, how will you stop him seizing what's left of the kingdom?"

Tripoli turned with a hard smile. "If that's what is bothering Balian, tell him not to worry himself on account of Saladin. He and I are good friends. When I am king, we will live at peace. No more invasions of Egypt, no more raids on the Red Sea, no more attacks on passing caravans. We will have nothing to fear."

Marta wished for one moment of poignant longing that she could believe him. Instead, she shook her head. "Maybe that's how it could be with the desert tribes, or with a different sultan. But Saladin needs a victory against us to justify his conquests. He always has. That won't change if you are king."

"You don't know what you're talking about." There had been a knock at the door, and now Tripoli raised his voice. "Come in! You, Aimon, take her to the gate and shut her out."

This was a signal discourtesy, but having been locked up, patronised and belittled, Marta had no particular wish to stay. Only to have some parting words.

"Not everyone can be brought to live at peace, my lord. The Saracens are at our very door, intent on our destruction. We must—"

The words failed on her lips as the door opened and Khalil ibn Hassan strode into the room.

For a moment, Marta thought she was seeing things, but Tripoli muttered "Devil take it," and those words told her everything. The sorcerer was really here. Gloved and booted for a journey in black robes and a burnished cuirass, with four attendants trailing behind him. An honoured guest in the heart of Tiberias. An embassy from Saladin.

This was the reason Tripoli did not fear to go to war with Guy of Lusignan, the reason Marta had been locked in the antechamber, lest she wander away from the room and stumble upon something she was not meant to see. The reason for the running feet and furtive whispers in the gatehouse when she arrived.

Strife. The Bessarion Lance had come off her shoulders somehow and was now clenched in her hands. Khalil's eyes fixed upon her and Marta took a step back.

"Go to the king, Marta Bessarion." Tripoli said, turning to grasp at her arm. "Go to Guy of Lusignan and tell him that war with me is war with Saladin."

Evidently, now that Tripoli had failed to keep his secret, he meant to threaten the king with it. Marta shook him off, impatient of the restraint on her spear arm. Khalil paid the count no attention, either. Doubtless he had been warned to keep out of her sight. So why was he here?

"Marta Bessarion," Khalil said quietly. "I thought I heard your voice."

Marta backed another step.

The sorcerer's eyes fell to the dagger she wore at her side and he actually smiled. "You received my birthday gift."

Numbers flashed through her mind. Five Saracens. Three Franks. One Marta Bessarion, her back against the wall. The odds were hardly to her advantage. In that moment of hesitation, a distant voice spoke directly to her mind.

Run, it shrieked.

In a flash Marta wheeled and seized the ring-latch on the door to the cabinet. It was still locked, but Marta felt something like fire and lightning running in her blood; something akin to the thrill that seized her in battle.

With one splintering, wrenching movement she tore the latch from the door as easily as she might tear a weed from a garden-bed. She hurled the iron ring full into Khalil's face and had the satisfaction of seeing him stagger into his attendants' arms with a cry of pain. Then she tore the door open, crossed the cabinet in two steps and was out on the loggia, racing for the downwards steps.

From the shouts in the antechamber, she had left Tripoli and his confederates in complete disarray. Pomers waited in the courtyard, his nose wet from the cistern where he had been drinking his fill after the journey from Nazareth. "Make way," Marta gasped, snatching the reins from the stable boy who held him.

No alarm rose behind her. No one stopped her at the palace gate, nor at the gate of the town. Still, Marta scarcely drew rein or breath until she was up in the hills and the trees arched over her, providing shadow and shelter. Then she pulled Pomers to a halt, gazing behind her at the homely, deceptive lights of Tiberias.

Maybe she ought to have stayed and fought. This was the second time Marta had been face to face with Khalil and had run away. She ought to have killed him, or at least set a time and place to meet him in battle. But his sudden appearance, when she was already surrounded by unfriendly faces, had been too much for her—and then there had been that shriek ringing soundlessly in her ears: *Run.*

She had experienced something like this before; it was just one more of the odd things that happened when you wielded an enchanted lance.

Far more worrying was the sorcerer al-Aziz Khalil paying Tiberias a visit. Marta bit her lip. Had Khalil stayed out of her sight, as he was no doubt meant to, she might have suspected Tripoli of nothing worse than wishful thinking. But this—Saracens in Tiberias—this was nothing short of treason.

"Strife," Marta muttered. Lord Balian would be crushed. Tripoli was more than a close friend; he was a *Watcher,* sworn to a righteous life of selfless service. A moment ago, hot with anger, Marta had been half inclined to ride back down the hill and challenge Khalil at once to a duel.

Now she felt as cold as the autumn wind scouring the hills. Division and betrayal—was this how kingdoms fell?

If it came to a battle Marta would have ample opportunity to kill her enemy. Yet battle must be averted at all costs now: they could not fight both Tripoli and Saladin.

She turned her horse's head towards Nazareth, praying that no accident would delay her.

Chapter XV.

Four hours later when Marta returned to Nazareth, she caught Lord Balian in the courtyard of the bishop's palace. He was leaving for the camp, outside the town, where the knights of the kingdom had mustered. "Did you speak to the king, my lord?" she asked breathlessly. "What did he say?"

Balian shook his head. "Not yet. It's been a busy day, and all the talk has been of camps and wells and roads."

"It's all useless," Marta said tightly. "We can't attack Tiberias. I've come from there with news the king must know at once."

"You went to *Tiberias?*" he asked sharply. When Marta did not answer, instead turning Pomers towards the palace, Balian hurried to catch her bridle. "It's nearly midnight, Marta. The king has retired and Miles just sent me away. Tell me instead."

It was Miles' name that decided her. She meant to see the king tonight, Miles or no Miles.

"It can't wait," she said, sliding from Pomers' back onto legs that felt stiff and stubby after so long on horseback.

Lord Balian laughed. "He'll be in his bath, Marta."

The baths—that was a useful thought. "Hold Pomers for me," was all she said, before heading towards the scent of wood smoke that poured from chimneys to one end of the palace. Nazareth was ruled by a bishop, not a lord, who had put his house at the king's disposal during the muster. But bishops, like other men, needed ovens to bake their bread and furnaces to heat their bathwater. Marta found the bathhouse itself not too far from the furnaces, faintly scented steam issuing from the grilles covering the windows. A lamp glimmered within, and when she put her nose against the finely-wrought iron whorls Marta saw that the king was in fact bathing in the small, steaming pool beneath the barrel-vaulted roof. His back was to her, little more visible than his head and those broad shoulders, of which Tripoli had spoken in such slighting terms.

Marta rapped against the iron grille. "My lord?" A startled splash rewarded her efforts. "It's me, Marta Bessarion. May I come in? I've just come from Tiberias with urgent news."

King Guy said something profane. "Don't you know what the time is?"

"It can't wait, my lord."

She heard a put-upon sigh. More water sloshed, and a moment or two later the back door leading from the bathhouse towards the furnaces opened. A wary Guy of Lusignan beckoned her inside. Beneath a robe lined with squirrel fur, he was dripping wet, but he had his sheathed sword under one arm. His eyes were wary as he scanned her from her steel gaiters to the Bessarion Lance across her shoulders and the fuzzy plaits wrapped around her temples.

"If the Watchers sent you here to kill me it will do them no good," the king said at length. "I'm only a sort of glorified henchman, and I'm not afraid to die."

"I'm not an Assassin," Marta said indignantly. How exactly like Queen Sibylla's husband to think that Lord Balian would send her to kill someone—or that she would be sufficiently lacking in her own judgement to comply. "I was telling the truth. I have news from Tiberias. This is what I *do*."

At first Guy seemed incredulous, but then understanding dawned and he looked almost pleased. "I knew I was inheriting the Leper King's crown, but I didn't know I was getting the White Watcher to boot. But you ought to have gone to my wife. She is the one who—"

"Last time I went to the queen, she stabbed me." Marta let the king digest that for a moment before going on. "You should know that Tiberias is full of Saracens, my lord. Al-Aziz Khalil himself is there. And Tripoli says that if he is attacked, Saladin will send reinforcements. He believes that Saladin will help him seize the throne."

"He *what?*" Guy stared, disbelieving. Then he buckled his sword-belt over the robe. "This is treason. If Tripoli thinks I am going to back down because of this—"

"You can't still mean to fight him," Marta protested. "This is madness."

"He's the felon, not me."

"But you are," Marta said, exasperated. "You and Queen Sibylla locked the gates of Ascalon against the Leper King, and you slaughtered the Bani Iaith at Darum to provoke him. You even tried to make your own alliance with the Saracens. King Baldwin had every reason to go to war with you, but he relented." She drew breath; it was an unusually long speech for her. "How can you expect to rule a kingdom on your own terms, my lord, and expect everyone to fall in with you, when the only pleasure you consult is your own?"

Guy's face had reddened, and Marta, who knew the young king to be arrogant and self-willed, braced herself for a reaction. Instead, he gulped and said, "That's fair, I suppose. What would you have me do?"

For a moment she was lost for words. Guy of Lusignan, asking her for counsel? Guy of Lusignan, able to be reasoned with when Raymond of Tripoli could not?

"Offer a diplomatic settlement," she said at length. Balian's suggestion occurred to her. "A marriage alliance with one of the stepsons, or something."

The king scowled. "My daughters are too young for marriage." This, too, was hypocritical given Isabella's untimely marriage, but Marta refrained from pointing it out. "And I don't trust Tripoli to see past his own ambitions. He misjudged Humphrey's willingness to be king, and he was caught by surprise when his supporters at Nablus chose to do me homage. Now he's committed the folly of an alliance with Saladin. How do we convince a man like this that we offer something better?"

"An alliance with the Saracens won't sit well with Tripoli's family and vassals," Marta said, recalling the deep lines in Countess Eschiva's face. "If you provide the way out, they will force him to take it."

The king rubbed his chin in thought. "I'll need to speak to my wife," he said at last. "Come with me."

Marta opened her mouth to refuse, but before she could say anything, the bathhouse door opened and Queen Sibylla herself stalked inside, followed by Miles of Plancy.

The queen was ready for bed in a fur-lined robe of her own, her black hair streaming down her back. White to the lips with anger, she seemed like an avenging angel. "What is the meaning of this, Guy?"

The king looked from his wife to Marta and back again. "My love, this is not what it appears to be—"

"It appears to *me* as though the little meddler is trying to persuade you to spare Tripoli."

"Ah. Well, honestly, I agree with her," King Guy said, recovering himself. "A diplomatic settlement—"

"And what guarantee do we have that Tripoli will be content with a settlement?" Queen Sibylla hissed. "He tried to take the throne six years ago and was foiled only by my marriage to *you*. If my brother had taught him a lesson then, you and I would not be forced to do so now."

"He's in league with Saladin, my lady," said Marta. "And he's allowed Saracens into Tiberias."

Queen Sibylla's mouth opened, but no words came forth. For a moment there was a silence in the bathhouse, broken only by the infrequent drip of condensed steam from the roof. Marta stole a glance at Miles and saw that even he had pursed his lips in a silent whistle.

"How do we know she's telling the truth?" the queen asked, still addressing the king, as though Marta was not even there.

"Your own scouts will confirm it," Marta said with a shrug.

The queen sent her a look that was almost sick with fear, and Marta knew that Sibylla believed her.

"We'll need to fight Saladin eventually," the king said apologetically. "But I'd prefer he not have one of the largest fiefs in the kingdom in his purse when we do."

Thinking that she had said everything that was necessary, Marta bowed and turned towards the door.

"Wait," Queen Sibylla said.

Marta turned back to look at her. That look still haunted the queen's eyes—she was sick with fear and a little desperation. Marta had no reason to think well of the queen and still less to like her, but she had always pitied her. It could not be easy to live at the mercy of a demon; it could not have been easy to live at the mercy of the Leper King, much though she had loved him. And perhaps, she thought, if King Guy could hear reason, could Queen Sibylla find in herself a desire to be free of her demon?

"Is there something I can help you with, my lady?"

The queen's eyes lost focus and roamed, distracted, into the shadows. Almost as though she thought someone might be concealed there, watching, listening. At last, she lifted her chin, and her voice, which had been so pleading a moment ago, was hard and cold as ever. "Have the sense not to interfere in my business again, Marta Bessarion."

Sighing, Marta bowed again and let herself out of the humid bathhouse. The chilly night air hit her like a slap, and a second shock followed when she realised that Miles had silently followed her into the courtyard.

Marta stopped, her back to Miles, scanning the courtyard for allies. Lord Balian had gone away, but he had left Pomers in the care of his squire, Ernoul, who would no doubt ensure she returned safely to the camp. For once, she felt grateful for the squire's quiet watchfulness.

"You've become quite the courtier," she said to the listening silence behind her.

"Neither the king nor the queen have any gift for dissembling," Miles said, circling to face her. He, too, must have been preparing for bed, for his customary embroidered tunic was gone, and he only wore a thin shirt and soft trousers. "I'm invaluable to them."

"I suppose it was your task to keep Lord Balian away from the king all day."

Miles laughed. "I do whatever the queen tells me. And she doesn't trust your precious Prester. If Balian thinks he can play both sides in furtherance of his own ambitions, he's about to find out just how mistaken he is."

And if Queen Sibylla thought Lord Balian was so rash, thought Marta with a sigh, she clearly had not been paying attention.

"I ought to congratulate you," she said bitterly. "Never mind that it will take the destruction of the entire kingdom to get your hands on it, you will have your fief at last."

"Yes, I thought that might sting." Miles grinned. "I have everything I ever wanted."

She marvelled once more that he thought she could begrudge him any good fortune. But she only said, "Except me."

The smile disappeared. "Yes," Miles said, "except you."

Chapter XVI.

Sibylla held her tongue only as long as it took her to find sanctuary in her bedchamber. Then she turned upon the fluttering feathers and drifting smoke that told her Lilith was nearby.

"Did you mean to tell me about this?"

"About what?" Lilith asked dreamily.

Sibylla pressed her lips together. Lilith knew full well what she meant. But the smoke and feathers were drifting towards the window and Sibylla knew she was in no position to make demands. "About Tripoli's alliance with Saladin."

"Oh, was the alliance with that rival of yours?"

"You're supposed to *tell* me these things," Sibylla growled, sinking onto her bed. "I rely on you."

"I believe that's a classic blunder," Lilith told her airily. "Over-reliance upon a trusted source of information. At least, that's what Qeteb is always telling me. I'm not your spy, mortal. I do only what pleases myself."

Of course Lilith was not her tool, but Sibylla did not believe for a moment that the demon was as ignorant as she pretended to be. Who but Tripoli would have made an alliance with Saladin? Was Lilith *trying* to embroil her in war?

"I can't afford," she said slowly, "to go to war with Tripoli and Saladin together."

"No fear of that," Lilith said. "Qeteb has no interest in having Tripoli as a client king."

"Qeteb," Sibylla repeated flatly.

"My counterpart," Lilith said with distaste. "He and his mortal familiar, the sorcerer al-Aziz, are using Saladin to build themselves an empire."

Another demon, working for the sultan? Sibylla's mouth was dry. Once she might have scoffed at such a notion, but since meeting Lilith she had learned not to discount such ideas. "Go on," she said.

"Qeteb is a much less charming companion than me," Lilith went on. "It's true, I require blood to sustain my power, but Qeteb requires tears. I make corpses, but Qeteb makes slaves. Those whom I feed upon suffer very quickly, but Qeteb's victims suffer slowly, without hope, for countless generations."

"I only want to know what it means for the war with Tripoli," Sibylla said, with grinding patience.

"The only way to legitimise Saladin's conquests is to wage war on the Franks," Lilith said with a shrug. "At present, among those you call the Saracens, a king makes good his claim not merely through such things as law or descent, but through the ferocity with which he wages war upon those of other faiths. There is a sultan in Anatolia, I hear, who has made great headway against the Greeks while Saladin has harassed and crushed his own co-religionists. Tongues have been wagging. The sum of it all is that Saladin will never leave your kingdom in peace, even if your renegade cousin is king. It would be as much as his own throne is worth."

"There can be no war with Tripoli," Sibylla said under her breath. She had half thought so in Acre, when Guy had called the muster; but the longer she had allowed herself to become accustomed to the idea, the better she had liked the thought of crushing Tripoli into the dust. But now… "You will ensure that there is no war."

"Preventing wars isn't my strong point," Lilith said, in a tone of complete boredom.

Sibylla's mouth tightened. "If Qeteb's strength is building empires and imposing order, Lilith, then what is yours? Chaos?"

The smoke and feathers shifted, unveiling a face that was in nearly every respect her own, but distorted with sharp-edged laughter. "Chaos? Order?" Lilith said. "What difference is there to you? Both of us love war and thrive on misery. Either way, mortals suffer."

Sibylla folded her arms, trying to determine her next steps. She could not afford to trust Lilith, yet surely this information must be good for *something.* If there were two demons on opposing sides, then certainly neither of them would make a kind or trustworthy ally. Or was *ally* the right word?

Familiar, she thought, *Lilith is my familiar.* It was folly, and Holy Church had forbidden anyone to think it, but she could not help the notion that struck her then: *I suppose that makes me a witch.*

Her brother would have ordered an exorcism and got himself cleansed of the monstrous creature long ago. But Sibylla was not her brother; she had never been strong enough, beloved enough—she had never been *man* enough for the kingdom.

She needed every advantage, no matter what it cost her in people and blood. For a moment, she remembered the tomb in the Holy Sepulchre where her son lay, but pushed the thought aside.

"What we need," Sibylla said, "is an external threat to force the kingdom back together. A *limited* external threat, just enough to bring Tripoli and Chatillon back with their tails between their legs."

"I can arrange that," Lilith said. "Nothing easier."

Sibylla held her breath for a moment. "Do so," she said at last. "But don't forget that it's in your interest to keep me and my kingdom standing. Who else will feed you so faithfully?"

Chapter XVII.

30 April, 1187—six months later

"The one advantage to this whole mess," Lord Balian said gloomily, "is that with Saladin now plainly mustering on the borders, the king and queen might finally be forced to meet Tripoli's demands."

Marta had caught him in the loggia in a rare moment of quiet. Sitting on one of the benches, he fondled a hound's ears and stared without quite seeing into the garden-courtyard. The sun had slid west towards the rim of the sky, casting the garden into shadow, yet Balian wore armour and a cloak. Within the hour he would ride north as one of the king's envoys to Tiberias.

Marta bit her lip. "You think the count's demands are reasonable?" Her pleas to the king six months before had been successful in staving off war, but not in bringing about a peace between the king and Tripoli. Negotiations had broken down when Tripoli laid claim to the royal fief of Beirut. Demanding a piece of the royal demesne was little better than demanding the king's own palace or crown, and not even Lord Balian had wondered at the king and queen's refusal. All winter, nothing had been done, and nothing had been settled.

"My faith, no. The very demand is insulting. How can Tripoli behave so madly?" Lord Balian fell silent, so that the distant chimes of armour and the slow clop of horses' hooves drifted up from the service courtyard—the sounds of men and horses being prepared for a journey. His face seemed perpetually strained these days, and was it only Marta's imagination, or had many more grey hairs appeared in the darkness of his temples over the past few months?

"If the king agrees, do you think Tripoli will make peace *now?*" she ventured. "Only because Saladin has mustered a great army, and refuses to renew the truce?"

"Well," Lord Balian said sadly. "We never really know anyone, do we?"

He had always looked on Tripoli as a friend.

Marta sighed and wished that she might reassure him, might point out that the count could be appealed to as a fellow Watcher, but she had lost all hope of that six months ago. She slid onto the bench beside him and said, "If Saladin is mustering to attack the kingdom, perhaps he'll relent."

Lord Balian shook his head. "It isn't only that Saladin is mustering. In Jerusalem they were saying he has sent an army to besiege Kerak and ravage Transjordan."

"I heard such a rumour," Marta said slowly. "Because of the breach of the truce?" In winter, Prince Reynald had seized another of the Saracen caravans travelling through Transjordan.

"Chatillon claimed he was not subject to the king, and had no truce with Saladin," Lord Balian said with a frown. "He also claimed that the caravan was well guarded by Turcomen knights, the ones they call Mamluks. Under the truce, the Saracens had the right to send caravans through Transjordan, but not knights."

Marta nodded. "So the caravan was a pretext for moving troops?"

"Perhaps. Or perhaps the caravan merely thought it required an escort. In any case it has provided Saladin with a pretext to take Transjordan, if not the entire kingdom." Lord Balian sighed. "None of this would have happened in the time of the Leper King."

Marta remembered the seraph's departure with a pang. Lord Balian was more correct than he could imagine.

"Do you remember the old Greek Messenger, who came to us on our first journey to Jerusalem and prophesied against the Watchers? And how she said that after the Leper King died, the fire would consume us?"

"They said that the world would end last September, too." Lord Balian sent her a sidelong glance. "What do you fear, Marta?"

You Watchers deal in power and politics, but it's all for your own benefit. What have you done to redeem this kingdom, to relieve the poor or free the captives? The old woman's words came back to her as though spoken yesterday. That day Lord Balian had promised to heed the Messenger's words. Meanwhile, Walter of Caesarea kept as his secretary the man who had done *that* to Persi and only God knew how many others; and Baldwin of Ramla had departed the kingdom in high dudgeon because he could not stomach some slight affront to his honour; and Raymond of Tripoli had committed treason because he thought he ought to have been king.

"I—I am afraid I have failed," she confessed. *I am afraid we have all failed, we who ought to have remained vigilant, we Watchers.*

Lord Balian sent her a startled look, and then put an arm around her shoulders. "Marta, Marta," he said. "Always trying to fix everything that's wrong with the world. Don't blame yourself, and don't be afraid."

He got up then, and went away to say his farewells to Queen Maria and the family, and to eat a quick supper before setting out; he meant to travel all night and meet with the other envoys at the Templar fortress of La Fève, before continuing towards Tiberias in the morning. Marta was not riding with him, for she was not gifted at diplomacy, and had already done what she could in that regard. Wearily, she got up and opened the door that ought to have led to her room.

It did not. It led to Khalil, instead.

He stood in the doorway and smiled at her. That smile was like the smile on the face of Death. Behind him was a tent, its walls lined with sumptuous hangings of striped silk. Other furnishings there were none, not even a carpet to cover the grass. Through the flap of the tent Marta caught a glimpse of a familiar sight—more tents, armed men, cooking-fires and servants to tend them, all lit up by the slanting golden light of sunset: the Saracen war-camp.

Marta recoiled a step but managed to catch herself before she could slam the door in her enemy's face. "No," she said, before he could speak, *"you may not enter."*

She had not given Khalil much thought in the months since Tiberias, content only to train and plan for the moment she would face him. That she *would* face him she felt certain: he would arrange it, sooner or later, if she did not.

"I don't want to hurt you," he said, as she was catching her breath. "I only want to talk."

"I'll only speak to you with steel," Marta hissed. She was not wearing her gauntlets, or she would have stripped one off to throw at him.

"I don't intend to fight you," he said, patiently. "There are other ways of settling our differences."

That took Marta's breath away. Khalil had slaughtered an entire town before her eyes and had attempted to sacrifice her family to demons. "No, there aren't," she said, catching the door to hurl it closed in his face.

"I have a hostage." As Khalil beckoned, a figure was shoved into the field of view; it fell to its knees. All the air left Marta's lungs in a rush. It was Miles, bound and bloodied and pale. Miles, staring at her in speechless appeal.

"I want to speak to you in person," Khalil repeated. "Come to the bridge of Jisr el-Majami tomorrow at noon, alone and ready to parley, and you will leave with Miles of Plancy."

Marta must have blinked, because between one moment and another, the vision had disappeared. She was looking into her own room.

* * *

Balian swivelled in his saddle to look back along the road he had travelled. It was a cool, fresh spring morning, and the low banks of fog clinging to the Samarian hills were all illuminated to a frothy gold by the slanting rays of the rising sun. In the broad and verdant Jezreel valley, through which the pale road striped like a ribbon, already the grass had begun to go tawny at the roots. In a few short weeks it would be scorched pale, and only the oaks and sycamores would provide a dark and dusty jolt of green in the summer landscape.

Behind Balian, the knights of his household moved steadily to the rhythm of their horses' hooves. Riding immediately behind him, his squire Ernoul stifled a yawn. Balian, who had spent the night keeping a prayerful vigil at the church in Sebastea, stifled another as he turned again to watch the road ahead. He was already looking forward to the morning's first halt, and an opportunity to stretch his cramped body. That would happen a little further up the valley at the Templar stronghold of La Fève, where Balian would meet with the other envoys sent by King Guy to make peace with Raymond of Tripoli. He would have been with them sooner, had he not been delayed in Nablus and Sebastea.

The sun rose higher, lighting up a world that still looked fresh and hopeful, despite the precarious state of the kingdom. Around them, the fog began to lift, revealing the distant bulk of the Little Hermon mountain, and the castle of La Fève like a black speck low on its westernmost spur.

As they drew nearer their rendezvous, Ernoul shaded his eyes with his hand, standing up in his stirrups. "My lord? It's very quiet at La Fève."

Balian narrowed his eyes at the distant castle, a ring of walls rising at a slight distance from the nearby village and church. At the wall's foot were clustered white shapes—the tents pitched by the other envoys. The Masters of the Temple and the Hospital, together with the archbishop of Tyre, had been in Nablus only the night before last, along with their attendants and twenty or so knights from their Orders.

The sun was high enough now that he could feel it burning into his right cheek, but any finer details eluded him. "How do you mean, quiet?" he asked Ernoul. "Your eyes are better than mine."

"No one is moving in the camp," Ernoul said. "I see no horses. No men on the battlements. No smoke from campfires."

Balian frowned. "That's odd. I *know* we arranged to meet here and go on to Tiberias together." If Saladin had come north…but no. Five days ago he was at Kerak.

By the time they reached the crossroads just south of the castle, the stillness had become eerie. Only small, inhuman sounds broke the silence: the soft flapping of canvas tents in the breeze; a mournful fowl honking somewhere in the marsh north of the castle, which at this time of year was full of standing water; the click of a hound's claws on the gravel as it left off nosing among the cooking-pots for scraps and trotted over to greet them, wagging its tail. But no voices, no footsteps.

Calling a halt, Balian sent two men as scouts up the mountain to the east, and another two down into the village, while Ernoul ventured into the camp to look inside the tents. The squire returned in a moment to report that they were empty, the belongings rolled and folded and neatly stowed. Now in the hush of the early morning, the silence almost began to frighten Balian. He wanted to call, or sing, even howl to fill it up.

Instead, he turned to look up at the fortress itself. The stronghold of La Fève had no keep: it was only a moated wall a little taller than a mounted man, pierced by a westward-facing gate. This was closed and silent. The battlements were empty.

"The banners are gone," Balian said softly. "Did you see any weapons or armour in the tents, Ernoul?"

"No, my lord."

"The horses are gone, too," added Samuel Arrabi. "Look here." He pointed to the hoofprints and droppings left around the empty pickets between the camp and the castle.

"Pray God it is not what I think," Balian said after a moment. "Hail the castle, Ernoul."

The squire cupped his hands around his mouth. "Ho, there! Lord Balian seeks entrance in the name of the king! Open up!"

Balian nearly jumped at his sudden shout; until now they had all been speaking in little more than whispers. If there had been dead men in the castle, he thought they might have started up at that summons. But living or otherwise, no one did. Only the wall threw back Ernoul's shout.

Presently Balian urged his horse to walk northwards along the brink of the moat, and the rest followed him. The wall was roughly square in shape, and on the north face they found a small postern standing ajar, with a foot-bridge leading across the moat towards the great cistern that captured some of the water from the marshes—a deep, open rectangle of water with a masonry parapet about it. Samuel Arrabi slipped down from his horse to study the churned-up mud near the parapet, and the caked earth on the foot-bridge. "Someone has been here to fetch water," he said. "Recently; this morning, I think."

Balian and his men gathered at the bridge-head, trying to glean some kind of message from the darkness beyond the half-open door.

"Ernoul," Balian said. His voice was thin in his own ears, hushed with dread. "Will you search La Fève for me?"

The squire paled but did not refuse. Dismounting, Ernoul crossed the foot-bridge, pushed the door open, and faded into the gloom of whatever lay beyond. For a heartbeat or two they heard his footsteps moving away from the door. Then silence fell; all they could do now was watch and wait.

What could have happened? If the envoys had simply determined to continue their journey, they would not have taken the castle garrison with them. Nor would they have left behind their tents and baggage. There was only one explanation that made sense to Balian—but that made no sense at all.

"It was to be a delegation of *peace*," he muttered. "Ridefort! What have you done?"

The sun crawled higher in the sky. Black midges, abandoning their play amidst the reeds of the wetland, came over to inspect the sweating horses and knights. The scouts returned with no news: no one in the village knew where the Masters and their men had gone, or why. The landscape was empty. Ernoul seemed to have been swallowed up alive by the castle.

Samuel Arrabi fidgeted with his reins. "Should I ride north? Try to spot them?"

"There may be a clue here in the castle. Have patience."

Arrabi bit his lip, and the other men stirred restlessly. To distract them, Balian said, "This reminds me of a tale Marta Bessarion once told me. Many years ago, a captain of the Greeks was on campaign in Persia, leading a band of scouts into the mountains east of Nineveh, when he came upon an empty and ruined caravanserai. A goat-herd warned them not to enter the place, but Marta's—the captain was not afraid. Leaving his men to watch the hills, he entered by the main gate, which stood partly opened."

"What did he find?" Arrabi asked politely.

"Nothing," Balian replied. "Only a walled courtyard, with rooms to lodge travellers. All of it empty, except for the jackals. But then there occurred a great marvel. The captain opened the first door he came to and looked out onto the Colonnaded Street of Antioch. The second door he tried led to the Forum of Theodosius in Constantinople. And the third led to Garden of the Indians in Ctesiphon."

Arrabi was interested despite himself. "What did the Greek captain do?"

"Seeing plainly that it was no natural habitation of men or God, he set fire to the place. The roof caved in; the doors collapsed, and the jackals fled yelping. Last of all, when there was nothing left but embers, something came out by the broken gate in the shape of a white stag, wholly untouched by the fire. It went up to the captain without fear and bowed its head to the ground. Then it ran away, into the mountains."

"And what did the captain make of that?"

"He said the world was full of secrets and powers, which none of us can fully understand."

The hinges of the postern creaked, and they turned to see Ernoul emerge from the castle.

"What news?" Balian asked, all alert again.

Ernoul crossed the foot-bridge and turned up a furrowed brow. "There are only two men in the castle, my lord. They were laid up in the infirmary with food and water nearby to hand. I questioned them but they do not know what has happened any more than you or I."

"They don't *know?*" Balian's mouth set tightly. "Then mount up and ride north. Perhaps we will find better news in Nazareth."

* * *

The old Roman bridge, which al-Aziz Khalil called the Jisr el-Majami and the Franks called the Bridge of Judaire, lay deep in the Jordan Valley, just within the borders of Galilee. As Marta descended into the valley, the air became hot and humid, almost suffocating with scarcely a breath of wind to stir it. She did not spare her mount for all that, pushing Pomers from a walk to a trot when she thought he could bear it. If Khalil intended to meet her at the bridge at noon, she did not mean to disappoint him.

Caution would have counselled her to ride more slowly, not to exhaust her horse before she faced her enemy. There was no particular need for haste; Khalil was anxious to speak to her, and she was anxious to fight him. Possibly the glimpse she had had of Miles was a lying illusion, created by one of the sorcerer's demons. Had Marta the time, she would have sent to Jerusalem to ascertain whether Miles was with the queen as usual, or whether Khalil had indeed spirited him away. Nothing dreadful would happen if she was half-an-hour late to the bridge; she ought to ride more slowly.

She did not.

The valley was a ribbon of lush green farmland between steep and tawny slopes. Marta passed the Hospitaller fortress of Belvoir, a formidable castle perched against the horizon on a buttress of the western hills, and presently arrived at the bridge itself - a pointed arch of dark stone, which spanned the river in one dizzying leap. Marta did not draw rein until she had ascended the western slope of the bridge and could see down the other side to where the pale road entered the northernmost reaches of Transjordan—the kingdom's border country, far distant from Prince Reynald's seat at Kerak, where there was no clear delineation between the king's authority and the sultan's.

There was no sign of Khalil on the far bank, even after she had ridden some way down the road and searched the shadows beneath the trees. Marta glanced at the sun. There was still half an hour left until noon: anxious for Miles, she had ridden too quickly and arrived before the appointed time.

As she walked Pomers back up the bridge, the slow clop of a horse's hooves came rising up the far slope to meet her. It must be the other solitary traveller whom she had glimpsed behind her on the road, Marta guessed, and by coincidence he happened to be making for the same bridge. Then she topped the rise and found herself face to face with Miles of Plancy.

Fully armed and sitting astride a war-horse, he was clearly in no kind of distress or durance. Or, indeed, in Khalil's company at all. For a moment, Marta simply felt weak with relief.

"Marta!" She could not quite tell if he was happy to see her or not. "What are *you* doing here?"

"I might ask the same," she parried. "I had a message to say that you had been captured."

She ought not to have said that, because it decided him that he was pleased to see her, after all.

"You came to rescue me again!" He gave her an infuriating grin. It had been some time since she had seen him like this, armoured and dusty, his face turning brown beneath the tow-coloured thatch of hair. "I knew you still cared for me."

Of course she still cared for him; she had never denied it. There was a wearying persistence to her feelings. She wished she might fall in love quickly with someone else, and drive out the old, comfortable, well-worn affection with a new. Until that happened, it seemed that her heart would always be tethered to his.

"Forget about that," she said. "Why are *you* here?"

"Forget that the White Watcher herself is in love with me? How could I do that?"

Marta forced herself to draw and release a slow breath. "For heaven's sake, Miles, stop preening and use your wits. Someone told me you had been captured, and that if I wanted to see you again I should meet them at the bridge of Judaire. The same person must have sent for you, too. Are you in league with the Saracens?"

"Indeed no," he said smoothly. "Tripoli summoned me on a matter of business, if you want to know. Since my fief is in his land, naturally I was eager to talk to him about it."

"You thought Tripoli would meet you *here?* At a bridge on the highway, in the middle of nowhere?" Marta threw out an arm to encompass the acres of green crops dotted infrequently with white farmhouses and villages, the massive distant hills, the vast blue arch of the sky. Then the truth struck her and took her breath away. "You're thinking of going over to him, aren't you? Are you mad? *No* one in the kingdom wants Tripoli on the throne; not even the Watchers. And he's in league—"

Marta caught herself.

"I only came to hear what he had to say," Miles said, looking discomfited. "Maybe I could have brought him to see sense."

"You couldn't," Marta said, once more gazing about the sun-drenched countryside, as though it might answer the questions that sprang up to plague her. "Tripoli's in league with al-Aziz Khalil, and they've worked together to decoy us here—but *why?*"

For a moment Miles only gave her a look of incomprehension. Then there was a distant sound of hoofbeats from the eastern bank of the river; and Marta turned to see a small cavalcade of horsemen riding towards her. At their head was Khalil, his fidgety horse flanked by two great beasts—on one hand a wolf the tawny colour of desert sand; on the other a leopard. With neither leash or muzzle, they paced silently at Khalil's side, and even at that distance Marta felt her skin prickle with disquiet. She thought she could feel their eyes fixed upon her.

Marta's hand clenched on the Bessarion Lance, and Pomers shifted uneasily beneath her, eyeing the wild beasts with terror. At the bridge-head, Khalil signalled his men to wait and rode forward with his beasts alone. There could not be more than a dozen men facing them, but twelve to two were fearful odds, and all of Khalil's mamluks were armed with wound crossbows.

It was a trap, but that was more or less what Marta had expected, and had accordingly taken her position at the cusp of the bridge where a quick retreat down the rising arch might shield her from the arrows of Khalil's men. But she wished Miles had not come; she could not face Khalil with the same reckless abandon if she had someone else to protect.

Perhaps that was the sorcerer's aim in summoning both of them to the bridge. He had gained Miles as a hostage, without going to the trouble of capturing him.

"You lied," Marta accused Khalil, as he approached and reined his horse in a pair of spear's-lengths away.

Now that she saw him in the daylight, Marta supposed he was well-dressed and well-groomed, in light mail armour and flowing black robes. She did not remember him being so young at Oliveta, and it discomfited her now that he appeared scarcely older than herself. When he smiled up at her with teeth almost predatory in their whiteness, that was even worse.

"In a sense I did," Khalil agreed, almost affably. "How else would I have gained the opportunity to speak with you?"

"I didn't come to *speak* with you," Marta said, and hurled her gauntlet at his face. "I challenge you to single combat."

Khalil took the blow with tranquillity. "You haven't heard what I came to say."

"Say it, then, and get it over with. But don't forget that I've struck you."

"Never," he said with silken mildness. "My offer is this. Hand over that weapon you hold, and I will allow both you and the Frank to leave in possession of your lives. Otherwise, you will be riddled with crossbow bolts before you can lift a finger."

His animals moved forward, teeth bared, hackles up, to circle them. Marta levelled the Bessarion Lance at the leopard's nose and it came to a halt, snarling up at her with sulphurous eyes. Despite the trickles of sweat running down her back and sternum beneath her armour, Marta felt that chill of fear sweep through her again. No mere animal should be so intelligent.

"I'm not giving you my father's lance," she said flatly.

"Be reasonable," said Khalil. "It isn't you my men have orders to shoot first."

"Don't listen to him," Miles said. He had been glancing from Marta to Khalil with a calculating look, as though gathering his bearings, and now slid his words in as smoothly as Queen Sibylla might slide in a knife. "You can't give up the Bessarion Lance for me."

"I don't mean to," Marta snapped. She might be fool enough to dash off to Miles' rescue, but she was hardly fool enough to give up her father's lance to save his neck. Or even her own.

"Then should I take it from your corpse?" Khalil inquired, still in that gentle, reasonable voice. He waved a hand, and his men raised their crossbows.

Before Marta could dare him to try, Miles said, "Give us a moment." To Marta he said, "Why don't you let me handle this? You can't bring a magic lance to a battle of wits and hope to win."

Marta shrugged. In fact, the sight of the crossbows had her flesh crawling from head to toe. Conventional arrows did little against good chainmail and a sturdy gambeson, and at worst she risked a mild injury to herself or a serious injury to her horse. But the new crossbows could hurl a short, thick bolt with vicious force through anything short of a wall. With twelve of them pointed towards herself and Miles, to fight would be suicidal.

If they *had* to talk to Khalil, Miles was by far the best person to do so.

Taking her shrug as assent, Miles sent her a sunny smile and turned to face Khalil. "You won't kill us," he announced with absolute confidence.

"I will, if you won't give me what I want," the sorcerer said. Marta was beginning to hate his habit of saying horrible things in such a mild voice. Did he think it was appropriate to threaten death, so long as one did it politely?

"You might kill *me*," Miles conceded. "You have no use for me, except to threaten mademoiselle here, which in itself is an excellent reason to keep me alive. But you certainly won't kill Marta. You want her alive. I wonder why that is?"

Khalil smiled faintly. "It is as I said. I don't mean any harm to you, Marta Bessarion. So long as you hand over the weapon—"

"If she hands over the weapon, what's to stop you ordering your men to attack her?" Miles asked. "Not to kill does not mean not to harm. With no guarantee of safety, she would be a fool to give up her best protection."

Khalil shrugged. "She would be a fool to presume on my patience much longer."

"He's not very good at this, is he?" Miles observed. Marta raised an incredulous eyebrow, and Miles went on. "He wants his own way, and he doesn't know the skill of bargaining to get it. My lord," he added to the sorcerer, "be reasonable. You'll need to offer some concessions. If you wanted the lady dead you would have killed her already, nor would you have bothered to lure me here. If you chose, you could certainly kill me, but then you would have nothing to hold over the lady's head, and she could easily do you a mortal injury before she died. And then you would have lost both the lady and the weapon, and your life to boot."

Khalil was not precisely frowning, but the smile had left his face. Marta repressed a sigh. Miles had only become more cunning and persuasive with the passing years; what a shame he put all that crooked intelligence to the service of his own appetites!

"What I propose," Miles added smoothly, "is that you should accede to the lady's wishes and face her in single combat. The winner gets to keep the Lance. Of course, if you should win, my lord, you won't have the lady. But it's by no means certain you'll get the Lance at all unless you consent to a fair fight."

"That's out of the question," Khalil said, with a dismissive flick of his hand. "I don't fight women."

"You won't fight this one, because you know she'll win," Miles taunted. "Not all the sultan's mamluks or all your demons could overcome her at Kerak."

The wolf growled and nipped at the heels of Miles' horse.

"I'll fight you fairly," Marta offered, as Miles tried to regain control of his mount. "With swords. No enchanted weapons."

"I won't fight today; I'm not equipped for combat," Khalil said. "I'll appoint a champion, and you can fight him for the Lance."

"I don't want to kill your *champion*," Marta said, showing her teeth in something that was not quite a smile.

"The beasts," Miles said suddenly, pointing to them. "She'll fight your beasts. That's only fair, to stake the Lance against your familiars."

Marta swallowed a protest. What was Miles playing at? Didn't he know that she had not overcome Khalil's familiars, the hairy man and the feathered woman, by her own power? Each time it had been the seraph, stepping in to save her. She did not know whether the creature would answer if she called upon it now.

Her protest was unnecessary, however, because Khalil's face shuttered. "No," he said flatly.

"You won't fight, and you won't try to kill us," Miles said. "It appears that we're stalemated." He turned to Marta. "We might as well leave. There's no point in staying"

All twelve crossbows were still levelled at them, but Miles was usually right about these things. With a warning glance in the sorcerer's direction, Marta turned her horse's head. All the way down the bridge and through the flat fields that lined both sides of the road, the skin on her back prickled with the expectation of piercing bolts which never came. Hurrying to a canter, neither she nor Miles slackened their pace nor looked back until they had reached a crossroads where the rising ground hid the bridge and the river from view.

For a moment they only waited and listened; and when no sound came to break the dead stillness of the day, Marta let out a sigh of relief. "We weren't followed," she said.

"I *told* you to let me handle it," Miles said with intolerable conceit. "You didn't think I could bring you out of that ambush without a scratch, did you?"

"If you'd had the wit to stay away in the first place, I could have killed him," she snapped. "Now I'm no further ahead than I was before."

"You could have died," Miles protested. "And the important thing is that Khalil *also* is no further ahead."

Marta frowned. "Is he not?" Khalil somehow had access to the house at Nablus: if he wanted to speak to her, there was no need to do so in person. "Why should he and Tripoli call us out to the bridge of Judaire for a half-baked attempt at a parley? I don't like it."

"Al-Aziz and Tripoli," Miles said thoughtfully. Then understanding dawned in his eyes. "Something is happening in Galilee. Something neither of them wants you to know about."

The thought of Tripoli and Khalil going to all these lengths for her sake was so absurd that Marta almost laughed. But then another thought occurred to her.

"Lord Balian," she said, "and the king's envoys!"

For a moment she stared at Miles in silent horror. Then, without another word, she turned her horse's head and took the north road towards Tiberias. After a moment, Miles followed.

Chapter XVIII.

Two hours' ride brought Marta and Miles to the southern shore of Lake Tiberias, where the waters flowed into the Jordan. There was another bridge here, at Senbra, and Marta turned aside to inspect the ground where the cobblestones of the bridge met the dust of the road. Hundreds of fresh hoofprints speckled, not just the road, but the ground to either side of it. A pile of fresh horse dung in the grass by the roadside removed all doubt that a great number of horsemen had recently passed into the kingdom from across the bridge.

"Saracens," Miles breathed. "So, this is what Khalil didn't want you interfering with."

It made a certain amount of sense, but Marta still had too many questions. "There must have been a few hundred of them at least. What are they doing, trespassing into the kingdom?"

"They haven't returned," Miles said, grinning. "What about it? Why don't we ride after them and see if we can spoil their fun?"

Did he think this was a laughing matter? Marta was about to retort, when movement in the trees along the shore of the lake caught her attention: distant moving figures, sunlight gleaming off burnished steel and silken surcoats.

"Quickly," she said, catching at his reins. "Take cover."

Between the river and the shore of the lake was a mound atop which had been built a minuscule village surrounded by olive-trees and date palms. It was surrounded by the ruined walls of older buildings, whose carved pillars and arches suggested a long-past grandeur. Barely a stone's throw from the road, these provided ample cover for two knights and their horses. Miles slipped from the saddle and rubbed his horse's nose, murmuring warnings for the beast to remain silent. Presently, hearing the rumble of a thousand hooves against the hard-packed dust of the road, they peered through the remains of a crumbling doorway to see the horsemen approach through the trees.

They were Saracens, of course: armed knights, riding slowly, as though they had all the time in the world and nothing to fear.

"Scouts," Marta murmured. "They must have come to spy out the land."

Both she and Miles knew it was too late now to do anything about it. The two of them could not engage half a thousand men, not without reinforcements. In another five minutes they would be across the bridge and fairly out of the kingdom.

"It's war," Miles said blankly, and unnecessarily. There was only one reason, after all, for the sultan to send a small army of scouts across the Jordan: he meant to follow them, and quickly.

As the Saracens cleared the last of the trees and came more clearly into view, however, the breath caught in Marta's throat. They carried round objects atop their spiked lances, ghastly and bleeding. Her hand clenched on Miles' shoulder, and he let out a low oath. There must be dozens of them. *Heads.*

As the column came level with their hiding-place, Marta saw the captives. They were roped together at the centre of the procession, strung out in a bloodied, shuffling column, at least a hundred knights and commoners. She put a hand across her mouth to stifle the sound of horror that bubbled up from within. Worse still was yet to come: bloody and distorted and raised aloft on a lance, Marta saw a face she knew—Roger des Moulins, the Master of the Hospital.

* * *

If Balian had travelled quickly this morning, he rode harder now with a mystery to solve. There was no more talk among the men as they hurried north along the Jezreel valley from La Fève, making towards Nazareth. Nine miles of road unspooled between them and the city of Christ's youth—nine miles that passed with nightmarish slowness despite the pace they kept, a tight steady trot rising periodically into a canter.

When the road abruptly climbed into stony hills and brought them opposite the slope on which the town was built, Ernoul swore under his breath.

"What is it?" Balian asked at once.

All of them had been riding with nerves on edge, watchful for danger. Ernoul pointed towards the unwalled white town with its citadel hovering protectively above. "I think Nazareth is empty, too."

Before either of them could speculate further, a solitary knight bearing the red cross of the Templars came riding to meet them. The moment he came within earshot, he waved frantically. "Wait there! Don't come any nearer!"

Balian signalled the halt, ignoring the way his heart sank into his gut. The lone Templar approached at a walk, man and beast both drooping with weariness. The horse was covered in great dark patches of sweat, and there was red on the knight's surcoat where no red should be.

"Christ have mercy," Balian murmured, but he restrained his worry and remained still until the knight approached. He could see from the man's face how terrible his tidings must be.

"What news?"

The Templar touched his lips with his tongue. "It's bad," he said.

"Tell me, where is the Master of the Hospital?"

"Dead, my lord. They—they cut off his head."

Balian swallowed hard. "What about the Master of the Temple? Where is he? Who did this?"

"Sir Gerard is alive, here in Nazareth. But grievously wounded. Only two others besides him and myself have escaped. It was…it was Saracens."

Saracens, across the Jordan, in *Galilee*? Balian felt ice slithering down his spine. The invasion—surely it could not already have begun?

"How many dead?" He could not stop until every last bitter drop had been wrung from the man.

"I cannot tell. All my convent—that is, the garrisons of La Fève and of Cara, eighty in all; and the ten Hospitallers; and the Master of the Hospital; and forty knights of Nazareth who joined us on our march north. Also countless people of the town were slaughtered or taken captive when they ran out to watch the battle and to spoil the Saracen knights."

"God have mercy," Balian whispered again. "Are the Saracens still in the kingdom?"

"We don't know, my lord. The count of Tripoli said that if we remained in our fortresses they would do us no harm."

This time the silence was almost sickening.

Tripoli.

Perhaps his lips shaped the words, but no sound escaped them.

"Amaury," Balian said at last, in a rasping voice. One of his sergeants pushed forward. "You have a name for courage. Return to Nablus with all speed. Take whichever horse is freshest. Have my wife the queen send me all my knights here at Nazareth, tonight." He turned back to the Templar. "Now, friend, take me to the Master of the Temple."

* * *

"It happened at the Springs of Cresson." Gerard of Ridefort, Master of the Temple, was still having his wounds dressed when the Templar knight ushered Balian into the room he had been given in the house of the bishop of Nazareth. There was a gash along the Master's forearm—an arrow had found a weak spot in his mail, sinking deep into the thigh—and his eyes were red with weeping. "When we reached La Fève, a messenger from Tiberias came to say that the count of Tripoli had permitted a party of Saracens to cross into his land, on condition that they did not attack any town or castle, and that, after spying out the land towards Acre, they would depart by sunset. So long as we remained within our walls, Tripoli said, we would be safe." He gave a scoffing laugh.

"Why didn't you?" Balian paced the room from window to door and back again.

"Do you jest? They might have seized Nazareth or Sephoria or Cana! How were we to trust Tripoli's words? The Temple must protect the holy places, or we are nothing."

"Saints above—you say there were seven *hundred* of them, and you had what, a hundred and forty?"

"We did not know their true numbers until it was already too late," Ridefort said wearily. "When we did, des Moulins would have had us withdraw, of course. But even then, they had stopped in the forest at Cresson to water their horses. The opportunity was *there*. Our first charge came within a hair of shattering them. They were forced to retreat, only to rally and form an ambush. Everything went wrong. It was a nightmare."

"You surely came away with more than three survivors," Balian said, desperately.

"No, for when our men tried to surrender, they were cut down where they stood. It is Saladin's custom to slaughter any of the Templars or Hospitallers who fall into his hands." The Master's voice broke. "If you had not stayed in Sebaste, my lord—"

Did Ridefort mean to blame him?

"Had I not stayed in Sebaste," Balian said coldly, "then I too would be dead, unless I had managed to stop you."

He left the room, but stopped in the loggia, grasping the balustrade and trying to think. What a senseless waste it had been! Damn Ridefort, for being fool enough to seek battle! One thing was so clear as to require no thought at all: Saladin would not content himself with an attack on Transjordan—he intended to strike at the kingdom itself, and Acre was his target.

War was upon them, and at the worst possible moment, with the kingdom divided and the Orders both decimated. Balian straightened. Nothing could be done until reinforcements arrived from Nablus. In the meantime, he had better see the bishop about organising what remained of Nazareth's defences.

* * *

"I suppose this is good-bye," Miles said, reining his horse in. Nablus lay before them, a froth of whitewashed houses covering the stony hills of Samaria, gilded by the afternoon sun. Marta allowed Pomers to amble to a halt of his own; she barely saw the town.

"I wonder if Tripoli knows," she said in a low voice. "I wonder if he watched them riding back across the Jordan, flaunting their trophies."

The sight at the bridge of Senbra on the previous afternoon had left them both speechless with horror; not even Miles had any pleasantries left in him after the sight of so many dead and captive men. They had pushed on again, anxiously following the pocked trail of the Saracen scouting-party up into the hills, past Cafarsset, and finally to the main road leading from Tiberias to Acre. It was the birds, in the slopes south of the road, which led them through hills thickly forested with pines and olive shrubs to the battlefield.

It had been a battle to turn black hair grey.

Marta had ridden through this valley six months before to plead with the count, and here, now, was the bitter fruit of Tripoli's treason. For a while, she and Miles simply roamed numbering the bodies fallen among the trees. At the lower, western end of the slope, most of the corpses were Saracen—Marta could imagine a first, victorious charge—but then they followed the hoofprints and litter of broken weapons up the slope until the horses began to baulk, frightened by an overpowering stench of blood on the wind. Readying the Bessarion Lance, Marta urged her horse on, circled a thicket, and found a little level place where a hundred or so knights of the Temple and of the Hospital lay together, efficiently beheaded.

As the White Watcher, Marta was not numbered among the eighty-five knights the fief of Nablus owed in knight service to the kingdom, and she had never fought beside them in battle. Nevertheless, she had often ridden out on errands such as this, helping to escort stragglers home after some defeat had scattered them. Well she knew the aftermath of a battle: the heavy coppery scent of fresh blood mingling with the stench of spilled guts and voided bowels; the caws of crows mingling with the groans and prayers of those who survived, which she had unconsciously looked for as she searched for the place. But on this battlefield there was not a whisper of sound. Even the crows were absent. Only a great black vulture rose ponderously from its perch atop the torn carcase of an unmoving horse, and flapped away through an opening in the trees.

Marta dismounted, secured Pomers to a branch, and walked among the corpses, feeling that, if nothing else, she must find des Moulins' body. But most of the dead knights' heads were missing, leaving only piles of anonymous trunks behind. Some of them had gone down fighting, still gripping swords and axes. Others were all hacked and bloody about their forearms, as though, having laid down their weapons in surrender, they had no other defence against slaughter.

"You can do nothing for them now," Miles had called to her. "Someone will send carts to collect the bodies."

He was right, much as it irked her to leave so many lying unburied and undefended. After a moment's debate, they had turned their horses' heads towards Nazareth, and arrived there once night had fallen. All the way, Marta had found herself gnawing her lip in silent vexation. If only the Bessarion Lance had been present at the battle, if only she had had the wit to realise what Khalil was playing at, things might have gone differently. It was just one more score to add to the sorcerer's account.

Lord Balian, in Nazareth, had explained what they did not know. The following morning, fifty knights arrived from Tiberias to escort the remaining envoys to meet with the count, and the work of collecting the bodies began. There was nothing Marta could do to help, so after seeing Lord Balian safely to Tiberias she had started for home.

All the way, Miles had followed her in a heavy silence. Now, hearing her question, he shrugged. "Tripoli? Don't waste your pity on that traitor. I know what you think of me, Marta, but no matter how desirous I might be for advancement, I'd never betray my own liege and people." He smiled grimly. "Tripoli's finished. He'll never be able to hold up his head again. If I were him I'd cut my throat."

"You wouldn't turn Mahometan and defect to Saladin instead?" Marta could feel the bitter twist in her smile. "He'd give you a fief, no doubt."

She half expected Miles to lash back at her with words more bitter still. Instead, he shook his head. "No," he said. "My name would be spat upon by every man of noble birth in the kingdom. How could I live knowing that?"

Marta shivered at the certainty in his voice.

"Won't you eat dinner with us before starting out again?" she asked, eager to change the subject.

Even then, he managed to give her that intolerable grin. "You can't bear to be parted from me, is that it?"

It was nothing of the sort; only for the past two days he had followed her like a dog, and she was surprised to find him so ready to leave her now.

"You must be hungry, and it's still a long road to Jerusalem."

"Thanks, but I'm afraid that Queen Maria will slip hemlock into my wine," he said. He did not press on at once, however, and seeing his face, Marta knew there was something else weighing on his mind.

"Be careful, Marta, won't you?" he said. "Not just about the war, I mean. Do you have any idea what Khalil wants with you?"

It was impossible, after all, to forget all the things that had passed between them. "I imagine you would know better than I," she said softly. "You once meant to help Queen Sibylla hand me over to him, after all."

Miles flushed. "I'll never win, with you," he said bitterly. "I don't know why I try."

He raked his weary horse's flanks with his spurs and went trotting down a path that bypassed the city for the south.

Marta sighed and went on down the main road, but Miles' words remained in her mind.

Upon returning to the palace, she went straight upstairs to her room, and stood before the closed door, her breath and heart quick with anticipation.

"Khalil, Khalil, Khalil," she muttered. "Come when I call you."

She whipped the door open. Only her room welcomed her. Whatever words of power it took to bridge the gap between Nablus and the sorcerer,

Marta did not know them.

"Face me in battle, you coward," she hissed, but the silence did not reply.

Marta sighed and dragged off her helm. It was all very well for Miles to tell her to be careful, she thought as she collected the things for her bath, but Khalil meant to hunt her down, and she would never be free of him until she had faced and killed him.

Chapter XIX.

A day after the defeat at Cresson, Sibylla broke down and summoned Lilith.

"Where have you been?" she demanded when the demon, a few minutes later, wisped into view among the shadows that crowded the borders of her room. "I gave you a task to do, and I haven't heard from you in months. For heaven's sake, tell me the news."

"I've been staying away from you," Lilith said blandly, little more than a voice from the corners of the room. The shadows thickened and rolled like fog above the sea on a cold morning, pulling at the corners of Sibylla's vision. "Haven't you been wearing a *hamsa* amulet? I took that to mean you'd like to see me as little as possible. I was only being mannerly."

Sibylla's face heated. As much as Lilith's presence tormented her, the demon's absence had been worse still. If there was to be a scorpion in her palace, Sibylla wanted it under her eye. "I wore that only to prevent you walking in on me whenever you please. But I took it off *weeks* ago."

"It doesn't prevent me walking anywhere, my sweet," Lilith whispered in a waft of cold air against her neck.

Sibylla jumped and turned. There was nothing behind her but her own black shadow. She drew a slow breath and said between her teeth, *"What of my husband?"*

With Saladin besieging Kerak and ravaging Transjordan, she and Guy had moved to Jerusalem whence they might be able to send relief. Instead, news from the envoys at Tiberias had sent Guy hastening towards the north: Saladin's men had struck like a thunderbolt from a clear sky. There had been a raid across the river, a battle, a slaughter. It was evident, now, that the whole kingdom was at risk. Old enmities must be forgotten. The king and the count must meet to make peace.

"Oh, it was an affecting scene," Lilith told her. "Tripoli and the lummox dismounted when they saw each other, and Tripoli went down on his knees in the road to ask pardon. There was hugging and kissing and no doubt a few decorous tears. They're at Nablus now, on their way back to Jerusalem together."

Sibylla sank into her chair. "Then Tripoli has submitted."

"Yes, he has expelled the Saracens from Tiberias and done homage to King Lummox. All it took was a little external threat, as you ordered." After moment's silence, Lilith spoke again. "Aren't you happy? You don't seem happy."

"Circumstanced as I am, happiness would be utterly unbecoming," Sibylla said coldly. "I requested a *limited* enemy threat, and now I have a full-blooded invasion on my hands. If you can't follow orders—"

"You wanted Tripoli's submission," Lilith snarled from the shadows. "And you were willing to use any means to force it, including an enemy attack. I accomplished the task with the loss of a mere hundred or so men, including the meddling Hospitaller Master, and you choose to blame me for an invasion everyone has known about for the past year? Ungrateful bitch."

"How *dare* you use such language to me?" Sibylla hissed, leaning forward in her chair. At those words, all light in the room seemed to dim. It felt suddenly impossible to breathe.

"Rid yourself of the delusion that the Poison Mother takes orders from a mortal flesh-sack," Lilith hissed in an unbearable, inhuman voice. Each word fell on Sibylla like a crushing labyrinth of stone. A moment later, she felt the room contract, as though something impossibly large and heavy had burst out of it, and its physical boundaries sprang back to their accustomed place. Sibylla took a breath, and another. Light returned; instead of roiling shadow, she could now see the dark straight lines of wall and ceiling and corner.

She tried to get out of her chair, but her hips clenched like a fist, making movement agony. Sibylla sank back. Lilith was correct: this was *her* fault. She had wanted to teach Tripoli a lesson, and she had done so, but at a horrible cost: one-tenth of the fighting strength of the entire kingdom, and that on the eve of an invasion. She had made them all weaker at a time when Saladin had never been stronger.

Sibylla felt trapped in a slow catastrophe of her own making, captain of a ship she had run aground. And because she was the captain, she could not escape, as others might. She closed her eyes, feeling pain radiating up and down her spine, seizing her head in a merciless grip. Queen at last, and she had never felt more helpless. Perhaps it had all been a mistake. Perhaps she ought to have gone to Nablus with the rest of them, forgotten all her clever, clever schemes, and come to some agreement with the Watcher faction— something that would have *preserved,* rather than destroyed the kingdom. Baldwin had always reminded her that the crown of Jerusalem was by election, not blood, and custody of the gold bauble itself did not mean one had the support to hold it. But what support could she have gained? The Watchers did not want outsiders, like Guy or her own Courtenay relatives, meddling in the affairs of Jerusalem. They were happy to let the whole kingdom dwindle and decay, just so long as they were left sitting atop the carcase. Perhaps someone might have been able to gain their support—someone like Miles of Plancy, with his tongue smooth as fresh butter—but Sibylla had never had that gift.

Sibylla spent a bad night, and was still in bed the following afternoon when the king and the count of Tripoli returned to Jerusalem, met by the patriarch in a lavish procession—of thanksgiving, Eraclius had said in his message to the palace. In her sunny, stifling room she tried to block out the sounds of celebration with a pillow clamped over her aching head. What fools they were, to dance and pipe when the waves were rising, and the kingdom sinking. Well, they would know their mistake soon enough.

Chapter XX.

Late June—two months later

"Long journey, mademoiselle?" the Nablus stable hand asked, inspecting Pomers with a raised eyebrow. The grey war-horse, dark with sweat and dust, had buried his nose in the trough to draw up prodigious amounts of water.

"Pretty far," Marta said. "North to Senbra and across the Jordan."

The stable hand sent her an inquiring look as he hauled the saddle, and the stinking blanket beneath, from Pomers' sturdy barrel. Marta did not elaborate. In fact, she had been much further than the Jordan: she had been up the Yarmouk River to the high plateau where Saladin had made his camp and was massing his army. She had not found a good vantage-point to spy out the camp itself, but nearby villagers had told of the largest army the sultan had ever gathered. Not much to report after a long, hard day in the saddle. She tossed a silver groat to the stable hand. "Rub him down well, Hugh," she requested. "And check his back for saddle-gall. It's been a long, hot day." She hesitated at the sight of a familiar mule in the courtyard. "Is Michael Zakar here?"

Hugh confirmed it, and Marta felt something in her heart lighten, like a bird taking flight. Two months since the disaster at the Springs of Cresson, war might be days or even hours away. The *arriere ban* had gone out weeks ago, and tomorrow morning Lord Balian would join King Guy at Sephoria with every able-bodied Christian in Nablus. She was grateful for this chance to bid her newfound family farewell.

Tucking her helm beneath one elbow, Marta hurried into the house. Before anything else, she must bathe. Michael, she was sure, would wait to see her.

The looms were both silent when she approached, still damp from her bath. Persi sat with Michael on the bench, speaking in low quiet voices. Marta stopped in the doorway, suddenly, wistfully hopeful. "I didn't mean to interrupt," she apologised when they looked up.

"It's all right," Persi said, sliding from the bench. Michael had kept his promise to keep coming to Nablus as though nothing had happened, but there was always something distant in Persi's manner these days when she spoke to him. Now she stood and said, "Michael was only telling me what he meant to do if the war goes badly. Sit down a moment. I'll run and get you some sherbet."

Obedient to Persi's order, Marta sank onto the bench of her own loom and said, "What do you mean, *if the war goes badly?* Even if Saladin makes it as far as Acre, do you really expect him to breach the walls?"

"If he gets as far as Acre, we will have enough problems without Saracens inside the walls," Michael told her. "If a siege develops, I may be best off shifting the entire workshop north, to Tripoli."

Count Raymond's capital in the Lebanon was famous for its weavers. "It would be convenient, no doubt," Marta said, trying not to feel bereft.

"I've asked Persi to come with me," Michael added. "As a weaver, that is. I know the White Watcher must stay with the kingdom, but—"

"But I don't mean to go," Persi interrupted from the doorway. She handed Marta a sweating glass of cold rosewater sherbet. "There are people here who need me."

Marta had the uncomfortable feeling that by *people* Persi meant herself. She accepted the glass and gulped the sweet, icy liquid, letting it spread a welcome chill through her body. "Persi, you should go. I have the Lance, but you're a weaver, not a warrior. Saladin is mustering the greatest army he's ever fielded."

"So is King Guy," Persi said. "Doesn't he have enough arrow fodder, without the White Watcher into the bargain? You've never ridden to battle before."

Marta heaved an inward sigh. Letting Persi know that she meant to ride with the host—a fact she had concealed scrupulously from Lord Balian—had been a mistake. "True, but there's never been an enemy like this before." The bell went for supper and Marta stood, aching and weary. "Are you staying the night, Michael?"

"Yes, I've taken a room in the town and will start home at first light tomorrow." Michael tucked their next batch of patterns into his wallet and bowed to Persi. "Please, think of what I've said."

"Time enough for that if things go badly."

He sighed. "Good-bye, then, and God keep you. Marta," he added, "will you walk with me?"

Marta exchanged a glance with Persi, who evidently took the point that Michael wished to speak with her friend alone. Persi's skin was too dark to show a blush, but Marta did not think she imagined the momentary flash of some complicated emotion in her eyes before the other girl inclined her head stiffly and turned to go. Was Persi envious?

As they passed through the passage leading to the service courtyard, Marta bit her lip. Eight months ago, she had blurted out Persi's secret to Michael, and since then she had not dared to raise the subject. She was conscious of having wronged Persi, and although she knew that it was far too late to undo the thing, absolute silence seemed the only amends she could make.

Until now, when Michael asked to speak to her alone.

"Is it about Jehan of Cacho?" Marta whispered.

Michael nodded. "I bribed a Caesarean official to inspect his bookkeeping. It turns out Cacho has been skimming money from his master and falsifying the accounts. A word dropped in the ear of rivals did the rest. He's been dismissed from his position in disgrace."

Marta stared. "Embezzlement? How did you know?"

Michael hitched a shoulder in a shrug. "I didn't. I only guessed that a man so practiced in helping himself to his master's serving-women would not have denied himself in other ways as well." He paused. "It isn't enough, of course."

"No," Marta agreed. It was more than she could have done; it might, at least, remove Cacho from his position of power. But it would not warn others of what he was, nor would it stop him harming others if he was ever presented with the opportunity. "How much was the bribe?"

Michael laughed under his breath. "Let me bear the weight of that, Marta. I'd hate to become accustomed to such a practice, for all that it served justice."

Another time, Marta might insist. At present, however, she was more concerned with the thought that Cacho might inveigle his way into some other position of power in the future. "Where is the man now?"

"He's a freeman and a Frank; where else do you think he is? The Temple has released a great sum of English gold with which to hire mercenaries in King Henry's name. Jehan of Cacho is now in Sephoria with the Plantagenet livery on his back."

"With good fortune, Saladin will rid the world of him," Marta said. "But if he survives the war...I don't know. Maybe I'll talk to Persi about laying a formal accusation."

Michael did not answer, and when she looked up at him inquiringly, she saw that his face had gone very serious.

"Marta," he said gently, "you've made enough decisions for Persi. Let her make this one, when she's ready."

She already felt the blood rising in her cheeks, but Michael was not finished.

"I didn't say it before—I was speechless at the time—but I'll say it now: Cacho already took Persi's choices away from her, and what you did, in telling me, was more of the same. I know you meant well, but Persi didn't need Cacho to be mildly inconvenienced in his career. She needed a friend she could *trust*."

Marta bit down on her lip. She had guessed something, these past months, of the wrong she had done, but this was worse than she had realised. Had she indeed repeated something of Cacho's crime? She began to feel sick with guilt. *You're so damned self-righteous,* Miles had said, and he was right.

"I didn't think," she said, bewildered. "No, that's not true. I *did* think; of myself, and not of her." And now, she thought wretchedly, Michael could never ask Persi to marry him again, and Persi would never know why he seemed to have lost interest in her, or have the chance to change her mind. She had ruined everything.

"I know you meant well," Michael said again, and Marta felt that it was more than she deserved. "But take it to heart. Speak to Persi as you like, but not to salve your own feelings." He put out his hand. "There, I've said what I must."

She took his hand. Her face was hot and her heart seemed to be a sucking void in her chest, but she said, "Faithful are the wounds of a friend. You're a true friend, Michael, and I'm proud to call you my cousin."

His hand tightened around hers. "Go in peace, and take care, Marta."

He began saddling his mule, which had been rubbed down and provided with provender during his visit. Marta went back into the house with dread clawing at her throat. She had betrayed Persi, whom she loved best in the world, whom she would rather have died than hurt again. She ought to confess. No, Michael was right—that would be to salve her own feelings again.

She reached the foot of the stairs leading up to the roof, where the family would take their meal in the cool of the early summer evening, when a voice spoke from the shadows.

"What did Michael want?"

Marta had not seen Persi sitting there at the foot of one of the great pillars supporting the loggia. Her friend looked almost sick. Marta knew what it felt like to carry love all bound up in her own heart, bitter and corrosive. She paused and said in as steady a voice as she could manage, "Michael is a sort of nephew of mine. Did you know that? He's descended from my little brother Paulus."

Persi managed a smile. "Marta, that's wonderful! Does *he* know that?"

"I didn't tell him exactly when I was born," Marta said mechanically. "But yes; I've claimed the relationship. He thinks me some sort of cousin."

"You should have told me!"

"It was a recent discovery. And…I know how you feel about him. I didn't like to broach the topic."

Persi did not answer for a moment. Then she said, "Is that why you are weeping?"

Marta had thought her face was in shadow. She opened her mouth to say that no, it was nothing, but that was impossible, because it *was* something. Her mind was a blank: she hesitated too long and saw the dawning realisation on Persi's face.

"Marta," she whispered, "you *didn't.*"

Strife. Marta could not answer; could not even *think* of an answer. In the silence, her face answered for her. Persi jumped to her feet, clasping her temples.

"You *told* Michael? After everything I said to you? Marta!"

"Forgive me, Persi," Marta blurted, unable to bear the look of betrayal on her face. "I've wronged you, I know. Don't blame Michael; he was just scolding me for it. But in truth he had already guessed as much."

"Stop it—I can't," Persi gasped, and then she turned and hurried up the steps. Her footsteps echoed in the loggia; then the door of their shared room slammed, and the latch snicked. Marta put a hand over her mouth. The house was still, only a few latecomers hurrying up the stairs to the roof, where the clink of dishes and low voices told where Lord Balian was eating his last meal at home, perhaps for some time, perhaps forever. Marta should be up there with them, seeing the last of Queen Maria and the children. Instead, she had dealt the final blow to their friendship. Persi would never go to Tripoli with Michael now, no matter how great the risk in the kingdom itself.

The door upstairs had only been slammed for as long as it might take to say a Paternoster before it slammed open again. "Where is he?" Persi demanded, leaning over the parapet.

Marta said without much hope, "Still in the courtyard, saddling his mule."

"All right," Persi said, and then she rushed down the steps. At the foot of them, she levelled a furious look at Marta. "I only asked you to weep for me," she said.

Then she went through the peristyle into the service courtyard, and Marta heard her voice, sharp and carrying on the still evening air: "A word with you, Michael."

"Marta?" Farther above, Lord Balian leaned from the parapet of the roof. "Aren't you coming to dinner?"

"I'm not hungry," she said through her tears.

An agitated voice near the stables echoed loudly for a moment, then hushed again. Lord Balian glanced in that direction. "Is everything all right out there?"

"I don't know," she murmured. As Lord Balian turned away again, Marta climbed the stair. She had half a mind to go to her room, but then she thought that Persi might want it to be alone in. Instead, she went to the roof, tucked herself into the darkest corner she could find and ate quietly.

The mood among Lord Balian and his knights was hopeful; Marta gathered that the kingdom had fielded every man it could spare, reducing every garrison to a skeleton. There were even several great lords from the West who had come to the kingdom over the past year or two, waiting for the truce to end so that they could win honour in fighting for the holy places. Meanwhile, the defeat at Cresson, despite the loss of lives, had brought the kingdom to a greater unity than it had enjoyed since the days of the Leper King.

Presently, Ernoul came over to sit beside Marta. "When this is over," he told her, "I'm going to be a knight. Lord Balian has promised it."

"He's very generous," Marta agreed, turning her face away and gazing across the parapet. From this vantage it was possible to catch a glimpse of the stables. Michael's mule was still tethered outside the low outbuilding, but she could neither see him or Persi, nor could she hear their voices. What had happened?

"I am to have a money fief," Ernoul went on, "and a village or two worth of revenue if one becomes available."

Marta could not help remembering the days when Miles was a squire and used to speak in the same way. "Money and station aren't everything,

Ernoul," she said. "If you lose your soul, what good is the rest of it?"

He reddened a little. "I meant to say, when we've defeated Saladin, times will be peaceful. Maybe the kingdom won't need the White Watcher so much, then."

"Would that it were true. Pardon me." Having filled another plate with food, Marta ventured downstairs and scratched on the door of her room before putting her head through. It was silent and empty. Marta sat on the bed, unpinning her muslin veil and running her hands through the thick strands of hair still damp from her bath. Across the courtyard, lamplight glowed in the children's room as their nurses put them to bed. She ought to say goodbye to them, too; but not tonight, distracted with worry. Somehow, she must put things right with Persi before she went away, even if it meant staying in Nablus an extra day or two. Marta had never been one to dwell in the past—for some time Persi and the Ibelins had been all the family she needed—but tonight she felt desolate, wishing she still had a mother and could go to her for advice. But of course, Rahel the Messenger was long dead, and even if there *was* a way back across the pathless gulf of time, Marta did not think she would take it. Not unless it was to tell the others that she was both well and happy—as happy as it was possible to be in this world. The thought was a startling one. She had loved her family, and still thought of them every day with gratitude and affection. Yet she would not have lived with them long in any case: she would have been married away to Constantinople or Alexandria, perhaps even as far as Carthage or Ravenna, and there she would have made a new life for herself. Perhaps one she would have enjoyed less than this one among the hills of Samaria, with Pomers and her father's lance.

But that meant she had no one to guide her now, and she had already made so many mistakes.

A murmur of voices rose from the courtyard. Marta went into the loggia and leaned over the balustrade. The days were just at their longest, but twilight had begun to descend and for a moment Marta could see nothing in the courtyard. Then the mulberry tree shook and Persi and Michael emerged from beneath it. They went to the covered lane and stopped just below the arch. For a moment they spoke in soft voices; then they parted, and Persi returned to the garden, before making her way up the stairs to the loggia. When she saw Marta, she stiffened a little.

Persi looked dreadful; there were signs of tears on her face, and from the way her lips were pulled tight, Marta knew she was still angry.

"I—I brought some food down from the roof," Marta whispered.

"Thanks," Persi said. She passed Marta, but at the door to their room she stopped, heaved a sigh, and turned.

"I'm going to Tripoli," she announced wearily, "with Michael. I'll likely be gone by the time you get back."

Marta pressed a hand against her mouth. "Persi. I can't tell you how sorry I am."

"I know. I forgive you—or at least, I mean to try. But I can't…" Persi didn't finish the sentence. She suddenly vanished into their room and slammed the door.

For a while Marta stood in the loggia, blotting her tears with her veil. She badly wanted to do something, to say something that would make everything all right. Now, at last, when she had taken away all other choices from both herself and Persi, all she could do was weep.

A breeze twitched the damp muslin from her hands and sent it flying down the loggia. Marta sighed and went after it, and a moment later found it in the hands of little John of Ibelin, in a shadowed corner near the children's rooms.

"I found your veil," he said, holding the scrap out to her.

Marta rearranged her face into a pitiful smile, glad for the darkness that concealed her tears. "Thank you. Shouldn't you be in bed?"

At nine years old, Lord Balian's heir had his father's tall stature and his mother's thoughtful eyes. "Yes, but I have a message for you." Suddenly, he launched himself against her and locked his arms around her waist. "Don't go away to the battle, Marta. Stay with us instead."

For a moment Marta could neither speak nor move. Then she put her hands on the boy's shoulders. "John, my love, who told you I was going to the battle?"

His shoulders jerked in a shrug. Marta patted him and looked out at the moon. Was it a message, or a *Message?* The boy had never demonstrated any kind of Watcher's Gift before. Living in a great house, secrets had a way of being overheard. Or perhaps young John had only drawn the natural conclusion from the fact that Lord Balian was taking the rest of his knights north to the muster, too.

"I go where I'm needed, chicken," she said, releasing him. "Now run back to bed before your nurse comes downstairs and finds you up."

By Terce the next morning, Lord Balian and his eighty-five knights were on their way to the muster at Sephoria. Marta rode with them—*to keep you company,* she said. But she wondered, as she left, whether she would ever see Nablus again, or set things right with Persi.

Chapter XXI.

"If we want to defeat Saladin, we must *force* battle upon him, the way we did at Montgisard." Gerard of Ridefort pounded a fist on the table. Two months since Cresson, the Master of the Temple seemed completely recovered from his wounds—recovered enough, indeed, that Sibylla thought he might be about to lunge across the table and strangle the count of Tripoli right there in the king's cabinet. "Saladin will never cross the hills to us, nor accept battle on our terms. Therefore, *we* must cross the hills to him."

Just this morning, word had reached Acre that the sultan had crossed the Jordan with a host numbering in the tens of thousands and made camp near the southern shore of Lake Tiberias, a reliable source of water. In the summer heat, any march undertaken by either side in the stony Galilean hills would be complicated by the need to source fresh water and shelter for thousands of heavily armed men and their horses.

"We should remain in camp at Sephoria, where the water is plentiful and our lines of supply are secure." Tripoli did not raise his voice, but his teeth showed in something very like a snarl. "Either Saladin will give in and cross the hills to us, giving battle on our terms—or he'll be forced to retreat without a victory, as he did seven years ago at Bethsan."

Sibylla glanced at Guy, who slumped silently in his chair with his mouth sunk in his hand. "I don't know if you recall, my lord," she said coldly, "but seven years ago when you gave my husband the same advice, you then returned home blaming him for cowardice and incompetence. With the result that he was then removed from the *bailliship* and ultimately, the succession."

Tripoli shot her a hostile glare. "I had presumed that my presence at this table meant that my advice was valued. Was I wrong?"

"Your advice is noted, but insufficient," Sibylla said. "What, are we to sit here and listen to minstrels while Saladin reduces Tiberias to ash and rubble, with your countess inside? That is not merely unknightly; it's an extravagance this kingdom can ill afford."

"Eschiva knows what to do," Tripoli said. "Saladin may take the town, but he will not take the citadel. And even if he does, she and the men may escape by ship across the lake. Give him one small victory, and his army will disperse, glutted on spoil and anxious for their crops and wives at home. Better to lose Tiberias than the kingdom."

"You *will* lose us the kingdom," Chatillon growled, speaking for the first time. "Only in bites and swallows rather than one fell stroke. Devil take it, man! Don't you know it's as much as Saladin's throne is worth to leave us in peace? Your strategy would give him Tiberias this year, Nazareth the year after, and Acre the year after that. Haven't we dawdled long enough?"

Chatillon, too, had returned to the fold. Saladin having retreated from the siege of Kerak, the prince arrived at Jerusalem with great fuss and pother, claiming—with magnanimous words and a flat, cold stare—that he had forgiven Sibylla her duplicity and meant to stand by the king. Guy had been loath to trust him again, but both he and Sibylla knew they could not do without the prince, nor the hundred and twenty knights he commanded.

"What does the Hospital say?" Tripoli turned on the Commander, William Borrel, who had been appointed custodian of the order after Cresson.

The lanky commander looked ill at ease; it could not be easy for any warrior to be thrust so suddenly into such a politically charged situation. "I agree with the Master of the Temple. Cresson must be avenged. Our honour is at stake."

"My lord." Tripoli now appealed directly to the king. "It's madness to take such risks, so long as we can protect the kingdom. Perhaps Saladin *will* return next year, and the year after—but in the meantime anything might happen. He may die. Help may come from the West. We may even find some way to arrange a peace."

"This man wears a sheep's pelt," Ridefort growled, "but beneath it is the hair of a wolf. How do we know he is not still in league with the enemy?"

Tripoli stood so suddenly that his chair toppled over with a bang against the flagstones. "You're a fool, Ridefort, trying so desperately to retrieve the honour you lost at Cresson that you're ready to burn down Christ's own patrimony to do it."

"That's enough for this morning," Guy said hastily, speaking for the first time. "We'll discuss this further once we've reached Sephoria and seen the lie of the land."

When the two of them were alone, Sibylla released a long, measured breath. Guy turned to her at once, concern etched in his gaze. "Are you in pain?"

"Nothing that matters," Sibylla said. The bout that had attacked her after Cresson was over, and she was gradually gaining strength. Still, the morning's debate had left her feeling bruised; she had found herself withdrawing from the conversation, imagining herself watching it all from a very great distance. "Tripoli has a nerve riding his high horse like this. Surely he knows he cannot expect to be trusted, after all he has done."

"Why not, my love?" Guy said thoughtfully. "He has expelled the Saracens from Tiberias and joined us, after all."

"Don't be foolish," Sibylla said, still numb and far away. "It's a change of policy, not a change of heart. After Cresson, Tripoli had no choice except to make peace. The Church threatened excommunication, his vassals rebellion. He's offended the Orders, and they own half of Tripoli itself now. He may no longer be in league with Saladin, but he might still bring you down the way he did seven years ago, with backbiting and undermining."

Her hands were warm. A gentle pressure squeezed them, calling her back to herself. When he saw that he had reclaimed her attention, Guy said, "It won't be like last time, when I had your brother to answer to. This time

I'm king and can make my own choices." He kissed her, before drawing back and searching her face with thoughtful eyes.

"What is it?" Sibylla asked, now fully in the moment again, and unsettled by that look.

His eyes dropped to their linked hands. "I think Tripoli is right."

"What?"

"A passive defence was good strategy seven years ago at Bethsan. It will be even better strategy now that Saladin has grown in strength, and with the hills so dry…"

"No," Sibylla said, wrenching her hands away from his. "Don't you see? That's Tripoli's gambit—to make you look like a coward and a fool. Haven't you noticed? The people have stopped bringing their charters to us for witness. They no longer believe the king can guarantee their rights against each other, let alone against Saladin. You need to appear strong. A timid man cannot hold power in this kingdom, no matter how wise and crafty."

"Sibylla. This isn't like you. You used to agree that what I did at Bethsan was for the best."

"That was before you became king and both Tripoli *and* Chatillon chose to rebel. I tell you, Guy, if you don't come back with a victory, you might as well not come back at all."

For a moment, Guy did not speak. Then he laughed, short and angry. "Then perhaps I won't come back," he said. He kissed her hands and followed Tripoli, Chatillon, and the others into the courtyard. Sibylla sat frozen, listening to the trumpets as the king left Acre for Sephoria. Guy had really left her, just like that, with a few angry words. Desperately, she tried to sift back through her words for the reason why he might have responded in such a way. What had she done? Now that she had made him king, was he, too, beginning to turn against her?

"Lilith," she said, but the demon was already there, sitting on the table, cross-legged, and wearing Sibylla's own face. "Go after them. Make sure there is a battle, a great victory."

Her own teeth flashed back at her in a wolfish grin. "I thought you'd never ask."

"Wait." Sibylla took a deep breath. Her mind felt clouded, as it often did when she was ill; at times she could scarcely remember her own name. She must be careful. Lilith would find some way to trick her. Even victory would be hollow if something happened to Guy. "Keep Guy safe. Guy must live and return to me."

Lilith flashed away, and Sibylla, gritting her teeth, rose from her chair. There was nothing more she could do.

Chapter XXII.

"At last I understand." In the shadow of the king's red pavilion, Marta jumped as the voice suddenly sounded at her shoulder. It was Miles of Plancy, of course. "To merit your attention, I ought to have made myself king."

Marta let out a sigh and turned towards Lord Balian's tent, which stood in the valley north of them. "Not now, Miles."

The king had pitched camp, not quite at Sephoria itself, but a mile south towards Nazareth, around the springs in the valley. No doubt the village was happy not to have thousands of knights, squires, sergeants and lightly-armed Syrian Turcopoles billeted among them—an army nearly as great as Saladin's own. This is what it must have been like when the Franks first came from the west, Marta thought, scanning the immense camp. Even Ramla had returned with fifty knights from Antioch.

Miles fell in step with her, his thumbs thrust into his sword-belt. "I just can't help noticing how you gravitate towards power."

She sent him a scornful look, lost in the gathering dusk. "Power means nothing to me."

"Oh? Is that why you can never be separated from that Lance?" He grinned. "What did you want with the king this time?"

"I was *summoned*," she said shortly. In the six days since she and Lord Balian had joined the camp at Sephoria, Marta had made nearly as many journeys across the Galilean hills, watching the Saracens' movements and reporting directly to the king. After crossing the Jordan, Saladin had moved west as far as the springs at Carfarsset. Yesterday—the kalends of

July—Saladin had made an attempt to draw the king into battle, advancing with part of his formidable army as far west as the springs at Turan. Despite much grumbling among the troops, however, King Guy had refused to be drawn out, and Saladin had marched back to his camp.

Today had been another long day in the saddle, and Marta felt weary in more than body. In another attempt to provoke a battle, Saladin had gone to Tiberias with a corps of engineers. Within hours he had undermined the wall, forced his way into the town, and sacked the place. Marta had watched from the hills as the smoke went up. That afternoon she descended to the lakeside town of Magdala, where fugitives told her that Countess Eschiva had retreated to the Tiberias citadel with her garrison and now begged the king to send relief, as was due her as a vassal.

"The king wanted my advice," she told Miles. She had barely had time to see to Javelin's care, peel off her armour and quench her thirst with water and salted lemons before the king's summons had dragged her aching bones up the hill to his tent. From the threshold, she had been able to glimpse Sephoria itself—its hilltop tower stood like a single stark cube against the darkening sky, with the smaller shapes of the village houses like children's blocks to the west.

What would happen to these people if they failed? What about Persi and Michael, and little John and the other children? At least the children had been packed off under Queen Maria's care to safety in Jerusalem; Marta breathed a prayer for their safety and peace. Then she ducked through the flap of the tent and found the king alone except for his brother Aimery who, as the constable, held command of the army.

At first, Marta had been sure there was some mistake, but then the king said, "Come in, Marta Bessarion." So she went in, shivering a little in her short men's tunic and trousers, both still damp with sweat.

On the long, broad table running the length of the tent's living-quarters, someone had upended a bowl of salt, dragging a stubby finger through it to create a crude map: a round blob for Lake Tiberias, a cross for their own camp, and a line stretching east from Sephoria to represent the road across the hills, forking in two halfway where one road ran due east to

Tiberias, while another bent south, through Cafarsset and Saladin's camp to the south end of the lake.

"The Master of the Temple has a plan," the king told her. "There's water here at Turan, halfway between Sephoria and the lake. If we advance to the springs, it may draw Saladin up from Cafarsset—and then we can charge up the valley and pin them against the ridge at the valley's end. If anything goes wrong, there are the springs at Turan to fall back to." He looked up at her, hopeful. "What does the White Watcher advise?"

The two men, both so much more experienced than herself, watched her with intent brown eyes. Marta felt fresh sweat prickling her fore-head. All week, every day, Lord Balian had been in the king's pavilion debating strategies with the other barons. This very evening he had been triumphant, saying that the king had certainly decided against marching out to do battle. And now this?

Marta swallowed—who was she to air an opinion? "I've been over the ground, my lord, if that's what you mean. It is as the Master of the Temple describes it, a valley leading to a ridge. It's very dry. I don't know what else to say. I'm not a commander."

"No," said the king, "but you are a Watcher. What do you say? Will heaven smile on this campaign?"

Not for the first time, Marta wished she were a Messenger like the old Greek woman, or a Perceptor like Persi, or at least still the recipient of a seraph's kiss. But she was just a foolish girl with a magic lance. Marta thought of Sibylla wrangling with Tripoli over the throne, and of Chatillon ordering her teeth ripped out, and of Jehan of Cacho swaggering it, no doubt, in the gules and gold of England. She thought of King Guy himself, riding to Darum to slaughter her friends, the Bani Iaith. She still did not know whether al-Na'im and his hospitable wife had survived.

After the Leper King, the fire.

"I don't know," she said slowly. "I don't know whether we deserve to win. It has been prophesied that a great disaster would come upon this kingdom after the death of the Leper King."

Even in the ruddy lamplight, she had thought that the king paled. But he said steadily, "A great disaster may yet befall if I do nothing. If I march tomorrow, will the White Watcher follow me?"

Marta did not hesitate. It was for this that she had followed Lord Balian to Sephoria, after all. "I will," she had told him, "but not for your sake. I fight only for the kingdom."

Now, picking her way across the stony ground between campfires, tents and slumbering bodies wrapped in cloaks, Marta wished the march could have been ordered not for tomorrow, but the day after, so that Javelin could be rested enough for the long, hot journey ahead of them. As it was, she would need to ride Pomers to war; a pang of foreboding struck her heart. She did not want the finest destrier in the kingdom, Baldwin's greatest gift, to perish on the battlefield or founder in the heat with thirst.

"Miles," she said, "did you ever receive that fief of Legione?"

"Yes; together with the three knights the village supports." Miles laughed. "A lazy lot, better used to boozing and dicing in the streets of Acre than sweating in harness. I've been whipping them into shape, believe me."

"Then tell them to fill up their water-bottles tonight," Marta said. "Not all the springs in these hills are properly replenished after the drought."

There was a moment's silence, and then Miles gave a low whistle. "Then it's true," he said. "We *are* going to cross the hills and bring Saladin to battle."

"Boast about it when you take off your armour, not when you put it on. It's too easy for battles to go badly."

"Battles go badly all the time." He slid her a sidelong glance. "But we'll have the White Watcher with us this time, won't we?"

By now, they had reached the dying campfire outside Lord Balian's tent. Marta lowered her voice; she could not afford word to get out that she meant to attend the battle. "Lord Balian has ordered me to retreat to Nablus should it come to a battle."

"Yes, but we both know you'll never do that," Miles said, with disconcerting accuracy. "You're spoiling for a fight with that sorcerer."

Marta pressed her lips together. "Don't forget what I said about the water."

"Ah, Marta!" An arm went around her waist. "I knew you still cared for me."

His hold was not so different from a wrestling grapple, and Marta reacted like lightning. Miles fell with a thud and Marta backed out of his reach. There was a blade in her hand somehow, though she did not recall reaching for it.

Miles sat up, saw her defensive stance, and gave a low chuckle. "You never cease to surprise me."

"Nor do you," she said.

He misunderstood her and smiled. "Then give me a kiss, for luck."

Had he always been like this, so utterly satisfied with himself? Her lip curled. "I didn't say the surprises were pleasant ones."

Turning her back on him, she ducked through the flap of Lord Balian's tent, all dark within and thick with snoring. Marta found the corner that had been partitioned off for her use, and crawled into her bedroll. It felt as though she had only just closed her eyes when a trumpet shattered the night air, and sounds of confusion filled the camp.

"What is it?" Ernoul was asking. "Is it an attack?" Armour jingled, weapons clinked, and flint and steel cracked as Lord Balian's household woke and fumbled for their gear.

A voice came barking out of the night. "Arm yourselves! Fill your water-skins, eat and make confession! We move out before dawn!"

At that, every soul in the tent fell silent. Then Lord Balian swore once, explosively.

* * *

Things moved quickly once the first shock of the king's order was past. Grim and silent, Lord Balian's men buckled on their weapons, packed their bedrolls, and yoked oxen to the baggage carts.

Yawning in the chill of the night, Marta donned her armour. It must have been around Vigils, some two or three hours before dawn. As the tent was taken down and folded into the ox-cart, Lord Balian put a hand on Marta's shoulder.

"Be off with you," he said. "You've done more than enough for us here."

Marta nodded silently, too overwhelmed to say anything. There was going to be a battle, and either of them might die or be captured. She could not imagine what her life might be like without him. "Be careful," she said at last.

"I will." He bent down to give her a swift, fierce hug. "But if anything happens to me, it puts my heart at rest to know you'll be watching over Queen Maria and the children."

Forcing a smile, Marta led Pomers away—but only as far as the next tent. In the chaotic darkness, no one noticed as she drew out a leathern shield cover blue as the sky and bound it to the rim of her white shield. Then she unfastened the white horsehair plume fixed to the head of the Bessarion Lance, stowing it into her saddlebag. After that, she had only to don her helmet, making sure its faceplate covered every inch of exposed skin. The disguise was simple enough, but effective among so many men recognisable only by their shields and liveries. When the trumpets called the men to form up, Marta rode sedately to join the king's squadron, where it was less likely she or her horse would be recognised.

The army contained three squadrons in all: Tripoli's men in the vanguard and the king's at the centre, with Lord Balian and Count Joscelin commanding the rear-guard. Together, they formed a great, lumbering procession that overflowed the road: knights and Turcopoles a-horse; squires leading the great padded war-horses which would only be mounted later, when the time came to charge; ox-wains carrying the baggage. Finally, in a glittering ring surrounding each column, the infantry walked: spearmen and archers whose task it was to protect the vulnerable horses until they could be deployed in a devastating charge. Only Marta had no spare horse; there was no squire to care for one, and she trusted the Bessarion Lance better than a fresh destrier.

Sunrise found the army on the road, thousands of hooves and feet raising a thick cloud of white dust in the broad, eastward-sloping valley. Clear hot light reflected from steel rings and plated cuirasses; at the head of the king's squadron the great gold-and-silver reliquary of the True Cross blazed like a beacon. Within a couple of hours, the heat intensified, until Marta was grateful for the shade of the oaks and pines thickly bordering the road. The ridge of Cresson, where the last battle had been lost, rose on their right and then fell behind as the army emerged from the forest into the broad, cultivated ground beneath the hills of Turan. An hour after Terce they reached the springs north of the village, and a halt was called to let the horses drink.

There had, as yet, been no sign of the enemy army, only the occasional distant glint of sun flashing upon a scout's cuirass in the hills.

The springs of Turan lay in a deep, green hollow, shadowed by hills and ancient olives. The army trampled the verge to mud within minutes, as though it was ready to swallow the place whole, olives and all. Marta dismounted to let Pomers rest while they waited their turn at the water. She was still waiting when she heard a commotion at the other side of the spring; and presently, voices calling for firewood. Some of the men attacked the olives, breaking off limbs and carrying them into the crowd.

"What is it?" Marta asked, as a sergeant in the king of England's livery rushed past her dragging a dead, fallen bough.

"They've caught an old Saracen witch and mean to burn her," the man panted, before rushing on.

A horrible premonition struck her. Marta swung up into the saddle again and laid about her with the haft of the Bessarion Lance. "Way! Make way!" she roared, and quickly cleared a path to the scene of the disturbance.

In the midst of a ring of sergeants and foot-soldiers, a bonfire had been hastily built from brushwood, and three of them were at work on it with tinder-boxes and dry grass. More men surrounded a bundle of old rags on the ground, striking it with feet and fists. As Marta struggled nearer, a stout wooden staff wielded by a gnarled old hand shot up and struck one of them in the face. He reeled back, clapping both hands to one eye. Panting and shaking, the victim scrambled to her feet and threw herself at the opening thus afforded.

The moment Marta saw that face, bleeding and desperate, she knew the end had really come.

It was the old woman, the Greek Messenger. For a moment Marta could say or do nothing at all. The two sergeants wrested her stick away from her and dragged her back towards the pyre, now a roar of leaping flames.

If you fail, the fire will consume me also.

So much noise. So much shouting: "Saracen whore. Let this teach you to cast spells on us!"

"Let go of her!" Marta shouted, urging Pomers through the screaming, gesturing, hateful ranks. Intent on their task, no one paid much attention to her. The sergeants threw the old woman bodily onto the fire. Blazing leaves and bits of bark spouted into the air. Until now Marta had not heard the old Messenger's voice, but the fire wrung a hoarse scream from her. The tangle of boughs cracked and scattered. The old woman scrambled out of the fire, tearing her flaming veil from her head and slapping at her smouldering robe. Red, shiny burns showed on her face and hands. Her old legs did not carry her far: they gave way, and she pitched into the hands of her tormentors.

"You fools," the old woman panted, "don't you know what you are doing?"

"Stop this at once!" Marta shrieked, breaking through the ring. She thrust one man away with the leaded butt of the Lance, but by that time the old woman was already in the fire again. Then Pomers was surrounded by bodies and grasping hands.

She had covered her shield and was no longer the White Watcher, whom all men respected. Men shouted at her, explaining that the old witch was in Saladin's pay, that she had been sent to curse the army while it slept. The acrid smell of burning hair was unbearable. Marta clapped her spurs to Pomers' flanks, making him rear up, lashing out with his hooves. The sergeants scattered. Marta slipped from the saddle, darted to the pyre, seized a wrinkled brown wrist and drew the old woman once more from the flames. The Messenger fell to the ground, but Marta could not tend to her with a crowd baying for her blood. Turning, she levelled the Lance at the seething mass.

"Keep back," Marta howled. "Keep back, or you die."

The crowd seethed in response, shouted, shook their fists, and cried: "Traitor."

Even with the Bessarion Lance, there was no way she could fight the whole Frankish army. Was this how she died—not duelling her enemy, but overwhelmed by the very people she was trying to save?

"One last message." The cracked old voice strained with agony as the Messenger raised herself from the ground, hair burned away, scalp bleeding. The crowd, astonishingly, hushed to listen. The old Greek's words were clear. "You have sealed your own fate. Disaster is upon you all, and many will fall. Flee now if you wish to save your lives."

Enraged, the men surged forward. Marta stepped to meet them, sweeping the Bessarion Lance before her. Men went down like ninepins. Then, from behind her back, there was a clanking rush of feet, and a horrible, wet, cracking sound. Marta screamed. A sergeant had buried his great Danish axe in the old woman's skull. She was dead by the time Marta turned.

Marta stared, letting the point of the Bessarion Lance sink into the dust. The sergeants closed around her, hoisting up the ghastly remains and throwing them, once more, into the fire.

Heat licked at Marta's skin.

If you fail, the fire will consume me also.

That distant voice broke into her shock. *What are you waiting for? Run!* Marta shook herself. For one moment the mob's attention was on the fire. In another they would remember her, the old woman's champion. She darted towards Pomers, leaped into the saddle, and retreated towards the spring, where the well-armed knights at the water's edge watched her approach with curiosity.

"What's happening over there?" one of them asked.

Concealed behind her faceplate, Marta could pretend not to have heard. Thankfully, another knight answered the question for her.

"The men say they've caught a witch. Superstitious idiots."

"That's not a good omen," said the first knight. "Men who are frightened out of their wits don't win battles."

With that, they took their horses down to drink. No one had done anything to help.

If you fail, the fire will consume me also.

The spring was reduced to a trampled muddy puddle long before the fire ceased to burn, or the fat to sputter, or the bones to crack. Long before the whole army had had the opportunity to drink, horns sounded and the army formed up to move on. Behind her faceplate, Marta gnawed her lip as the men took their places, knights at the centre, footmen lining the column's flanks.

If you fail...

She *had* failed. Marta had never felt more helpless. She had feared a second Oliveta, but what would Oliveta be compared to this? For a moment she considered turning her back on them, fleeing to Acre and following Persi and Michael Zakar to Tripoli. But what then? Khalil was still alive and looking for her; someday he would find her.

There was no way out but ahead.

Chapter XXIII.

The enemy struck as soon as they left the springs.

Mounted skirmishers poured through the wooded slopes to the right—bearded Turcomans in fur-lined hats and dusty broadcloth coats, their long braids flying behind them as they loosed their darts and wheeled away again; moustachioed ghulams in mail coifs and lamellar breastplates over brightly-coloured tunics, dashing in on sinewy horses to rake the column with curved sabre and tiger-head mace; Arabs with fluttering turbans, round shields and stiff sheepskin surcoats probing the infantry with their lances.

At first these were only light, teasing attacks—nothing a massed charge of infantry could come to grips with; and thus they could only be endured. But then, as the valley narrowed towards the ridge of Manescalcia, the attacks suddenly thickened. Shouts of warning ran down the column as a whole company of archers poured from the southern hills and raced towards the army. As they neared, the brassy morning air hissed and glinted with their arrows.

"Hold ranks!" The shout was passed down the column. Marta raised her shield. Horses screamed and men howled as the arrows thudded home all around her. Beyond the screen of infantry, shrill war-cries and pounding hooves tore past—a cloud of dust that ripped at the Frankish flank with blade and mace. To Marta's right, the screen broke. She responded without thinking, levelling her spear and spurring Pomers through the frayed infantry, into the storm. Dust billowed around her. Towards her they came: shadowy shapes on horseback, bared teeth, flashing swords. Marta levelled the Bessarion Lance and shot through them like an arrow, tearing one man from his saddle. She let the Lance swing down, behind and over, to come back to rest: bloody and sharp and thirsty for more. Blows glanced off her shield. With a change of weight she twitched Pomers aside just in time to escape being spitted on some lance as keen and thirsty as her own. Then, the dust-cloud thinned and she plunged out into the sun again, and the infantry (who had just finished burning their Messenger) cheered and opened their ranks to welcome her inside the column again.

The skirmishers vanished into the hills again as quickly as they had come, allowing a brief lull. By now the column was strung out across the valley for perhaps a mile, slowed by those constant, wearing attacks. Bodies lay in the road, impeding their progress—mostly horses riddled with arrows. Marta's throat was coated in dust; she took a precious mouthful of water and felt grit between her teeth as she recapped the bottle. Her hands were still shaking, and sweat had run into her eyes.

The next attack slammed into the line further ahead, near the white-and-gold royal standard. The True Cross in its golden reliquary reeled a little, flashing in the sun. A shudder and surge ran through the entire column; then it came to a halt altogether. "Way!" Marta shouted hoarsely, and the infantry parted, letting her through.

She caught the skirmishers withdrawing and sent them on their way with bloodshed. When she turned, she found that she was not alone. Four other knights had followed her from the column, one of them bearing a shield with a black left-sloping bar across it.

"Get back!" she shouted to them, as some of the fleeing Saracens turned, drawing their bows. By some miracle, none of their arrows touched her. Marta laughed recklessly as she returned to the column. Not even Pomers was scratched, though his breath thundered like a bellows, and his coat was a lathered mess of sweat. She must not ask too much of him, not if she wanted him to last the day. She herself felt almost suffocated with the heat.

Undoing her steel mitts, she turned to the knight who had stuck closest to her across the deadly ground beyond the column. "Are you out of your mind, Miles? Why are you following me?"

"Are you out of yours?" he retorted. Under his steel cap, his face was red and perspiring. "I recognised Pomers and thought you'd appreciate the support."

Marta pulled off her gloves and shoved back the sleeves of her gambeson as far as they would go, dribbling a little precious water over the flushed skin beneath. Cool relief trickled through her overheated body. "You know you don't have what it takes."

"That's why I stayed with *you.*" He pulled at his water-bottle, and when he lowered it, there was a peculiar light in his eyes. "Didn't you see? The arrows don't reach you, Marta. They turn aside. They splinter in the air." He gestured towards the heavens. "Someone is watching over you."

Miles looked as he had the night of their escape from Kerak, when he had first witnessed the power of the Lance. Awed, almost reverent. Marta only felt sick and dizzy. She had seen power like that before, and on that occasion it had not been the work of anything heavenly.

Khalil wanted her alive, and at any cost. But *why?* Where *was* he?

"All right," she said slowly. "Five are better than one. But tell your men to stick close to me."

She shifted inside her armour, feeling the sticky gambeson chafe her arms. She would be one great heat rash when this was over.

At least they were approaching the ridge now, according to King Guy's plans, and the true battle could begin.

* * *

The battle could not begin, because the Master of the Temple had underestimated the sheer choking number of Saladin's light cavalry, and because the king had been fool enough to listen to him, and because Saladin, damn him, was far too wily to commit his main forces to a frontal attack but merely contented himself with this nipping and growling.

Balian was not a swearing man ordinarily, but this was enough to make a saint curse. All they had needed to do was sit snugly in their camp at

Sephoria until the sultan made a mistake or went away. Instead, they had committed themselves to this grinding march, at the height of summer, in dry country. Saladin hardly needed to exert himself: just enough harassment to slow their march to a crawl, and he could wait for the sun to do the rest.

Meanwhile, Balian was forced to watch as his rear-guard shredded from a capable fighting force to a blood-streaked rabble. The enemy skirmishers concentrated the brunt of their attack here, where the Temple and the Hospital formed a solid, steel core to the column. At first the rear-guard slowed; then it came to a standstill.

Now, Balian met with the king and Tripoli under the True Cross, their conference conducted in shouts simply to be heard over the chaos of Saracen attack.

"The rear-guard is melting," Balian howled. "We're sustaining the brunt of these attacks. We must have lost a tenth of our horses already, and walking in this heat is impossible."

"Where's Ridefort?" the king yelled, pink and clammy as the rest of them.

"Yes, and where's the battle he promised us?" Tripoli scoffed. "This is the ridge of Manescalcia, after all!"

The Master of the Temple had elected to stay with his suffering men. "He says we can't deploy for battle under these conditions!" Balian gestured to the rear. "The Saracens have us hemmed in so that we couldn't possibly ready the destriers!"

Without destriers there could be no charge, and with no charge there could be no battle. There was a long silence. "Could we retreat?" the king asked.

Balian shook his head. "They've closed the valley behind us."

The king was silent as the reality of their situation sunk in. There was no going back, but with the rear-guard already exhausted, going on was risky. As for staying put, that meant more of the same. And it was only noon, with the hottest part of the day still before them.

Marta had warned of disaster; Balian knew he ought to have paid better attention. This was partly his own fault. If King Guy could have trusted him and Tripoli to put the good of the kingdom above their own political ambitions, he might have been able to take their advice.

Swallowing his dread with an effort, Balian asked, "How far to Tiberias?"

"Eight miles," Tripoli shouted.

The king digested this in the same blank silence. It had taken them three hours to traverse as many miles since Turan. At this rate they would die of heat long before they reached the lake. "There must be some water nearer than that."

Everyone looked at Tripoli, who gestured towards the ridge where the valley of Manescalcia sloped up to the sky. "There are some small springs at Hattin, a village north of the road. Just about three miles away."

"We'll have to divert," the king decided, and it was such an obvious choice that no one had any objection to make. "What did you call the village? Hattin?"

That, Balian thought, would be a fittingly humble name for a graveyard.

If they made it so far.

* * *

Marta's head pounded. This was worse than Arabia. Then, at least, it had been winter, and the desert heat was bearable. Today, with no shade and no water, she was slowly suffocating beneath layers of armour and padding.

They had skewed north and were headed uphill—away from the road and across thin scorched grass up a slope that never seemed to end. There was supposed to be water ahead somewhere, but the men around her, knights and sergeants alike, looked utterly despairing. The change of direction had, at first, thrown them into confusion. Meanwhile, the Saracens made constant quick, stinging charges, causing the line to sway and stagger and wellnigh collapse on itself. Beset by skirmishers both behind and ahead, their pace slowed, often stopping altogether. The rear-guard, it seemed, was struggling to keep up. Marta could not guess how many bodies now littered the stony hills behind, fallen to arrows or slings or heat.

"Ready to charge again?" Miles asked her. He was missing one of his knights, who had lost his horse to a stray arrow and been forced to join the infantry. But he was a thick man and unaccustomed to exerting himself in the heat. Complaining of spasms and cramps, he had quickly fallen behind. Miles had told him to take refuge on one of the ox-carts. Marta could only hope the knight had made it.

Now, she inspected Miles for the tell-tale signs of heat-sickness. He seemed fatigued, like everyone else, but was still perspiring freely: the sweat had made black runnels of mud through the grey dust that caked him. "Feeling all right? Not faint or dizzy?"

"I'm not a child, Marta. Come on."

Marta had lost count of how many charges she had led that afternoon; the hottest part of the day had dragged by in one long nightmare. Since it was now Nones, however, and the sun had at last begun to descend among the low rolling hills at their backs, she could only hope that the day would soon begin to cool.

"Stay close," she told him, and lifted her voice to cry "Way! Way! Let us out!"

The infantry drew aside again, managing to raise a faint cheer for Sir Miles—they did not, of course, recognise the White Watcher. Gallant despite his exhaustion, Pomers quickened to a gallop.

Miles moved with her. He had stuck to her all day like a burr, for once giving up his needling remarks, but she could not help suspecting his motives in sticking so closely by her side. Protection from stray arrows was not the whole of it: the men were shouting his name. *Miles of Plancy, Miles the Lion.* He might live, or he might die, but after this day people would make songs about Miles of Plancy, too.

Bursting from the column, they drove straight into an unsuspecting onslaught of Turkish ghulams, the sultan's elite heavy cavalry. Marta drove through them obliquely, taking care not to be drawn into their centre. Thrown into confusion, the ghulams wheeled away and fled back into the south hills rather than continue their assault. This time the cheering from the column was louder, and Marta felt a momentary taste of hope. If

Saladin let off pressure for a moment, if the army could get remounted and deploy for a charge, then surely some victory could be won.

The spear in her hand vibrated like a plucked harp-string. That familiar voice echoed in her ears. *Look up! Beware!*

Marta obeyed without thinking. Her heart stood still as she saw what was coming towards her. A nightmarish figure took shape in the quivering afternoon heat: a tall, gaunt figure which stalked down the Frankish column, twice the height of a man, clad in scales and hair. A single Polyphemus-like eye burned in its forehead; the other was set red and malevolent in its chest. It wielded a horn bow, arrow after invisible arrow striking men and horses. They reeled, paled, fell out of rank.

Marta's throat went even drier. She had met this creature before, when its arrows nearly killed Miles and herself in Arabia. She was almost certain she had met it again at the bridge of Judaire in the shape of a desert wolf. A midday spirit, it wielded as its weapons despair and acedia, pestilence and heat sickness. Marta swerved away from the column, away from Miles, towards the gaunt apparition. A hoarse cry burst from her throat as she approached, and she hurled the Bessarion Lance with all her might.

This time the dread thing neither saw her onslaught, nor stepped aside to avoid it. All its attention was on its prey in the column. The spear flew through the eye at its heart with no more effect than if she had tossed it through a shadow.

But the terrible eye rolled and fixed on Marta.

Strife. She had no seraph's kiss to protect her now, and the Lance had flown from her hand and vanished. She was defenceless.

She was still hurtling towards it. But Pomers seemed, like his mistress, to see the great enemy. With a snort of terror he threw himself into a sliding stop. Marta reeled in the saddle. When she looked up again, the phantom had disappeared. The Bessarion Lance was there a stone's throw away, stuck in the ground, ripe for the plucking. Between one heartbeat and another she imagined it being snatched away from her, leaving her unarmed in this hell. With a gasp, Marta plunged forward to retrieve it.

The haft smacked into her hand and all was well again. Somewhere behind, Miles shouted her name; then his horse flashed up beside Pomers and he was grabbing her rein, pulling them back into the column barely in time to evade another charge of enemy skirmishers.

"What do you think you're doing?" he shouted at her over the thunder, the crunch and shriek of the charge.

"I *saw* something," she protested, trying to regain control of her reins. "A monster, a demon…"

His eyes widened. "You're addled by the heat. Saint George…" He thrust out an open hand. "You can't fight like this. Give me the Lance."

"What?"

"Give it to me!" He lunged at her to grab the haft, and all the tentative friendliness that had sprung up between them these past few weeks evaporated. Marta swept up the lead-lined butt to strike his wrist aside. The blow broke his hold on Pomers' rein, and despite the jostling, tight-packed throng managed to put a little distance between them.

"Never," Marta hissed. Her head throbbed relentlessly, her gambeson was chafing her raw, and she felt as though she might suffocate in her armour. Still, she would rather die than entrust the Bessarion Lance to Miles. Sooner than do so, she would fight her way to the rear-guard and hand it over to Lord Balian, even if she got a scolding in return. "If this is the help you mean to give, I don't need it."

"You fool. You'll get us all killed if it falls into enemy hands."

"What, aren't you enjoying yourself, Miles?" she spat back at him. "Was this a worthy price for your soul, this chance to defend a fief of your own?"

She charged from the column again, choosing a thin spot where the infantry's formation had been unpicked by the sultan's horse archers. This time, Miles did not follow her.

The afternoon continued: charge and countercharge, volleys of arrows exchanged, advances so slight as to be nearly pointless, the army hemmed in too closely to deploy or manoeuvre. The sun began to decline behind them, burning in its shroud of dust like the red-rimmed eye in a demon's breast. Such had been the intensity of the fighting that since midday the army had scarcely advanced a mile. For some time now it had been clear that the springs at Hattin were as far out of reach as Tiberias itself. Yet at last they attained the high plateau around Manescalcia, where the king called a halt and the Templars, at last, were able to charge from the rear-guard. But the enemy melted away, swallowed the charge, and gave nothing back.

There was nothing left but to pitch camp. The small, whitewashed houses of Manescalcia village had been deserted by their inhabitants, and within a few minutes the few wells were scraped utterly dry. For the rest of the afternoon, until the sun was a blaze of fire on the western horizon, all forward movement ceased: the army simply stood passive and bristling as the enemy nipped and bit.

Night came at last. A cool breeze sprang up. The enemy inched closer and set up their own camps just out of bowshot. Marta could hear their voices when the wind stilled, and smell their campfires. The king posted no scouts, for not even a cat could have slipped through Saladin's cordon, and the encircled army occupied the sort of high, sloping ground that made it difficult to see far in any direction. Yet someone who had climbed a pine-tree said that there was a thick haze to the east, around the village of Lubia less than two miles away.

Marta did not need to be told the significance of that. The horsemen who had made the day such torment had merely been the sultan's vanguard. Exhausted as the Franks were, they had not even begun to reckon with the enemy's main army.

She unsaddled Pomers and rubbed him down; put the brackish remnants of her water into her helmet so that he could wet his lips; and slumped into the dust to gnaw on a handful of dates and almonds. She kept her face averted as Ernoul and Samuel Arrabi went by carrying a precious ration of water to the gold-and-gules Ibelin tent. At this point, letting Lord Balian know she was trapped in the host with him would add little to her own comfort and only worry him. She had money with her; she would beg or buy a collop of meat from the sergeants who, having roasted a Messenger this morning, were now doing the same to a goat-kid over a nearby fire.

Once it was dark enough to conceal her from the men, Marta pulled off her mail coif and loosened her hair from the thick braid coiled around her head. Unbound, the sweaty mass lay limp and sticky on her neck. She rested her head on Pomers' saddle, but there was no hope of sleep. All night, the Saracens kept up an incessant drumming and singing. Marta itched unbearably under her armour: tormented by thirst, she could not work the slightest moisture into her mouth.

Maybe she would die tomorrow—maybe the whole kingdom would be lost—but despite the warnings that now seemed so clear, Marta could not regret what she had done. She could not consign her people to al-Aziz Khalil, nor to a sultan who had spilled countless of his own peoples' blood to build himself an empire. Not without striking a blow in their defence.

And she could not quite bring herself to believe that the Bessarion Lance could fail her.

The night passed restlessly: if it was not someone groaning for the misery of their wounds, it was some too-loud confession of sins or a fight breaking out over the last few mouthfuls of water at the bottom of someone's bottle. Marta closed her eyes and tried to close her ears, knowing that she would be the better next morning for pretending to sleep, even if the reality evaded her. It must have been some hours before dawn when she slipped into a half-waking dream.

Marta thought she stood on a craggy hill overlooking Lake Tiberias, which shone like silk beneath the thin light of the crescent moon. A dark cloud hung over the town itself, smoke from the plundered carcase. Her mouth itched and burned with the taste of ashes.

A voice spoke in her ear. "You can save them, if you wish. I'll help you."

Marta turned and found herself facing the feathered woman she had seen looming behind Queen Sibylla on the day of her coronation. Her lips felt weighted, but she forced out the words anyway. "I don't need your help."

"Ungrateful child!" the woman said, with a pretence of kindness that made Marta's skin crawl. "Don't you know who has been shielding you from arrows all day? I ought to abandon you; then you'd—"

"Bear me a message to Khalil, who calls himself the Mighty," Marta interrupted her. "I, Marta Bessarion, say that he is a dog and a bloody tyrant, and that he has no right to more of Galilee than will serve as his grave. I am ready to prove the same on his body in combat, or to declare him a coward if he does not answer this challenge with sword and spear, tomorrow, in the field."

The feathered woman smiled, and although she had looked like any mortal woman a moment ago, now her teeth were gleaming sharp. "That is your message for him. Will you hear the message he has for you?"

"No," Marta said. "Go away, in God's name, and let me sleep."

Chapter XXIV.

The hot clear light of another merciless day roused Marta before sunrise. Her mouth tasted like a sarcophagus, but the Bessarion Lance was still in her hand: not even sleep had loosened her grip upon it. Clumsy in haste, she braided her hair and pinned it around her head. Two coifs went over it, one of sweat-stained linen and then another of fine chain mail. Having checked that her helm, saddlebags, and saddle were all in place, she went to see Pomers.

He was picketed with some of the other horses at the centre of the camp, and Marta inspected his flanks and hooves sadly. His shoes were sound enough, but as she had feared, the saddle had galled his back, rubbing hair from the skin. He twitched with pain as she settled the still-damp saddle blanket across the sores.

"Give me one more day," she whispered, sorry for what she must do to him. As she said the words a terrible premonition settled over her: one more day was all any of them could take. One more day to complete their ruin.

"Strike camp! Mount your destriers!" Already the order was being shouted through the camp. Marta sighed and buckled on her saddle.

The enemy was still close but out of view, concealed by slopes and trees. They did not attack at once but drew off to allow Tripoli's vanguard to move out, aiming up the long slope of the plateau towards the village of Hattin. From previous journeys, Marta knew the place: there was a shrine there to Saint Jethro, and a spring that flowed down through a steep gulley towards the north. A little to the east of the village, the plateau reared up and ended with two craggy bridge-heads to nowhere: the Horns of Hattin, which overlooked the lowlands of Tiberias, Magdala and the raw-silk blue of the lake. She thought she might have visited the Horns last night, in her dream.

Before they reached Hattin and its water, they must cross three miles of open land: hemmed in on the left by the forested hills around the village of Nimrin and on the right by Saladin's main force at Lubia; harassed behind by the sultan's left wing and opposed in their march by his right.

Now that the vanguard was on its way, it was time for the king's squadron to form up and move out. "No rounceys! Mount your destriers!" Constable Aimery shouted. Marta settled into her saddle with a stifled groan as all yesterday's aches, bruises, and blisters complained. Then they started resolutely into the cloud of dust raised by Tripoli's advance.

Scarcely had the march begun, when some of the knights and Turcopoles in the king's host began pointing at the pine-clad hills to the left. Marta pushed her way through the column to see. When she did see, her mouth dropped open.

A caravan had come into view: five camels roped together, circling their rear and heading towards the wooded hills beneath Nimrin. And those great, damp skins, one hanging from each side of the saddle, could only be one thing…

As they watched, a camel was detached from the caravan and a white-turbaned driver rode it nearer.

"It's water," someone gasped. The column swayed towards the camel, yearning. "Hold your line!" the constable shouted.

"Way!" Marta cried. Bursting through the infantry, she galloped headlong for the approaching camel. The driver saw her coming and unsheathed his straight sword. Marta screamed at him, unconsciously urging Pomers to greater speed as the camel driver slashed first to one skin, then the other. Great silver curtains gushed from the skins and flooded the dust. With a mocking wave, the driver turned his camel and fled.

Pomers pulled to a halt and nosed the damp earth, desperate for water. Numb, Marta sat atop him watching the water-laden caravan as it went away from her, into the hills. The air hissed with arrows, but she paid no attention as they burst to shivers in the air around her.

One horseman, who had been following the caravan, stopped. Across the quarter-mile dividing them, their eyes met.

Marta tensed. From turban to saddlecloth the Saracen wore unrelieved black; only his polished cuirass of lamellar plates flashed with light in the morning sun. Although she was not quite close enough to see his face, the set of his shoulders was unmistakable.

Couching her spear, Marta raked Pomers' flanks with her spurs and swooped upon Khalil like an eagle. She had scarcely crossed half the distance between them when a company of Turcoman archers flowed out from behind the village and raced towards her. Marta cut her way through them, but by the time she got clear and the dust had settled, Khalil had vanished.

Marta hesitated, but there was no sign of her quarry and she was dangerously far from the column. Instead of pursuing, she turned and fled back to the army.

The reason for the water caravan soon became clear. Smoke started to belch from the forested hills to the left in a thick, suffocating cloud that blew across the dry plateau, enveloping the army, stinging their eyes and making them cough and retch in the heat. Some of the sultan's followers must have been in the hills all night building fires and wetting the brushwood to elicit smoke.

After the Leper King, the fire.

Still Saladin did not strike them, his skirmishers only testing the Franks' resolve, probing their defences. It had been one matter to harry an army whose knights were unprepared for battle, but every man was on his war-horse this morning.

Just after Terce, the storm broke.

From the south, the Saracen drums rolled nearer. The cavalry attacks imperceptibly thickened until Lord Balian's rear-guard and the king's central squadron were beset with rolling charges, relentless as the waves of the sea. Step by step, the incoming tide swept them up the plateau. Arrows filled the air, felling horses, bristling from hauberks.

The drums rolled nearer still. Somewhere in Tripoli's vanguard, a trumpet screamed and there came the thunder of a charge. The next moment another trumpet sounded; the knights of the king's squadron turned to face the south, and the infantry wall in front of her suddenly parted. Another blast, and Marta was carried out with the rest of the king's knights. More trumpets blew from the rear-guard, but Marta scarcely noticed whether the military Orders were making a charge of their own: she was caught in a rolling tide of steel and horseflesh, so closely packed that other men's stirrups battered her own. Despite his thirst, Pomers gave a war-cry of his own, a roar that shook the heavens. Their impetus was irresistible: before the tightly packed Frankish onslaught, the ranks of the enemy scattered and fled.

Marta had often suspected that the power of the Lance conferred strength not just on the wielder but also her mount, and now, as Pomers steadily outstripped the other horses, she thought it must be true. In the smoke and dust, Saracen knights loomed up ahead of her, Arab and ghulam cavaliers wielding spears and sabres. She and Pomers moved in perfect unison, the Bessarion Lance hurling opponent after opponent from his horse.

Then she saw the man in black.

The king's trumpet blew and the onslaught slackened. With consummate discipline, the knights of the kingdom checked their horses and fell back, leaving a trampled field of bodies and blood behind them. The shattered Saracens turned, making for the place where, somewhere upslope, half concealed by the smoke, Saladin must have been rallying his broken troops. Following them would be hazardous, of course, but Marta had no thoughts of danger: she only had Khalil *there*, in front of her.

She raised her arm to throw the Lance like a javelin.

Marta, no! Stop!

The voice went through her like a spear itself, and starbursts of blinding colour burst behind her eyes. Marta blinked, shaking her aching head to clear it. The next instant the black-clad man was upon her. Catching his sword-blow on her shield, Marta converted her attack from an overarm cast to a downward-stabbing blow. The Saracen crumpled, sliding to the ground. For a moment the Lance caught in his collarbone; Marta wrenched it free and circled to check her handiwork.

It was not Khalil at all. His turban was not even black—it was green.

Not Khalil—then why had she thought it was? Marta raked her spurs along Pomers' flanks, hastening to join the retreat. Was it just a cunning illusion, like the one which had shown her Miles in Khalil's power? She might have cast away the Bessarion Lance for nothing, the way she had almost lost it yesterday trying to fight the hairy demon.

Was this Khalil's strategy? Was he trying to draw her out, to part her from her weapon, to render her helpless?

Marta was dry-hot, too thirsty to sweat, but she felt as chilled as if she had been picked up and tossed bodily into Lake Tiberias.

* * *

By the king's orders, Balian was supposed to be in the rear-guard with the Templars, the Hospitallers, and Count Joscelin. That last part still held true: Joscelin was here on his left hand, eyes red with smoke and hollow with dread. But the military Orders were long out of sight, swallowed up in one of their charges. As for being the rear-guard, Balian was no longer sure he had an army to protect any more.

The battle had gone on for hours now, charge and countercharge, rally and retreat, all of it done in the suffocating cloud of smoke that continued to pour down from the hills. In that mirk there was no telling whether the king was still fighting, let alone Tripoli and the vanguard.

"Does anyone know what is happening?" Balian demanded, but of course no one could answer him.

Then, as it did periodically, the breeze shifted, the smoke and dust thinned, and Balian caught a clear glimpse of the two Horns directly northeast. The king's squadron must have been pushed in that direction: Balian glimpsed the banner of the kingdom and the glint of the Holy Cross

216

at the centre of a massive scrum below the peaks. The battlefield between them had degenerated into pockets of iron resistance. A great number of infantry seemed to have collected upon the northernmost peak of the Horns, but of Tripoli there was no sign.

Balian turned to Count Joscelin, the swarthy old man who had come to the kingdom a landless fugitive and had accumulated himself a great lordship from the leavings of other men; the one who had led Isabella to her marriage with Humphrey, who had snatched Jerusalem for Sibylla and made Guy king. He would never forget what Joscelin had done, but today it was as much as either of them could do to survive.

"Where's Ridefort?" Balian howled.

"I don't know. He never returned from that last charge."

"And Tripoli?"

"I haven't seen him since the beginning. Someone said he'd run away."

Saints and angels, Balian thought. Tripoli had to have made that first charge with the vanguard, most likely towards Hattin village. Then what? Had he broken through the cordon now strangling them, or been swallowed up and annihilated?

His thoughts were interrupted by Joscelin's hand closing on his arm. The other count pointed south as the wind lifted the veil of smoke surrounding them. All day, Saladin's left wing had clustered on their heels. All day, the Frankish rear-guard been struggling to keep up with the king's squadron, to keep moving north. Now, as the cloud lifted, it was possible to see that the Saracen cordon behind them had worn thin. Imperceptibly, the majority of the battle had concentrated upon the struggle around the Holy Cross at the foot of the Horns.

Joscelin's eyes met Balian's. With one accord they glanced again towards the Horns. The smoke-cloud rolled low again, blotting the Holy Cross from view. Once again, they were alone on the battlefield, cut off from their fellows, crippled and surrounded.

Except, just possibly, for the road behind them.

"We could save some of the men," Joscelin said in a strained voice.

Or they could stay and try to relieve the king, to salvage the battle. If they fled now, Balian knew exactly how it would seem. People already whispered how convenient it was that he had managed to avoid the disaster at Cresson; how the traitor Tripoli had been one of his nearest friends. Abandon the battle now, and those voices would only gain strength.

But the battle was hopeless, and had been since the moment they failed to bring Saladin to battle yesterday as planned. If Balian stayed, he had nothing but death or captivity to look forward to.

The kingdom would be better off without Guy of Lusignan anyway.

Balian's throat was dry and raw, and he had to swallow once or twice before he could make himself heard.

"Have the men turn south," he told his trumpeter. "And sound the charge."

* * *

Downslope of the main battle, a trumpet blew the charge, and Marta let out a sob of relief. "Listen to that! It's Lord Balian, with the rear-guard!" she called out to the knight beside her—who happened to be Miles of Plancy.

Somehow, despite their quarrel yesterday, he had ended up by her side again. Marta presumed he still wished to avoid arrows.

There was a note of despair in his voice. "They'll never make it," he predicted. Then, suddenly he burst out, "What the devil?"

The clouds parted just long enough to show the rear-guard in bloody shreds streaming, not towards them, but away, down the hill and back into the thick of the smoke.

"The *bastards!*" Miles was almost wailing. "Deserters! Come back! Devil take it, Ibelin!"

It was only a glimpse, there and then gone again, but it scraped the heart out of Marta, like a spoon scooping seeds from a melon.

"There's your Prester Balian for you," Miles growled. "A coward."

She should have swallowed her pride and told him where she was. Lord Balian would never have gone away and left them if he had known *she* was here.

Would he?

She glanced around her. Only the king's squadron now seemed to hold any semblance of order, standing its ground in a beleaguered ring about the True Cross and the royal standard. The vanguard was long gone, its cavalry fled north through Hattin village, its infantry retreating to the north peak of the Horns. The king had sent messages begging them to come down and fight, but they stubbornly remained there, too scared to fight and too exhausted to flee. It was now at least twenty-four hours since many of them had tasted water.

Even as Marta watched, trumpets blew and the king's and constable's men began to move around the ring of defence, shouting for them to retreat upslope to the southern Horn.

As the retreat began, hurried on its way by the Saracen pressure, Miles shook his head. "This is the end."

Perhaps it was, Marta thought. Perhaps Persi had always been right—that the kingdom itself did not deserve to stand. Perhaps Lord Balian *was* a coward and deserter, but she still hoped he would escape. She had failed to save her new home, just as she had been unable to save the old. The thought was as bitter as death, but she would yet snatch one comfort from the wreckage of this day.

She would punish Khalil for what he had done to both.

"It's not the end yet," she told Miles. The wind having changed, more of the battlefield was becoming visible at every moment, and the Saracens were now well within view. Marta pointed towards a distant banner directly opposite, where a kingly figure in a tall yellow cap stood watching them from the midst of his advisors. At the sultan's side was a black turban; she was *almost* sure it was Khalil. "Before we die, let's kill the sorcerer."

The Frankish retreat came to a halt on the south horn. From here all of them could see Lake Tiberias, deceptively near and glistening with tantalising promise. The low flat lands surrounding the lake were hazy-blue and peaceful in the stifling mid-afternoon heat, but there was no way down the Horns' plunging slope and craggy, tumbled rocks to the plain below. The only way out was the gentle slope to the west, now choked with the enemy.

A slope which would add power to any charge launched from this peak.

Word came that a charge was indeed to be organised, and to provide a rallying-point, the king ordered his red tent pitched—it was remarkable, Marta supposed, that they still had luggage at all.

Pushing her way to the front of the line, Marta could not help noticing how many of the men were visibly sick with heat, drooping beneath the weight of their armour with pale skin and vacant looks. Marta herself could hardly have looked any better: no water had touched her lips since the previous evening. After two days of bitter fighting, only the magic of the Bessarion Lance kept her from utter collapse.

The Saracens drew off a little, gathering for their own final assault. It was then that Marta caught sight of Khalil. Horsemen and clouds of dust parted to reveal him astride his chestnut horse, clad head to foot in black and watching her with hungry eyes.

The Bessarion Lance thrummed in her hands, scarcely less eager than herself to fly. With a hoarse yell of "Way! Way!" Marta plunged through the scattering infantry.

Had she been thinking, she would never have done something so mad: she could not pierce the shield-wall at a moment like this without leaving the rest of the army exposed or precipitating a premature charge. Yet all she could see was Khalil. She rode him down and felt the crunch and jerk as the Bessarion Lance pierced his body and slid out again. Once more she spared a glance behind and saw, to her horror, that she had been tricked again: she had killed the wrong man. Marta saw his pale bloody face on the ground as she flashed past. But there was no stopping now: there was thunder behind her—the other knights had also charged. And ahead of them was Saladin's eagle standard. The tall yellow cap she had seen before was there, but the black turban was some way to the right. Veering towards it, Marta was separated from the charge. She was alone in the battle and weapons of every sort were splitting and breaking around her. Marta hurled the next Khalil from his horse and that one was equally as false.

"Coward," she screamed, pulling Pomers into a tight circle around the broken body. She tore her helm from her head, lifting it in the air. "Look!" she shrieked at the hostile faces surrounding her. "Al-Aziz Khalil is afraid to face a woman!"

Something constricted around her body and Marta looked down with a gasp of shock to find a lasso binding her. The next moment it went taut and dragged her from her horse. Marta hit the ground, her thighs burning from the effort to cling to her saddle, but oh, they had underestimated the Bessarion Lance. She rolled, got to her feet, and tore the rope from her body as though it had been a mere thread. Three men had already darted between herself and Pomers. She used the Lance to sweep them aside, scooped up her fallen helmet, trod on the back of another as he struggled to rise and was astride the horse again in a moment.

"A lasso?" she shouted over her shoulder as she spurred Pomers towards the king's red tent. "Is that all you can do?"

By the time she and Pomers made back within the safety of the shield wall, she was still laughing, half intoxicated with danger. But as she drew rein again, she found herself dizzy with exhaustion.

There was a limit, even to the power of the Bessarion Lance.

"Marta! What are you playing at?"

Miles, she thought vacantly, had so much smoke and dust and dried blood on his face that if not for the terror in his eyes, he might have been sculpted from clay.

"For God's sake pull yourself together," he told her, seizing her shoulder and giving her a shake. "First you charge before the signal, and then you ride off into the thick of the enemy—that's suicide! Are you trying to *help* them win?"

He's right, you know. You're playing right into Khalil's hands.

She did not know where the whisper came from, but Marta stopped laughing that very moment. Khalil had been using his doubles to lure her away from the charge and its target, Saladin himself. He had not just been trying to part her from the Bessarion Lance—he had kept her so busy that she forgot to help the rest of the army.

Another charge formed, exhausted knights massing together behind the shield-wall. The sultan's banner was so close. If they could get at him—if they could kill Saladin—then perhaps whoever was left in the kingdom might avail themselves of the resulting chaos, take back Tiberias and defend whatever was left.

Marta had covered her shield with sky-blue leather, now grimy and stained and scarred with many blows. Now, she ripped the cover free and tossed it away. "It won't happen again," she promised.

For the first time in many hours, a look of hope eased the strain in Miles' face. "Marta the Knight! Marta the Knight!" he shouted. "The White Watcher is here!"

Others turned, saw her shield, heard his shouting and joined in. *"White Watcher! White Watcher!"* Every one of them must have heard the songs and stories about her. They stood back, clearing a path for her to the place of honour at the front of the charge. As she took her place, Marta tipped back her faceplated helmet and nodded to them bashfully.

She must not chase Khalil again, since he was too great a coward to face her himself. She must do what she could for the kingdom.

The trumpet blew. The infantry parted. The charge thundered into battle.

Marta and Pomers moved at one easy pace, striking down enemy after enemy on their way towards the eagle banner. Beneath it, now within bowshot, the sultan sat atop a beautiful Arab horse. If he felt any fear at the sight of the Frankish charge, he did not show it. Marta unhorsed a Saracen knight in heavy armour, and then nothing but a little open ground, and the sultan's court guard in figured silk and furred caps, stood between her and the dignitaries beneath the banner. She spurred Pomers again and thundered towards them.

White-hot pain pierced her spear arm and Marta lost her grip on the Bessarion Lance.

She felt it happen, not because she was aware of her hands unclenching, but because she suddenly wanted to faint from pain and exhaustion. Looking down, she saw with horror that her arm was pierced through by an arrow; her hand was empty.

Pomers slackened to a trot, then a walk. Saracen knights charged past her, one of them swinging a mace as he went. Fire burst across her vision as the blow glanced from her helmet. The world slipped sideways. The ground came up to meet her.

When the shock passed, Marta got her sound arm beneath her and shoved herself up, searching for the Lance. The ground was littered with bodies and horses, broken weapons and spent arrows and big, fly-speckled slurries of dust and blood. The rest of the Frankish charge stood at a standstill a little further up the slope. Marta was alone except for Miles, who was struggling with his fallen horse ten or fifteen paces off. As she watched, he dragged his foot out from beneath the writhing beast, limped one step and then another, stooped to the ground, and raised the Bessarion Lance in both hands.

A horrible premonition came over her.

"Miles," she howled, ravaging her throat. She tried to put her weight on her wounded arm and pitched forward onto her face. She spat dirt and staggered to her feet.

There was only one horse still on its feet, and Miles was nearer to it than she. He caught Pomers by the reins and vaulted into the saddle.

"Miles!" The sound of battle was far away, but he did not seem to hear her pleas. She reeled across the ground and caught Pomers' rein. "Miles, for pity's sake, don't leave, it's me, it's me—" but her voice was an unrecognisable rasp. Miles looked down at her with eyes blazing red and desperate, and swung the lead-weighted haft of the Bessarion Lance.

White light exploded across her vision. And then—nothing.

Chapter XXV.

Marta lay in a red haze of pain.

Her head felt as though it had been split open. Her right arm throbbed fiercely. Her skin was on fire, the heat so all-consuming she could scarcely breathe. Even blinking hurt, her eyeballs scratchy and dry.

She moved, trying to find a more comfortable position, but the effort was too much for her stomach and she jerked onto her side, retching. There was nothing to speak of in her gut, but she spat bile and leaned on her sound left arm, panting quick and shallow. The drums pounding nearby only made her feel sicker, before she remembered that they were enemy drums, and some feeble awareness of her situation flooded back to her.

Blearily, Marta gazed up the slope. Weapons were still clashing, the king's trumpet vainly trying to rally his knights. But the battle had rolled away from her. The red tent was a splash of glaring colour against the fading sky of afternoon. Even as she watched, the tent fell, and a cheer rose from the sultan's guards.

Marta fainted again. This time when she woke, silence struck her. For one moment she thought the whole day had been some dreadful dream, and that she was still lying snug in camp at Manescalcia, ready to get up and fight a battle. Then not far away a voice called feebly for water and help, and she knew it was no dream.

Peeling open her sore eyes, Marta struggled to her knees. A pair of feet in scale chausses halted before her. She blinked at them, uncomprehending.

"Marta Bessarion. You're awake."

The voice, speaking in purely accented Arabic, was straight out of her nightmares. The next instant, her helm came off. Marta looked up into the face she had been seeking all day—black beard, smooth skin, lordly nose; not a thread of silver in his hair.

The sorcerer, Khalil ibn Hassan.

Suddenly the day seemed less of a loss. Marta's left hand clenched around the carnelian dagger. Too intent to notice the pain, she grasped his belt with her right hand and slipped the little blade beneath the hem of his lamellar cuirass and into his belly.

Hot blood seeped between her fingers. Khalil grunted with pain and caught her wrist before she could rip his guts all the way open. For a moment neither of them moved. Trembling, sick with exhaustion as she was, Marta did not dare to release her grip—awaiting the moment that he would crumple to the earth, clutching his stomach.

Instead, his grip on her wrist tightened and he dragged the little dagger out of the wound. There ought to have been a gush of blood, but none came. Apart from the red stickiness on her fingers, it was as though she had never struck him at all.

"It's dishonourable to stab a man with a blade he bestowed as a gift," Khalil said, releasing her. "Keep it, anyway. It won't hurt me."

He unhooked a leathern bottle from his belt, unstoppered it, and offered it to her. Marta stilled. If Khalil offered her water, it meant he was not going to kill her. Or, more to the point, that he was not going to offer her the chance to kill him.

"You're afraid of me," she rasped. After shouting for two days straight, her voice was unrecognisable. "I challenged you to a battle three times and you spent the whole time *hiding*. Coward."

There were three or four other men with Khalil, heavily armed mamluks with round shields, wearing brightly coloured tunics over their mail. They looked apprehensive when she spoke, as she had intended they should. But Khalil did not react.

"I told you I would not stoop to fight a woman. Since you're in no condition to do so at present, you might as well drink. Where is the weapon?"

His cold, even question caught her by surprise. Marta laughed, recklessly grateful for one thing at least. "The Lance? I suppose it's halfway to Acre by now. It's slipped through your fingers. *Again.*"

Undoubtedly, she would be held to ransom, perhaps in exchange for the Bessarion Lance. Later she would reckon with the problem of how to extricate herself from Khalil's custody without giving him what he wanted in return. Later, too, she would let herself rage at Miles for taking the Lance, striking her down, and abandoning her. If he had fled the battle and escaped, however, then he had not only ensured that the Bessarion Lance slipped through Khalil's fingers; for the time being, he had saved her life.

Meanwhile she could *smell* the water and would go mad if she did not drink it. Marta snatched the bottle from the sorcerer's hands and poured it down her throat, swallowing in great eager gulps. Warm and brackish though it was, it flooded her body like a healing tide and was gone long before she was satisfied.

Khalil did not respond to her taunts about the Lance, either. Taking her good arm, he pulled her to her feet, and strode down the slope to where the sultan's camp was being pitched. The mamluks closed in behind. Marta was forced to follow, her hand still sticky with his blood, barely able to keep her own feet.

Failure tasted like bile, and dirt, and blood. She had been so sure she could bring Khalil to battle and defeat him—and all he had needed to do to frustrate her plans was to stay out of reach. Marta kept stumbling over men and horses, all hacked and trampled. This was defeat, nearer and uglier than she had ever seen it before. Not all of them were the king's Franks and Syrians either; many were Turks and Saracens from the sultan's army. A little south of the carnage, where the Saracen tents were being pitched, a heap of weapons was growing; knights and Turcopoles were being led past it and made to throw down whatever blades they carried. Marta remembered the slaughter at Cresson, remembered the Master of the Temple saying that it was Saladin's practice to execute any Templars or Hospitallers that fell into his power. Some said he did not stop there: that he killed Turcopoles, too, out of hand. The kingdom's light cavalry consisted of many Syrians, few of whom had the ability to pay great ransoms. Few, too, had ever been Mahometans or even descended from Mahometans; yet the sultan treated all of them as apostates, punishable by death. Sickened, Marta wondered whether Samuel Arrabi and his father were among the prisoners; whether they were light-skinned enough to pass as Franks.

Khalil did not pause, hauling her towards the great tent where Saladin's banner floated. Another knot of prisoners was herded up near the tent, some sitting, some standing, all looking in the glare of the fading day like the stones and pillars of a ruined city. These were knights in fine armour, Templars and Hospitallers and lords—elite prisoners.

As they approached the tent, a knight staggered backwards out of the tent as though he had been struck. The sultan followed him with a drawn sword, the point of which was already bright with blood. The knight fell to his knees in the dust and Saladin struck again, slicing the head from the body.

Marta scarcely needed the insignia on the man's breast to tell her who it had been. Reynald of Chatillon, at last, had met his reward.

"Keep the head," the sultan ordered, handing his bloodied sword to a servant. "I swore to kill this man once I had him in my power, and I would have it known in Damascus that I keep my oaths."

King Guy stumbled out of the sultan's pavilion in his wake, halting when he saw the prince's corpse. His face was pale as milk, and for a moment he shuddered like the hills in an earthquake.

"Don't be afraid," Saladin told the king. "Did I not give you water to drink?" He turned towards Khalil, ignoring the captive king and the other anxious Frankish faces clustered behind him. Marta recognised Humphrey of Toron, blinking like an owl, together with the Master of the Temple, the Commander of the Hospital, and old William of Montferrat.

"Khalil ibn Hassan." Saladin clapped his hands on Khalil's shoulders. "The blessing of God be upon you, my friend! Ask of me anything this day, and I will give it with an open hand."

Khalil bowed his head. "Two things, my lord. First, this woman."

The sultan took a second look at Marta, and his eyebrows went up. He shook his head. "Glory to God, these Franks! You know you may take any prisoner of your own, Khalil, but this one will be trouble to you if she lives. There are other women among the prisoners taken at Tiberias, modest and soft, who have been ladies and nuns."

"True, my lord. But there is more honour in taming a cheetah than a house-cat."

Marta listened without quite believing what they were saying. Jerusalem, the law made relations between Christians and Saracens punishable by death—but the Saracen law was different, allowing a man four wives and unnumbered slaves. She was being handed over to Khalil—

No. It could not be true, Khalil would not want her for *that.*

"On your own head be it," the sultan said. "And the second thing?"

"Give me your leave to depart. I would return to Damascus."

That bothered the sultan far more than the fate of a single prisoner. He frowned. "God willing, I have the conquest of a kingdom to complete. I require your presence."

"You shall have it, my lord. You know I am never far from your side."

Saladin hesitated, but then waved a hand in assent. "Then go, but I will hold you to that promise."

Khalil bowed, drawing Marta with him into what had become the main thoroughfare of the rapidly pitched camp. Marta followed, every step jarring agony from the arrow that still pierced her right arm. "Where are you taking me?" she asked, but Khalil did not answer, and it was as much as she could do now to remain on her feet.

It was as Miles had pointed out at the bridge of Judaire. Khalil wanted more than the Lance—he wanted her alive. But *why?*

He led her in at the door of a tent. Beyond, the space was dark, smelling of herbs and incense. Otherwise, it was almost completely empty, only grass underfoot—a familiar sight from the evening before Cresson. As Marta's eyes adjusted to the darkness, Khalil released her and moved towards a doorway that had been set up in the centre of the tent. Made of oiled and exquisitely carved wood in the shape of a round arch, it had one great heavy slab of limestone for a threshold and a curtain over it of beautifully figured silk. Marta blinked at the curtain. She was sure she had woven it herself once, years ago. It had been in the house at Nablus when Saladin occupied the place, but it was gone by the time he left.

Khalil muttered something under his breath, something she did not hear over the sound of hooves galloping past outside. He twitched back the curtain and opened a door beyond. A ray of light flooded into the darkened tent as Khalil pulled her forward again. Marta's feet tripped over the stone threshold, and when her sight cleared, she found herself in the courtyard she had glimpsed once or twice before. Instantly, the noise of drums, wailing and horse hooves ceased, and the stench of smoke and blood faded from the air: she heard only a distant murmur like the bustle of a peaceful city. High walls rose around her, many of the windows masked with wooden lattices. A staircase to one side of the courtyard led up to the great square loggia decorated with potted palms and lamps of coloured glass. An orange-tree had been planted at the centre of the courtyard, and a serpentine mosaic girdled its roots.

The place was quiet and watchful, scented with citrus. For a moment Khalil released her to speak to a white-bearded, turbaned man who came puffing from one of the lower chambers, followed by more servants and soldiers.

She was not left in peace for long. Khalil gestured at her, completing his instructions. "Take her to Arwa to treat her wound and clean her up."

"Why?" Marta rasped. It was like a bad dream: she could hardly even speak. "Why have you brought me here?"

Khalil turned to her again. "I don't mean to hurt you."

His words were too cool to be believed; a word of empty comfort flung to a child. But seven years had passed for her since Marta had first met this man, and she was no longer a child. She put the bloody dagger to her own throat and said just as coolly, "Tell me plainly what you want with me, or I will cut my own throat where I stand."

Khalil looked at her in much the same way he had looked at her so long ago, that first evening in Oliveta when she had thrown the same knife at him. First with curiosity, and then with slow reassessment. "Leave us," he told the servants. When they were alone, he moved a step towards her, and Marta backed away.

Khalil sighed and stripped off his gloves, one by one. Nothing could have prepared her for his next words, spoken in the same passionless voice.

"I seek your hand in marriage, Marta Bessarion."

"What?" she whispered.

He drew something from his littlest finger, something that glinted in the light. "I am not mocking you. Whatever is the customary gift among your people, I am ready to fulfill."

He held it out to her—a plain gold wedding-ring sized for a woman. Marta stared, uncomprehending. Somewhere up in the eaves of the house, sleepy and content, a dove cooed. The sound was like an enchantment. She lowered the knife from her throat, too tired to hold it there any longer.

"Do not refuse me," Khalil added.

"Or what?" she rasped. "Will you force me?"

At that he looked offended. "You are Marta Bessarion, a lady of high renown. I seek an honourable marriage by free consent. Have I not told you I mean you no harm?"

"Free consent, from a captive?" Marta laughed, reckless though she stood on a blade's edge. Lashing out with her sound arm, she struck his hand and sent the ring skipping across the flagstones. "Do as you like, Khalil ibn Hassan. Conduct yourself like the dog you are, but I have no fear of you. I will *never* consent to be your wife."

Khalil gave a sharp-edged smile. "You will," he said with utter confidence. "I'll make it worth your while. Ghassan!" he added in a shout, making her jump. The old chamberlain must have been waiting, for he reappeared at once. "Take her away; I'll deal with this one later."

He stayed only a moment longer, searching her face as though he expected to break her will with a gaze. "I mean it kindly," he said, for her ears alone. "One day you will understand that. One day I will see you weep for love of me."

Chapter XXVI.

In the king's house in Acre, Sibylla sat in an open window, her hands idle and her veins ready to crawl out of her body, so anxious was she to be up and doing.

Yesterday morning at dawn, a messenger came from Sephoria to say that Guy had set out across the hills towards Tiberias in hope of bringing Saladin to battle. It was sunset now on the second day, and no news had come. The whole land was holding its breath, men and animals slow and sleepy in the heat. Now, with the sun going down in a sky so clear it seemed to be made of glass, all blue and gold and speckled with distant light, Sibylla could no longer bear the wait.

"Lilith," she called, not daring to raise her voice above a whisper. *"Lilith. Where are you?"*

There was a shimmer in the air and a figure took languid shape on her bed, a monstrous heap of claws and feathers with an ugly, blood-soaked beak. There was nothing womanly about the demon tonight.

Sibylla approached, trembling. "What news of the battle?"

She was answered by a drowsy squawk. Blood smeared onto her pillow. Sibylla recoiled. The bird went back to sleep.

Sibylla had bathed and changed into clean clothes; her hair was still damp. Nevertheless, she tied it into braids, wrapped a veil around her head, and went down into the courtyard of the palace.

"Saddle my horse," she ordered.

The palace stood near the north wall of the city, surrounded by a moat and castellated walls, defended by a strong citadel. Sibylla had always felt at home here, but tonight something about the walls and the fortress made her feel as though she was suffocating. While her horse was saddled, her lady Sara and half a dozen sergeants made their own preparations. Hardly caring whether they followed, Sibylla set off through the great north gate and the prosperous, growing suburbs beyond the wall. From there she took the road leading southeast towards Nazareth, the road down which Guy must have ridden a week ago when he had left her so coldly, with their disagreement poisoning the air behind him. She thought of Lilith, bloody and sleeping. Dread fastened upon her heart and squeezed.

They rode for an hour while the sunset faded into darkness, through vineyards and orchards and sugarcane plantations. At last, there were worried murmurings from her escort, and Sara stirred her mount into a trot to approach her. "My lady, we should not stray far from the city."

Sibylla ought to have sent a messenger to Sephoria, not blundered out upon the road herself. She reined in, knowing her servants were right, but unwilling to turn and immure herself again within those suffocating walls, in the small room where Lilith lay sleeping off her feast.

At last, when she was about to turn her horse's head for home, Sibylla heard a distant sound from the east. "What's that?"

Everyone stilled and listened. "It's nothing, my lady," Sara said gently.

Sibylla knew the woman was wrong, but disdained to say so. Instead, she waited until the hoofbeats came nearer, and the truth was incontrovertible.

"Who goes there?" the captain of her sergeants called, urging his horse ahead of her.

"Miles of Plancy," an exhausted voice called out of the night. "Please, of your courtesy, take me to—"

"Plancy," Sibylla cut in, afraid that she might scream if he did not get to the point. "What news of the battle?"

The sergeants let him come nearer. He was riding a grey horse she thought she recognised, but the beast was lathered, ready to founder; Miles himself was bloody and despairing.

Sibylla scarcely needed him to speak then, but he did, anyway, in words that dropped upon her like stones.

"It was a terrible defeat, my lady. I fear the enemy will soon be at the gates of Acre."

Chapter XXVII.

Sibylla knew it was her own fault. She had demanded a battle of Guy, against his own and half the kingdom's better judgement, and he had given it.

Her room was a prison where she sat by the hour, staring at the whitewashed wall. She had not slept the night after Miles came, nor the night after that. Every few hours, new stragglers found their way to the palace, laden with yet more terrible news.

The True Cross had been lost. The relic discovered beneath the Holy Sepulchre when Godfrey first liberated Jerusalem, carried into battle at the head of the army as a standard and a talisman, had fallen into the hands of the enemy. They said Saladin meant to send it to Damascus for public display, to be spat upon and beaten. Guy would always be remembered as the one who had lost it.

It was not yet clear who had been killed, who had been captured, and who had escaped. Some said Guy had been slain in the battle. Others said he had been beheaded at the door of the sultan's tent. It was said that some of the lords had escaped to the north and were still at large: Tripoli and Balian of Ibelin, the very men who had denied her the throne and attempted to break her marriage.

Sibylla had been unable to speak to Lilith, otherwise she might already have had answers. It was like waiting for a hidden scorpion to strike; each time she glanced at her bed she still saw matted feathers, a sharp beak, and smears of blood.

This is not like you, Guy had said to her before he went away. He did not know that Lilith wore her face, whispered in her mind, slept in her bed. There was less and less room in Sibylla's own life for herself.

It was her fault—that is what Lilith would say, were she truly here. It was Sibylla who spilled the blood of the Bedouin at Darum, and Sibylla who, in seeking to become queen, had sought help from Lilith and not the Watchers. She had always promised herself that in the end she would do enough good to outweigh the evil she momentarily committed. Perhaps that was not the way of things, after all. Perhaps, no matter how much penance one did after the fact, one had still committed the crime and must reap the consequences to the bitter end.

Very far away, the door opened and a voice said in her ear, "My lady, the Saracens are approaching the city."

"Let the viscount make whatever arrangements he sees fit," Sibylla said automatically, as she had whenever such things were said to her. One thing was clear: she had ceased to be capable of ruling. The solution was easy and came as a relief. She must remove herself from power. Better to abandon authority than to misuse it.

"My lady," the voice said again, and hesitated. "Sibylla, it's me."

She looked up into Uncle Joscelin's lined face; he seemed to have aged ten years in a week. "Uncle! You're here?"

"And in the nick of time," he said. Sibylla hated the pitying way he looked at her and her surroundings, this stuffy little room and the chair she had not moved from in hours. It was clear that she had done nothing at all. Why did he not see that this was the best thing she *could* do?

"Do you mean to defend the city?" she asked.

"Saints, no. How? We have barely enough men to garrison the royal house, let alone the city walls. Balian of Ibelin took most of what was left of the rear-guard to Tyre, and I haven't enough men to supply the shortfall. All we can do is hand the city over."

"Tyre," she said numbly. Another city in the royal demesne, further north on the coast. Smaller than Acre, it would be easier to garrison; more distant, too, which gave its defenders a better opportunity to fall back and regroup while Saladin concentrated upon the richer prize of Acre.

Ibelin had abandoned her and the whole city without a second thought.

"I'll need the key to the city gates," Joscelin prompted her.

"The viscount will have one."

"Yes, but he won't give it up without an order from you."

If it was her decision she would never surrender, but Sibylla smothered this instinct. "Then send him to me."

She had lost the kingdom. Any more interference, and what fresh disaster might result?

* * *

Some time later, Sibylla awoke to a commotion in the city. As always when her illness troubled her, the sleep had not left her feeling refreshed, and she lay in her chair blinking for a moment, aware of a sound that had been going on for some time and was becoming louder—shouting, hammering. The smell of smoke jolted her fully awake. Dragging herself from her chair, Sibylla hobbled to the window. Black smoke billowed into the sky from somewhere nearer the harbour. The palace gate had been shut and barred. Guards ran to and fro in the courtyard; an oxcart piled high with blocks of limestone from one of the city's building projects was hauled in front of the gate as a barricade, the wheels chocked to hold it immobile. The roofs of nearby houses bristled with shouting people.

Sibylla staggered towards her chair again and struck the bell that stood beside it. Alix entered at once. "What is it?" Sibylla gasped. "Have the Saracens come?"

"No, my lady, but—"

"Where is my uncle?"

"He's just returned."

She was not wearing a veil and her hair was a lank mess, but Sibylla rushed from the room anyway. Joscelin was in the cabinet with the viscount, who ruled Acre while the king was not in residence, and one or two others. "What is going on?" she demanded. "Why is the city on fire?"

"It isn't the Saracens," Joscelin said, looking harassed. "I rode out and gave the key to Saladin's nephew, who is pitching camp just beyond the walls. But the people found out, and now they're rioting."

Someone put a chair behind her, but Sibylla did not sit. "Why?"

"I don't know. I was just going out to speak with them."

"You didn't consult with the city before handing over the key?"

Joscelin exchanged guilty glances with the viscount.

Sibylla cursed herself for falling asleep. Of course the people had rebelled. Had the past year taught her uncle *nothing?* One could issue orders, one could sit on a throne and wear a crown, but that was not true authority. True authority came when people obeyed you, not because of who you were, but because they saw you had their interests at heart.

Sibylla would be no good at this, but Guy was missing, and the people would have little confidence in her uncle at present. "I'll speak to them. Alix, fetch a comb and a veil. Sir Walter," she added to the viscount, "take me where I can speak to the burgesses."

That happened to be the wall between the two gatehouses. Sir Walter, nervous, told her to remain behind the cover of two shields carried by his knights, but Sibylla had no intention of hiding. When she showed herself and raised her hand, the angry, protesting crowd beyond the gate hushed expectantly.

They waited for her to speak, but showing herself was as much as Sibylla could manage at present. She was in no state to shout at them. Instead, she had Sir Walter announce that the queen would receive representatives. It took the crowd only moments to select their speakers: a priest from the Order of the Hospital, a rich Pisan merchant, and a judge from one of the courts of the Syrians. Sir Walter had his men admit them via the wicket-gate, and they met Sibylla with profound bows in the gatehouse.

From the chair where she had half collapsed, Sibylla inspected them severely. "What is the meaning of this uproar? Who has set these fires?"

The Syrian gulped, and the priest stammered, but the Pisan merchant, whom Sibylla knew of—a commoner richer than many princes—stuck out his burly, silk-encased chest and said, "We won't surrender. We'd sooner burn the city over our own heads, than hand it over to the enemy."

"What *nonsense*," Sibylla said. "Don't you understand that there is no garrison?"

"Yes, but it isn't nonsense, my lady," the Syrian judge said apologetically. "What will happen to our families once the Saracens are inside the city? Will our laws be respected, the way the Franks have respected them?"

"Will our churches be permitted to remain churches?" the priest added.

"And don't forget our property," the merchant put in. "The markets across the sea have been quiet this year, so our warehouses are full of goods. I have a fortune's worth sitting here in sugar alone. How dare the count of Courtenay hand all this over to the Saracens?"

"I'm sure my uncle would have negotiated such terms as he was able," Sibylla said, with more confidence than she felt. "Uncle?"

Joscelin cleared his throat. "Saladin's nephew promised us to spare the lives of the Franks within the city, my lady."

"Just the Franks? What about us Syrians?" the judge asked, paling. "What about the Mahometan sects Saladin oppresses, the Shi'i and Isma'ili and Druze—"

"And what about our *goods*," the merchant bellowed.

"What guarantee do we have," the priest said slowly, "that Saladin will even respect the promises made by his nephew?"

"We can defend the city," the merchant said, slapping a meaty hand over the sword he wore on his hip. "Every man of us can fight."

Sibylla, who had spent her entire adult life in the company of scarred men whose swords bore a patina of heavy use, could not help noticing how shiny and new the merchant's weapon looked. That thought checked the leap of her heart, the eagerness that flashed through her to fight to the last drop.

"Man the walls with untrained burgesses?" Sibylla said levelly. "Do any of you have hauberks at home?"

"I have," the merchant insisted, but the priest and the judge shook their heads.

And then, between one blink and the next, Lilith was in the room. "Do what they say, Sibylla. I'll help you."

Like you helped at the battle? Sibylla might have asked, had they been alone. But that was hardly the point. Lilith had just confirmed a dreadful suspicion that had been growing on her for some days, something so blindingly obvious and cunningly cruel that she would never forgive herself for being party to it.

She was a fool, a *fool,* and the kingdom would have been better off with Tripoli as its king.

Sibylla wore her face like a mask. "Please tell the people of the city that I regret failing to consult with them before sending my uncle to arrange the surrender. If we can get guarantees that *all* the people, laws, property, and churches of Acre will be respected, will you consent to surrender?"

The priest and the judge nodded eagerly.

"You can tell Saladin we'll destroy the whole city if he refuses," the merchant growled.

"Write that down," Sibylla said to the scribe in the corner. "Fellows, you will present these terms to the people of Acre, and if they are approved, my uncle shall take them himself directly to Saladin. This time he will deal with no underlings."

That seemed to satisfy the representatives, who bowed and desired God to bless her. Uncle Joscelin, as he escorted her back across the courtyard to the palace, was less approving. "It sets a bad precedent," he fretted. "Consulting with commoners? You'll have the burgesses forming communes next, and demanding to set up republics, the way they have in Pisa and Genoa."

"That's much more likely to be Saladin's problem than mine," Sibylla retorted. She brushed past him and practically fled to her room, slamming the door behind her—but this time it was not to hide.

"Lilith," she hissed through her teeth. "I know you're here."

There was no response. Sibylla felt as though she was going mad, but enough was enough.

"You lied to me," she accused the empty room.

"Really?" Lilith blinked into view, hands on hips. "I am a demon and you are surprised to learn I have *lied?*"

Today Lilith's appearance was like looking into the clearest mirror ever devised. The demon had even reproduced the faint pimple on Sibylla's chin. The resemblance made her dizzy, but Sibylla clenched her teeth.

"Each time you've promised to help me, the result has been strife, war, and death. You offered to spare the lives of my people and take the lives of the Saracens. Twenty thousand men of this kingdom are *gone*, Lilith. Now I'm supposed to rely on you to defend Acre?"

The demon pouted, an expression Sibylla doubted had ever crossed her own face. "I'm a demon, not a captain. Providing enough troops and water for an attack on Saladin was your husband's responsibility, not mine."

Sibylla closed her eyes. "Is Guy alive?"

"I don't know if I ought to answer that."

Then he *was* alive. If he was dead, Lilith would have told her outright, just to see her suffer. "Thank God," she muttered, and opened her eyes again. "You don't care to give us peace or victory, do you? All your desire is simply to feed upon suffering. You care not whom you kill. *You* did this to us."

Lilith laughed, and the illusion of humanity shredded; feathers drifted from her arms when she pointed at Sibylla. "*You* did this to yourself. *You* were fool enough to believe in me. You, who think yourself so clever. What did you expect, my love? Why should I do anything for you, and not myself? Why should I be any more selfless than you have been?"

Some dusty crippled thing in the corner of Sibylla's heart told her that Lilith's words were true. She, not just Lilith, had behaved like a demon, willing to sacrifice brother and children and Guy himself so that she could wield the power she believed she deserved. And now she knew that everything she had said to excuse it was wrong. There was no gain for her in alliance with Lilith: only destruction.

"Leave," she whispered. "Leave me, and never return. I don't want your help. I renounce your friendship."

Lilith sneered. "Renounce all you like, it will take more than a good luck charm to keep me at bay. There's no way out for you; don't you realise that? You've given yourself into my power. Soon, I will be the queen of this kingdom, and you will only be a memory in your husband's dreams."

With these words, Lilith disappeared. Sibylla knew with a sinking heart that she would return. She paced her room in a fever of worry.

Soon, I will be the queen of this kingdom.

Of one thing she was absolutely certain. The kingdom must not be ruled by those who would exploit and destroy it. That meant Lilith. That meant Saladin. That might even mean herself, but the people had appealed to her today and she found that she must not fail them.

Think. Sibylla tipped her head back to regard the coffered ceiling, once noisy with colour but now painted a soothing white, like the rest of the room. She certainly could not defend Acre, but perhaps Tripoli and Ibelin had the right idea in withdrawing to Tyre. Her thoughts went to Ascalon, her own city on the coast, further south. It had a harbour, and therefore would be difficult to isolate or starve. Its strong fortifications had been built and maintained with care. The garrison would be thin, but by retreating there with the garrison of Acre she would buy time and consolidate her shattered forces.

It was the best choice—that made it the only choice. Sibylla threw open her door and went into the antechamber, frightening her attendants to their feet. "Where's the viscount?"

"He's out on the wall, my lady. The city is still restless." Miles of Plancy, pale and listless, had been infesting the palace while he recovered from his wounds. He looked nearly as bad as she felt, but Sibylla judged that action would be the best medicine for both of them.

"I have orders," Sibylla said. "First: have my ship prepared for a voyage to Ascalon. The whole household and the whole garrison at a minimum must come with us. Any knights, sergeants, or Turcopoles in the city must take passage, together with as much weaponry as we can lay our hands on. Second: send out messengers, courageous men who know the land well, to find anyone who has fled the battle. Tell them their queen summons them to Ascalon for the defence of the kingdom. Someone must also go to Tyre to request the lords there for what assistance they can spare."

"I can go to Tyre myself," Plancy offered.

"No. For you I have a special mission." Except for a few desperate weeks when the Leper King had tried to part her from Guy, Sibylla had always worn an onyx signet ring on her thumb. Now she touched it, tracing the calligraphy etched into its surface. "You are to carry a message for me to Masyaf of the Assassins."

A deafening silence fell over the room. Headquartered far to the north in the mountains of Syria, the Assassins were a Mahometan sect who protected themselves from the persecution of their co-religionists and the interference of others by placing spies in great households. For years their agents might serve faithfully, only to cut your throat the moment you did something to offend them.

Sibylla was reasonably sure she had none in her own entourage, but only because the one in her household had already tried—and failed only by a whisker—to kill her.

Plancy's face was a study. "What message am I to give to the Assassins?"

"You will hand a sealed packet to their master, and then come home again," Sibylla said. "Make ready, and I will prepare the packet."

None of this would solve the greatest problem she faced, however. Rightly or wrongly, she was the queen of this kingdom, not Lilith. She could not simply remove herself from authority; therefore, she must somehow remove Lilith. If she could not remove Lilith herself, she must seek help, no matter from whom.

"One more thing," she added. "Where is Marta Bessarion? I need her urgently."

Plancy turned white, so that for a moment she thought he was about to be sick.

"Don't tell me something's happened to her," Sibylla said numbly. Marta Bessarion was the only Watcher she could still trust.

Plancy forced a sickly smile. "No, no—my wound caught me, that's all. Marta Bessarion? An excellent notion. I'm sure that with the kingdom at stake, she'll be more than willing to put past disagreements aside. Lord Balian sent her home before the battle, of course. I've no doubt you'll find her at Nablus, or Jerusalem."

Chapter XXVIII.

9 July—five days after the battle

Marta's nightmares of battle and blood and burning flesh gave way to a dream. She stood in a shadowy hall of massive stone pillars holding up the vaults of some dark and distant roof. At the centre was a sigil drawn on the flagstones, a calligraphic knot of looping words just like the one Khalil had used to summon Lilith in Oliveta, so many years before.

This sigil was blackened and blasted and smoking, and at its fractured centre a woman lay. If there had been fire it did not quite seem to have touched her, for despite the hot vapours rising from her body, her brown skin and night-dark hair were both sound, and her tunic of green silk was unscorched. Marta knew well how it looked—and smelled—when a woman really burned.

She approached the sigil, and the nearer she came the larger the woman, whose back was towards her, seemed to grow, until she seemed like a small mountain, a fallen giantess.

But before she could catch a glimpse of the woman's face, Marta woke to a reality scarcely more comforting than the nightmares. She opened her eyes to find herself on the divan in the women's quarters, a dim funereal room she recalled glimpsing in moments of clarity between dreams. Her whole body was a mass of aches, her skin covered in red welts from two days of wearing armour in the heat without changing or washing, and the wound in her arm was a slow, steady throb.

"She's awake," a voice said. Someone who smelled of parchment and ink bent over her, gentle hands touching her forehead.

"The fever is past," another voice said. "Here, drink this."

A cup was put to her lips and a little lemon water trickled in. Marta's heart gave a lurch, reminding her that she was surrounded by enemies. Who knew what else was in the draught? Lashing out with her good arm, she sent the cup flying and staggered off the divan, fists outstretched in an attempt to ward off any counterattack.

She was sore everywhere, but her head, as fiercely as it ached, was clearer than it had been in days. Three faces looked back at her, shadowy in the dim light. Khalil's women.

"Careful," one of them said, hurrying towards her as she reeled with dizziness. "You've been very sick, and you—"

"Keep your distance," Marta snarled, recovering herself with an effort. She glanced around. The place was like a tomb, its walls grey and black bands of stone. The enormous pendant lamp hanging from the ceiling was unlit. Only the more transient furnishings—cushions and divans and chests—gave the place any feeling of life.

A fourth woman sat spinning in the window, but even that was covered by a wooden lattice, a barrier against the sun, the wind and the sky.

Using her good arm, Marta dragged the woman away from the window, upsetting the basket of fluffy undyed flax that sat beside her. A wooden casket stood on the broad sill and Marta picked it up, dashing it against the lattice, once, twice, thrice, until a corner of the wooden screen peeled away from the window-frame. After that she had to stop, panting, almost fainting.

The other women were making some sort of urgent protest. The spinner—a woman about her own age or a year or two younger—tried to seize her. Marta thrust her away with an elbow, jammed the casket into the gap she had made in the lattice to hold it open, and slipped through the gap like a fish through a net.

She landed with both feet on a stone ledge beneath the window and ducked beneath the splintered fringe of the lattice. Her foot slipped and for an endless moment she found herself on the edge of the world, falling into a measureless void.

Marta screamed. Her fingertips caught in the lattice, and one of her feet was still on the ledge, so that she found herself suspended by finger and toe from the frowning stone wall that fortified the nearly-sheer face of a mountain. Under her weight, the lattice peeled away from the window a little further. The casket she had used as a wedge came free and plunged straight down for twenty feet before bursting upon the rocks. Its contents, bright thread, spilled in a crazy web across the jagged stones; but its heavy pieces skipped and jumped down the precipice, tumbling and turning, until they became too small to see.

Was she still dreaming? She had to be. This was not Damascus. There was an eagle hovering in the sky just at eye level, its hunting gaze fixed upon the rocky valley impossibly far below. The house of Khalil's women was just a little box of stone deposited at the peak of a narrow ridge somewhere in the mountains, only God knew where.

Sobbing, Marta clawed herself back onto the narrow ledge and inside the lattice and into the hands of Khalil's women, who helped pull her back across the broad sill of the window. Safe, she slid down the wall, wrapped her arms around her knees and tried to breathe without shaking.

"The *fool*," one of them—the spinner—hissed. "She'll get all of us killed!"

"There's a mountain!" Marta gasped, trying to calm her heart. "Where did the *mountain* come from?"

"The house is magical," one of the older women told her. Now that she was nearer, Marta thought that she must be in her early forties, with the soft, unweathered skin and comfortable figure of a rich man's wife. Her clothes were similar to the ones Marta herself now wore: a flowing tunic with lavish bands of embroidery at the cuffs, hem and throat. The skirts stopped about mid-calf, showing off flowing trousers below. Her hair had been divided into four braided locks, and there were bangles on both her arms.

She nodded towards a heavy wooden door at the far end of the room. "That door leads to the quarters of al-Aziz, in Damascus, but he keeps his women's quarters here in the mountains. God knows where the barracks is, where he trains his mamluks. Believe us when we say there is no way off the mountain, except by magic, through that door."

"You aren't the first to try," put in another of the women—the one who smelled like parchment. She was ten or fifteen years younger than the first, thin and almost severe in her dress, without the ornaments or jewels worn by the first speaker. She clicked her ink-stained fingers at another woman, a serving-girl from the look of her worn clothing and bared feet. "Go and fetch food, Bahar. Here, let me see your arm."

It was this one who, at Khalil's command, had removed the arrow and bound up the wound that first evening when she was sent to the women's quarters. Instinctively, Marta pulled away. "Don't touch me."

"I'm trying to help," the woman said, but fell silent when the eldest of them put a hand on her arm.

"I am Halimah bint Rashid," the eldest said. "I was born in Masyaf to the Sheik of the Assassins, and when I was young my father gave me as a wife to al-Aziz. My sisters lived in Masyaf and Aleppo, the mothers of many fine sons who worshipped them. In the days before I was given to al-Aziz, they often visited Masyaf with their children. We drank tea and sherbet and painted each other's hands with henna. Since the day I came into this house, I have not been permitted to see them once."

"I am Arwa bint an-Nasih al-Hanbali," the thin woman said, blinking owlishly. "I was born in Damascus, but my father was a great scholar who travelled far and did not deny his daughters the honour of sitting with him at the feet of his own teachers. My sister, Amat al-Latif, is a great scholar in her own right and the companion and advisor to one of the sultan's own sisters. On our travels through the desert, we would lie awake in our tent, reciting to each other everything we had learned: verses of the Quran, hadith, and the commentaries of learned men—but my favourite was the poetry. Sometimes I receive a letter from my sister and am permitted to send one in return, but since the day I came into this house, I have not seen her face once."

The youngest woman, the spinner, was plump and deep-bosomed, with curling hair and a sulky, discontented mouth. She might have been the most beautiful of all of them, if not for the deep shadows beneath her eyes and the pale exhaustion in her face. She held a distaff tucked beneath her elbow and had begun working with it again the moment Marta returned through the window. When they all looked at her, she scoffed a little and said, "I am Fayruz al-Shiraziyya, the daughter of no one, and I was given to al-Aziz as a gift. The only sisters I know are the other dancing girls in the palace of the sultan of Baghdad. They were whores and I do not miss them."

"The point is," Halimah said, clearing her throat gently, "in this house we have no one but each other."

"Let me know when you're ready to have your dressings changed," Arwa said, standing back.

Perhaps it was not Arwa's fault that, when Khalil gave an order, she was expected to obey.

Marta said very softly, "I am Marta, the daughter of John Bessarion. Many years ago, I lost my whole family because of Khalil ibn Hassan, and now he has taken me away from the second family I found for myself."

They exchanged looks. "Al-Aziz has been seeking you a long time," Halimah said. "Three years ago, he turned down a marriage alliance with the family of Saladin himself so that he would be free to marry you when he had the chance. He can be a hard man when he is not given his own way. The best thing is to yield."

"I can't do that," Marta said in a voice thick with anger. "I won't marry him. I won't let him think for a moment that he has any right to me."

"Sometimes it is battle enough simply to remain alive," Arwa said. "Marry him. It's only for a while, anyway. When we are old, he will divorce us and let us go. A man like him doesn't age; he doesn't want a house full of old women."

"But where will you go?" Marta was horrified.

"Back to our fathers. Or maybe our sisters will take us in."

Marta could not help but look at Fayruz, who had claimed to be the daughter and sister of nobody. Her full lips had thinned. She spun as though her life depended upon it.

Dimly she remembered them all hovering near her bed for days. All of them had been spinning, except Arwa, and she was continually muttering, reciting proverbs and poems under her breath.

To change the subject, because she had no intention of taking their advice, Marta said, "You are very diligent. Does Khalil require you to spin?"

Fayruz curled her lip, and Halimah and Arwa looked at each other. "No," Arwa said, "but in this house it is always advisable to remain busy with some work."

There was a silence. Fayruz pressed her lips together. None of them seemed willing to speak, until Halimah said, "It pleases al-Aziz to seek alliances with djinn and afrit. They have a—certain influence over the women of the house, but we have found that they can be warded off."

"Any small, productive, repeated labour will avert the evil eye," Arwa put in. "Rote learning, spinning and weaving, whittling or tilling the earth."

Marta remembered fleeing across the desert of Arabia. Her guide, Omar, had ridden with whittling-knife and wood in hand, always with one eye for the sky where a black vulture hovered, watching them like an evil omen.

Her throat went a little dry as she remembered the feathered woman falling like a bolt of lightning from that same sky. She had never thought to ask Omar what his purpose was; she had presumed he was only fidgeting to allay his own nervousness.

"I'm not afraid of the evil eye," Marta said. As a Watcher, she was not subject to evil spirits.

"You should be," Fayruz said, sniffing. "Al-Aziz has sold all his women to the Poison Mother."

"Fayruz," Halimah said warningly.

"What? She's bound to find out eventually. The bargain is this," Fayruz added, addressing Marta. "The Poison Mother gives al-Aziz immortality, power and magic. In exchange, should any of his wives conceive, the Poison Mother comes to feed upon the child's life."

Marta half expected the other wives to demur, but Halimah made no protest, and Arwa murmured, "To God we belong, and to God we return!"

It struck her then: that was why it was so quiet here. It was not just because there were no footsteps or voices in the streets beyond the walls, and not just because the serving-girls must be hard at work in the kitchens of the Damascus wing.

There were no children.

That was why they would have to go back to their fathers' houses when they were old, or else beg for lodging with their sisters. That was why Halimah envied her sisters the sons who adored them.

"Oh," Marta whispered.

"What does an immortal want with sons?" Halimah said drearily. "Al-Aziz will never die, and has no need of heirs. His servants are all-seeing and can dart from Cairo to Baghdad in the blink of an eye. He does not even need trustworthy relatives to look after his interests in distant cities. To an immortal, offspring would only threaten his power."

"None of us can remain busy forever," Arwa said, and Marta thought she looked meaningfully at Fayruz. "Sooner or later, we slip up or nod off, we stumble in our recitations or drop the spindle. Then the Poison Mother sees us and takes what we have been trying to hide. And even if we manage to fool the Poison Mother, we cannot fool al-Aziz. You can't stop it, you know. And he won't treat you any the better for managing to disobey him."

Fayruz half turned away. Marta saw the protective hand that drifted to her belly and was pierced by sudden understanding. Fayruz had no sisters or parents waiting for her return. Without a son, she would be utterly destitute once Khalil tired of her.

A thought struck Marta, so horrible that it took her breath away. If she *was* forced to marry Khalil, she might really conceive his child. She might *bear* Khalil's child, because the Poison Mother could never touch her. What would they say of her at home, then? That, preferring dishonour to death, she had willingly chosen Khalil's bed over her own grave?

No—they would say that in any case, no matter what she swore to the contrary. Marta thought she might be sick. No wonder the other wives counselled her to marry him—but Marta could not do that either. Not when Khalil reduced his wives to breeding-ewes endlessly producing lambs for slaughter, because he would deny himself no pleasure, and because in the bloody marketplace between seen and unseen, it gave him power.

Marta would cut her own throat sooner than marry such a man, but sooner than cut her own throat, she would cut his.

That thought steadied her. Khalil had refused to meet her in battle, and now she had no lance. Even the carnelian dagger had failed to kill him. But there had to be a way; otherwise, all this would be in vain—and she could not allow that. Marta Bessarion would endure anything if she could only be the death of Khalil.

No man could live forever.

* * *

Halimah had pointed out the door leading to the Damascus part of the house. It was not locked at all, but when Marta threw it open that afternoon when no one was looking, all it showed was a blank wall of stone. Later, when evening arrived, the door opened again, and this time Marta's insides became a slithering knot of dread as she glimpsed Khalil's sumptuous quarters, with its woven hangings and its low, silk-covered bed.

Two of Khalil's personal guards entered the room—Nubian eunuchs, boyish and smooth-cheeked. They singled her out at once, bowing. "Bint Bessarion, you are awaited in the loggia."

Marta felt that if she let go of the storm of anger she had been weaving around herself all day, she might run, or vomit, or fall down and weep. It was one thing to swear vengeance on her enemy; it was quite another to face him and carry it out. Despite her defiance in the courtyard, she did fear him. He meant to break her spirit, and he was able to do it, too. He was stronger than she in almost every way.

Marta might have allowed the thought to overwhelm her, but instead, very deliberately, she fed it to her anger. She spun it into iron thread and wove it into a hauberk of adamant, and she followed the Nubians out of the harem on the mountain, into the house at Damascus.

Khalil sat in the loggia, a single rectangular platform at one side of the house that overlooked the courtyard through a pair of immense round arches. Cross-legged on a divan, he leaned over the immense silver bowl of water, almost a pool, that sat before him. After a moment, Marta realised that it reflected the shape of the doorway in the tent in Saladin's army, and that a muffled voice was speaking from it.

"—to do what must be done, of course," Saladin said. "They send their holy men to fight us, and so I had *my* holy men, the qadis and scholars, carry out the executions. Those who had the stomach for it."

The sultan was speaking of the captives of the Temple and the Hospital, Marta realised with dread. He had slaughtered them all, but with intentional cruelty: by men who were not even trained to give a clean death with the blade.

She spun it into anger, wove it into armour.

The guards left her standing before Khalil and went to guard the steps leading into the courtyard. Khalil paid her no heed, but Marta did not mind. She crossed to the balustrade overlooking the courtyard. Every archway leading from the courtyard was an entrance to some shadowed lower room; there was no obvious way out into the street. She smelled hot fragrant spices from somewhere ahead—the kitchen, of course, would have its own entrance to the street. All she needed to do was follow her nose some time when the guards were not stationed at the foot of the stairs and Khalil was not watching her.

Behind her, Khalil asked, "Has my lord secured Acre?"

"My nephew received the key to the city, all praise to God, but the populace has staged some sort of insurrection and set fire to the city. They demand guarantees for themselves, their laws, and their property. I am inclined to grant them what they ask."

Marta's heart twisted. Had she gone home, as Lord Balian had intended, then she might still be in the kingdom now, helping to shore up what was left.

Khalil said, "My advice is likewise. Keep them alive and respect their property. Unbelievers make good subjects because they are subject to higher taxes."

"Also do not forget, my friend: *the merciful will be shown mercy by the Most Merciful.* Is your business in Damascus completed?"

"Not yet, my lord. But should my presence be required, I will come to you at once."

The water rippled softly. Marta had been standing with her back to Khalil, looking over the courtyard. Then the divan creaked. Marta turned, her stomach knotting tight with fear, as Khalil rose and approached.

She forced herself to stand her ground—what else could she do? Her right arm was cradled in a makeshift sling against her breast, still aching from the strain it had sustained when she had nearly thrown herself off the mountain.

"What do you think?" Khalil asked.

She thought that she wanted to kill him and that only the necessity of finding out how held her here.

"Well?" he prompted, when she did not reply. "If the people of Acre are given the chance to save their lives and property, will they submit?"

"Why do you ask me?"

"Because you have been in Acre. You know the city. You can judge their mood." After a pause Khalil went on. "And because, as my wife, you would be my trusted advisor in all matters relating to your people."

Marta stared. Was Khalil trying to *bribe* her? Offering power and influence in exchange for granting him a form of legitimacy—not just as her husband, but as a ruler?

Wrath almost suffocated her. How little he knew her! She would not acknowledge even Queen Sibylla's right to rule over a people whom she mistreated; how much less would she acknowledge Khalil?

"Your wives you keep locked away, even from their own families. Why should I believe that you would offer me anything more?"

Khalil smiled indulgently. "You are forthright and spirited. This is one of the things I like about you."

Marta remembered his wives, sad and grave, counselling her that Khalil was a hard man when crossed. No doubt he did like a woman to be forthright and spirited; it was an additional pleasure to subdue her. Her teeth ground. "Answer me."

"I ask only your consent to make you my wife and lady. Don't you believe that that in itself might be worth something to me?"

"As revenge?"

"As aid and companionship, rather," he said, imperturbable as ever. "I spent four hundred and sixty-two years alone in the mountains, imprisoned in stone. I spent eighty-nine years building myself this empire. There is not a soul alive who can comprehend the nature of my power or the immensity of my experience. Only you were there from the beginning. You are the only witness to my glory."

Marta's incredulity must have shown on her face. Did Khalil expect her to while away the evenings singing the praises of her enemy? "You want a court minstrel, not a wife."

"You remind me of your brother, you know."

The quiet observation hit her like a spear and Marta, for an instant, forgot to breathe. She would *not* ask about her brother. Khalil wanted her to, but she would not play his game. Then suddenly she realised what it might mean if Lukas or Paulus had come into his hands. Which of them was it? What had he done to them?

Khalil smiled. "You must be curious how I came to be here."

She could not possibly be less curious about *him*. "That part is obvious," she said thickly. "You lived. Like a cockroach."

He crossed his arms and said, "Your brother Lukas is dead. Time would have felled him, even if I had not."

Marta did not move a muscle. She must show him no weakness. She took every emotion and spun it into anger.

"Your mother and siblings are also dead," Khalil said. "You are the last of Rahel's children now. A shame. Your father is the last to be accounted for."

"Everyone dies eventually," Marta said in a low voice. "But you're wrong. I'm not the last of Rahel's children." She thought with fierce pride of Michael Zakar.

Khalil went on without acknowledging her words. "I've dealt with your family before, to mutual benefit. Eighty-eight years ago, your brother

Lukas found me trapped in the ruins of Oliveta. In those days he was young and filled with anger, like yourself. That made him weak. In exchange for the weapon your father hid from me, he sold himself to the demon Lilith."

You're wrong, Marta wanted to say. *Lukas would never be so foolish.* But would he? She remembered his frustration over being forbidden to fight; his resentment that the homeland their family ruled had been taken away from him; the way their parents shook their heads and tried to reason with him.

"For nearly five hundred years, as I told you, I sat in the ruins of that city, turned to stone from the waist down, subject to the summer sun and the winter snow. Unable to eat, to drink, to sleep—and above all, unable to die. There was one way I might be freed, and that was if one of the souls I had tried to sacrifice on the sigil should return and give me water to drink.

"Like you, your brother tried to kill me. Like you, he failed. I then told him the secret of my release."

Each word was like a hammer-blow, merciless.

No, Marta thought. No, no, *no.*

"Your brother desired the Lance. He bargained with the afrit Lilith to get it, and Lilith held him to that bargain. When Lukas Bessarion gave me water to drink, I rose and lived once more in the world of men. Without your brother, I might still be sitting there today. Without our bargain, you would not have the Lance. I allowed him the weapon; he rescued me from endless torment."

It was a lie. It *had* to be a lie.

Oh, *God* above, Lukas!

Khalil leaned down to gaze into her eyes. "Marta Bessarion, do you weep for me?"

It took her a moment to recall what he had said when she first refused his ring. *I will see you weep for love of me.* The memory steeled her: the tears prickling at her eyes dried in the quick blaze of her wrath, and she bared her teeth at him.

"Not for a moment," she hissed. "Are you done?"

He straightened a little, unfolding his arms and arranging his lips once more in that deathlike smile.

"I returned to the world of men, but the world of men had forgotten me. Every soul I had once known was dead. I was friendless, fatherless, houseless; every man's slave, and Lilith's slave most of all." He tilted his head towards her. "But you have known that, too. Even now, at the sultan's right hand, I am always alone. I have allies, but no friends; wives, but no lovers; slaves to tend my whims, but no intimates, to share sorrow or joy."

The realisation dawned upon Marta that he was, in some measure, sincere. How many cold and lonely nights had he spent in perfecting this speech? She ground her teeth together. If Khalil was alone, he had no one to blame for it but himself.

"We've done unpardonable things to each other in the past, but we can end it now, Marta Bessarion. We are both alone, you and I, and you need me as much as I need you. I offer you a place at my side, not as a plaything like the rest of the women in the mountain wing, but as a queen and counsellor. In exchange, give me your bloodline, adept in magic. Give me your free and voluntary faith. Most of all, give me your tears."

By the time he finished speaking, his voice was almost pleading, and the smile that sat so ill on his lips had vanished. He extended his hand towards her; and Marta, speechless, backed away. None of Khalil's words made sense. Adept in magic? Could that be his explanation of the seraph's display of power at Kerak?

"I can't," she said blankly. "You've just told me you don't want another slave, but that's what you've made of me."

"I *tried* to speak with you," Khalil said. "You only wished to fight."

Biting back her angry words, Marta looked in despair to the heavens. As though in answer to her silent prayer, an idea formed in her head—something she could offer him, with which to drive a bargain, as Miles had advised on the bridge of Judaire. "If you're oppressed by demons, I can rid you of them."

"That state of affairs has changed. The afrits are no longer a problem."

"Aren't they?" Marta did not trouble to keep the scorn out of her voice. "Then you are aware, of course, that the one with feathers is in league with

Queen Sibylla of Jerusalem, and has been for two years at least."

From his momentary silence, she saw that he did not. Khalil forced a smile. "What makes you think so?"

"She was in the Holy Sepulchre at the queen's coronation," Marta said.

"I see," Khalil said, politely sceptical, but evidently ready to change the subject. "In the meantime, think on what I have said." He clapped his hands together, and the guards below came to attention.

"Fetch the prisoner," Khalil called to them. He turned back to Marta. "My last gift was not acceptable to you. Perhaps this will be."

She scoffed. "Another slave?"

"A captive," Khalil said. "One for whom I have spent much of the past week in searching."

One of the doors below opened and Marta leaned over the balustrade. For a moment she half expected it to be Lord Balian—or worse, if it meant the capture of the Bessarion Lance, Miles.

When the guards hauled a bloodied man into the courtyard, however, it took her a long moment to recognise him. Last time she saw him, this man had been sleek and satisfied. Now thick grime and blood coated his face, and his teeth were bared in a rictus of fear. Only the red livery he wore tripped her memory.

Jehan of Cacho.

This was some sort of ghastly mockery, that she should be trapped between Persi's enemy and her own.

Khalil smiled, as satisfied as Cacho himself had been that hot summer's day in the hills above Caesarea.

"You wanted this man dead, I know." At a motion of Khalil's hand, the guards drew their swords. "Marta Bessarion is here, Frank. Kneel. Let me see you beg her for your life."

At once, Cacho collapsed to his knees, his face crumpling. "Have mercy, mademoiselle," he wailed. "Take pity! You wouldn't expect an ordinary sinner to live the life of a monk, would you? *Mea culpa, mea culpa!* Let me go, and I'll publish a confession. I'll cross the sea and never return."

"Very prettily said," Khalil approved. He glanced at Marta, who was still frozen with shock. "She doesn't speak. Perhaps her heart is hardened against you."

Sobbing, Cacho fell on his face.

Khalil turned to Marta with a wolfish smile. "What do you say? Shall you give the order, or shall I?"

Marta could not say a word—what could she say? Cacho ought to die. She wanted him dead. If she begged Khalil to have his men break every bone in the wretch's body, Khalil would do it gladly, because it was he who held all the power here; the choice he offered was a mere pretence.

"Why ask me? I'm your prisoner as much as he is. No doubt you will deal with both of us as you like."

Khalil gave an indulgent laugh. "I only wish him to know himself at your mercy. Which, as of course you withhold—"

He signalled to his guards, a slice of his hand across the throat. One of the guards dragged the grovelling prisoner back to his knees. Even as Cacho stretched out supplicating hands, the other guard swung with a single deft stroke of the sword. His wail cut off in a gurgle and his head and body made two distinct *thumps* on the flagstones.

Marta crammed a hand against her mouth. She had seen men beheaded before, and would gladly have beheaded this one herself. But this...

The first guard cleaned his sword. The second took a sack from his belt, slipped the head within, and tossed it up, into Khalil's waiting hands.

"Marry me," he said, presenting her with the hot, dripping, reeking thing. "Swear to serve me, and we will deal with all your enemies thus."

Who did he think her enemy was, if not himself? Marta felt dizzy from the half-dozen different emotions seething within her: shock, disgust, horror. A fierce and staggering triumph, at seeing the man who had called Persi a liar grovelling for his life. Above all, rage at the man who stood before her, offering her Cacho's head, as though he was guiltless. It had all been a trick. Khalil wanted her to beg him for justice. He wanted her to accept his gift and legitimise his authority.

Marta spun it all into armour. She could not afford to lose herself in passion. "How," she managed in a strained whisper. "How did you *know?*"

"Ah," Khalil said complacently. "Have you not seen that my house has many doors and windows, which lead to distant lands? All I required was a chip of stone from your doorway."

For so many months, Marta had felt that something was wrong with the house in Nablus, that it was no longer safe, that she was being watched. It was true; she *was* being watched. Khalil stood proudly smiling as though he had done something worth boasting about.

"There's only one man's head I want," she hissed, "and as God is my witness, I will have it."

Khalil laughed. "There's the cheetah I trapped," he said. Still smiling, he turned to signal his guards. "We're done for now. Take her back to the women's quarters. See that she does no harm to herself or the others."

Chapter XXIX.

"Come and eat," Halimah invited an hour or so later, when female servants came up from the kitchens laden with trays of richly scented food, and the wives sat down to eat. "You need to regain your strength."

Marta made no reply, only continuing her pacing from one end of the common room to another under the watchful eyes of Khalil's guards. Her stomach tightened at the scent of food. She had not eaten a square meal in at least a week, since departing Nablus. Her heart twisted; she wanted to tell Lord Balian she was alive. She wanted Persi to hold her. She wanted to stop feeling as though her gut was a nest of snakes. Then, perhaps, she could eat.

Acre was about to surrender—they would be fools not to, especially if the sultan offered the inhabitants their lives. And she, like a fool, had lost her temper with Khalil when she ought to have been flattering him into telling her the secret of his immortality. Why must she be a hammer, meeting every battle head-on?

Cross-legged at the table with the other wives, Fayruz must have been thinking similarly. She snickered and said, "Defy al-Aziz, and he'll tire of you soon enough. Then he'll turn to his loyal wives for comfort."

"God is merciful, but it's true," Halimah said heavily. She too had not been eating, but instead watched Marta pace. "You know that al-Aziz would sooner kill you than let you escape."

In any game of hammers, Khalil was bound to win.

Marta shuddered to think what he might do to break her will. She had lived among men of war all her life and knew there was a limit to what anyone could bear. She certainly was not fool enough to imagine that Khalil could not break her, if he really tried. He had determined to get her willing loyalty; and in order to do so, sooner or later he would grind her into the dust. Perhaps she would be on her knees like Jehan of Cacho, begging for her life and kissing his hand. Or perhaps she would be dead.

Long before that happened, she must find the answer she needed, and escape this hell.

In the meantime, she had to survive and endure. The way Persi had. The way Halimah and Arwa and Fayruz had.

Marta made herself kneel at the table. Her stomach would not tolerate much food, but she made herself eat at least a little.

* * *

Marta dreamed of the woman in green silk, lying amidst clouds of smoke and steam on a shattered pavement in a shadowed hall. At first, her body glowed like an amber stone with heat; but she cooled quickly, until only warm brown skin remained.

Abruptly, a door closed between Marta and the sleeper. Now she stood in the courtyard of the Damascus house. Marta turned. The orange-tree at the centre of the courtyard glowed with light, its fruit like lanterns. Marta cradled one in her palm. At her touch, its light increased and her hand also became a lantern, all fiercely golden and veined with red, with shadows where the bones fanned out from her wrists.

She knew it was a dream by her right arm, which ached with only a ghost of pain.

A white snake lay coiled about the roots of the tree, and in her bones Marta felt that to pluck such a fruit, without permission, would be a great trespass. As she released it, her hand dimmed, like the woman in the green tunic, to shadowy flesh. She crossed the courtyard to another corner and opened a door there, hoping to find the kitchens and a way out into the street. Instead, a gust of wind blew in her face and Marta found herself looking across the massive ramparts of a castle which towered over the hill upon which it stood, the village at its feet and the ring of moon-silvered mountains that surrounded it.

She closed the door and stepped back. Her heart was beating hard, remembering her father's story of the caravanserai in the Persian mountains. *The house is magical,* Halimah had said.

It was only a dream, Marta reassured herself. She moved to another door, the white snake following her. This opened into a dark passage. Marta and her silent, serpentine companion mounted the steps at the end and wandered through one large, echoing room after another, all done in sombre black and white marble with darkened lamps, gorgeous and echoing. The rooms were clean, but evidently unused. There were no inhabitants to fill them, only the trophies of Khalil's conquests: chests and silks and carved wooden furniture; tapestries from the north, ivory from the south; suits of armour from the west and porcelain vases from the farthest east. The windows were covered in wooden lattices. Marta put her eye to one and peered out into a broad square lined with folded stalls beneath the shadow of a mosque.

In the next room she looked out a new window into a moonlit courtyard with a mulberry-tree in the midst of it. She caught her breath. It was Nablus, flaming with torches. Servants rushed to and fro, carrying bundles and sleepy children. In the loggia, Persi bent over a chest, muttering under her breath as she pressed down bolts of rich cloth and tried to strap the lip shut. Michael Zakar ran up the steps and picked the whole chest up with a grunt: *Hurry, Persi; we need to go.* Persi followed him downstairs, protesting something about her loom. Below, Queen Maria stood by the mulberry tree with a black veil pulled deeply forward over her head. She gazed about the courtyard; then she took the hands of her youngest children, Philip and Margaret, and followed Persi and Michael into the service courtyard, leaving the house empty and dark.

Marta left the window and went on. In time, she approached a door, half open with rays of warm golden lamplight streaming through it. The soft sound of voices spilled from it. Marta stopped short. This was the door leading to Khalil's apartment from the women's quarters—except that this time she was approaching it from the Damascus part of the house, not the mountain wing.

It was only a dream, she told herself again. There was no danger.

Khalil's voice was a rumble of displeasure layered over the brisk squeak of chalk. "If Lilith will no longer come when I call, she'll need to be dealt with."

"I never liked this triumvirate anyway. Lilith is nothing but a liability. She's never cared for what we're trying to build."

There was an inhuman quality to this second voice. Marta put her face against the gap in the door and stifled a gasp at the sight that met her eyes. Khalil was on his knees putting the finishing touches to a white sigil; prowling around the outer circumference of his design was the same hairy man she had seen twice now, first in the desert of Arabia and then at the battle in Galilee.

The eye in the creature's head was fixed on Khalil, but the other roamed the room. Marta withdrew behind the door.

Lilith, she thought, as Khalil's chalk ceased its chattering, and his shadow on the wall stood and lengthened. She had heard the name before, and its attendant stories. The one with a taste for children, whom Khalil's wives called the Poison Mother.

The feathered woman, who had Queen Sibylla under her thumb.

"She has only ever been biding her time to betray us," the hairy man added.

"And you have not?" Khalil asked. From the way his brows knitted, Marta wondered whether he recalled what she had told him about Lilith's alliance with Queen Sibylla.

The hairy man ignored the barb. "The time is ripe to cut her loose, now, while the sultan trusts us. What if she chooses to defect to the Franks? If she thinks they can get the better of us, she'll help them and turn on us."

"She'll serve them the same way, if it suits her," Khalil said. "Enough, Qeteb. If I cut Lilith loose, who will act as spy? After so many years concerning herself with mortal affairs, she's far better attuned to them than you are."

He began muttering some incantation under his breath, too soft to hear. Only at the end did he raise his voice. "Lilith! Hear me and attend!"

A cold wind blew through the room. If Marta had not kept her toe against it, even her heavy wooden door would have slammed shut. Then a familiar voice spoke.

"I hear and obey." It was the faintly mocking voice of the one who had come to her in the night before the defeat. "Ah, what a hurry you're in, my esteemed friends."

"It's been more than a week since you reported," the hairy man said sharply. "Never forget that we tolerate you only as long as you are useful."

"It is because I'm being *useful* that I haven't reported," the other demon retorted. "Obviously. You were more fun, al-Aziz, before you took up with this god of public servants."

"In those days I was under your thumb," Khalil said coldly, "so pardon me if I do not willingly return to them. Your report?"

Lilith let out an exasperated and peculiarly human-sounding sigh. "Upon Acre's surrender, the queen has withdrawn to Ascalon and is preparing for a siege. However, the majority of the knights who survived the battle at Hattin have gone to Tyre. The garrisons of all the kingdom are depleted and the sultan has captured all of Samaria and Galilee. In Nablus, where the Muslims are numerous, the people revolted and have submitted to the sultan."

It was hard to imagine so many of the people she knew in Nablus rising up against their Frankish neighbours. All this time, had she and her foster-family only been tolerated and flattered, not loved? All this time, had the people she thought of as neighbours been so discontent?

Marta thought of Hind, the woman who had murdered her husband and become a bandit, and realised she did not know.

Khalil spoke. "The sultan tells me he is now besieging Toron. What is the mood among the defenders?"

"Panic," Lilith answered with relish. "They wait only to discover whether the lords in Tyre will send help. When no help comes, they will surrender and beg safe-conduct."

"Good," Khalil said. "Go to Tyre and spread fear there. Have them surrender quickly, before help can arrive from across the sea."

Marta was only a dream, listening in on a dream. But Lilith said, "A word of advice to you before I depart again to waste my time on *useless* pursuits: your djinn is untrustworthy, and Qeteb is deaf as well as blind. But I hear a mouse behind the door."

Without another word, the feathered woman vanished. Marta dared not wait for the sorcerer's reaction. *Wake up!* she shrieked at herself, and the next moment she jerked upright in her own bed, far from Damascus, in the women's quarters on the mountain.

Sweat beaded her skin despite the coolness of the night. Marta's heart raced, recalling how vivid and detailed the dream had been. Could it have been real? Could she have really listened in on a conversation between Khalil and his familiars?

Could she really have been caught by Lilith?

Again, Marta felt that someone was watching her.

Halimah had been right—this house was indeed magic. Doors led where they should not. Windows looked into streets and courtyards in distant cities. Perhaps she could also roam it in her sleep, and eavesdrop on the enemy. There was more than one way to use a hammer, after all.

A glow of light showed behind the curtain at her doorway, a warm beacon in the watchful darkness. Marta got up, pulling a robe around her shoulders. The common room was empty of anything but shadows, but the doorway next to her own was open, and lamplight streamed out. Fayruz sat within, propped up against the wall, nodding over her spindle.

Marta cleared her throat and Fayruz startled awake with a gasp, clutching her spindle and setting the bobbin whirling again before blinking up at Marta. "You! What are you creeping about like that for? You startled me!"

In the two weeks since Marta had come to the house of Khalil, Fayruz's belly had become clearly visible beneath her tunic. Had Khalil summoned her—which he had not—he would surely have recognised her condition. These days, Fayruz rarely emerged from her room, but when she did, her eyes were shadowed with exhaustion. The other wives whispered that she snatched sleep only during the day; Arwa and Halimah always made sure that Fayruz was awake before laying down their own work.

A stab of pity and remorse went through Marta and she went to her own room just long enough to retrieve the spindle she kept there, along with its tuft of raw cotton. Then she returned to kneel before Fayruz.

"Go to sleep," Marta told her. "I'll watch over you."

"I'll take care of myself, thanks."

"It's all right," Marta assured her, settling cross-legged on a cushion opposite Fayruz, and setting her own bobbin twirling. "I won't sleep again tonight, anyway. Bad dreams."

Fayruz shot her a narrowed glare and enunciated every word clearly. "I don't want you here. Leave."

The other woman's distrust stung a little. Marta sighed. "Forgive me; only I thought you looked so tired, and—"

"Stop it," Fayruz spat. "Stop pretending you care."

Marta's mouth fell open. "Well, I don't particularly. But—"

"You make me sick," Fayruz said. "Do you think, because you're the present favourite, you'll rule this roost much longer? If I bear Khalil's child, I won't be a nobody anymore. I'll be better than all of you put together."

Marta was not sure where to start. "I'm not Khalil's favourite. I've refused everything he's asked."

"He only sees you these days."

He could not have summoned her more than twice, and Marta could only be grateful for such fitful attention. "I wish to heaven he wouldn't. Fayruz, what makes you think he'll let the child live? I mean," she added hastily, "of course we must protect it. But if Khalil does not scruple to hand his own offspring to Lilith before they're born, what would prevent him doing so after?"

Fayruz smiled tightly. "Because he is so very righteous in his own eyes, of course. He would never stoop to *murder*."

She laughed, drawing her knees up as though to cradle her belly since both her hands were occupied. Marta thought of the satisfaction with which Khalil had sentenced Jehan of Cacho to death, of the confidence with which he had handed the head to her as a gift.

Yes, she decided, Khalil was such a hypocrite as to feed his children to Lilith and pretend that his hands were clean. He would even take pride in such a thing. *I may not want my children, but at least I don't allow them to suffer—to be abandoned or sold or strangled like kittens.*

"You said I don't care, but I do," Marta said softly. "I care about Khalil."

Fayruz blinked at her. "You *love* the toad?"

"No. I care that he should pay for everything he has done to the four of us and God knows how many others. I care that his demons should not consume another life. I care that, before I die, I shall bathe my lance in his blood. And on that Lance, Fayruz, I swear to you that I will guard your child."

Fayruz stared at her, almost fearful. Then she forced a smile. "You're mad."

"I'm very angry," Marta said, feeling almost apologetic.

"I can see that." Fayruz spun in silence for a while, and then she put down her spindle. "Very well. Let me lie down, just for a moment."

Fayruz must have been exhausted; she scarcely moved for the remainder of the night. At dawn, Marta was still spinning when the female slaves of the house—who occupied their own, smaller rooms beneath the finer quarters allotted to the wives and Marta—filed up from below to begin cleaning the common room. One of them slipped with her broom and knocked a small table awry. The sound made Fayruz jump.

"How long was I asleep?" she hissed, blinking at the servants at work outside.

Marta stifled a yawn. "All night. It's nearly time for dawn prayers." Indeed, within a few moments, Arwa popped out of her own room, cleared her throat, and began reciting the Mahometan call to prayer. The clear, fine voice echoed through the whole house, hastening Bahar and the three other servant-maids to finish their tasks and take their place kneeling behind the three wives. As she led the prayers, Arwa stood facing in a direction which told Marta that they were any distance due north of Mecca.

That placed them, most likely, in the Syrian mountains. There were, of course, mountains immediately north of Mecca itself; but Marta did not think Khalil would keep his women too far away from Damascus.

The first time she had been a prisoner among Saracen women, Marta had joined them in their prayers, not knowing their language or the difference between their religion and hers. These days she knelt apart from them, also facing south, but in the direction where she presumed Jerusalem lay, and said her own prayers in silence.

She kept the Watcher's Mark on her forearm covered, too, for it had made her no friends among the weavers in Cacho. That was no wonder, if they had last seen the mark on Jehan of Cacho. This morning, instead of praying, Marta found herself tracing the eight-spoked wheel through the muslin sleeve that covered it. Watchers were supposed to perform deeds of practical charity. The old Messenger, who had burned at Turan before the battle, had reproached the Watchers of Jerusalem for putting their own political interests above their duties as Watchers. Had Marta done the same? No doubt it was an act of practical charity to banish Khalil from the world; but she had allowed Fayruz, who was surely desperately in need of help, to sit up night after night trying to protect her child from Lilith. Fayruz was a more honourable warrior than herself, she judged with self-reproach: here was Marta sleeping peacefully all night and plotting revenge all day, looking forward to a single stroke of her spear—or sword, as the seraph had predicted—by which she would end Khalil's life; meanwhile Fayruz, all alone, without weapons or training, without armour or Christ, was doing battle every night, tirelessly, for the life of her child. Marta was covered in shame.

"Fayruz, you're looking a little more refreshed this morning," Halimah said encouragingly when all the servants had gone to their duties in the Damascus wing. Only the youngest remained, a Kurdish girl who was helping Halimah wind skeins of thread onto a host of wooden bobbins that lay in a basket. "Is the baby all right?"

"Still kicking." Fayruz touched her belly. She looked at Marta, and although she said nothing, Marta thought she could read a little begrudging gratitude in the other woman's eyes.

It was invitation enough: she had been looking for an opportunity to speak.

"We can save the child," Marta declared. "Khalil won't kill her once she's born."

"Who's *she?*" Fayruz muttered. "I'm having a *son.*"

Otherwise, there was a reluctant silence for a moment until Arwa said, "If al-Aziz catches sight of Fayruz, he'll know what we've done, and all of us will suffer for it."

"He hasn't so far," Marta said, "and I'm sure I can continue to keep his attention for four or five months, or however long it is." *Strife,* she thought, the moment the words were out of her mouth. Had she just sentenced herself to remain in this house for five months? Would she never learn to think before she spoke? But she had made her promise and must keep it. If she learned the secret of Khalil's immortality before Fayruz had her baby, and if the opportunity presented itself to escape, she would simply have to convince Fayruz to escape alongside her.

Marta took a deep breath. "Besides, we're all suffering anyway. At least, this way, it'll mean something. If we break the day into four watches, one of us can always be working to protect Fayruz from Lilith. Halimah, if you can work all morning, and Arwa, if you can recite all afternoon, then Fayruz can take the first part of the night, and I'll take the second. If we all share the load, we can all find enough rest. And we'll show Khalil he isn't master here, after all."

Halimah looked aghast. "Don't say such things, Marta. Al-Aziz *is* master here." She sent a worried glance at Fayruz. "I don't know. It seems wrong, somehow."

Arwa was the one who came to their rescue. "Wrong?" she asked in a low voice that vibrated with anger. "Wrong of us to protect our own flesh and blood, when al-Aziz would feed it to afrits? Don't you know why so many powerful men have worshipped the Poison Mother? It isn't just pleasure she promises them; it's power. It's the certainty that no matter what they do in the dark, they will never fear the consequences because

Lilith is there to consume the result. No, Marta is right. Khalil insults us by treating us like this. Not as wives, but as livestock."

"Women call on her too," Halimah said, faintly protesting.

"Women call on the Poison Mother like a beast stuck in a trap screams in desperation, because they think she will set them free," Fayruz said, angrily. "Will you help guard my baby, Halimah, or will I summon the Poison Mother here and now, and beg for her aid? Perhaps, if I offer *you*, she'll let my child live!" She brandished a pair of scissors like a dagger.

Halimah flinched and bit her lip. Marta, watching her, felt for the woman, who had lived in Khalil's shadow longer than the rest of them had; it was no wonder if she had learned to appease him. Marta almost wished she could learn to do the same.

"It isn't right," Halimah said at last, in a whisper. "It *isn't* right to treat us like this…consorting with djinn and afrit…is it, Arwa?"

Arwa pursed her lips. "I have always been taught," she said carefully, "that Muslims worship but one God, and to do otherwise is to be otherwise."

"Then in the name of God, the Gracious, the Merciful…all right. I'll help you."

Her words, soft as they were, resounded loudly in the silence. Halimah glanced towards the door to Damascus, as though, now they had made up their minds to defy their lord, she half expected him to burst in on them with fury and bloodshed. But nothing happened. Halimah went on winding bobbins, and Fayruz curled up on the divan to nap. Arwa sat cross-legged on the cushioned window-seat—the lattice had been repaired since Marta's attack—and began to write.

Glad to give her reddened fingers a rest from spinning, Marta set down her own spindle and followed Arwa to the window.

"What are you working on?" she asked, squinting at the neat lines of ornate calligraphy. She could speak the Saracen tongue in a rough and ready way, but she had never learned to read it.

"Only a poem," Arwa said with a sad smile. "I should like to write commentaries and histories, God willing, but to do such things one ought to travel—to interview scholars and men of public life."

"Will you read it to me?"

"It isn't finished yet," Arwa said shyly. "Do you love poetry very much?"

"I like it, though I don't always understand it. Unless it is about knights and combats."

Arwa bit her lip. "Well, in that case, you won't judge mine too harshly. It's about home." And she cleared her throat and read softly:

Sooner than live in a tall palace, I'd dwell in a lively house.
Sooner than hold a purring kitten, I'd keep a dog to call travellers home.
Sooner than twirl in a muslin dress, I'd wear a homespun frock.
Sooner than gobble a loaf in splendour, I'd scrape up breadcrumbs from a bare table.
Sooner than hear the chime of timbrels, I'd whistle with the wind through the chinks in my wall.
Sooner than command my slaves, I'd laugh with my handsome kinsmen.

Give me a simple life in the country and no soft living.
All my heart is there, in the noblest of homes.

"It's beautiful," Marta said, biting her lip to keep it from trembling. While Arwa read, she could not help remembering summers on her father's estate near Ibelin, running barefoot through the vineyards and swimming in the sea with her brother Lukas.

Lukas: brother, traitor, and one more of the sorcerer's victims, if what Khalil said was true. Oh, he would regret telling her of his misdeeds.

"You look tired." Arwa had missed nothing of the expressions playing across Marta's face. "You should rest."

The kind words were a balm to her: Marta gulped, suddenly afraid that she might burst into tears. Yet if she broke, she would never put herself together again; and she had a task to do first.

"When I slept last night, I had strange dreams. I thought I walked through the house, and its doors took me to strange places. I overheard Khalil speaking with his familiars."

Arwa paled. "I take refuge in God from the accursed devil! You shouldn't speak of such things!"

"It was only a dream," Marta said, trying to pretend that she believed it.

"*Only* a dream!" Arwa repeated, shaking her head. She leaned forward, whispering. "Even if that were true, Marta, we told you the house is magic. You ought to be careful. Only the house's master can command the house; but it has a mind of its own and *we* are not its master. You never know what memories or dreams, visions or premonitions might be lurking here in the shadows."

Arwa's advice, and the way it was given, reminded her with a stab of Persi. Marta could feel that her smile was all wrong, twisted with longing and regret; but she smiled it anyway. "What is *careful?* I'm not sure I know."

"It means, stay away from the in-between places," Arwa told her, ever practical. "Don't linger in doors and windows. Especially not at sunrise and sunset. And the borderland between sleep and waking is dangerous too. You'll be watching Fayruz all night; take care to remain vigilant at dawn."

"I'll bear it in mind," Marta said. Retreating to her room, she sank onto the bed and watched the sun cast patterns of light through the lattice. So, Arwa believed she really *had* roamed the house in the night, eavesdropping on Khalil and his familiars—Lilith and Qeteb.

For an instant she had thought herself capable of driving a wedge between Khalil and at least one of his familiars, but she was no Miles, capable of convincing any man that the sky was green and the grass blue. Khalil had not even been willing to listen to Qeteb when he unwittingly repeated Marta's warning. She recalled Lilith's report on the progress of the war. The details had been clear and convincing, confirming the guesses Marta had made on her own about how things were likely to unfold after the disaster at Hattin: depopulated garrisons choosing to surrender because they were not strong enough to defend themselves. She should be there. She owed it to the kingdom—to the oath she had made to Baldwin—to be there.

Worse, Lilith knew she had been listening in on the conversation with

Khalil. What if Khalil learned of the dream-walker haunting him? Marta did not believe that any demon could hurt her, but they might report her to Khalil, and he was quite capable of doing so.

What happened when Khalil came to see her, not as a plaything, but a threat?

"Fayruz, what if we could leave this place for good?" she asked the other woman that night, when she came to begin her watch.

"But we can't," Fayruz pointed out, still diligently plying her spindle. "There are only two doors into the Damascus wing of the house, and those are both kept locked, or guarded when they're opened. Even if we got out of the women's quarters, we'd still be in the house. Even if we got out of the house, we'd still be in Damascus."

Marta smiled. It was she who had spirited Miles out of the heart of Arabia. It was she who had rescued Persi from Ascalon and then snatched herself and the Bessarion Lance out of the queen's own citadel. She said only, "I've done such things before. The first step would be changing places one morning with a pair of the kitchen slaves. Even if Khalil allows him to live, do you want your child to live at that man's disposal?"

Fayruz was silent. At length she shook her head. "He'd be taken away from me. Sold as a slave, or else turned into the image of his father."

"I have friends on the Coast," Marta said. "You would be welcomed. A place would be found for you."

At least, she thought it would. She would no longer be praised as Marta the Knight, the kingdom's virgin saint, but surely Persi and Michael would not turn their backs upon a pair of fugitives.

Fayruz shuddered a little. "No, I can't. If al-Aziz catches us, he'll kill us."

"At least then we would escape this place."

"You're mad," Fayruz said again, with conviction. "It's not too bad here, if you can manage to be the favourite. If you want to help me, just spin and let me sleep."

Marta bit her lip, but perhaps Fayruz was correct. The best way to free any of them was to kill Khalil, and her best chance at *that* lay here, in the shadows of the house of her captivity.

Marta set her bobbin whirling and Fayruz curled into her divan, tying a scarf over her eyes to block out the lamplight. Deliberately, Marta settled herself in the window. The bobbin rose and fell between her fingers. She waited.

Hours went by, the dreariest part of the night. Marta watched and prayed and spun; but when dawn arrived, soft footsteps stole into the common room. With the work of tidying safely afoot in the next room, she set down her spindle, settled against the window-frame, and let her heavy eyelids droop.

Stay away from the in-between places, Arwa had said.

She smiled to herself.

The light brightened through the window, and Marta began to hear a noise like weeping. No—moans of pain. A horrible sound, hardly human, and punctuated by rhythmic thwacking sounds.

A latch on the lattice had not been there before. Marta opened the shutter and looked down into an outer service courtyard of the Damascus house. The sun was a blinding glare in the sky above. The courtyard was a dry and dusty spot between the stables and the house, with tall posts—training-pells battered with sword-cuts—lining one side of it. Today, a man sagged against one of them, held upright only by the leather thongs around his wrists. His back was blotched and welted from beating; here and there a red trickle ran from a split in the skin.

Khalil strode into the courtyard, dragging a woman with him. At the sight of the bound man, she gave a wail and crammed the back of her hand against her mouth.

Khalil released the woman, letting her fall into the dust. In a voice like stones grinding together, he said, *"You* did this."

Marta had no desire to watch, but she could not look away, either.

"Stop," the woman begged. "Have mercy. He did nothing, *nothing,* except take pity on a kinswoman."

"He made off with you, into the desert," Khalil said. "It took me three days and a pack of dogs to hunt you down. Is this what you call *nothing,* wife of al-Aziz?" He turned to the mamluk who stood by the beaten man, a thin rod in his hand. "Did I give you leave to stop?"

"He's fainted, my lord."

"I can see that. *Continue.*"

The woman darted to her feet. Before the thin rod could strike the prisoner again, she threw herself over him like a shield.

Crack. The rod caught her across the shoulders, eliciting a high, sharp cry. The mamluk recoiled, dropping the rod as though it had stung him.

There was a moment's silence. The mamluk stared at Khalil in mute terror.

"You'll pay for that," Khalil told him gently. "No one strikes her but me."

The woman rocked to and fro, holding the prisoner in her arms. From her vantage-point at the window, Marta could just make out her words.

"I'm so sorry. I'm so sorry. I'm so sorry…"

The beaten man lifted his head, looked up at her with dull and accepting eyes, like one who has been condemned to death and hopes for it to come quickly.

Khalil said: "Give me your sword." The mamluk offered it with a bow. And then, with a brilliant flash in the sunlight, he thrust the blade through the woman and the man in a single stroke, and deep into the pell.

Marta clapped her hand over her mouth and fumbled for the shutters.

Below, Khalil said to his mamluk, "Have the bodies taken to the women's quarters. Make sure the rest of my wives see the just penalty for disobedience."

Marta slammed the lattice shut with a jerk that woke her from her dream. In the common room, Arwa was calling the adhan. Fayruz turned over, then sat up with a jerk at the sight of Marta's face.

"You didn't fall asleep, did you?"

"Maybe for a moment," Marta confessed, slipping down from the window-ledge. "But only once the maids were already cleaning."

She rushed out of Fayruz's room and into her own, jerking the curtain shut behind her. Each time she closed her eyes she could see that man and woman nailed against the pell, their blood mingling.

No wonder Fayruz did not dare to flee, if that was how Khalil dealt with those who tried.

No wonder Arwa warned her against drowsing in the window at sunrise.

Marta pressed a hand against her mouth. Blood rushed in her ears, but now the feeling of being watched that had so unsettled her in Nablus was almost comforting.

The house had listened to her. The house had warned her. *The house has a mind of its own.*

Stay or go—and she could not go, not without Fayruz—it was a dangerous game she was playing. Khalil would be no kinder to one who subverted his house, than he had been to the wife who had suborned his guard.

Yet she now had a plan, and an ally. She felt more alive than she had since the battle.

Marta placed her open palm against the lintel of her own window. "Thank you," she whispered. "I'll heed your warnings. But I won't stop until Khalil is dead. You understand that, don't you?"

Chapter XXX.

Mid-August—five weeks after the battle

Balian arrived in the palace of Tyre that evening at an angry trot. "My lord of Sidon!" he roared even before he had passed the gate. *"My lord of Sidon!"*

Five weeks since the battle, and four weeks of being holed up like rats in Tyre. Watching helplessly as the cities and castles of the kingdom fell like ninepins. All of Galilee and Samaria was gone; thank God Maria and the children had made it to Jerusalem in safety. Acre was handed over, Jaffa slaughtered, Toron seized, Beirut surrendered. With no one to defend them, the kingdom's cities had no choice but to surrender one by one—in just five weeks!

At the centre of the palace courtyard, a knot of fellow lords had gathered in hushed conversation. "Sidon!" Balian shouted again, reining in, and motioning the men behind him to spread out, blocking the gateway. "What do you think you're doing, man?"

The lords turned towards him, their faces pale and blurred in the twilight—Reynald of Sidon, Joscelin of Courtenay, the viscount of Tyre. Tripoli himself was long gone—Balian knew not whether it was his health or spirit that had broken, but he had fled north to Tripoli weeks ago, a shattered man. Whispers of treachery and even a few clods and rotting vegetables had hastened him through the city to his ship. By now everyone in the kingdom knew about the count's charge at Hattin, which had taken him and the whole of the vanguard straight through the Saracen army and down to the open lowlands beyond. The Saracens had not dared to stand firm in his path, and they had closed up behind to forbid his return.

Tripoli claimed it would have been suicide to turn back, that he had saved his life and the lives of all his knights. Balian had said nothing to condemn his friend—in the end, he and Joscelin of Courtenay had made the same choice—but he said nothing in Tripoli's favour, either. He and Joscelin had waited hours longer to abandon the battle. Either way, what did it matter now? All that did matter was that those who had survived should now stand together and refuse Saladin a single inch more of land.

"Where's Archbishop Joscius?" Balian snapped, dismounting and tossing his reins to Ernoul. "He should be part of this, too."

"He's here," the Archbishop said breathlessly. One of the senior-most church officials in the kingdom, Joscius must have run on foot from his own palace the moment he received Balian's message. Others hurried through the gate to join them: Walter of Caesarea, the acting heads of the Temple and the Hospital, Hugh and Raoul of Galilee.

Sidon folded his arms stubbornly as Balian stalked forward to meet him at the courtyard's centre. "What is this, Ibelin? An ambush?"

"Treachery, maybe," Balian said.

Sidon's hand went to the hilt of his sword. "Do you care to make that good, my lord?"

Balian swallowed his rage. "First show these good men what your sergeant there is carrying."

Sidon flushed and looked stubborn, but the viscount of Tyre—the royal governor of the city, who with Sidon had been in command since Tripoli's departure—silently took the bundle from the Sidon's messenger and shook it out. Golden eagles fluttered in the fading evening light.

The archbishop gave an audible gasp at the sight of Saladin's standard. "What is this?"

Balian gave a sharp laugh. "Sidon would hand this city over to Saladin without striking a single blow in its defence."

"Saladin is coming to besiege us in Tyre," Sidon said with a scowl. "We cannot sustain a siege without help, and where should help come from?"

Five weeks could scarcely have permitted news of the defeat to cross the sea—let alone brought any real help. One could not inspire, muster, provision, and ship a whole army in five weeks. If help did come from the west, it would not be for years.

"Queen Sibylla's orders," Courtenay added smoothly, "are for all her vassals to send her aid in Ascalon."

"You speak like cowards," Balian said. "We are to send the queen reinforcements, but if Saladin camps outside Tyre, a strong and defensible city, we are to give it up?"

"Death before dishonour!" Hugh of Galilee agreed.

"Or if not death, then at least a reasonable show of force," Raoul amended with a twist of his thin, mocking lips.

"Who made *you* vassals?" Sidon snarled at them.

"And who made *you* king?" Balian demanded.

"One might ask you the same," Joscelin put in. "Your voice alone settles nothing, Balian, no more than ours does."

"So, you acknowledge yourselves in the wrong," Balian said, triumphant. "Let us put it to the vote, as ought to have been done from the start." He turned to face the other lords, wellnigh everyone left with standing in the kingdom. "What do you say, my lords? Should Tyre be surrendered?"

Silence.

"Our duty is to guard the holy places," said the acting master of the Hospital at last. "That means we prioritise Jerusalem, not Tyre."

Archbishop Joscius shook his head. "This city doesn't belong to any of us; it belongs to the queen. I recall too well what happened the last time one of us refused a royal order."

Balian could hardly believe his ears. "Caesarea?" he appealed.

"Oh, by Saint Maurice." Lord Walter was indecisive. "It depends on whether we can get anyone to help us."

"And if no one comes?" Sidon challenged.

"Oh, good Lord in heaven, then put up the banner, I suppose."

Balian felt the whole situation slipping out of his hands. *No.* He had spent too much time biting his tongue and deferring to others; he would never forgive himself for letting Ridefort persuade King Guy to cross the hills to that terrible defeat. Giving in now was wrong, he was sure of it.

He was a Watcher—Prester Balian, guardian of the whole kingdom. He had to go on fighting, no matter the cost.

Even as Balian hesitated, he became aware of a sound in the distance. Shouting. Cheering. A joyful sound, such as he had given up any hope of hearing again.

In a flash he guessed what it was.

"Someone *is* coming," he said. "A ship was sighted this afternoon, waiting for the tide to enter the harbour."

"More fugitives from Beirut, no doubt," Courtenay said.

That was one of the reasons they could defend Tyre: it was now bursting with the evacuated garrisons of Tiberias, Toron, Beirut. This ship, however, had not come from Beirut.

"It came from the south, not the north."

"Then it's most likely someone from Ascalon. And in any case what difference could one ship make?" Joscius said heavily. He stopped. "What is that sound? Some disturbance in the city…"

All of them could hear it now. They looked at each other in silence as the sound of chanting came nearer. When it swept into the square beyond the gate, the viscount seemed to wake from a dream. "Gatekeepers, stand by!" he called to the guards on duty. Balian, who thought he recognised the word the crowd was chanting, rushed to his horse and urged it towards the gate.

A flood of horsemen, their gear winking and clinking bravely in the evening light, entered the square with the townspeople running and cheering beside them. Their emblem was one Balian had seen before. The man at their head sat atop a shining black horse which had clearly not been ridden fast or far. He was in his late thirties: fair-haired, handsome, gladder and more carefree than any man should be these days. The man reined his horse to a halt under the gate and smiled at all the lords within, watching him with silent bewilderment.

"Hail, friends! I am Conrad of Montferrat, recently landed on these shores."

"Who?" Archbishop Joscius demanded, pushing past Balian's stirrup to squint up at the newcomer.

Balian opened his mouth to explain, but Montferrat forestalled him.

"I am the brother of Longsword, who was married to your queen for three short months before his death, whose son was your king for a year, whose father fought beside you and was captured at the great battle." This time his voice carried clearly in the hushed square. His teeth flashed in a vulpine smile. "And I am also the newly appointed lord of this city."

It was the archbishop who recovered his wits first. "Indeed? Do you have a charter from the queen?"

"Perhaps he has a charter from the sultan," Balian said, with withering scorn directed at Sidon and Courtenay. The viscount tried to hide the eagle banner behind his back.

"Not from the queen," Montferrat said with another flashing grin. "The people of your city came out to my ship in boats while I was still debating whether Tyre was safe for landing. They told me that if I did not come ashore, the city would be handed over to the sultan. But if I did come ashore, they would do me homage and make me and my heirs the lords of it. So I have come to take possession of my city."

Balian laughed, as he had not expected to laugh again. "For my part I am ready to do you homage, my lord."

"You can't do this," Courtenay protested. "This is a royal city!"

"Not anymore," Raoul of Tiberias said. By far the quickest-witted of his siblings, he made a sudden snatch and shouldered his way forward, shaking out the eagle banner of the sultan so that it glittered in the torchlight. "The queen has given Tyre to Saladin!"

"For shame!" a burgess yelled from the crowd.

"It was *my* decision," Sidon protested. "Not the queen's!"

It was the truth, but it was also a transparent attempt to save the queen's honour; Balian found that he could very happily see Queen Sibylla blamed, even falsely, for the needless surrender of another city. "Then shame on you also!" he shouted, and the people of the city took up the cry.

"Shame, shame!"

To that thunderous chant, Montferrat took the banner of Saladin and drew his dagger from his belt. With one slash he opened the banner down the centre and then ripped it cleanly in two. The pieces streamed from his fists in a salute given to the shouting people, then he tossed them onto the flagstones and trampled them beneath his horse's feet.

"My lord," he said, turning to Balian, "if it has come to this, we must be sword-brothers."

With a chime of armour, Balian clasped Montferrat's arm. "As David and Jonathan, my lord."

Before the night was out, everyone but Sidon and Courtenay had sworn homage to Montferrat as the kingdom's new *bailli*, for as the uncle of one king and the brother-in-law of another he was surely the best choice. Afterwards, they all sat up late into the night telling Montferrat the terrible news of the battle. When Balian finally sought his bed, he opened again the letter which had come into the city by sea some weeks before.

He lifted the paper to his nostrils, still faintly able to catch the scent of *her*. Maria, his Greek queen, separated from him by the sultan's armies and the length and breadth of a land that had become a battlefield. Smoothing out the letter, he read the words for the twentieth time.

Maria Comnena, former queen of Jerusalem, to her beloved and venerable lord Balian of Ibelin, all good wishes sent in genuine affection.

Your news has restored life to me, for at first there was no word of you after the battle, and I can scarcely refrain from weeping when I think of the dangers you have suffered. The children are in good health, except that Philip has had a fever, which alarmed us, but all is now well. Here in Jerusalem all is dolor and weeping. There are not five knights in the city, and if Saladin should take Ascalon we will not defend ourselves long. Send us word whether you will have us stay in Jerusalem, or meet you in Ascalon, or come to you in Tyre. I have had a mass of thanksgiving sung in the Church of the Madeleine for your escape, and also have endowed the new chapel of Saint Nicholas for a new altar-cloth.

Balian put the letter down again. There was no word in it of Marta

Bessarion, but doubtless she was watching over his family. If she was one of fewer than five knights left in Jerusalem, she would of course feel obliged to stay. It was only a shame they did not have two, or three, or several hundred White Watchers in the kingdom to save them now.

With Tyre safe under Montferrat's command, Balian could surely afford to leave the city and undertake the perilous journey south to Jerusalem. He would need a promise of safe-conduct from the sultan, but that would pose little difficulty: he had known Saladin personally since his days as King Amalric's ambassador of choice, and the sultan's generosity was a point of pride. Now would be the perfect moment at which to bring his family to safety in the north.

To say nothing of the White Watcher herself—that is, if Marta would consent to leave Jerusalem.

Tucking the letter away, Balian retired to his lonely bed and went to sleep thinking hopefully of seeing Queen Maria again soon—and of bringing the Bessarion Lance north.

Chapter XXXI.

"Of course, Jerusalem is the ultimate goal, my lord, but the wisest course would be to capture Tyre *now,* before its garrison can be strengthened further."

In Khalil's apartments, the sorcerer stood over his silver basin, speaking by magic across a staggering distance to Saladin in his camp outside Tyre. Nearby, Marta sat cross-legged before the low round table where dinner had been prepared. Khalil, as urbane as ever, had signalled her to take her seat while he finished his conversation. Hungry though she was after hours of listening to him confer with the sultan, Marta did not dare to touch the food until he was ready. She thought she had best refrain from making him unnecessarily angry, if there was any hope of that.

Every good knight must learn to pick his battles—Marta could accept that—but most knights got to fight their battles with armour made of steel. All she had was wrath.

Besides, from here she could get a look at the sigil that, for reasons known only to Khalil, had been painted upon the floor beneath the bed.

"I can't afford to lose momentum," Saladin said from beyond the water. "Tyre will not fall readily into my lap. There's a certain Lord William among the prisoners we took at Hattin, whose son has already arrived from the west and taken command of Tyre. An unbeliever, and very cruel. Truly, it will take a long and determined siege, at a time when my men are already begging to go home to their wives and their harvests. If you were here you would understand."

So, Khalil had not been with the sultan. Nor had he been in Damascus in the six weeks since the battle, except on fleeting visits. From what Marta heard in the women's quarters, Khalil had always lived like this, constantly moving from place to place, unpredictable and reclusive.

Halimah said the house had wings in Cairo and Baghdad as well as in Damascus.

Arwa said a sorcerer's life was one of perilous balance, the scrupulous maintenance of perfect rituals in his alliances with afrits—what Marta called demons—even as he simultaneously pursued a life of erratic deviation to escape the manipulations of others. Arwa said that what she and the other wives did was the antidote to both these extremes: small, profitable labours undertaken towards a definite goal, for simple joy and beauty.

Anti-magic, Fayruz called it, and the name stuck.

"If I take Jerusalem, God willing, my name will be made and my men will be loyal forever," Saladin added. "I have sworn an oath to do it. If I turn aside to take Tyre, if I let the momentum slip through my fingers, I may never have another opportunity."

Marta closed her eyes, willing the sultan to do as Khalil advised, to stop in Tyre and waste his advantage in siege and pestilence until help could come from beyond the sea. It could not be that Jerusalem, her home in two lifetimes, should fall to invaders in both.

But Khalil bowed and said, "No doubt my lord knows best how to conduct the war," and that seemed to settle the question.

"One more thing," the sultan put in. "You are on good terms with the Old Man of the Mountain, I believe. I'm told that before Acre's surrender, a single messenger was sent from the city to Masyaf of the Assassins. What do you make of this, al-Aziz? Has the Old Man reneged on his allegiance?"

"I have no knowledge of the Assassins' doings, my lord," Khalil said. As Khalil was married to the Old Man's daughter, Marta knew this must be a transparent falsehood. Perhaps Saladin was not aware of Halimah's background; perhaps he did not even know of her existence.

Wrapping her arms around her knees, Marta continued her inspection of the sigil on the floor. It was a ring of writing surrounding the bed, done not in chalk but in white paint; its lines formed a web beneath the bed itself.

Did this have something to do with Khalil's immortality? No—it was unlikely that Khalil would leave the secret of his immortality written on the floor for anyone to see. Marta wished she had taken the trouble to learn the Arabic script. She would ask Arwa to teach her, and in time, perhaps she would be able to tell what it said. She had asked the house itself, but it had not answered her. There were other things it could not tell her, either: where Lord Balian and Queen Maria were; whether the children were well; whether Persi had gone to Tripoli. Its view, Marta surmised, must be limited to things that had taken place within the house itself, or in the places to which it was connected, like the courtyard of the Nablus house.

Khalil bowed his farewells to the sultan; now he cast a handful of salt into his basin, banishing the vision. Marta watched as he moved to a window and muttered some incantation. Then he opened the wooden shutters and Marta looked into a vast and dim audience-hall.

"I must speak with your lord," Khalil told someone within. The sorcerer stood like a cat watching a mouse's hole until an aging man appeared. His garments were sumptuous, but his face was coarse from indulgent living.

So this was the master of the famous Assassins, Marta thought, biting her lip in fascination. Halimah's father, the Old Man of the Mountain whose men were so famously devoted to him, it was said they would cast themselves to their deaths at their lord's merest gesture.

"Whatever token you may have received from the Frankish queen," Khalil said without preamble, "you must not answer it. Saladin is our ally, and the time has not yet come to remove him."

"I'm perfectly aware of that, al-Aziz," the Old Man said. "But Saladin is not the only one who holds my pledge, and this one was given to the Franks long ago, before Saladin was the thorn in my paw. I would not have it said my promises went for naught."

"The politic ruler knows when to delay the fulfilment of old promises when a new loyalty becomes more pressing," Khalil said, smoothly.

The Old Man shrugged. "What should I do, then? Shall I have the messenger knifed and repossess the token?"

Khalil considered this a while. "No," he said at length. "Return the token. There's a newcomer among the Franks, one who seems ready to consider himself a king. If the Franks quarrel among themselves, their queen may wish to have the ring redeemed on behalf of one of her own co-religionists. Best not to discourage her."

He closed and latched the shutters. Marta braced herself as Khalil sank gracefully onto the cushions opposite her at the table: her heart began to race, but she forced herself to breathe slowly.

Khalil said, as he often did after conducting his business in her presence, "What do you think?"

She dug her fingernails into her palms and said: "You're lying to the sultan. Rashid al-Din is your father-in-law and you told him you had no dealings with him."

"Very good," Khalil said with the gall to sound both surprised and pleased. "You've been interrogating my other wives."

She had befriended them, not interrogated them. What else did Khalil think they found to do with their time, imprisoned as they were? But she was not here to talk about herself; she was here to talk about Khalil. She glanced up at him. "What would Saladin think of you if he discovered the truth?"

"He'd call it treachery." Khalil broke a piece of crisp, fresh bread and dipped it into spiced oil, using his left hand to hold back his sleeve of black silk as he did so. Marta recognised the weaving as her own work—one of the bolts of cloth that had been stolen from Nablus during the occupation two years ago. He wore it like a trophy. "Saladin believes I brokered a peace between himself and the Old Man. He doesn't know that both the peace, and the assassination attempts that came before it, were at my command. Now he believes he owes the security of his empire to me."

"Whom do you really serve, then?"

"Myself. I have not built this great empire for *Saladin*."

"So when the time comes, you'll snap your fingers, and an Assassin will cut the sultan's throat." Marta did not trouble to disguise the scorn in her voice.

Khalil only smiled. "Close, but not quite. A hundred Assassins will cut the throats of the sultan's entire clan, and then I will be sultan."

Marta swallowed hard. "Why are you telling me all this?"

"Because I want you to know me as I know you."

And because, she added silently, for all his talk of making her his lady, he never meant to let her escape this house alive. Perhaps he could tell from the look on her face what she was thinking; perhaps that was what made him smile again.

"I gave you a ring, and you refused it. I gave you the head of your enemy, and you hissed at me like a wildcat. Tell me, Marta Bessarion, what gift will you accept from me? What *do* you want?"

Why did he want, not merely her captivity, but her consent?

"From you?" She shivered. "Nothing but my freedom and my lance." *And your head on the point of it.*

"Freedom is a bargain I make with all my wives, in time."

"You mean, you turn them out when they're old and weak and have no sons to care for them," Marta said hotly. "I want better than that."

His eyes sparked. "Shall I give you a son, then?"

Marta went absolutely stiff and cold. From a long distance she heard herself say, "He would not be *my* son."

Khalil frowned. "Of course he would be your son. You would have given birth to him."

And he would never let her have any other claim on the child. Marta closed her eyes. Perhaps Khalil was simply like other powerful men she had known. Even the Leper King had not, at first, understood that a man could not demand both to be feared as a master, and loved as an equal. "I don't want your son."

"What then? Should I make you immortal, as I am? I have done that for no other woman." A pause. "Except for Rabia, who made me believe she loved me. But then she ran away with one of my slaves, so that I was forced to repossess the gift of her life."

Marta remembered her dream, the beating, the sword piercing two hearts in the same moment. Part of her wanted to scream, but part was sufficiently far away to hear the words and reply calmly. "You found a way to kill her, even though she was immortal?"

"I don't want to speak of her," Khalil said with a dismissive flick of the fingers. "What do you say to immortality?"

It was merely another bribe, worse than the others. If Khalil made her immortal, he could rule her forever. She would lose even the hope of being cast off like the other wives. Marta said, "If it can be taken away at any moment, it isn't immortality." *And if it can be taken away, then you are not so safe as you think.*

"Then there's nothing I can give you." Khalil frowned. "Certainly not the Lance. That is *mine.*"

"It's my father's," Marta blurted: she had strangled so many things behind her teeth that she could not help letting this one slip.

"On the contrary," Khalil said, amused. "It is very much my own. Who do you think created it?"

Marta had nothing to say to that. She had first seen the Bessarion Lance when her father brought it home after the great battle at Yarmouk—a battle she shuddered to think of, for she knew now what kinds of battles lose kingdoms. "If you had created a lance that made you invincible, then how did you come to lose it?"

"How did *you* come to lose it? By treachery, of course. Why else should I have hunted your family for centuries?" At the look on her face, he laughed. "You don't believe me? Come."

Khalil got to his feet and beckoned her into the loggia. "The stars are right," he said. "By luck, it might even be the very day." He pulled her after him, down the stairs and into the courtyard with its orange-tree. The door set beneath the stairs was the same through which they had come from the sultan's camp. Khalil set his palm against it and turned to Marta.

"I built this house with stone quarried from the battlefield, so that I could always return there. Open the path, Ibrahim."

The door rattled softly against its hinges as though a distant wind was shaking it. Khalil seized the latch and threw it open, drawing Marta behind him into the hustle and bustle of a Saracen camp at night. Dawn must not be far off, as it was in the house at Damascus, but the most Marta could gather of the place was that it must be somewhere on an arid, windy plateau, with dust and dead grass everywhere underfoot. The camp was a rough-and-ready affair with tents of goatskin leather. Women, unveiled and weathered, were cooking at the campfires, balancing children on their hips. Men ate or performed their prayers, their mail glinting beneath voluminous robes, their pointed helmets swathed in a loose, turban-like headdress. Marta flinched as someone strode towards them carrying a great round shield. She expected to be tossed aside by it, but instead it passed through her as though she was a ghost.

"It's only a memory," Khalil told her. "We are not truly here. Look. Here comes your father now."

He pointed at two figures, a man and a woman, hurrying from the lower ground towards what the stars told her was the south. The woman was in vigorous middle age, with greying hair and weathered skin; but her tunic was a vivid shade of green that instantly reminded Marta of the colossal woman in her dream. Yet it was the man who interested her most.

"That's not my father," she said, when he was near enough to make out the man's muffling robes and headdress. She remembered him as a great tall man with a close-cropped silvery beard and immaculate robes of bleached wool. This stranger was of no particularly imposing stature, and what could be seen of his face and hands beneath his robes was filthy; he skulked behind the woman with his eyes fixed on the ground.

Khalil said nothing, but his smile was grim.

Outside one of the tents, the woman signalled the stranger to halt. He waited, his bloodshot eyes flickering watchfully about the camp, until the woman beckoned him to enter.

"He's gone," the woman said with evident relief. "Morning council is the only time of day he's parted from it."

The stranger nodded curtly and moved into the tent. "Where is it?" he asked, pushing back the hood he wore. Lamplight fell across his face.

Marta's heart stopped. *"Abba?"*

It *was* her father. The abyss of time was bridged in a moment: once again she was a child, and here was a world of love and safety. Marta reached out to touch him, but like a nightmare, her fingers went through him like smoke.

"Here beneath the carpet," said the woman, rolling back the heavy, well-worn mat covering the ground. Near the bed a shallow groove had been cut into the hard-packed earth, and her father fell to his knee with an exclamation of satisfaction, lifting out a familiar oiled haft and ripple-patterned blade.

Hundreds of years and battles later, the Bessarion Lance still looked as pristine now as it had then. Not a speck of rust marred its blade; not a splinter had come away from its haft. Her father touched it lovingly, and the look on his face told Marta that beyond a doubt that he knew what it could do.

He turned to the woman. "I owe you endless thanks for this."

She looked up at him, almost pleading. "You'll do as you promised?"

His nod was little more than a tuck of the chin. "You haven't told me your name."

"Soraya."

"Then, Soraya, you can trust in me. As soon as this fight is done, I'll fulfil my vow."

He had looked at Marta the same way when he promised he would come home alive from the battle. She had believed him then; of course this Soraya believed him now.

Soraya released the haft. "There's one more thing you must know, Greek. The moment the spear leaves the tent, in the hands of anyone other than the master, I must fly and tell him at once. Do you understand?"

"Yes."

"I'm not sure you do," she murmured. "You will have less time than you think. The moment you leave the tent, you will be hunted. I cannot shield you from that."

Khalil spoke in a low growl. "I will have my revenge for that, too."

Of course, the woman in the memory did not hear him. "Do not look back. Do not turn aside. Do not stop until he is dead. *Now go.*"

John Bessarion hurried out of the tent, into the darkness. A sound of distress escaped Marta's throat, but there was no point in following him.

For a moment Soraya remained in the tent, her jaw locked, sweat beading on her temples. After a moment, involuntarily, one foot inched forward, then another. Then, like an automaton, she marched out into the camp.

Almost at once a commotion started. In the distance the memory of Khalil's own voice began shouting, something about thieves and spies.

"You see," the present Khalil said to Marta, "how many of my women have betrayed me."

How strange, she thought, *that the one thing all of them should have in common is you.* He seized her hand and they went out again into the breaking dawn. The camp was in an uproar, the memory of Khalil striding towards the tent with Soraya at his side. He had his grip on her, too. At the door of the tent he looked in, saw the upturned carpet, and turned on the woman.

"Who was it? Answer me!"

"I don't know. It was a Greek."

"And his name?"

"I told you I don't know."

"How much does he know?"

"I—I told him—where to find the Lance." Again, she seemed to be battling some unseen compulsion. But if her lips betrayed her, her hands did not: even as the words struggled out, she snatched the knife from her master's belt and slashed it across her own throat. There was a little spray of blood, but it quickly became dust drifting in the air.

The memory of Khalil shouted, grabbing for the knife a moment too late. It was as though Soraya turned first to stone, then to dust, and then to a cloud drifting in the wind. Marta's surprise squeaked in her throat as Soraya crumbled through her master's hands, leaving him staring, stricken, into the air.

"That was the master-stroke," the present Khalil said into Marta's ear.

"After that, the slave was gone and of course there was no catching the thief."

Abruptly the vision faded. Marta blinked. She and Khalil stood in the courtyard of the Damascus house, beneath the orange tree, just about dawn.

Thief, she thought desolately. Where had she *thought* the Bessarion Lance came from? It was magic; Marta had always known that. She had never quite believed that it was holy and blessed, so of course it must be tainted. Of course it was Khalil's. Of course a slave woman had bled to get it away from him. Did her father know what great price had been paid for his lance?

"How now, are you weeping?" Khalil asked, half mocking.

This was a part of the game he played with her—a reminder that he planned to break her spirit and meant to keep on until he succeeded. "Not for you," Marta said fiercely, dry-eyed. "Did she die, then?"

"The slave? No. It takes more than that to destroy one of her kind."

"And what kind would that be?" Marta demanded, but he had already lost interest in her.

"The sun is rising, and look at you," he declared, seeming for the first time to notice that she wore neither shoes nor veil. "Back to the women's quarters with you; you're not fit to be seen."

* * *

Morning prayer would begin shortly. Marta had been in Damascus for hours, leaving Fayruz to watch and spin alone the whole night long. Snatching fresh clothes from her room, Marta went downstairs to the bathhouse, where the water was cold but fresh and invigorating.

War. Assassins. Khalil's offer of immortality. *I was forced to repossess the gift of her life.*

That meant it could be done, though Khalil had refused to elaborate when she asked him. Instead, he had attempted to distract her with talk of the Bessarion Lance and a demonstration of his power.

If he would not tell her, then she needed to find someone who would: and this time, he *had* let something slip: the name of the djinn of the house.

Clean and clothed, with the murmurs of morning prayer echoing softly above, Marta laid a palm against the window-lattice. The rising sun was a red ball impaled on the rim of the mountains. She closed her eyes.

"Ibrahim," she said. "Open a path."

Nothing.

"Ibrahim, open a window."

Nothing.

"Ibrahim…please…answer me…"

Nothing. The sun shrugged free of the mountains and rose into the sky. Marta's shoulders sank.

When she turned, Fayruz stood at the bath-house door, eyes wide and speechless.

"What do you think you're doing?" she hissed.

Chapter XXXII.

Balian came to Jerusalem like a bird flying on the wings of a storm. When he reined in before the Jaffa Gate, it was closed—the countryside around empty and silent, outlying hospices and monasteries shut up and barricaded.

All Balian had was his sword, five knights of his own household, and a flimsy piece of paper bearing Saladin's guarantee of safe-conduct. It felt like running through thorns naked, as he had commented uneasily to Conrad of Montferrat, in Tyre, before setting out.

"You should be used to it by now," Montferrat had taunted.

Balian had only shrugged. "You find us in times fit for songs and legends, my lord."

Not that Montferrat had not shown himself more than equal to them. When he had returned Saladin's banner to the Saracens—in pieces, tossed into the dry moat outside the city's walls—the sultan had sent for Montferrat's father, and had paraded the old marquis outside the city walls, promising his freedom in return for the city. But by that time, young Montferrat had been given the best possible incentive to defend Tyre, and that was Tyre herself.

Even faced with his father, Montferrat had stood firm. "Tyre is mine. And I will not give even the smallest stone of this city for a man so old and worthless."

Balian had been a little shocked, for by law, a son who refused to ransom his father or mother was to be stripped of his inheritance. Yet the old marquis had laughed.

"That's my boy." His words had carried quite clearly to the battlements. "A cold-blooded bastard, like his old man. I could have told you it was no use."

Saladin must have made some signal, for an archer among his men laid an arrow to the string and stood ready to draw at the old marquis. "There is no reason for both of you to die together."

At that, Montferrat snatched a crossbow from a sergeant standing near him, levelled it at his father and pulled the trigger so that the bolt skidded into the dirt at his feet. "Devil take it," he bawled. "I missed. Give me another."

The Saracens seized their prisoner and fled back into their camp, while Saladin hastily withdrew, shaking his head in disbelief. Montferrat had turned from the wall and laughed until the tears ran down his face.

"You called his bluff," Balian said in wonder.

"The marquis of Montferrat is too valuable a prisoner to kill. I wonder what the old carpet-seller will do now?" Montferrat crowed, leading the way down into the street. Balian knew he ought to reprove the count for referring to a man of Saladin's nobility and wisdom as an old carpet-seller, but there was something intoxicating in Montferrat's contempt for the man.

The sultan had mustered his men and continued south, past devastated Jaffa to Ascalon. The second largest city in the kingdom after Acre, with formidable defences, Ascalon was the strategic key to the entire southern half of the kingdom. Balian understood why Queen Sibylla should choose the city to stage her own final stand, but if Saladin should batter or bargain his way in at those gates, it was certain he would then turn his attention to the greatest prize of all: Jerusalem, where Maria and the children waited.

There was only one way to get them to safety. Leaving them there was unthinkable: other cities might surrender in peace, but Jerusalem was sacred and her bloody conquest, ninety years before, had rankled in the Saracens' memory. If she fell by storm, the aftermath would be equally bloody.

Balian sent to Saladin, asking for a safe-conduct to fetch his wife and children from the city. And the sultan had been gracious. Balian could take only a small escort, and he could spend no more than a single night within the city, but he could travel from Ascalon to Jerusalem and back again with his wife, children, servants, and property.

"I'd never do that for a woman," Montferrat commented. "This Greek princess has the whip-hand of you, my friend."

Montferrat had been offered a Greek princess of his own—Theodora, the sister of the present emperor—but had abandoned her in Constantinople when her dowry proved inadequate.

Balian smiled at his wine glass. "You sound like my brother. I don't think he's ever really loved a woman. Have you?"

"Yes, but I outgrew it."

"What happened to her?"

A yawn. "She married the baker."

Balian snorted. "A burgess' daughter?"

"I was young, and she was pretty." Montferrat gave a shrug. "She had the whip-hand of me, too. But I was a boy, then. It was nothing."

"Or maybe it was something, and every man who truly loves gives his lady the whip-hand. Mankind certainly got the whip-hand of Christ, and she was none too gentle on him, they say."

"You're a devout man, to take *that* example," Montferrat said, with a startled laugh.

"In these times you have to be, my lord."

Now, days later, Balian halted at the east gate of Jerusalem with a sigh of relief. A ship had carried him from Tyre to Ascalon, but the overland journey from the queen's city to Jerusalem had taken him through land that had once belonged to him and his family—Ibelin, Ramla, Mirabel— land now empty and desolate, abandoned by many of its inhabitants and roamed by the enemy.

Ernoul hailed the gatehouse, a massive stone fortification which formed a northern outcrop of the Tower of David, Jerusalem's ancient citadel. He had only to give Balian's name to bring the gate's dejected keepers to life.

"It *is* him, God be praised! Fetch the Patriarch! Tell the viscount! God takes pity on us!"

Balian's heart sank and he turned to his men—Ernoul, Matthew and Samuel Arrabi, Ranier of Nablus, and Thomas Patrick. "No loose chatter about our errand," he warned. They were doubly sworn not to remain in Jerusalem: in Ascalon, Queen Sibylla had urged him to return quickly, to join in the defence of that city. He could not be everywhere at once.

The gate opened.

Balian was a defeated knight, coming with a tiny retinue by the grace of an apparently omnipotent invader. As he entered the city, however, the people flocked into the streets to give him a conqueror's welcome: wealthy Syrian burgesses fretful for their homes and livelihoods; Italian merchants trapped away from their native seaports by Saladin's patrols; peasants who had fled their neighbouring villages to the safety of the city walls; the priests and nuns of every sect, from Maronites to Premonstratensians; pilgrims from the uttermost parts of the earth, who in better years would already be taking ship in the autumn sailing. Beggars, bakers, alewives, and shepherds flocked into the narrow, honey-coloured streets until his horse could barely make headway, calling his name and pelting him with flowers. Nevertheless, in all that crowd Balian saw no soldiers, no knights, and precious few men of fighting age. Those had all marched away to Hattin.

His heart plunged, but he fastened a smile onto his face and nodded graciously as he forged his way down the David Street towards the Ibelin house where Maria, he was sure, must be waiting for him. The crowd, seeing his direction, received entirely the wrong idea.

"To the Patriarch! To the Patriarch!" they chanted, and when they reached the Street of the Patriarch opposite the church of St James the Martyr, instead of allowing him to proceed towards the Temple Street house, they swept him up towards the Holy Sepulchre and the patriarchate beside it. Balian allowed the tide to take him, only looking back from time to time to make sure his men were still about him. Soon enough they were carried up the steps and deposited at the gate of the patriarchate on the Street of the Sepulchre where, to Balian's amazement, he found Eraclius waiting for him on the steps with tears in his eyes and outstretched arms.

"My son," he said.

Somehow, that made it all seem less like a dream and more like reality. Balian had little enough reason to like the silver-tongued, worldly old patriarch, but at the sight of Eraclius' face he felt his own crumple. He fell into the old priest's arms and embraced him like one of his own brothers.

* * *

"Tomorrow?" The Patriarch was aghast. "You're leaving *tomorrow?*"

In the Patriarch's cabinet, Balian fidgeted with his cup of wine, unwilling to sit or drink when he had such a blow to deal the old man. "I am sorry, truly. Before I was permitted to come here, I had to go to Saladin and swear on the Gospels that I would travel with only a small escort and stay no longer than one night in the city."

Eraclius looked haunted. "Once he has taken Ascalon, Saladin will come for Jerusalem. There is no one in the city capable of organising a defence. If you leave us, you take our last hope with you."

Balian shifted uncomfortably. "I swore."

"To Saladin, a conqueror. That cannot bind you. I'll absolve you."

"I knew what I was getting myself into," Balian said, although he had not for a moment imagined just how difficult it would be. "Besides, you need more than a commander. How many knights are there in the city?"

The Patriarch shook his head. "Two, maybe three. The king stripped the garrison bare before he went away."

No survivors had returned to the city from the battle, then. Most must have gathered at Tyre or Ascalon, the two centres of resistance. Balian felt almost sick to think that the greatest army ever fielded by the kingdom had been thus squandered. Patriarch Eraclius, who had crowned Queen Sibylla and her husband in the first place, must bear at least some of the blame for that.

He folded his arms. "You expect me to defend this place with seven or eight knights?" Even with Marta Bessarion as one of them, it was hardly possible.

"Someone must!" The Patriarch scrubbed a hand down his face, so that for a moment every line stretched and sagged. When he reappeared, he said tiredly, "Have you seen your wife yet?"

Balian shook his head. "I came only to conduct her and her household to Ascalon, my lord."

"So, she will go to safety, leaving the rest of us in danger."

"Safety," Balian spat, and suddenly his temper had frayed to pieces. He slammed his hands on the table. "Safety! You think a fifty-mile journey through Saracen-infested country is *safety?*"

The Patriarch lifted tired eyes. "And yet you expose your wife to it, sooner than leave her with us?"

Balian had no answer for that. He felt his shoulders slump; at last, he backed away and went to the window, looking into a cramped little courtyard where some of the Augustinian canons of the Sepulchre had gathered in their plain black cassocks, murmuring amongst themselves and sending anxious glances towards the very room in which he stood.

"No matter what I do," Balian said heavily, "the holy places will be trampled, and some of these people will die. If I leave, Saladin will besiege them, and they will die or go into captivity. If I stay, I am only one man. He will still besiege us and we will still die or go into captivity. The one difference is that, if I remain, I will subject my wife and children to the same fate, and forswear myself, and be remembered to all ages as the man who lost Jerusalem."

"What difference can one man make?" the Patriarch whispered. "That was what I asked myself when she crowned Guy of Lusignan."

Balian stared at the Patriarch, unsure of what he had heard.

But Eraclius only looked up at him and said, "Go find your wife." He ushered Balian outside into the courtyard, and when the crowd in the street began to call Balian's name, held up his hand for silence.

"Tell them, Lord Balian, what you have told me."

Balian wished he did not have to do it like this, but he had been a coward long enough. "Good people," he said in a scratchy voice that he scarcely recognised as his own, "I cannot stay with you. I have sworn an oath to remain no more than a single night in the city."

Complete silence greeted his words, then muttering as those who had heard him passed the news on to those standing further off, who might not have heard. Balian beckoned his men and ventured into the street again. All the way to Temple Street he felt their reproachful silence on him like a burden: it was as though he had come to the Patriarchate in a bridal procession and was leaving it for a burial.

He expected to find that word of his arrival had made its way to the house in Temple Street ahead of him. Instead, the porter at the gate paled as though he had seen a ghost. Inside the courtyard, someone shrieked, "Lord Balian!" and set a little dog barking wildly. Isabella hurled herself down the stairs from the loggia and threw her arms around him, sniffling wetly into his neck.

"You've come for us," she sobbed, and then pulled away from him, scanning his weary knights. She blinked two or three times and then said, "Wait—where's Marta? Didn't she come with you from Tyre?"

Balian's heart turned to ice as he inspected the house, as though despite Isabella's words, he might still catch Marta Bessarion peeping out shyly from behind a door or a potted lemon-tree. Instead, Queen Maria leaned from the loggia, a hand to her mouth, her eyes shimmering with gladness. The children and their nurse, the servants, the few sergeants he had left behind in Nablus to guard his family all spilled into the courtyard to welcome him. None were the fosterling he had hoped to see, and suddenly the moment of homecoming was hollow indeed.

"Is Marta not here?" His lips were numb as he spoke the words. "I sent her *here*."

No one answered.

* * *

Balian did not tell his wife what the Patriarch had asked of him until he woke in the night to find her curled against him, staring towards the window with wide-awake eyes.

"They want you to stay and help them," said Queen Maria.

Her words fell into the silence between them and hung there. Balian shifted himself a little higher on the pillows to put his arm around her.

"How did you know?"

She sighed. "It happened while you were going through the house marking things to take. A messenger arrived from the Patriarch to say that the people had gone to him and begged him to make you stay. There was talk of sealing the gates to hold you in the city against your will."

"And?"

"What do you mean, *and?*" She had been tracing meditative circles on his chest with her fingers. Now she smacked him lightly with the palm of her hand. "You know what I mean. Do you intend to stay?"

"Uff! Do you want me to stay?"

She let her head fall back onto his shoulder. "No," she said in a muffled voice. "I want you to take me and the children away before something terrible happens. That's what I want."

This morning, it had been possible to imagine going away and leaving Jerusalem to get on without him, because after all Marta Bessarion would surely be here, and would surely refuse to leave the city, with her enchanted spear that could never be defeated in battle. But Marta Bessarion was not here. On the first day of the battle, somewhere between Sephoria and Nablus, she and the Lance had disappeared like a dream in the night.

"She rode to the battle," Queen Maria had said when they realised she was missing. "She rode to the battle and something terrible has happened to her."

Balian could not bring himself to believe it. Surely Marta could not have been defeated—not with the Lance. If the White Watcher had been at the battle, he would doubtless have noticed. No—likely Miles of Plancy had got himself captured, like the young fool he was and, like another, Marta had ridden off to Damascus to rescue him. In time she would return; she always had before.

The alternative was that she had vanished as suddenly as she had once appeared in his life—that she had gone back to whatever place she had originated from, taking the Bessarion Lance with her. That would be a catastrophe, but a fitting one, since God no longer smiled on them.

Balian did not know what to think, but he was certain that if somewhere in the world Marta was alive, she would return.

Meanwhile, here was Jerusalem with all its people, looking to him for help. "You'd have me let the people and the city of Christ shift for themselves?"

"I have been their queen. I suppose I should care for them," Maria acknowledged. "But they chose Sibylla. They never cared for me." She patted his chest. "What does your own heart tell you?"

He watched the darkness. "I made an oath to Saladin, of which the Patriarch offered to absolve me. What do you think?"

"*Can* an oath bind a man if it was made to an enemy? To an unbeliever?" Maria shook her head. "Sometimes I miss my own people. We Greeks have never been so nice on such matters."

His scruples withered. After all, he had promised himself he would allow nothing to stand in the way of his service to his people. If he could not break an oath on the personal authority of the Patriarch of Jerusalem, on whose authority *could* he do it?

"The Patriarch said something strange to me, Maria. When I asked him what one man could do, he said he asked himself the same question concerning Guy's kingship. That he thought one man could make little difference to the kingdom."

"Ha!" she said, stiffening in the crook of his arm. Beyond the thin partition that screened their bed from the rest of the room, their personal servants snorted and shifted and moved.

"Hush," he begged her. But she turned over, pushing herself up onto her elbows so that she could look directly into his eyes.

"How dare he?" she hissed. "What he means is that now King Guy has single-handedly destroyed the kingdom, he expects *you* single-handedly to save it. What a nerve! And he'll blame you, too, no doubt, should you fail. Never mind that it's easier to destroy a thing than it is to preserve it."

He smoothed back the fall of hair tickling his chest, smiling. "It's the closest thing we'll ever get to an apology, I think."

She stilled. He felt the warmth of her breath as she let out a puff of understanding. "You *want* to stay. Balian…"

"Maybe I can't do anything, Maria. But I promised myself I would stop at nothing for the sake of the kingdom. How can I refuse when I'm all they have left?" It was too dark to read her expression, so when Balian spoke again it was uncertainly. "Don't be afraid."

As always, Maria hated being thought a coward. "Not for myself. For the children. For you, serving yourself up to Saladin an oath breaker and rebel."

"Saladin will understand. He'll release me. It isn't as though I can make any difference. Maybe he'll still let me send you and the children to Ascalon." He did not mention that Queen Sibylla still expected him to join her own defence. It mattered nothing to him, and it would matter less to Maria.

"We can't count on that," she said in a tiny stiff voice.

"Then tell me to take you away from here, and I'll do it."

From her silence, he knew she was tempted. Balian drew breath to tell her he yielded, but she heard it and spoke first.

"How could I hold up my head if I knew I had forced you to turn your back on your duty?" She leaned down and kissed him. There was salt on her face. He got his arm around her waist and crushed her close.

Life was so fragile these days. Peace, so fleeting. And love, so agonisingly precious.

Chapter XXXIII.

"What do you think you're *doing?*" Fayruz's whisper cut like a knife through the stillness of the bathhouse.

Marta's heart raced as the other woman came closer.

"You didn't come last night," Fayruz accused. "I thought you were helping me save my child."

"I couldn't," Marta explained, weak with relief that Fayruz had not caught her trying to wake the house. "I was in Damascus all night. It was already dawn when I came back."

"Al-Aziz had you all night?" Fayruz looked exhausted, her eyes bloodshot with lack of sleep, but they narrowed on her suspiciously. She barely heard Marta's protests. "As long as I'm in this condition, I'll stay out of his sight, and he'll favour you. But don't get comfortable."

Comfortable? With her enemy?

"When all this is over," Fayruz said softly, "you will leave al-Aziz to me. *I* will be his favourite, as I was before you came."

Marta had no intention of leaving Khalil alive at all if she could help it—surely Fayruz knew that. Did the woman think to save him? "You value the favours of a man who will cast you off when he tires of you?"

Her hand fluttered towards her belly. *"Yes.* What else do I have?"

At first Marta felt only pity. Fayruz had made a terrible gamble to secure her own future. *If* Khalil forgave her for bringing her child to birth, and *if* the child was a boy, and *if* Khalil acknowledged his son, then she would be somebody's mother.

Fayruz said, "If you ever feel tempted to supplant me, know that I will tell al-Aziz you're trying to seduce his djinn."

Marta stared. "His djinn?"

"Ibrahim, the slave of the house." Fayruz lifted a sardonic eyebrow. "Where did you *think* the magic came from? But it won't help: the djinn won't obey just anyone."

She had, after all, been caught. "I'm not trying to seduce him. I only want to talk to him."

"To a man like Khalil, there's no difference. Why risk it?"

Marta tipped her head back, looking to the domed roof above them with its many round perforations, now admitting the pale light of morning, so that the whole room lit up in soft pink and gold. "Because we're alike, Ibrahim and I," she told the house. "Because we're both slaves."

She hoped—oh, she hoped—that the djinn could hear what she did not say: *maybe the two of us can help each other.*

Abruptly, Fayruz screamed.

Marta turned back to her just in time to see the other woman recoil as a pale flicker vanished into the shadows behind one of the bathhouse's pillars. "What is it?"

"A white snake," Fayruz said. She was about to say something more, but cut herself off with a shudder. "You don't know what you've done."

Marta had seen a white snake twice now: once at the house of Nablus and again in her dreams, coiled at the base of the glowing orange-tree. She brushed past Fayruz and stepped cautiously around the pillar, searching the shadows for the creature. There were wooden benches pushed against the wall, and baskets beneath them with a litter of ointments and combs, razors and sugaring-cloths, perfumes and soaps—everything eight women might require to wash, groom, and anoint themselves.

Before Marta could move the baskets to see behind them, Fayruz seized her wrist. "Stop," she said in a choking voice. "Don't you understand? If you go where you shouldn't, you'll bring disaster on all of us. Khalil will hold *all* of us responsible."

In that at least, Fayruz was correct: if Marta managed to slip from Khalil's grasp—whether by a plunge down the cliffs from the window, as had nearly happened in her first week, or by subverting his servants as Rabia had done—then Khalil would undoubtedly seek a scapegoat in the women's quarters. She must be careful, or all her efforts to save the baby would come to nothing.

Marta said no more about it, but allowed Fayruz to lead her upstairs. Worn out by all that had happened, she spent most of that day in a broken sleep, plagued by bad dreams. The day after, she asked Arwa to teach her how to read in the Arabic language, and Halimah to tell her what she knew of the Assassins.

"There are many foolish stories about my people," Halimah said, scoffing. "It is not true that my father buys the loyalty of his followers with pleasure gardens and hashish."

"But your people *are* very loyal," Marta hazarded a guess. "They'd have to be, to do what they do."

"My people are considered heretics by everyone," Halimah said, throwing a peculiarly distrustful look at Arwa, who pursed her lips. "We do what we must to survive. My father's partisans must be able to live a false life for years at a time, to serve foreign lords, and then to slaughter them without hesitation should they become a threat."

"No wonder Khalil wants them in his pocket."

"He won't get them," Halimah said with a flash of obstinacy. "We follow the commands of the Hidden Imam, who lives in secret until the day of his revelation. The Assassins will never bow to another, except for a time, as it suits us."

"How," Marta inquired, "does the Hidden Imam transmit his commands?"

"Through my father, who is the only one who knows his identity and hiding place."

Fayruz, dozing on the divan, cracked open her eye and said, "Ha! A likely story."

Halimah flushed. Arwa put down her pen and said, "Fayruz has a point. If only the Old Man has access to your Hidden Imam, then your Imam is not really the Imam. The Old Man is, since he can pass off his own whims as the will of God."

Marta herself was inclined to think that Khalil ibn Hassan himself was, or had supplanted, the Hidden Imam. Yet as Arwa and Halimah descended into outright quarrelling, Marta began to doubt it. Khalil would never be satisfied with ruling as the Hidden Imam, sharing even nominal power with the Old Man.

"Then what *is* Khalil's relation to them?" she asked the room at large. No one answered. Arwa was in the middle of an elaborate argument, proving that although it was a sin to call a fellow Muslim a heretic, the Assassins were undeniably murderous lunatics whose beliefs were not aligned with the sunna. Halimah kept interrupting, and Fayruz had got up and gone into her room in an attempt to find some quiet.

The answer came that night, after she fell asleep.

As usual, her dreams began with the woman in green silk. Circling the woman, Marta caught a glimpse of her sleeping face. It was young and lovely. For some reason—perhaps the distinctive, vivid green of her tunic—Marta had expected to see Soraya, the ugly, weathered woman who had helped her father take the Bessarion Lance.

Or perhaps she should call it the ibn-Hassan Lance?

That thought was like a heat rash beneath her armour—as galling as the thought that one of the Watchers might have ordered the murder of Miles' father. She did not want to think of her father's lance as having anything to do with Khalil, nor his demons.

It would not bother Persi, who after all had never had a very high opinion of the Lance. *Not every problem can be solved with a lance,* she would have said. Still, Marta would never think of her father as a common thief. John Bessarion had done no wrong in taking the Lance, on that she would stake her honour. Those who abused their power did not deserve to have it, and Marta thought the slave-woman Soraya, who had sacrificed herself to put the weapon beyond Khalil's reach, would agree with her. Yet she would never be able to forget that the Lance was Khalil's creation.

All the sweeter, when I use it to kill him.

As before, a door closed on the low hall where the great woman in the green tunic lay. Marta turned to find herself in the courtyard of the

Damascus house. In her dream it was nearly sunset and Khalil was crossing the courtyard beneath the glowing orange-tree with a stone ashlar balanced on his shoulder. The hairy man and the feathered woman—Qeteb and Lilith—followed him, each of them dressed for war with quivers at their thighs and bows in their hands. Qeteb's cuirass had an eye-shaped opening in the centre, with a perforated lattice across it. Marta followed, her heart beating fast for fear of discovery. She could not work anti-magic in her sleep.

Khalil went directly to the door that had, on a former occasion, led her out into the great castle in the mountains. This evening the door stood open, allowing Marta a glimpse of a passageway beyond. At the end of the passageway a low doorway led into a well-lit room full of voices, the clanking of dishes and the chopping of knives—it was the kitchen, for which she had been searching.

Khalil was not interested in the servants. He halted outside the passageway, where a section of the stone threshold had been cut out, the shattered remnants lying in a pile of white stone dust to one side of the door. Now, Khalil lifted the stone he carried on his shoulder, checked the intricate words that had been carved into its sides, and fitted it carefully into the hollowed threshold.

Smoothing his hand over the stone, he muttered some words. The house shivered a little when he was done. When he stood, Marta could scarcely have told that a piece of the threshold had been replaced.

Khalil closed the door, opened it again, and stepped out onto the terrace of the mountain castle.

Qeteb, Lilith and, last of all, Marta, followed him out of a small door in an outbuilding and crossed the terrace towards the keep, a massive honey-coloured structure flanked by four great towers and approached by a double staircase. In the left-hand doorway, a sleepy guard startled and challenged the intruder.

"Take me to see the Old Man of the Mountain," Khalil said to the guard. He held out his hands, showing that he was unarmed and, so far as mortal eyes could tell, completely alone. "I've come as an ambassador from

Saladin."

Mystified, the Assassin led Khalil into the dim keep. Their path twisted and turned on itself through a dark vestibule, past a dripping cistern, into first one and then another long, vaulted hall. This was a place built for defence, not for comfort, lined with loopholes that denied the enemy a clear approach and provided the defence with everything they might need for barricade or ambush. Masyaf, Marta judged, was the definition of impregnable.

An ancient cross had been carved into the stone at one end of one of the halls and Marta realised, with a sting of surprise, that the castle must have been built by her own people for the Roman emperor.

Khalil was told to wait in a great echoing hall lit by high slitted windows. A cushioned and canopied divan stood towards the north wall: the Old Man's seat of judgement. Left alone with his familiars, Khalil went to the divan and sat upon it, strumming his fingers gently upon his knees as he waited for the Old Man to arrive.

Presently, a crowd of men burst into the hall, all of them armed with swords and knives. Marta knew then that she was seeing a memory, for the Old Man at their head was clearly ten years younger, fewer lines in his skin and less silver in his beard.

He came to a complete halt when he saw Khalil sitting on his throne.

"Who are you?" the Old Man of the Mountain challenged, "and how did you get into my palace?"

"All you need know of me, Rashid al-Din Sinan," Khalil said, "is that I have had the means of entry for a very long time. Until now, you never made yourself troublesome enough to merit my attention."

Reaching into the purse he carried at his side, Khalil extracted a knife with a distinctive pattern on its blade. Marta had once seen one like it, in the streets of Acre, when she and Persi had been attacked by the Assassin planted in Sibylla's household. Now, Khalil threw the weapon on the ground between himself and Sinan, followed by—of all things—two cakes of bread.

"These things appeared last night in the tent of the sultan Saladin." Khalil leaned forward, lacing his fingers together across his knees. "You *dared* to threaten one of my servants."

Sinan's face barely flickered at Khalil's claimed mastery of the sultan. "He dared to lay siege to my city," the Old Man stated. He clicked his fingers to the men around him. "Tonight, he'll find your head on his pillow."

Five of his men stepped forward. Khalil lifted a lazy finger, and Qeteb and Lilith responded with a quick-fire volley of arrows. What happened next was horrible, even to Marta who had seen more than one battlefield. Struck by unseen darts, the five Assassins faltered and fell to their knees. Their skin reddened, then paled. They began to vomit, to tear at their armour, to gasp for air. Within moments, those who had not died lay moaning on the pavement.

Sinan stared at the devastation wrought, apparently, by one small movement of Khalil's finger. The remaining men of his entourage backed away, nervous. Khalil smiled.

"Let us discuss the matter like men of sense. There's no need to test the loyalty of your men."

"My men would cast themselves from the mountain at my command," Sinan boasted. He turned to the flinching Assassins. "What are you waiting for? *Take him.*"

So it proved: the Assassins charged Khalil in a single mass, but these fared no better than the last. Lilith and Qeteb's bows sang, and one by one the Assassins fell.

"Close the door," Khalil told Lilith, and a wind swept the hall, slamming its door shut, shaking the latch into its groove.

Sinan's face paled as he realised that he was now shut in alone with the sorcerer. He grasped his sword, but did not dare to draw it.

Khalil, in response, rose from the divan. "You asked who I was," he announced. "Think of me as your Hidden One."

"The Hidden One reveals himself *only* to me," Sinan growled. "And you are not he."

"I am the Hidden One now," Khalil repeated gently, "but when you address me, you may call me al-Aziz. From now on you will carry out *my* commands. Obey me, and true power will be yours." He stopped in front of the Old Man, within reach of his sword. "Look pleasant when I speak to you, Sinan. Or should I replace you?"

Sinan refused to look pleasant—indeed Marta doubted it was within his power to do so. Yet he said, "I concede. But I will obey *you*—not the sultan."

"Make what arrangements you like with the sultan," Khalil said with a shrug. "So long as you come to an alliance with him, I will be satisfied."

Khalil brushed past the Old Man, signalling with a wave of his hand for Lilith to open the door again. Marta half expected the dream to relinquish her there, but instead it carried her on Khalil's heels, past nervous Assassins who had witnessed the carnage from the outer hall, back through the twisting passage and across the high terrace to the door with the broken threshold.

Khalil closed the door on Masyaf of the Assassins and stood in the courtyard of his own house with his head bowed in thought.

"The sultan will be awaiting your report," Qeteb said in his harsh, sudden voice.

"I'm aware," Khalil answered, but he did not hurry towards the loggia and his basin. Instead, he said: "Sinan did not lie concerning the loyalty of his men. When the time comes to make myself sultan, I will want such devoted followers."

Lilith sniffed. "Much good they did the Old Man, dying on his floor like that. You want an immortal."

"An immortal is difficult to make and unruly once made," Khalil said, frowning. "I do not know whether I am capable of inspiring such loyalty."

"You have power, and that is equally good," Qeteb said. "You've bound more than one djinn to your will already."

There was silence.

"You should consider it," Lilith urged—clearly this was the continuation of an argument that had been made before. "Just imagine: your very own mamluk, ruthless, immortal, and loyal as an Assassin."

"I've told you a hundred times I'm not interested in creating more djinn."

Khalil said, but he spoke slowly, his eyes far away, as though he saw what Lilith described—and was fascinated by it.

"Lilith's plan was to create a race of them," Qeteb said. "To fill the world with chaos and provoke another cataclysm. But a single djinn, bound and controlled by magic, would scarcely be a threat to the world. Such a puppet might be a greater asset than the Lance ever was."

Khalil stroked his beard. "Neither of you can now take human shape, as you did when you fathered the first races of djinn."

"Of course not," Lilith said. In her excitement, she became less human. Feathers thickened over her body, consuming her lamellar cuirass. Her beaked helm grew curving and sharp. "One of us would need to possess you. After that it would only be a matter of finding the right mother."

Marta woke in a sweat with Lilith's words echoing in her ears. *The right mother.* Her stomach churned, but there was no time to indulge in speculation. It was midnight, and the full moon was at its zenith. Picking up her spindle, she hurried into Fayruz's room.

"Don't forget that if anything happens to this child while I'm asleep," Fayruz said, jabbing a finger towards Marta, "I'll tell al-Aziz what you've been doing with his djinn."

With that she rolled herself in her blanket. Marta did not bother to reply, instead taking her place sitting in the window.

Djinn, she thought with a shiver, remembering Lilith's excitement over the plan to which Qeteb had alluded so flippantly. She did not for a moment believe in a second cataclysm, any more than she had believed in the end of the world when it had been predicted last year by the astrologers. Yet it made Marta shudder to think that there were beings still abroad in the world who had been there before the Flood, corrupting humanity and generating monsters—if that was truly the origin of the djinn they spoke of. Now, though diminished in power, were they still desperately trying to reproduce past victories?

They would be stopped—of that she had no doubt. Yet perhaps it had fallen to her to stop them. Why else should she have been brought here, to the heart of the enemy's power? The house—Ibrahim—had shown her how Khalil planned to build his empire.

Now, smoothing her hand against the window-jamb, she whispered her questions. "Who are you? How do the doors work? How can I stop Khalil? Has he already made his djinn?"

Fayruz lay breathing steadily, unhearing. Marta spoke more softly, her lips nearly brushing the stone.

"If you really want to help me, why can't you let me *out?*"

No answer came that night, and weeks more passed, bringing only fragmentary dreams in answer: visions of Nablus, of Masyaf, of Saladin's camp. Woven in among them was always the woman in the green tunic. Unseen and unnoticed, Marta watched from her dreams as Saladin marched through the kingdom unopposed, reached Ascalon, and laid siege to it. Early in September Lord Balian himself came to the sultan at the head of a delegation of Jerusalemites. There was an eclipse of the sun that day, and he met the sultan in semi-darkness.

"I have summoned you here to show you that I have conquered all the land," Saladin told her foster-father. Lord Balian's hair was going grey and there were new hard lines around his mouth. "Only Jerusalem now withstands me. You would do well to surrender now, while you still may."

"I am commissioned to say that we will never surrender Christ's city," Lord Balian said. "It is the house of God."

"It is the house of God in my religion as well as yours," Saladin told him. "Because of this I would not lay siege against it, nor fill it with blood. It would be more fitting to hand it over peacefully. Here is the bargain I will make with you: I will give you six months' truce. If, after that time, no army has come to relieve you, then you will open your gates to me, and I will have you and all your goods escorted out in peace and taken to the lands of your co-religionists in Tripoli or Antioch or across the sea."

"Our co-religionists would spit in our faces if they found that we had given up Our Lord's sepulchre so readily," Lord Balian said. "We refuse your terms."

He turned away, but the sultan stopped him with a word.

"Then you had best send your wife and children to Tripoli," Saladin said.

"Do it now. There will be no chance later."

Chapter XXXIV.

4 September—two months after the battle

The third time Sibylla caught her ladies whispering nervously about the eclipse and what an evil omen it was, she jammed her needle into the hooped linen she was embroidering and stormed out of her Ascalon house, refusing to let any of them follow her.

Ascalon had no citadel: instead, two massive towers defended the south gate, serving as the closest thing Sibylla had to a keep. She climbed one of them, soon reaching the cupola. Shaded from the sun and open to the sea winds, the tower had once a favourite place from which to survey her county and think. Now it only brought back bitter memories of the day she had made the worst mistake of her life.

Marta Bessarion *and* the girl's lance had been here on this tower, and she had lost them both. So desperate had she been to regain some measure of command over her own fate, she had ordered Guy to lead an attack on the inoffensive Bedouin who had received her brother's permission—and guarantee of safe-conduct—to graze their livestock in the royal demesne of Darum.

Ever since, Lilith had haunted her.

In the half-light of the eclipse, the town stretched away to the north, sprawled at the edge of the sea like mildew. Somewhere to the northeast, in that distant pall of untimely dusk, Saladin was encamped with his army. Even now she could hear, far and faint, the thud of his mangonels battering through her walls as inexorably as they had battered through two lines of outerworks.

Somewhere in that darkness, her envoys were negotiating the city's surrender.

Somewhere in that darkness, Guy—her Guy—was waiting to come back to her.

Sibylla closed her eyes, feeling unutterably weary. Two weeks ago, when the sultan first arrived outside her walls, he had brought Guy out and paraded him before the wall. Guy, blank in the face, had summoned the city to surrender. Sibylla and her commanders had refused out of hand, of course; it was obvious that the king was acting under duress and not of his own volition.

Apparently, when similarly confronted with his own father, Conrad of Montferrat—her brother-in-law by her first marriage to Longsword—had shot at the old man. Sibylla indulged in no such japes. She had not even deigned to show the enemy her face, remaining resolutely in her own house, despite the overwhelming urge to see Guy for herself and ensure to her satisfaction that he was well. It was the only proper thing to do, of course, and she would do it again. But part of her had become tender of late—self-critical. It was doubtless irrational, but a corner of her aching heart whispered that perhaps Guy would have preferred her to shoot at him.

None of it had helped. After two weeks of fierce fighting, of barely sleeping and eating, of meeting with counts and viscounts, making decisions with feverish speed and utter certainty—as though she was not engaged in fighting for an entire kingdom but only riding to a hunt in fair weather across broken ground—the wall of Ascalon was about to be ground to flinders.

If only she could retrieve Guy from captivity, Sibylla would never again meddle in the affairs of the realm. Without her—without Lilith—the kingdom might just have a chance. But Sibylla had not been able even to ransom Guy.

"What more do I need?" Sibylla whispered. She had lost Acre, and now she was losing Ascalon. She had bought time, she had gathered small reinforcements, she had manned the walls with willing commoners, she had even sent the onyx ring to the Assassins, but it had been for naught: the Old Man of the Mountain had returned her token, saying that Saladin was his ally and could not be touched.

"You need *me*," a voice said in reply. There was a rush of wind behind her, and the sound of great claws scratching against the stones, as though an immense bird of prey had settled on the parapet behind her. Sibylla startled. She had tucked a bit of linen into her belt when she stormed out of the house—a band of blackwork to ornament a shirt-collar. Retrieving it with shaking fingers, she went on stitching even though, in the untimely dark, she had to hold the work almost to her nose in order to see it. After a few stitches, she dared a glance over her shoulder.

The cupola was empty: no great bird of prey loomed over her. Although her neck burned, her eyes itchy and blurred from focusing on fine stitches from dawn till well into the night, Sibylla sighed with relief. Constant work was the only way she had found to ward Lilith away from her, to ensure that her thoughts remained her own.

She wondered what would happen when she became too exhausted to work.

It was about Nones when Plancy climbed the tower to report on the success of his meeting with Saladin.

"Did you see the king?" Sibylla asked, not looking up from her work.

"We spoke to King Guy personally," Plancy said, bowing. "He told us that, since the walls were about to fall, it was best to surrender. Unless we do, the sultan will destroy the city and slaughter everyone in it, as was done at Jaffa."

The city had paid brutally for its defiance, yet some of Sibylla's commanders had attempted to argue that Ascalon's wall could be reinforced and the city held. Sibylla suspected Lilith's influence there.

"We also spoke to the sultan," Plancy went on, when Sibylla did not respond. "As one might expect, he wishes to protect his co-religionists in this city from pillage and slaughter. If we surrender, he's willing to offer safe conduct both to the garrison and to any Franks who wish to leave."

"And the king?" If Saladin thought she meant to give up the second greatest city in the kingdom without getting something to show for it, he was very much mistaken.

"Will be released to us." Plancy grimaced. "But not for another year, at least. The sultan said this was because we might have surrendered sooner, but chose not to."

In her outrage, Sibylla forgot her stitching altogether. "He *dares?* What does he think I am, an unruly servant who must be chastised for tardiness?"

Miles looked uncomfortable. "I objected, my lady, but it did no good."

Sibylla covered her face with one hand. All her hopes were pinned upon getting Guy back, and now even that hope was gone. She was too sick, too tired and too bedevilled to rule this kingdom herself. As long as she was alone, she would continue surrendering it piece by piece.

"Really," Lilith said in her ear, "you should let me help you, since no one else will."

She lifted her head and found Lilith in Sibylla's own form perched beside her on the parapet. She had ceased her work, just for a moment, and here was the demon to haunt her again. Suddenly she felt she would rather be damned than work another stitch.

"How is Guy?" she murmured.

Thinking she had spoken to him, Plancy was the first to answer. "Very low in spirits. He begged me to tell you he was sorry."

For what? she thought. All the wrong was Sibylla's doing, not Guy's.

"Oh, he knows full well that he's lost you your kingdom," Lilith said with malice. "I've seen it before, what it does to a man to lose a battle so badly. He'll never hold his head up again."

"What can I do?"

Plancy began to talk about the sultan's guarantees of safe-conduct. Instead of listening, Sibylla looked into Lilith's eyes and listened to thoughts dull with despair: *Nothing matters any more. The only thing I can do is show Saladin what I think of him. Defy him. Let him take Ascalon over the dead bodies of everyone in it.*

This isn't like you, Guy had told her before he marched away to the battle from which it seemed he would never return.

Sibylla turned away from Lilith and found herself breathing as hard as though she had run a race. Unsteadily, she picked up her embroidery—the light was getting stronger again now as the sun slipped from its hiding-place—and began to work again. Within moments she was able to think more clearly.

"We'll go to Jerusalem," she said, stopping Miles mid-sentence.

Silence hung over the tower.

"That's the other thing," Miles said uncomfortably. "Jerusalem is next."

"That's why we must go there."

"When I was in the sultan's camp I saw Lord Balian waiting to speak with Saladin. He'd been summoned from Jerusalem. Saladin told him to surrender or be killed, and Balian refused."

Sibylla's lips tightened, her aching neck bent studiously over her work. "We'll go to Jerusalem," she repeated.

"That's really not necessary, my lady. Not with Lord Balian undertaking the defence—"

"No. We can help each other, he and I." Sibylla took a deep breath. "Balian needs men, and my presence in Jerusalem will stiffen the defence. I demanded to rule this kingdom when it was at peace. Now that it's at war, I cannot abandon it."

* * *

Three days later, Sibylla arrived in Jerusalem to learn that Balian of Ibelin was holding council in her own palace—in fact in her father's old cabinet. Restraining the acid words that rose to her lips, Sibylla beckoned her own men—her castellan Joscelin of Samosac and Miles of Plancy—to follow her to the cabinet.

The sight that greeted her was a sombre one. Ibelin, who had been speaking in a leaden, hopeless voice, quickly stopped whatever he had been saying. The Patriarch had his chin buried in his hand. Ibelin's two knights—Thomas Patricius and Ranier of Nablus—seemed plunged in melancholy.

Sibylla spoke more gently than she had intended. "God keep you, friends. What news?"

"My lady!" the Patriarch gasped, jumping from his chair and offering it to her. "They didn't tell us you had come."

Ibelin turned, looked at her twice as though unable to believe his eyes, and got heavily to his feet. "Queen Sibylla," he began. Then he caught a glimpse of Plancy behind her, and that robbed him of speech once more. "Sir Miles," he said once he had recovered himself. "It rejoices me to see you alive and in freedom. Where is Marta the Knight?"

Sibylla sank gratefully into the chair she had been offered. She carried her embroidery hoop in one hand and quickly began stitching again, clutching the needle as a drowning woman might clutch at driftwood. Her household had noticed her compulsive stitching, of course; she had heard them whispering about it. Well, let them whisper. It kept Lilith at bay, and made her feel safe.

"Well, Plancy?" Balian demanded, as the silence lengthened. "If you know where Marta Bessarion is, tell me!"

"How should I know?" Plancy retorted. His voice was strained. "You know what she thinks of me."

As the thread slid beneath Sibylla's fingers, she risked a glance at her knight. Plancy stood with his arms crossed and his face reddened.

"Don't hedge with me," Ibelin said in a growl that made her bones rattle. "When did you last see her?"

"On the eve of the battle, when she said you were sending her home to Nablus."

Sibylla, who had been about to interrupt—surely one woman's where-abouts could not be the most pressing question of the day—nearly stopped stitching. There was a false note in Plancy's voice. Why should he lie about this, of all things?

Ibelin did not challenge the lie, but he was not satisfied, either. "She never returned home. Until this moment I nearly believed you must have been taken captive to Damascus, and that she had gone to fetch you back."

Plancy said nothing, and Sibylla was forced to keep her attention on her work.

Ibelin's next words were dangerously soft. "How *did* you escape the battle, Plancy?"

Plancy flushed, but he spoke bitterly. "The same way you escaped it, my lord—through cowardice and treachery, abandoning my fellows to their destruction. Is that what you wished to hear me say?"

Ibelin reddened in turn, but Sibylla cleared her throat before he could retort. The argument had already gone too far: she could not have Ibelin picking quarrels with her followers when the kingdom might depend on their being able to work together.

"The battle is over and done," she said, coldly. "All of us have things to reproach ourselves for; me as much as anyone. Please, let us not weary ourselves with the past."

Ibelin's jaw bulged, but he bowed and took his seat again, staring dejectedly at the table. Sibylla placed her needle for the thousandth time already that day, and tried to find a more comfortable angle for her aching neck. She wished she did not need to stitch. Now, when it was most necessary to be honest with him, to watch his face for the play of expression, she was compelled to pay attention to her work.

"You and I must be friends, if we can," Sibylla added. "We both share the same goal: the preservation of this kingdom. Balian of Ibelin, you swore fealty to my husband and not to myself, but today I ask you: will you serve me?"

As the thread slid beneath her fingers, she risked another glance into his eyes.

Ibelin frowned. "You are the king's wife and the source of his authority. I already hazarded my life in battle on your behalf; I will not desert you now."

It was not the answer she hoped for. The plan she had made was a good one—Sibylla was sure of that—but she did not know whether Balian would assent to it.

Patriarch Eraclius cleared his throat. "We have a few dozen knights, my lady, since Lord Balian has knighted every man in the city of sufficiently noble birth. There is armour and arrows for everybody, but not many seasoned warriors. If you have brought with you knights and sergeants from Ascalon…"

"I have," Sibylla said. "All who were left of the garrison of Acre, all who were left of the garrison of Ascalon, and some few stragglers who returned from the battle." She stabbed the linen and drew the thread through. "They won't make any difference, you understand."

There was an echoing silence.

"I beg your pardon?" Eraclius stammered.

"It's simple fact," Sibylla said calmly. Things which seemed obvious to her often needed to be spelled out in simple words to others. "Jerusalem is stocked with the fugitives of all Judaea. Since we are inland and Saladin holds the coast, we have no means of supply. Montferrat in Tyre, who has accumulated for himself much of what remains of the fighting strength of the kingdom, is either unable or unwilling to relieve us. And these walls are no match for Saladin's mangonels."

"This is Christ's city; he will help us." Balian spoke stubbornly.

"May it be so," Sibylla said—she had heard of stranger things happening. "But in the natural way of things, according to all reason, the city will fall. And it will do us no good to delude ourselves otherwise."

No one objected to this. Sibylla drew a deep breath and stitched on. "Therefore, the only thing we can really hope to achieve is to defend ourselves long enough to win some concessions in our surrender."

Ibelin sent her a wary look. "Such as? Don't forget that I've already refused one opportunity to treat, and Saladin has no obligation to offer a second chance."

"He will, though," Sibylla answered. "We cannot defeat Saladin, but we are quite capable of selling him victory at a greater price than he cares to pay. He will deal with us if it means he gets Jerusalem without needing to fight for it."

"You cannot be serious," Ibelin said. This was a side of him she had never seen before—something in him had broken, leaving him harsh and angry.

"Jerusalem belongs to Christ, and you would barter her away without a blow struck in her defence?"

"Doesn't Holy Writ tell us," Sibylla said evenly, "that it is Jerusalem above and not below, which is the mother of us all? I tell you I *will* barter this city to Saladin, and I will make him pay dearly for it, if not in blood. I will demand Acre. I will demand Ascalon. I will demand the king, the Master of the Temple, and other captives. I will demand a truce for two years. It will be a noble exchange worthy of the holiest of cities."

Ibelin must have been staggered by her vision: for a moment he made no reply, save to pull at his beard. For a moment Sibylla thought he would agree; and she saw herself securing a strip of the coast with which to reconquer and defend her lost kingdom.

Then Ibelin shook his head. "We are in too weak a position. Why should Saladin treat with us at all? His spies will surely inform him of our weakness, and he is too cunning to make us any great concession."

"If we want an inch from Saladin, we must demand a mile."

She made the mistake of looking Ibelin in the eye as she spoke, and he scrutinised her before shaking his head.

"You're tired, my lady," he said gently. "You look as though you haven't slept in weeks. You'll think more clearly when you've rested. Leave the defence of the city to me, and we'll discuss our negotiations with Saladin when the time comes."

Sibylla would happily have driven her needle into him. Instead, stabbing her linen, she ran the sharp metal into her own thumb. She pulled it out again silently, refusing to show a single sign of discomfort: he would only consider it proof of her exhaustion and a further excuse to set her at naught.

"See to the defence, then," she ordered him coldly. "You are dismissed."

Ibelin took his knights and left. Patriarch Eraclius got up, then, bowing to her as though to take his leave.

"What, my lord? No opinion of your own?" Sibylla asked him, angry that he had not spoken in support of her plan.

He grimaced. "Well, it's one thing to bargain the city away by your own cold logic, my lady. But I'm the Patriarch—how can I agree to hand Christ's city to the Saracens? I fear the people will never countenance it."

They had not been able to countenance it in Acre, either; that withered her anger. Sibylla bowed her head. "Of course, my lord."

The Patriarch went out, and only when she was alone with her own men did Sibylla put her smarting finger in her mouth.

She might have tried to conceal her pain, but if Ibelin had looked down he must surely have seen the tell-tale smear of blood across the snowy linen of her work.

Chapter XXXV.

It was like being trapped in a bad dream, to believe with every fibre of her body that a certain thing was best for the kingdom but to have no power of doing it.

Yet that was how Sibylla had wrecked the kingdom in the first place: by doing what she was convinced was right at the cost of riding roughshod over wills, hearts, even lives. Perhaps, now, the best thing she could do was nothing at all.

Sibylla took a long, slow breath in the wake of the Patriarch's departure. Samosac, her castellan from Ascalon, said, "Shall I go to the citadel, my lady?"

"Do so," Sibylla said, "and ask to receive the command of it. Plancy, stay with me."

Samosac departed and Sibylla sent Plancy to fetch her chaplain, thinking that she ought to have some letters written; she ought to speak with some of the city hospices about food and water supplies, together with other things that might be needful to see the populace through a siege. After that, she ought to go out to see that the children had been settled into their quarters. For now, Sibylla went on stitching, hiding the smear of blood behind more black stitches, and ruminating upon what she had heard and seen.

Samosac returned from his errand before she had finished dictating her first message. With one look at his face, she could tell the news was bad.

"The Tower of David is manned by Ibelin's people," he told her. "They refused to hand it over. They further said they would supply the palace guard."

That would make Sibylla, in effect, a prisoner in Ibelin's city. "Since I have given Ibelin the command of the defence, he has a right to control of the citadel," Sibylla said, shrugging. "But not even Ibelin will have the audacity to insist on controlling my personal guard. Arrange it, Samosac."

The former castellan bowed himself out.

"Have you instructions for me?" Plancy asked.

Sibylla spared him a long look. It was Plancy who had chiefly occupied her thoughts in the wake of her meeting with Balian. She needed a guard, and there were few knights of any experience in the city, but she did not know whether she could trust him. From the very beginning he had been all too willing to betray his friends for the sake of his own advancement, and she had always considered him treacherous and unscrupulous, not to be relied upon if her ascendancy faded.

Now she certainly was not in the ascendant, and Plancy had lied to her as well as to Ibelin, when she had asked him if he knew the whereabouts of Marta Bessarion.

"What do you want to do?" she asked him.

His eyes flickered uneasily away from hers. "Put me on the wall, my lady. I want to fight."

Plancy had fought at Ascalon, commanding the outworks and doing such feats as had people drinking to his health in the wine shops. No one had ever accused him of physical cowardice, and in the coming siege such prowess would be necessary. "Granted. I'll ask Ibelin's leave for it."

He bowed. "You won't regret it, my lady. If Saladin won't come to terms, we'll force him to it on the field. We'll get the kingdom back for you."

This was so deluded that Sibylla wanted to laugh. "You think we can retake the kingdom? Don't gull yourself, Plancy. Saladin has us where he wants us. We'll be lucky to salvage a rump of the kingdom, much less take it back in its entirety." At the look on his face, she did laugh. "Your precious fief is *gone*. Fight never so bravely, you won't get it back."

He bit his lip until it turned pale. Was he admitting to himself at last that he had traded love for power and ended up with neither? Sibylla did not pity him for it, any more than she pitied herself. In the end, she had made a similar bargain herself.

Or perhaps it was the battle that troubled him. Plancy had been left behind after a charge and counterattack, or so he had told Sibylla. He had managed to escape in the lull as the front of battle swept past him, overwhelming the king's tent.

"How *did* you escape the battle, Miles of Plancy?" she asked him.

This time, he was on his guard. "It's as I told you: once the king's standard fell, I found a horse and escaped."

"A horse fit for a king," Sibylla observed. "I have seen it; very like a destrier my brother had. When he could no longer ride, he made a gift of the horse to the White Watcher." That discomfited him: Plancy turned absolutely white. Sibylla continued, merciless: "You really don't know where to find Marta Bessarion?"

From pallor, he turned red. "Devil take it, why should I know that? We're barely on speaking terms."

"Everyone knows what she did for you." It felt good to watch him squirm; it was a sort of vicarious penance. Everyone knew what Guy of Lusignan had done for her, too. "Find me a Watcher. Not one of their great lords, but some holy fool like the Bessarion. Didn't she have associates? One of them was Nubian."

"Persi of Silimi." Plancy bit his lip, evidently reluctant. "I doubt she's in the city, my lady, but I'll see who I can find."

* * *

It took Plancy a week and a reminder to produce a Watcher, but Sibylla's persistence was rewarded one cloudy afternoon in mid-September when she was sitting in the loggia working, as ever, on some piece of embroidery. She had other guests that day. Isabella had come, bored and listless, fretting that she missed Humphrey. With her came Stephanie of Milly, Humphrey's mother, whose silence echoed like an endlessly repressed scream.

Then Plancy entered into the courtyard below, accompanied by a man and a woman in gorgeous festive clothing. The woman's dress was saffron-dyed yellow veined with blue and vermilion, and the white veil covering her face sparkled at the borders with silver. Plancy came up the stairs and bowed to Sibylla. "I found the Watcher we spoke of, my lady."

The woman and her escort followed Plancy up the stairs like a summer sunrise. Sibylla said, "I expressly requested a Watcher of *humble* station."

But Isabella's mouth dropped open at the sight of the woman. "Why, it's *Persi!*" she erupted in delight. She got up and threw her arms around the newcomer. "Persi, you look so fine! I didn't know you had come to Jerusalem. Why did you never come to see me? And where is Marta, for nobody seems to know?"

The weaver's eyes darkened with pain. "I wish to God I could answer," she said, extracting herself from Isabella's embrace. "I came to Jerusalem with Queen Maria, since the country wasn't safe for travel to Tripoli. As for the finery…" She glanced at the man at her side, a Syrian by the looks of him. "I *was* getting married today."

Isabella screamed. "And you never invited *me?* To whom? Is this your young man? What is his name?" She thrust her hand into her purse and came out with a handful of silver. "Ah, this is not enough for a gift. Let me run home and get you something. Where is the feast to be held? Will there be dancing? Should I bring minstrels? *Do* say I can come. It will take my mind off poor Humphrey. I won't bring above six others. *Please.*"

Six additional guests, including a bored princess, might be a stretch even for a well-to-do burgess wedding; but Persi only hesitated a moment, exchanging a glance with the young Syrian. "Of course you must. We were married in the porch of Saint Elias in the Juiverie Quarter; the feast is at a house in the same street." Pushing back her veil, the Nubian turned and fixed Sibylla with a wary gaze. "We had better not remain here long. Our guests will come to find us if we are not soon returned."

Now that she saw Persi's face, Sibylla seemed to remember that she had once held the woman hostage. All that seemed a lifetime ago to her now, but evidently the memory was still quite fresh to the woman before her. "I will not keep you long," she said. She had intended to ask the Watcher to join her in her cabinet, but perhaps that would be too threatening. Instead, she nodded towards the loggia that ran the length of the palace, fronting onto the garden. "Walk with me."

Persi of Silimi followed her silently, a blaze of overwhelming colour in the corner of Sibylla's eye. When they had left the others sufficiently far behind, Sibylla cleared her throat.

"They tell me you're a Watcher. Don't be afraid: I must ask your help." Sibylla hesitated. *She'll tell,* a voice whispered. *She hates you; you can see it in her eyes. It'll be all over the city by sunset.*

She could not trust her own thoughts: not when she was unprotected like this. Nor could she spend the rest of her life feverishly doing needlework. She must trust *someone.*

"I have a demon," Sibylla said, her voice cold and hard, daring Persi to laugh. "It has clouded my wits, killed my children and destroyed my kingdom." No reply. Sibylla risked a sidelong glance. "You don't seem shocked."

"No," Persi said. "It's no news to me, my lady. I've seen Lilith's mark on you for a very long time."

"Don't speak that name!"

"I won't if it troubles you."

Sibylla envied the Nubian's easy confidence. She lifted her chin, trying to remind herself that despite everything, she was still a queen. "I had you in my power once. Now you have me in yours. Ask anything you like, have your triumph, but for the sake of the kingdom, I beg you to help me."

They reached the end of the loggia and halted. Persi let out a sigh. "What do you expect me to do?"

"I expect nothing and demand nothing. But since I am queen, I must have my wits about me. I can't have that creature turning everything I do to evil."

Persi heaved another sigh. "Allow me to speak freely?"

"Of course." Sibylla said, but the Watcher's reluctance already filled her with foreboding.

"My lady, your deeds were already evil before Lilith claimed you. Such a situation does not come about by chance. She only availed herself of an opportunity *you* provided."

Beyond the loggia, the clouds began to weep, unburdening themselves of the first rain of the season in slow, fat, heavy drops that spotted the warm stone of the pavement below. Sibylla watched them fall and wondered whether the Nubian meant to say that she had no hope at all.

Persi went on: "I can *try* to rid you of Lilith, but why should she give up her lawful prey? As long as any part of you still believes you have the right to rule as you like, without reference to God or man, I might as well save my breath."

"I am the anointed queen of this kingdom," Sibylla said. She might have made up her mind to relinquish the rule of the kingdom for Guy the moment he could be returned from captivity, but that choice belonged to her, not this upstart weaver. "I hold authority. It is my right to rule."

"Authority must hang on *something*," Persi rejoined. "Don't you remember Our Lord saying that in his kingdom, the greatest of all should be those with no more power than the humblest of servants?"

"Do not lecture me," Sibylla said, so coldly that it was only later that she recognised what she felt as anger. "Tell me what to do and I'll do it."

"The best advice I can give you is this: think on your sins."

"This is nonsense. If I'd called a priest, he would already have performed an exorcism."

"Then I cannot conceive why you dragged me away from my own wedding feast."

Sibylla bit down on her lower lip until she almost expected to taste blood. Then, very icily, she said, "Pray don't let me keep you from it."

She had not called a priest because so many of those she knew were like Eraclius: worldly men with smooth tongues and broken vows, jewelled fingers and concubines. Lilith would laugh such a man to scorn. And Sibylla was very much afraid that if she summoned the genuine sort, he would give her the same advice Persi had just done.

They went back to the others in a frigid silence, where the young Syrian extended a protective arm towards his bride, although Sibylla noticed that he took care not to actually touch her.

Plancy nodded to the pair. "Shall I take you back to your wedding?"

"Please don't bother," said Persi. She was halfway down the steps when she turned back. "Sir Miles, is it true what they're saying? That you know what happened to Marta Bessarion?"

Plancy stiffened. "It's a lie. Who says that?"

Persi watched him in silence, at her leisure. Then, when Sibylla half expected an outburst, she shook her head. "It's only a rumour. I thought there might be some truth in it."

Her tone was carefully uninflected, making the words ambiguous. This said, she picked up the front of her skirts and disappeared with her bridegroom. Eager to attend the wedding feast, Isabella dragged her mother-in-law away at once. As for Plancy, he seemed lost in turbulent thoughts. Sibylla was pleased to let him stew; she had not yet determined what use might be made of his evident guilt.

The real question was, what could she do about Lilith? Sibylla shrank from the idea of seeking help elsewhere; it was too much to risk her plight becoming known, when she had no guarantee the attempt would succeed.

She must go on working; that was all. Her neck ached, her sight was shortening, and her fingers were covered in irritated bumps from the constant slither of thread; but it was a small enough price to pay for peace and clarity of mind—at least during the day.

The night was another matter.

"You went to the Watchers," Lilith accused when Sibylla finally slipped into uneasy dreams. *I saw you with the Nubian weaver. You're trying to get rid of me. And here I thought we were such excellent friends.*

Sibylla did not speak—the weight of the demon on her chest had pressed all the voice out of her.

Lilith stared down out of Sibylla's own eyes, cold and angry. "How shall I punish you? There are so many ways. Shall I strike your daughters with pestilence? No, that wouldn't bother you, would it? There's the handsome dullard, moping and pining in Nablus. It would take only a very little more to make him cut his own throat."

Sibylla tried to answer, but she only began to suffocate instead. Terror seized her, shaking her out of her dream, but even in waking there was no relief. In the darkness, Lilith loomed over her with vengeful eyes and bared teeth.

For a moment Sibylla felt dizzy and sick. All afternoon, since the confrontation with Persi, her aches had flared up again. By now it felt as though someone had seized the back of her head in a vice; the effort of sitting up in bed had sent pain radiating down her spine.

"Or," Lilith went on, "should I end this pleasant dalliance and take possession of you entirely?"

Sibylla put a hand over her mouth to keep from screaming. *It's a bluff.* She did not know where that thought came from, but it steadied her at once. If Lilith had been granted the right to possess her entirely, she would of course have done so by now.

Lilith was only trying to frighten her.

Lilith was feeling threatened.

"I'm not afraid of you," Sibylla whispered, "and after what you've done to my kingdom, I'm done trusting you."

"What *I've* done to your kingdom?" Lilith sounded offended. "You understand, don't you, that old things must be torn down before new things can be built? Have patience. I mean to turn all this to your account."

"Do you expect me to believe this, when all you have done is destroy me?"

"Very well. What should I do to prove my usefulness?"

"I beg your pardon?"

"I'm not a mortal," Lilith said with a shrug. "I don't understand what your kind wants. So test me. Let me prove I take your part."

This was folly. And yet...

"All right," Sibylla said. "Take away the pain. Make me well."

"Is that all?"

Sibylla closed her eyes for a moment. If the pain did not lessen soon, she would be confined to bed for days, exhausted and sick, unable even to embroider. Easy prey to Lilith's taunts.

"Take it away," she whispered, "and I might actually believe you mean me well."

"Oh, very well," Lilith said, pouting. The next instant Sibylla could almost believe she had died and left her mortal body behind. She felt weary—as though sinking into bed after a long day's journey—but the lack of any sort of pain, the consciousness of complete comfort and rest, brought tears to her eyes. For a moment she could scarcely speak.

"You—you could have done this at any time," she accused.

"Well, but you never asked." Lilith got off the bed and crossed her arms. "Isn't it better to be with me than without me? Think on *that* before you decide whether to have me banished."

She disappeared, and Sibylla gasped as, in the blink of an eye, all the pain and sickness rushed back to her. "Lilith," she begged. *"Lilith,* please." But there was no answer. At last, the demon had chosen to ignore her.

Less than a week later, Saladin arrived outside the wall of Jerusalem.

Chapter XXXVI.

Late September—three months after the battle

In her dreams, Marta followed Khalil through the courtyard of his house and on through the low door by which she had first entered it.

A falcon rode on his wrist. Marta followed as he carried the bird across the stone threshold into the empty tent with its wall-less door.

Beyond, Saladin's camp was in an uproar. Drums, horns, and the sound of battle filled the air. Khalil stalked through the cacophony towards the distant walls of Jerusalem. Although it was now beset with enemies, Marta recognised Saint Stephen's Gate at once. Saladin's petraries and mangonels thrummed ceaselessly, flinging stones and javelins into the city from behind barricades cut from thorn-bushes. His archers stood ranked behind a shield-wall, filling the sky with falling arrows. Between them and the wall, in and around the scarred and blackened ruins of the Madeleine, some fierce struggle was going on: a Frankish knight led a charge aiming east towards Saladin's lines, and none could stand before him.

Jerusalem, her home—Jerusalem, which Baldwin had begged her to protect—was fighting for her life and there was nothing, *nothing* Marta could do about it.

Ask something of me, Baldwin had begged her, when he could not give her his life.

Give me your tears, she had said, because when there was nothing else one could do, one could still weep, and sometimes tears were better than actions.

But Marta could do more than weep: she could also bear witness.

She followed Khalil to the awning beneath which the sultan watched the battle. "You are late," Saladin greeted him. "They have nearly been among our tents."

Khalil bowed, then beckoned to the demons who walked beside him. Qeteb and Lilith leaped into the sky. Qeteb shot like an arrow into the clouds, causing them to fray and dissipate, so that the morning sun shone fiercely into the defenders' eyes. Lilith blew, and a dry wind whipped towards the city wall, carrying billowing clouds of dust.

The cloud of dust enveloped the charge. Awful sounds came from within it; then, the cloud thinned and the Franks were retreating. For a moment Marta caught a clearer glimpse of their leader, a man on a white horse with a black bar across his shield.

Miles? And—was that Pomers?

At this distance it was too far to say for sure, but none had stood before that lance. It *had* to be Miles. Amidst all her bitterness, Marta felt a moment's brittle satisfaction: he and Pomers had lived, and the Bessarion Lance was here after all, defending Jerusalem as it ought to be.

"Tell me what is happening in the city," Saladin ordered, as the sally was pushed back from the sultan's camp. Khalil threw his falcon into the air and took his seat on a mat. His head fell back, watching the bird. His lips moved in silent command.

Marta, who had seen this trick before, and who was only a dream herself, leaped into the air after the falcon. Together they wheeled up past arrow-range and hovered over the city, allowing Khalil to see within. Within, Jerusalem was scarred with falling stones, and the Juiverie Quarter near the north wall was speckled with the bodies of those who had been cut down by the sultan's ceaseless arrows.

A stone from the mangonels struck a tower on the salient just east of the Saint Stephen Gate; it smashed free a wooden hoarding which had been put up to protect the defenders, and the whole thing fell with such a crash that both the defenders and the attackers cried out and trembled and fled. Still the bombardment went mercilessly on, and Marta, hovering above the city in her dream, watched with hot eyes that could not weep.

* * *

During the first week of the siege, Saladin had made camp outside the David Gate, where the ground was too rough to allow him to bring his siege engines close to the wall. Every day, Sibylla watched from her window in the palace as Ibelin's men marched out on sallies to harass the enemy.

During the second week of the siege, Saladin packed up his camp and there was fervid rejoicing—until he marched only as far as Saint Stephen's Gate on the north wall, where the more level ground allowed him to bring up his terrible engines to unleash stone and fire upon the city.

When the sultan's sappers undermined the wall and collapsed a part of it, despair settled over Jerusalem: it felt as though the world was about to end. From the palace, Sibylla watched women going up the road towards the Holy Sepulchre with their children, carrying basins and tubs.

"What are they doing?" she asked her attendants.

"They're going to Cavalry, my lady, to make offerings and do penance."

Sibylla looked down on the endless stream of women and children. So many, so helpless in the face of the coming sack. They knew well enough that their defiance would only purchase them death and suffering and horrors enough to make the ears bleed that heard of them. And here she was among them, together with her daughters.

She contemplated what would happen to her when the city fell: how, unlike the other women in Jerusalem, her station would probably spare her death or ill-treatment; how Guy would ransom her back and think no more of it; how tongues would wag behind her back nevertheless; how her chastity would be cast in doubt; how it would be whispered that her daughters, children though they were, had been taught wantonness in captivity; how they, like Sibylla's great-aunt Yveta, would be forced to take refuge in a convent since no man would wish to marry them.

It would make no difference to Sibylla, because she had half a mind to take the veil anyway. Guy was no Baldwin the First, to lock his wife into a convent merely because she had been captured by pirates, yet she must already have irreparably damaged his trust in her and there was surely no other future left for her. Still, for her daughters she felt an unaccustomed stab of pity. It would be hard for them, always to be tainted by something that was not their fault. Something that, if anyone, *she* herself was to blame for.

"Prepare Melisende and Beatrix to go out," Sibylla ordered softly. "Dress them plainly."

Disguising herself in a black veil and mantle, and supporting her aching body on a staff, Sibylla went out into the streets half an hour later with Beatrix's hand within her own and Melisende trotting beside her, carrying a tin basin someone had found in the stables. "Where are we going, my lady?" she asked, but Sibylla did not answer.

Two sergeants followed them at a distance. Sibylla had adamantly refused to let her own guards escort her, and this was confirmation of a thing she had already guessed: that Ibelin had ordered some of his own men to watch her. Sibylla wanted to laugh. Did Ibelin really suppose that here, at the end of her reign and the kingdom and the world, she could do anything more to hurt him?

All along the Street of the Patriarch, on the steps leading up to the great pool, in the street outside it and the open space around the Holy Sepulchre, the women of the city had filled their tubs with water and children. It was an eerie sight, the silence broken only by splashing and weeping. Sibylla waited her turn on the steps to fill her basin, and because she did not have the strength to carry it down the steps into the street again once she had filled it, she let it stand on the edge of the cistern.

"Come here, Melisende," she told her elder daughter.

Melisende began to sniffle, but she stepped into the tub and wound her arms about her knees. Sibylla poured water over her until the child was soaked through and shivering. When Sibylla took out her spring shears, both girls began to cry.

"Don't cut off my hair, mama!" someone else's child begged behind them. Her own daughters said nothing. They only called her *my lady,* not *mama.*

"I only want to spare you," Sibylla told them. She could not tell them from what. Nor could she comfort them: who was she to them? The stranger who dictated their lives, the chess mistress holding them in reserve, to be moved onto the board as soon as they were ready to be used?

So she said nothing further, although her heart was in her mouth and she felt so very, very afraid for them. Instead, she seized Melisende's dark and dripping locks and cut them off, one by one, close to the scalp. Only when the girl was cropped close, like a boy, did she let her out of the basin and put Beatrix into it. When both children were washed and shorn, she emptied the basin and folded the dripping locks into her mantle.

The Holy Sepulchre was full of prayers and weeping, as dim and noisy and stuffy as it ever had been. Piled on the Stone of Anointing were thousands of damp little bundles of hair, from long black plaits to fair, wisping curls. Sibylla looked up after she had laid her daughters' hair with the rest and saw through the crowd, just for a moment, the ornate tomb of carved stone she had made for her little son, Baldwin the Fifth. He had been so small and so weak, and every day of his life she had been his enemy. She had not even been able to comfort him as he lay dying, and now the sense of shame and regret she felt was almost stifling. Impulsively, Sibylla put her arms around her daughters and pulled them close to her heart. They stiffened in surprise, but did not protest. Then she took their hands and led them away.

She was passing the main gate of the Hospital when a woman stepped in front of her and said, "My lady." It was Persi the Nubian, carrying a basket on each arm that was full of freshly rolled bandages.

Encumbered by two children, a staff, a basin, and an overwhelming weariness, Sibylla did not try to escape. But she said faintly, "You must have mistaken me for someone else."

"I think not," Persi said, frowning at Sibylla's veiled forehead. "My lady, you must take care. Whatever Lilith has promised you is a lie. Whatever she offers you, there will be a price more than you can pay."

With that, Persi bobbed a bow and disappeared into the Hospital, leaving Sibylla free to move on.

Persi was right, of course. But the promise of a strong and painless future was more than Sibylla could resist, and with the city on the point of destruction, what was the point in scruples? If Lilith ever returned, Sibylla was bound to give in. It was only a matter of time. She should never have confided in the Watcher.

Returning to the palace, Sibylla gave the children back to the care of their nurse, who held up her hands in horror at the mess she had made of their heads. She was passing back through the loggia to her own room when she overheard voices below, in the courtyard, where Ibelin had just returned from a meeting with the Patriarch.

"Not now, Ernoul. What, Christ's city on the point of falling, and you want to talk about Miles of Plancy?"

"But my lord, they're saying he wields the Bessarion Lance."

The Bessarion Lance? Sibylla knew the significance of that weapon; few better. She leaned over the loggia parapet as Ibelin swivelled to tower over one of his youngest knights.

"What did you say?" Ibelin's voice was very quiet.

"I tried to get a closer look at it," Ernoul said, "but he keeps his lance covered unless he's on the battlefield, using it to sweep the enemy before him."

That would explain why Plancy had begged to be sent to fight. Sibylla felt a tickle of excitement. So, Sir Miles had escaped the battle, not just with Marta Bessarion's horse, but with her lance, too. Certainly, there was some advantage to be gained from this.

Ibelin still did not say anything, so Ernoul went on. "He's done things like this before, my lord. None can say how he escaped the great battle, but everyone remembers how he returned alone from Arabia, although he went there with a hundred other men."

"Enough!" Ibelin said at last with a growl. "I know you love Marta as much as the rest of us, Sir Ernoul, but you've allowed your jealousy to blind you. Marta would never allow the Lance to pass out of her possession. If she is not with us, it is because she has business elsewhere. In the meantime, I have a city to save, if I can."

Ibelin was deluding himself, clearly unable or unwilling to face the likelihood that his fosterling had been killed or captured. Sibylla shook her head. Of course Plancy had taken the little Bessarion's enchanted lance and left her to rot. He always was remarkably cold-blooded.

She turned in surprise as Ibelin, having sent Ernoul about his business, mounted the stairs to the upper palace and made towards her. "My lady, a word?"

Having seized control of the city, Ibelin had so far conducted the siege without consulting Sibylla at all, claiming all the while to act in her name. Sibylla had permitted it without a word of protest. Even had she thought herself better equipped than him to command the siege—which she now had every reason to doubt—the city could not possibly defend itself with a divided leadership. A lesson learned painfully late.

Instead, Sibylla contented herself coordinating matters of provision and visiting the city's hospitals, when she was not prevented by her own sickness. Feeding, clothing, and treating the city's swollen population was as important a task as conducting the siege, and the queen's oversight meant that any urgent needs would be quickly seen to. Still, she was Amalric's daughter, and it was a humiliation nonetheless.

"The wall has been undermined," Ibelin told her without preamble, his face dour beneath its beard. "You should know that I am going to see the sultan tomorrow, but since we refused his offer of quarter three weeks ago at Ascalon, he will be within his rights to slaughter us all. Naturally his men wish to avenge the siege of eighty years ago."

Sibylla did not need Ibelin's reminder that when Godfrey and Saint-Gilles first came out of the west, Jerusalem had fallen in a terrible bloodletting; certainly the Mahometans had not forgotten it. Of course they wanted their vengeance. That was one of the reasons she had kept her mouth shut while Ibelin ruled the roost in her city.

"Well?" she said. "Why come to me now?"

Ibelin looked away, unable to meet her eyes. "I need your help."

For a moment Sibylla forgot to draw breath. It had come, the moment she had been expecting the whole siege. Quicker, even, than she had expected, but then Ibelin had never been as stubborn as Tripoli. She felt no triumph. This was no victory.

"You expect me to save this city single-handed, when you and all your knights have failed?"

Ibelin looked her full in the eyes. "You saved Acre and Ascalon."

Sibylla lost her voice entirely. She had *lost* Acre and Ascalon, traded cities for lives. But then, a city was more than its walls and roofs, more even than its trade and garrison. Before anything else, a city was its people.

She cleared her throat. "My advice has not changed. Offer Saladin Jerusalem in exchange for Acre and the lives of all these people."

Ibelin's mouth tightened. "He'll laugh in my face."

"Quite likely he will," Sibylla said. "But then you must tell him this: that if he refuses, you will do as the burgesses of the city advised you to do, just this morning."

"How do you know—"

"I have servants, Ibelin, and I have not forgotten that I am queen in this city, even if others have." He reddened, but she went on. "Tell him, then, that you'll sally forth with every man who can hold a sword to defend the city where Christ died, so that each of you will kill ten of the enemy before you fall. Tell him that sooner than allow your women and children to be taken into captivity and lost to Christ, the men of Jerusalem will slaughter them all with their own hands. And tell him that you will first burn to the ground the holy places claimed by his co-religionists—the Temple of the Lord and of Solomon."

Ibelin stared at her. Sibylla did not see why he should find the notion so shocking. It was not as though she meant the plan to be carried out. Saladin's victory would be substantially less if the very holy places he meant to capture had been destroyed before being handed over. Conqueror though he was, from previous negotiations over Acre and Ascalon she knew Saladin preferred honourable surrender to bloody subjection.

"He *will* agree," Sibylla said. "But make the offer quickly, while there is still time. Once his knights force their way into the city, there will be no chance to make our threats good."

* * *

In the sultan's camp, Khalil opened his eyes with a gasp. As his consciousness returned to his body, Marta's dream snatched her back to his unwitting side.

By now, the fighting outside the city wall had calmed. The awning under which the sultan had stood watching the Frankish sortie was almost empty, now inhabited only by one or two of the sultan's commanders and their servants.

A Turkish squire plucked at the sorcerer's elbow—no doubt it was this that had woken him. "My lord," the young man said, bowing low, "you're wanted urgently in the sultan's tent. An envoy has come from the city."

Khalil rose, tossing the boy his glove and lure with instructions to retrieve the falcon and return it to his tent. Still dreaming herself, Marta drifted behind as he returned to Saladin's great pavilion of Saladin, where a weary Frankish knight stood leaning upon a spear whose point had been shrouded in a long, thin bag of leather.

"My lord misunderstands," the knight was saying to the sultan as Khalil and Marta arrived. "No one in Jerusalem sent me; I'm acting on my own behalf." His shoulders hunched, nervous, furtive. "There is a secret which, if it is known, will cause all men to spit on my name. Since I cannot keep it hidden if the fighting goes on much longer, I've come to offer the great Sultan Saladin my help in subduing this city."

Marta could not see the knight's face, but the very set of his shoulders was as familiar to her as the back of her own hand, and the voice had once spoken in all her dreams.

Miles.

Chapter XXXVII.

"Marta." Fayruz's voice broke in on her dreams, warning her that it was midnight, time for her watch to begin. Waking to find tears on her cheeks, Marta rubbed them away at once. She would not weep, she *would* not, not even though Jerusalem was on the point of a brutal sack and Miles was ready to commit some new treachery.

Marta sat up in bed, wincing as she put pressure on a skinned left elbow—the fruit of the previous day's exertions.

By now she was reasonably familiar with the layout of the Damascus house, as well as the women's quarters here on the mountain. Yesterday morning she had beaten open a corner of the lattice in Arwa's room, meaning to slip out onto the roof which it overlooked in an attempt to reconnoitre the women's quarters. For surely there must be some way down the mountain, however difficult, however well hidden. Even if the house had been built by workmen who travelled by magic, one person at least needed to visit the mountaintop first, to construct a doorway and take a piece of stone, and that meant there must be a path.

Yet if there was a path, Marta had not found it. Instead, the window had led her directly into a place she had only seen before in her dreams. One moment she had been putting a bare foot out into the autumn sun, spreading her toes to grip the rough warm tiles surrounding the perforated dome of the hammam roof. The next, having wriggled herself through the jagged gap between lattice and window-jamb, she found herself looking down into a bare stone hall, the undercroft of some great house, which had been set up as a training-room for warriors: it contained hacked training pells and racks of weapons. Her foot now knocked against the smooth stone wall, so high up that if she overbalanced and lost her perch straddling Arwa's window-sill, she would surely beat out her brains on the pavement far below. It was in recoiling through the broken lattice into Arwa's room that she had scraped her elbow.

Now, cradling the tender spot, she blinked up at Fayruz in her doorway. "Where does Khalil train his mamluks?"

"God have mercy!" Fayruz hissed. "Be quiet! Are you *trying* to get me killed?"

It was only then that Marta registered the light burning in the common room. Beyond Fayruz, twin shadows loomed—the eunuchs who guarded Khalil's private quarters.

She did not need Fayruz to clear her throat and announce, "Al-Aziz is waiting for you."

Marta turned to stone. It was midnight and she was tired; she did not want to go to Khalil, did not want to walk the blade's edge between appeasing him and arousing the wrath she knew must be waiting, ready to erupt against her.

But Marta had no choice in the matter, and that was the worst thing of all. She quickly dragged a comb through her hair and dressed herself before following the guards through the door that led to Damascus.

Khalil did not come to his room at once, but when he did, she saw at a glance that he was in a triumphant mood. "Eat with me," he ordered, seating himself cross-legged before a low round table which had been spread with food while Marta waited.

Silently, she sat down opposite him. With her gut in knots of tension, the smell of the food made her sick. One of the servants put a sweating glass before her, sherbet cooled with snow. A drop ran down onto the table. *A table thou preparest me in the presence of mine enemies.* The words came unbidden into her head. For a moment the world hollowed out before her like a mask she wore—a mask that looked like defeat from her side but might in truth be something else entirely.

The moment passed. If it was something else, she could not see it; not when she felt so weary.

"Congratulate me," Khalil told her. "By tomorrow, God willing, Jerusalem will be mine."

"I congratulate you," she said dully, "on reducing to your will a city that knows you not and loves you not."

Of course Miles would betray Jerusalem, she thought. In the midst of a siege, the Bessarion Lance could not be an easy secret to keep. Had rumours already begun to fly, that Miles of Plancy now wielded the White Watcher's Lance?

I'd never betray my own people, he had once said, in the days before betraying her. *My name would be spat upon by every man of noble birth in the kingdom. How could I live knowing that?*

She ought not to feel sorry for him, but she did. He must truly feel desperate.

There was a sharp *click* as Khalil placed his cup on the table and stared her down with cold hostility. Her words had not pleased him.

"Jerusalem is nothing to me. Consent to be my wife, and when I am sultan I will confer it upon you."

Marta repressed both her shudder and her hot refusal. "I am your prisoner. Why must you have my consent?"

"There must be something you want from me."

He knew very well what she had requested; only he was determined to make her say it again. Marta stared at the untouched food between them and said, "I want my freedom. I want to go home in peace."

"Didn't you hear me the first time? You shall go home. I'll give you Nablus. I'll give you Jerusalem. I'll give you the whole damned kingdom to do with as you like."

"As your wife."

"That goes without saying."

She closed her eyes. His voice had taken on a loud, hectoring tone. Marta felt unwell, and knowing that his patience was at last wearing thin only made her more weary.

"I won't live under your shadow. I'd sooner beg on the streets in Paris, or Silimi."

"This is foolishness," Khalil said, frowning. "Everyone must live under the shadow of another. That is the natural order of things. What other choice is there? Lilith's chaos?"

"So, I'm to be a worshipper of Lilith, merely because I refuse to be your wife?" If he was losing patience, so was she.

"You'll be lucky if anyone else wants you. Or do you imagine that you will go back to being the least of Ibelin's daughters?" Khalil scoffed. "Even that is a false hope. If you go home, it will be presumed by all that you spent your time in captivity earning your survival on your back. I mean to do you a favour, you obstinate girl. The choice is simple: you can be my wife, or you can be any man's whore."

Marta felt that she was watching them both from a very long distance away, half deafened by the rushing of blood in her own ears.

That won't happen to me, she had told herself. *I'll still be the White Watcher. As long as they need me, they'll never speak a word against me.*

Don't think about it, she had told herself. *Sufficient to the day is the evil thereof.*

But he was right; she knew he was right. More highly placed ladies than herself had lost everything after a stint in captivity; had been shut up in convents for the rest of their lives, no matter what had or had not happened to them.

"Ibelin was a poor father to you," Khalil added, evidently relishing the look on her face. "He neglected you, allowing you to rove at will about the countryside, prey to anyone who passed by. I would not neglect you. I would make you rich and powerful and immortal."

How could she make him understand that Lord Balian's neglect, as he called it, suited her better than his care?

"What you call freedom doesn't exist," he went on. "The truth is this: everyone lives in the shadow of someone greater, and everyone has inferiors living in their own shadow. I cannot offer you a life free of superiors, but I can offer you such numbers of inferiors as will make you the queen of Jerusalem and even the world. When Qeteb has made me emperor, you shall be empress. You will hold the greatest rank it is possible for a woman to have."

"Do you believe Qeteb to be an angel, that you build him an empire?"

His scowl deepened at her question. "He is a more natural creature than the Poison Mother."

Marta shook her head. Qeteb's order was as monstrous as Lilith's chaos. She would choose neither of them. Wrong did not become right merely because it was *orderly*.

Khalil's hand slammed on the table, making her jump. "For the last time, will you consent to be my wife?"

Endure, Persi had said, and Marta had tried to endure. But she was too tired now to mince her words, and she was not yet sufficiently cowed to have no words left at all. There was one part of herself that was still within her power, and that she refused to give him.

"I'd sooner have married Jehan of Cacho," she said.

Khalil's hand tightened slowly, till the knuckles went white on the handle of his knife. Marta could not breathe. The room seethed and darkened with his black mood; his violence, which had hung over her all these weeks, unspoken and unacted, was finally ready to break free.

"Take her away!" Khalil shouted. The two eunuchs on duty in the loggia silently reappeared.

Marta stood, her heart hammering. Khalil levelled his long forefinger at her.

"You ought to have accepted my gifts," he warned before the guards marched her back to the women's quarters.

She could not have slept, even if it was not past time to watch over Fayruz and spin her anti-magic. Her defiance had earned her another night's respite, but she had seen a new, more threatening side to Khalil tonight. At first her defiance had charmed him, but by now he had expected her to weaken.

Had he really expected her to jump at the chance of ruling Jerusalem? No doubt in name only. In Mahometan realms there had, as yet, been no Melisendes or Irenes or Zoes, and he had made it clear to her where her place was in Qeteb's "natural order of things." Nor would Marta have accepted the offer had it been made in earnest: she was no Sibylla either, and had no desire for temporal power. Now that she had definitely rejected all he could offer her in the way of enticement the courtship was finally over, and the terror would commence.

With Fayruz asleep, Marta looked up, into the shadows of the roof. "Sir God, help me," she whispered. "Time is running out for me. How can I destroy him when I'm utterly broken?"

Dawn came, and with it the soft sounds of the servants sweeping the common room. Knowing that Bahar and the other girls would see to the safety of Fayruz and her baby, Marta tiptoed towards her own room. At the threshold, a pale flicker of movement caught her attention.

A white snake lay coiled in her doorway.

"Ibrahim?" Marta whispered.

Lazily, the serpent uncoiled and went ahead of her beneath the curtain into her room. After a moment its head reappeared, forked tongue flickering in and out, for all the world as though it was waiting for her.

Marta pinched herself until she was sure she was not dreaming. Then she set her bobbin spinning, lifted the curtain, and stepped through, not into her own room, but into the Damascus courtyard. There was the orange tree, now past its season for fruit; but instead of a serpentine mosaic, it was ringed by one of Khalil's painted sigils. In every other respect the courtyard was as she knew it. Stars glittered in the sky overhead; a light shone from the loggia behind. The cool fingers of the breeze stroked her skin, aromatic with the scent of citrus. Beyond the walls of the house she could dimly hear footsteps and voices in the street.

It was no dream: she was really *here,* in the Damascus courtyard, at dawn.

By now Marta knew which of the doors led towards the street. She threw herself at the latch and rattled it, thinking only of her escape.

"Keep spinning." It was a man's voice, low and melodious with an accent very like Persi's. "This is only a memory, and there's no way out for you here."

Marta turned, but although she could have sworn the voice spoke in her very ear, there was only the white snake threaded between her feet, watching her with unblinking black eyes. Her heart gave an awful leap as she realised how vulnerable she might be, if one of Khalil's familiars caught sight of her intruding where she should not be.

"What is it?" she asked when the bobbin was spinning properly again. "Why now?"

"The stars are right," the voice said simply.

With that, the door in front of her opened and a man came hesitantly through from the street. Tall and nearly as dark-skinned as Persi herself, he was dressed like a rich merchant in a thick jacket of cotton damask.

The light from the loggia fell on his wondering, upturned face. Then, a shadow flitted by the great illuminated arches and footsteps pattered on the stair that led into the courtyard.

"You came," said a breathless, husky voice. Marta startled as she recognised Lilith, the feathered woman. All her monstrousness had been folded away somewhere out of sight: she was clothed decently, not in slick black feathers that gleamed iridescent in the light, but in a blue tunic so deep it was nearly black, her hair smoothed down beneath the veil that wrapped her head. "Come quickly, my love: I've been waiting too long already."

"Wait… You did not tell me you were a lady," the Nubian man objected, in the same voice that had spoken in her ear a moment ago. Ibrahim, as he had once been, looked up at the house as though overawed by it. "I have no wish to offend some great lord."

Lilith laughed, taking hold of him and drawing him into the courtyard. "You were eager enough when you thought me the wife of some ordinary merchant. Are you afraid? I have made five prayers today, and purified myself before all of them. My husband has gone on a long journey, and will not return for a month or more. Yield, yield, half-breed: I have perfumed my bed with myrrh and aloes, the shrouds are fresh and new, and the embalmers are waiting."

"Shrouds?" Ibrahim said faintly. He tried to disentangle himself from the woman, but she held him fast; with a strength belied by her small stature,

Lilith bent his elbow and forced him to his knees.

"Shrouds," she repeated, leaning down so that her face was on a level with his. Her teeth had grown long and sharp, dripping with saliva. "Or was it sheets? I cannot remember the words you flesh creatures use."

Ibrahim's face was an image of terror. Lilith scoffed. "I expected more of a fight," she said, pulling off her veil and snapping it taut, like a rope.

Its border was embroidered in silver letters. The djinn took one look at it and scrambled backwards across the pavement. Finding his feet, he turned towards the door; but Qeteb stood blocking his escape.

For a moment the djinn froze. "You," Ibrahim said. He drew his sword, the blade of which was scored with its own spell, and fell upon Qeteb with a white flash of steel.

Casually, the hairy man seized the blade, snapping it in two. Ibrahim fell back with a gasp as the demon threw away the steel.

"Never forget: I gave you your life and I can take it again," Qeteb said in a whisper like the fall of sand. Then he planted his palm against Ibrahim's chest and threw him bodily against the orange-tree, and Lilith seized him, binding the djinn to the tree using the flimsy muslin scarf.

"Too easy," Lilith said disdainfully, stepping away from the captive, who seemed incapable of escaping his spelled bonds.

All this time, the thread hummed smoothly through Marta's fingers, and the white snake remained so still and cool about her ankles that she almost thought it had died, or fallen asleep.

"This is why djinn make better slaves than mortals," Qeteb said meaningfully to someone who stood in the loggia, watching. Marta's skin prickled as she recognised Khalil. "As our descendants, they are subject to us."

"But not to me," Khalil replied to Qeteb's observation, descending the steps into the courtyard. Marta knew it was the demons she should fear, but when Khalil's gaze swept across the place where she stood, the thread hitched in her fingers and her bobbin stuttered.

The sorcerer walked into the courtyard and faced the trembling djinn. "Ibrahim ibn Salim ibn Qeteb, in the name of your father Qeteb I summon you from your body and bid you to dwell in this house."

A wind sprang up. What happened next was exactly like what had happened in the camp at Yarmouk, when the woman Soraya had killed herself: the djinn's body stiffened, desiccated and blew away into dust. The whole house groaned and trembled; the orange-tree threw up its hands, tossing the pale undersides of its leaves in the lamplight. Marta's thread blew and tangled, and the bobbin jerked to a halt.

Lilith turned and looked directly into Marta's eyes.

Chapter XXXVIII.

"Lilith." In the midnight shadows, with the doors locked and her servants chattering quietly in the anteroom, Sibylla's voice was only a guilty whisper. "Lilith, *please.*"

Ibelin had gone to negotiate with Saladin as Sibylla recommended, but the attempt was a laughable failure. He found the sultan watching as his men assaulted the wall.

You want peace with me now? the sultan had asked. *It is too late. Look: the city is mine. My men have surmounted the wall. There is my banner upon your battlement.*

But even as they watched, the ladders were thrown down, the wall retaken, the banners tossed into the ditch after the retreating Saracens.

Now will you receive my embassy, my lord? Ibelin had asked politely.

But the sultan only scowled at the Frankish envoy. *It makes no difference. I still have agents within the city. It is my duty to exact vengeance for the Muslims Godfrey slew in the streets and even upon the Haram al-Sharif, which you call the Temple Mount. My victory is assured. I need not make bargains with you.*

"There you have it," Ibelin had told Sibylla, when he returned with the heavy news. "So much for Saladin's vaunted generosity."

"Every man forsakes virtue when it suits him to do so," Sibylla responded. "It simply means that we must make it worth Saladin's while to embrace it again."

"And how will you do that?" asked the sceptical Ibelin.

Sibylla had refused to answer. She would never confess to anyone, not even her priest, what she meant to do now.

"Lilith," she said more loudly, grinding her teeth. "I'm ready to make terms."

In a blink the demon faced her. "You must have missed me," Lilith taunted. "Are you ready for me to take your pain?"

Sibylla's nails dug into her palms. "No. That's a luxury I can't afford. If you truly wish to prove your usefulness, do as I ask. Save me and my people from death and captivity."

Lilith clicked her tongue. "Sibylla, Sibylla. Why would I do that?"

"You *wanted* a war," Sibylla said fiercely. "You cannot have a war when all my people are dead."

"On the contrary! As I understand it, once Jerusalem falls, the first war Saladin will have on his hands will be the one the rest of your people bring from across the sea. I must give them something to avenge, you know."

Sibylla was speechless, scarcely able to believe what she was hearing. This time she knew who she was dealing with: she begged Lilith's help in the utter certainty that the gift would rebound on her with greater disaster, the way it had at the great battle. Yet now Lilith would not grant her even a treacherous boon.

"Oh, don't worry, I'll take care of *you*," Lilith said contemptuously. "Such a massacre as Saladin means to carry out in this city will rid you of your enemy Ibelin, and of your sister Isabella, who is your last remaining rival for the throne. But more than that: there's a great deal of power generated by the shedding of much blood. It will be enough to bind you and me forever, to make you immortal, perhaps even to destroy Saladin and his entire army. After that, we could have anything we wanted. Damascus. Egypt. Anatolia."

At that moment the notion was not entirely abhorrent. Sibylla saw herself a queen—ageless, painless, ruling an empire that extended from Jerusalem to cover the earth. But she could not imagine Guy reigning by her side. The years had softened her husband's heart and hardened his resolve. After all that had happened, he would never trust her again; and in that, he would surely be right.

Sibylla touched her lips with her tongue. "All I want from you is the salvation of this city."

"Didn't you hear what Saladin told Ibelin? The city has already been handed over to him."

"That's impossible. None of these people would do such a thing." She picked up the embroidery hoop, which had been gathering dust in a corner for weeks, and raised it like a buckler. "If you cannot give me what I ask, you had best go."

Lilith began to laugh. "You're deluded. Don't you know? One of your own precious knights has already sold the city to Saladin in exchange for a fief. Even now, he plans to admit the sultan's men by the postern of the Madeleine. There's no escape from this. Give in. Let me make you strong enough to withstand the sultan and every other enemy you have."

Once, the prospect might have tempted her, but she could not do it; she could not consign Jerusalem to another desecration of blood. If the holy city had been entrusted to her, it was not for her own sake. Right now, protecting the holy places meant giving them up—and rescuing the people was more important than remaining their queen.

She had been willing to bargain with Lilith one last time, if only Lilith would help her to rescue the people. But of course Lilith cared nothing for the people; she cared only for destruction and desecration.

Sibylla had been a fool to hope for more. Only now, in the clarity of despair, did an alternative take shadowy form in her mind. A name to match with the deeds Lilith had described. *One of your own precious knights.* She knew precisely whom.

"Plancy," she breathed, and threw open the door to the antechamber, startling the guards and ladies outside. "Where is Miles of Plancy? Does anyone know?"

"You won't stop him," Lilith said, appearing at her elbow. "He has the enchanted lance he stole from Marta Bessarion."

"Plancy didn't fight on the wall today," one of her guards volunteered, when the question was put to him. "He's been at the citadel, checking that its inner defences are strong."

Or rather, scouting them for the sultan, for when the city's walls were breached and the last defenders withdrew to the Tower of David to make their final stand. Sibylla could have marvelled at his cool betrayal, but she was surely the one who had taught him such games. "Find Ibelin. Tell him to come to me at once. Yes, I know it's late. Wake him if you must."

Sibylla withdrew to her room and sat down to begin stitching. The pattern grew under her fingers, almost without thinking. Black thread scrawled across the fabric, creating intersecting lines and geometric flowers. She had a plan, pitifully thin, but it was all she had left. Ibelin's stubbornness and Plancy's treachery meant she would no longer be able to salvage Acre as a beachhead from which to reconquer her kingdom, or even to establish some kind of protection for the holy places and their inhabitants.

The most she could now hope for was to keep the people alive and free—and she did not even know whether she would be able to do that.

* * *

Jerusalem at Vigils was dark and silent, watching in dread for the morning. As Balian paused in the torchlit courtyard to take off his cloak and gloves and hand them to a page, he prayed that Queen Sibylla had sent for him with some solution in mind. He was supposed to meet the sultan again at dawn, and he had no notion what to say.

Somewhere in the palace, a door creaked and footsteps echoed in a stairwell. Ernoul's hand touched his arm in a silent warning. Balian saw a man start across the courtyard pulling a deep hood over his face. Torchlight glinted off steel gaiters, the sort of equipment only a highly-ranked knight would possess. In his right hand, the stranger carried a lance whose point was covered with a long, thin leather bag.

What was a knight doing sneaking out of the palace at Vigils?

"God keep you, Plancy," he called on a whim. The knight stopped in his tracks and after a long, breathless moment, turned to face him.

"And you, Lord Balian."

"Where are you off to at this hour?"

"It's the queen's business, my lord."

"Then you'd better be about it," Balian said. He did not trust Plancy; even if he had trusted the young knight, he would not have trusted the queen. Under his breath, he muttered, "Send someone to follow him, Ernoul."

Upstairs, Queen Sibylla awaited him in her antechamber. It was as bright as day in there: full of lamps, as though she meant to burn all the oil before it could fall into Saladin's hands. She did not look up when he entered—she had taken to her needle again, and had her serving-women hard at work too.

"You summoned me, my lady?"

"Do you know where Miles of Plancy is?" she demanded.

"I passed him just now in the courtyard. On an errand of yours, he told me."

"Yes, of course he would say that." She darted a glance up at him, quick and sharp as her own needle. "Plancy lied. I did not order and do not condone his actions."

In the echoing silence, Balian's heart stood still with dread. "Say what you have to say."

The queen bent her head over her work. "Did you see his lance? It is the same once wielded by your fosterling, Marta Bessarion."

Ernoul did not speak, but he sent Balian a glance pale with anger.

"Find him and bring him to me," Balian said softly. As the door slammed behind the younger knight, he said, "What more do you know? Where is Marta?"

"At first, all I knew was what I overheard from your knight there." Sibylla nodded in the direction of the departed Ernoul. "Nothing but hearsay and rumours. It occurred to me, though, that when Sir Miles returned from the battle, he was riding a very fine grey destrier, the very image of the one my brother gave to Marta Bessarion."

Pomers. "Devil take it," Balian whispered.

The queen went on. "I have now questioned my knights. One of them told me that, at the very end of the battle when all hope was lost, the

White Watcher appeared to lead the men of the kingdom in one final charge. They nearly reached the banners of Saladin himself, but there was a counterattack and my fellow was struck from his horse. When he opened his eyes, he saw the White Watcher's lance stuck in the earth, right before his eyes. Just as he was about to reach for it, Plancy snatched it for himself. Another knight seized his bridle and begged him to stay. Plancy struck the man down as he fled."

Balian felt as though he had turned to stone. "And Marta?"

The queen's lip curled. "Who knows? But one who would strike down his own friends to flee a battle is capable of any villainy."

"I'm going to hang him," Balian said thickly, wheeling for the door. Within five minutes Ernoul had set out with a squad of sergeants on Plancy's trail. Within half an hour they led Miles of Plancy led back to the palace, dazed and bleeding.

In the peristyle, Ernoul unshrouded the Bessarion Lance and offered it to Balian with a flourish. "He tried to use it to defend himself, my lord. So I had Bertrand fire a warning bolt from his crossbow."

"A very gentle warning," Balian said, observing the bloody gash in Plancy's side. He took the weapon from Ernoul, and his gut curdled as he recognised the damascened steel of the blade, the familiar, silk-smooth wood of the haft. *Marta, Marta, what has become of you?*

"Release me at once," Plancy groaned, pressing a hand to his bloodied side. "How dare you waylay one of the queen's servants on the queen's business?"

"Tell me how you came to be in possession of the Bessarion Lance," Balian responded, very gently.

In the torchlight, Plancy's face shuttered. "I didn't know it was the Bessarion Lance."

"Don't lie to me."

Plancy squirmed. "I didn't know it at *first*, I mean. I found it on the battlefield. No one was near it. No one claimed it. There was no time to stop and ask. You were there! You saw what the fighting was like!"

He had, and the thought that Marta had been in the middle of that, lost in it, was like thorns in his gut. Balian let out a breath. This was why he had refused to believe Ernoul, to imagine that she had come to grief.

He still did not want to believe it.

"You returned from that battle with Marta's lance and Marta's horse," he said. "What am I to make of this? Did you rob her corpse? Did you kill her yourself? Or did you take what you wanted and abandon her to captivity?"

Beads of sweat formed on Plancy's forehead. "Why blame *me* for her misfortune? You knew what she was like. You even encouraged her to ride around with this trumpery weapon and consider herself invincible."

"You seem to think," Balian said, his gentleness now withering cold, "that I would have countenanced *any* of this. It was not on *my* account that she rode to Arabia four years ago. If she was at the battle it was only because of *you.*"

"*You* were the first to abandon her! *You* turned tail and fled, like a coward! She saw it, you know. You ought to have seen the look on her face!"

Plancy's words ran echoing rings around the silent dark of the peristyle. They struck Balian like arrows to the heart.

"So," Balian managed to say, over the bitterness of his own shame, "you *knew* she was there. You were at her side."

A terrible awareness of his mistake spread over the young knight's face Guilt followed. "No! No, it wasn't like that." Plancy gulped. "I did fight by her side. We were both in the king's division, and I followed her on all her sorties. But then, during the battle itself, I lost track of her. I swear to you, when I took the horse and the Lance, I didn't know if she was dead or alive."

"Then what happened?" The queen's account had not spared the young knight, and Balian did not mean to spare him either. "Take care how you answer, boy. You were not the only witness to survive the battle."

At that, Plancy went as pale as paper. For a moment Balian thought he would refuse to answer; but with a ragged breath that was almost a sob, he said: "Then a knight begged me not to leave her on the battlefield." He buried his face in his hands. "It was Marta."

Balian stared, the hairs on his neck prickling. This, the queen had *not* told him. Possibly she had not known.

"It was *Marta* who stopped you? It was *Marta* you struck down with her own lance?"

He moved almost without thinking, catching the young man by his surcoat and slamming him against the wall. Plancy kept his hands pressed to his face. The wet glimmer of tears between his fingers served only to disgust Balian more.

"Look me in the eye," he growled.

Plancy dropped his hands and hung there against the wall, unresisting. For the first time Balian had some notion of the torment the young knight must have suffered; in his heart, he could find only a grim satisfaction.

"Tell the truth," he whispered. *"Did you kill her?"*

Plancy's chest heaved. "Oh, my lord, no. I struck her with the haft. I l—" His voice faded. He turned his head away. "I left her alive. For *them.*"

There was a sword on Balian's hip crying out for Plancy's blood, but the last thing he wanted was to grant this traitor the mercy of death. Balian let go of Plancy and stepped back, folding his arms to keep them away from his sword.

"I have never heard of a more shameful thing. You ought to be led through the city with your shield reversed."

"Kill me now," Plancy groaned, collapsing onto his knees.

His grovelling only incensed Balian. Had Plancy truly been truly sorry for his actions, he would not have spent months trying to conceal them. Nor would Balian have needed to drag the truth out of him.

"Get up," he bellowed. "You've been a beast; now act the man. Stand to hear your sentence."

Ernoul dragged Plancy to his feet. He obeyed meekly, to all appearances utterly broken.

Not broken enough. Balian meant to grind him into dust—Plancy, and his treachery, and his accusations against Balian himself.

"I will not grant you the mercy of a quick death," Balian declared. "I will make it clearly known in the city what you have done. I will make it known that your life is sacred. Then, if I have any influence at all with the sultan, you shall go alive into captivity, and may God have mercy on your soul."

He turned on his heel, but Plancy fought against the hands that restrained him, sobbing "No! Not that! Kill me first, and then dishonour me!"

"You aren't worth it," Balian sneered.

"But I've done worse," Plancy blurted. "I've betrayed the city to Saladin."

* * *

Time stretched out. In the end, the matter was dealt with quicker than Sibylla had expected, yet each minute passed like aeons. She stifled her yawns and stitched on, determined not to relax her vigilance until she was sure the city was safe.

Presently, the door shook to knocking and Ibelin stalked into the room, his anger belied by the redness of his eyes. He glared at her, but said nothing.

"You found Plancy?" Sibylla ventured. "Is he secure?"

"Did you know?" Ibelin demanded, answering her question with another. "Did you know he had sold the city?"

Sibylla placed her needle. "Yes, but I—"

"But you didn't tell me." Ibelin waited for a leaden moment. "Was it *your* notion, then? What did you profit from it? Did you trade the lives of all these people for the freedom of that fool you married?"

She had been afraid of this misaimed wrath. Ibelin had made it clear he did not want her help defending the city, so Sibylla had been obliged to use whatever weapon she could. Having interrogated her knights, she had found proof of Plancy's behaviour towards Marta Bessarion. She had no proof of his dealings with Saladin, not unless he confessed. Which, it now seemed, he had.

"If you'll listen a moment, I can explain."

"No," Ibelin growled. He turned to the door, where his own men waited— *how many of them?* Sibylla suddenly wondered, with a jumping heart.

"You are to take over the guarding of the palace. Lock up anyone who resists. As for the queen..." Ibelin cast a glance at her over his shoulder. "Seal her into this room. Allow her no companions. No one is to enter or leave the palace until I have met with Saladin."

Chapter XXXIX.

Marta did not remain in the courtyard to learn whether Lilith had really discovered her. Instead, she fled through the nearest door and found herself in the shadows of the women's quarters. Bahar and her girls were still busy cleaning; Arwa had just emerged yawning from her room, ready to issue the adhan. All the same, Marta fumbled with her spindle, hastily setting the bobbin spinning, and daring to breathe only once the thread was again humming between her fingers.

Had Lilith truly caught her trespassing upon Ibrahim's memory? What would the consequences be, now that Khalil's patience had worn thin?

Her time might be short: now that she knew the djinn's true name, she must seize her opportunity at once.

Still spinning, Marta hurried downstairs to the bathhouse, where during the dawn prayer she would be assured of privacy. "Ibrahim ibn Salim ibn Qeteb, peace be upon you."

There was no answer, but the light that fell in patches through the dome of the hammam shivered a little, as though the house itself had drawn breath.

"Ibrahim ibn Salim ibn Qeteb, in God's name I beg you come to me."

Another breath, another shiver.

"Ibrahim ibn Salim ibn Qeteb, I have seen your captivity and you have seen mine. Come: let us each bear witness."

The water in the great tiled pool boiled, and in the steam a gigantic, yet insubstantial shape took form. Marta retreated a step, but she never stopped spinning, and the thread ran smooth through her fingers.

Made of wisps and memories, the great djinn towered over her, still wearing the brocaded coat he had worn in the memory of the courtyard.

"Daughter of the enemy of my enemy: do you seek death, that you summon me by my true name? The master of the house will not countenance my speaking to you face to face."

Despite the danger, Marta could not overcome her own delight. "You came," she said, beaming up at him. "At last. *Thank* you."

"I *said*," the djinn growled, "do you seek death?"

He bent over her, all heat and wrath and noise. Entranced, Marta wished to pass a hand through him, to see whether the figure was tangible, but that seemed impolite somehow.

"Not death," she said, "but knowledge."

"You ought to have been content to share my dreams," Ibrahim said, a little sulkily. His deep, soft voice was enough to make the stones hum. "Al-Aziz will strip me of my past if he finds that I have helped you."

This was puzzling. "You showed me your true name. What else was I meant to do with it?"

"I showed you the key to the magic of the house," Ibrahim retorted. "Do you imagine I could not have spoken to you freely at any time? Each of us wants our revenge on al-Aziz, and I will help as I can, but I cannot speak to you face to face. Be patient for a year, and learn from the visions I send you when the stars are right."

Be patient? For a *year*? Marta thought that she might scream. "I can't," she choked. "I don't have a year; I'll be lucky to last a week. Don't go! I can destroy Khalil; only I *must* have answers to my questions."

If her hands had been free, she would have clasped them, but since they were busy with the anti-magic of spinning, she could only beg with her eyes.

"Three questions," Ibrahim said reluctantly. "No more. And consider them carefully: you must never summon me again."

"How can you be freed?" Marta asked at once, anxious that he might change his mind.

He blinked. "This is your first question? I warned you—"

"You have been my friend in this house," Marta told him. "I cannot go away and leave you in Khalil's power. I swear on my lance that I will set you free."

Between the promise she had made to Fayruz and the promise she now made to the djinn, part of her wondered whether she would have the chance to go away at all. Yet promise or not, she could not have left him. Not after all he had done for her.

Ibrahim seemed staggered by the vow. At last, he cleared his throat and said, "First you must banish the afrit whose name binds me to the vessel, and then you must destroy the vessel."

Marta opened her mouth, but caught herself just in time, before she wasted a question. Ibrahim smiled wryly before adding: "In my case, the afrit is Lilith, and the vessel is the orange-tree in the courtyard."

Exorcise Lilith and destroy an entire tree, in a part of the house she had not set foot in without Khalil at her side? Marta swallowed, confronted with the immensity of her task. Still, daunting as it might be, such a task was surely not impossible. Two more questions burned on her tongue.

"What is the nature of the Bessarion Lance? Khalil claimed to have created it."

"He did." Ibrahim was silent a moment. Then he said, "Khalil's lance is the vessel of a spirit far greater and older even than myself. That is what I have been trying to show you, every night as you dream."

"The woman in green," Marta whispered, and his look confirmed it. Marta had suspected as much, since she had learned the nature of the house. But she had hoped, oh, she had hoped it was not true. She did not like to think of the Lance as a slave.

"I don't understand what a djinn is."

"Is that your third question?"

"No. Disregard it if you wish."

Instead, he answered. "There are divers explanations. Some say we were the offspring of afrit and men; others say we are a third race altogether, creatures of smokeless fire."

"Nephilim," Marta conjectured.

"One thing is certain: that most of the ancient lineages of my people died out years ago—hunted, enslaved, and killed. Those who are left are rare, imprisoned within different vessels, or flown altogether from the world of earth and flesh." He hesitated. "It is thought, by some, that a new lineage of djinn might be created, but only if a mortal sorcerer was to render his body for a time to his familiar. In theory, a child conceived in such a state would inherit something of the nature of the afrit."

One of us would need to possess you, Lilith's voice said in her memory. *After that it would only be a matter of finding the right mother.*

Marta's heart stood still. "Why would anyone take such a dreadful risk?"

"Because he would then have a new djinn to enslave."

Marta remembered the sigil painted across the floor beneath Khalil's low bed, with writing she had not yet had the opportunity to decipher. She remembered Qeteb's words: *Just imagine, your very own mamluk, ruthless, immortal, and loyal as an Assassin.*

"You think he's going to try it," she whispered. "You think he's going to create a nephil—a djinn." And then with a jolt that made her sick, she understood. "Fayruz! He *knows*—he's been *letting* us protect her."

"Child," Ibrahim began sadly. But then his voice changed, becoming sharp with warning. "Your spinning!"

She looked down at her hands. The bobbin swung motionless from her right hand. As she startled and tried to catch it, it pulled free from the puff of cotton on her spindle, ran across the floor and dropped into the pool.

The anti-magic had broken.

"I must go," Ibrahim said.

"Wait," she gasped, falling on her knees, ready to follow the bobbin into the water. "I haven't asked my third question."

Before she had finished speaking, a new voice intruded upon them.

"Ah! I thought I heard a mouse creeping where she shouldn't."

Marta bolted upright with a gasp. It was Lilith, a seething knot of feathers and darkness among the shadows of the doorway; Lilith, in the shape of the harpy she had first seen at the destruction of Oliveta.

With a sickening jolt, her heart began to beat again. "Poison Mother,"

Marta whispered. *"I know you."*

For some reason, the creature seemed surprised. "Oh ho, and she has eyes in her head as well as ears! Leave us, half-breed."

"No, *wait*," Marta protested, but it made no difference. Ibrahim vanished as suddenly as he had come, and she was left alone facing the shadows of the doorway where Lilith stood wrapped in coiling darkness.

"You think very highly of yourself, giving orders to *my* slave."

"On the contrary, it's him I think highly of."

"Forget about Ibrahim," Lilith told her. "You want to leave this house? Good. Follow me. I'll take you to your old home in Nablus. From there, you can surely find your way to Jerusalem."

Marta stared. "What?"

"You heard," Lilith said. "Come, quickly, while you have the opportunity."

"Why?"

"Maybe I've taken pity on you."

Lilith was a demon; pity could have no place in her heart. This was a trap, unless she was really trying to get Marta out of the house for some private reason of her own. Had she for one moment trusted Lilith, she would have followed with a sob of gratitude, but that was clearly impossible. Ibrahim was still a slave. Fayruz still had another three or even four months to go before giving birth—perhaps to a djinn.

And Marta still did not know how to kill Khalil.

"That's impossible," she said. "Don't insult me with such offers."

"Come! I know you've been intriguing against me—eavesdropping in your dreams, telling al-Aziz about my alliance with the fearful queen. Do you think I mean to let this go on? If you're wise, you'll bargain with me. Or shall I report to Khalil at once?"

It felt as though someone had scooped out her insides with a spoon. "I cannot stop you."

"He'll believe me. I'll tell him everything—about you, about Ibrahim, about the brat you're trying to hide."

"Yes, in God's name; now *go.*"

Lilith vanished. The shadows dissipated from the passage. Marta drew a long, shaking breath; and then she remembered Lilith's parting words.

The baby—Lilith knew about Fayruz's baby.

"Oh, strife," she whispered; and without waiting to retrieve the bobbin from the pool, she rushed for the door.

Chapter XL.

Upstairs, the prayers were just finishing. Marta dragged Fayruz into her own room, yanked the curtain shut, and seized the other woman by the shoulders.

"Lilith knows, and it's my fault. I'm so sorry."

"How?" A look of despair came over Fayruz's face. "You couldn't even watch through the night?"

"Never mind how," Marta said. She dared not say what she feared, that Lilith might have overlooked their fumbles and spared the child for the sake of Khalil's spell. "I promise I will get you and your baby out of this house, but you need to come with me *today.*"

Fayruz shrugged free of Marta's grip. "You're mad. Where to?"

Marta had spent time thinking about this. There must be Watchers in Damascus. All she needed to do was show her Mark and someone would direct her to the rest of her people. They would surely help her.

Surely.

"There are people in this city who will protect us."

Fayruz snorted. "The people that can protect us from al-Aziz don't exist."

"Fayruz." Marta gave her a little shake. "Khalil will have no mercy. Lilith will take your baby unless you come with me *now.*"

Fayruz bit her lip, her eyes flickering from Marta to the door and then back again. Her calculations brought her swiftly to a decision. "All right," she said. "What's your plan?"

The plan was to waylay Bahar and one of the other kitchen girls, begging them to trade places with herself and Fayruz. Their black veils and plain, homespun coats would cover Marta and Fayruz from head to foot, allowing only their eyes and hands to be seen. Even inside the house, Khalil's servants were held to an unusual standard of modesty, but it would work in their favour now, the voluminous robes managing to somewhat conceal the swelling of Fayruz's pregnant belly.

Bahar agreed, terrified and reluctant though she was. In order to give the slaves an excuse, Marta put both girls into a storeroom and locked the door behind them, advising them to tell their master she had overpowered them.

Fayruz looked at her sceptically, but Marta shrugged. "He will believe it. In this way he is afraid of me himself."

She would have liked to bid goodbye to Arwa and Halimah, but the fewer people knew of their escape, the better. Instead, she and Fayruz ventured to the door leading into the kitchens. Images of Rabia's death floated through her mind; it took Marta a moment to work up the courage to knock. But when the guards opened the door from the kitchen side, they barely looked at her or at Fayruz, still less scrutinising them in any detail. Marta led the way into the kitchen and found the two other slave girls hard at work, grinding flour and pounding sesame seeds into a paste.

"You're late," a man scolded them. This must be the cook, Marta surmised: a pudgy man who, like the guards, barely spared a glance for them. He flapped a hand at them. "Go on. The master won't be happy if the sweeping isn't done within the hour."

Bahar had warned them not to reply to their orders except with obedience. Marta bobbed her head and, still carrying the brooms that had recently been used to clean the women's quarters, she led Fayruz out the opposite kitchen door.

Khalil's house was nearly as quiet during the day as it was in her dreams at night. Fayruz panted hard behind her as Marta led her, not to the great shadowy apartments on the first floor, but down the stairs to the small rear courtyard: the dusty, utilitarian place where she had witnessed the deaths of Rabia and her guard. There, to the left of the hacked pells, a small wicket door led out through the bolted gate into the street. It stood half open, and—God be thanked—unguarded. In the stable, a buzz of talk and laughter told where the porter had gone; he must be helping some farmer unload a cart of horse feed or some such thing.

Marta could have wept with relief. The only other thing she could have begged for was a mule for Fayruz to ride upon, but as it was they would have to rely on their legs. One quick dash, and they would be free. Home was so close she could *smell* it.

"Quickly," she whispered to Fayruz, but even as she darted towards the gate, the porter emerged from the stables and let out a shout of alarm, grabbing for his sword. He was nearer the door than she, and Marta, with a sob of despair, came to a halt. She had no weapon to use, nothing except the broom she carried, and that was no substitute for the Bessarion Lance.

Even as she hesitated, two hands fastened in her coat.

"Help! Help!" Fayruz shouted. "The master's slave is trying to escape!"

Marta twisted. "Fayruz! What are you *doing?*"

"Saving my baby," the other woman panted. "It's too late—it's no use—"

Men boiled out of the stables, two more guards and a big, burly mamluk in a gorgeous brocaded tunic. Fayruz released her and Marta staggered away, almost drunkenly raising her broom. But freedom was so close—and she had faced greater odds before.

"Saint Martha," she breathed in supplication and raced for the gate, but one of the guards threw himself in front of her. Marta swept up her broomstick and splintered it across his head. He staggered sideways and fell to one knee, momentarily stunned. A hand closed on her right arm and she swung around, transferring her broken broomstick to her left hand. Now little more than a long splinter, she rammed it under his arm and into his ribs with all her might. Against his finely woven mail, the point snapped with the impact; but the blunt force of it dislodged his grip, and Marta staggered free.

Her one remaining opponent was the mamluk, who now came towards her brandishing a spear. In desperation, Marta threw the splintered end of her broomstick to her left hand, and with her right drew the carnelian dagger. It was no good, of course. One could not wield a dagger against a lance. The mamluk swept the haft almost lazily, catching her across the midsection. The flagstones reared up and Marta tumbled in the dust, bent double with agony and fighting to draw breath.

Dimly she was aware of the sorcerer's men standing over her, weapons ready; of the wicket-door being shut and locked; of the guards' hushed voices becoming silent altogether; and of a shadow falling across her, somehow making it harder to breathe, before two bruising hands lifted her up—Khalil. He carried her into the house like a child.

"Let me go," she rasped, despite her tormented lungs. He only tightened his grip painfully, and she fell back against his shoulder.

Behind, two guards flanked a pale, terrified-looking Fayruz.

Khalil stepped through the door of his room into the women's quarters. Halimah and Arwa jumped to their feet with cries of surprise and alarm. Khalil spared no glance for either of them, instead kneeling to deposit Marta on the same divan she had occupied in her first days, when she had been sick with fever and Arwa had nursed her. Still gasping for breath, Marta pulled herself to a sitting position. Fayruz stumbled into the room behind them, escorted by the eunuch guards, and Khalil turned upon her.

"What is the meaning of *this?*" he demanded, stripping the black coat from her. Beneath, the bright, gauzy silks of the women's quarters could not conceal her condition. Whatever Khalil had been about to say caught in his throat.

"What's this? A *child?*"

Fayruz opened her mouth; only a sob came out.

"Lilith!" Khalil snapped his fingers. Fayruz began to wail, but no Lilith appeared.

Khalil cursed, unsheathing the little knife at his belt—Marta's carnelian dagger. Putting a nick in the tip of his forefinger, he scrawled quick bloody words on the wall. *"Lilith!"* he bellowed.

The feathered woman appeared at once, springing from the bloodied wall. Her eyes rolled and fixed on Marta, but it was to Khalil that she spoke. "How dare you, al-Aziz?" she snarled. "I'm not your slave!"

She vanished immediately, but Khalil dragged her back with another shout: whatever spell he had worked with his blood seemed enough, for the moment, to compel her obedience.

"My whole household is conspiring against me, and now you *dare* to join them?" Khalil growled. "Look at this. One of my wives is with child. Why did you conceal this from me? Why did you not take care of it?"

"Because she's been hiding it from me!" Lilith shrieked, before vanishing a second time.

If the demon seemed terrified, that was nothing compared to the wives. Fayruz threw herself on her knees. "My lord," she gasped. "I only wanted to please you. Did I not prevent your slave from escaping?"

"You expect me to *reward* your disobedience?" Khalil stepped towards her, the carnelian dagger steady in his fist. Fayruz keened, a despairing wail that went straight to Marta's heart. Staggering from the divan, she stepped between them almost before she knew what she was doing.

"We all did it," Marta rasped. "We took turns hiding the baby from Lilith. It was my idea. Punish me, not her."

She scarcely knew what she was saying. Perhaps she wanted him to provoke him—to bring down upon her head the violence that had been hanging over her so long. Or perhaps she only wanted Khalil to know that he could trust *none* of them.

His dark eyes searched her upturned face. "You weep," he taunted her.

"You dream," she spat.

But he only laughed, quick and hard. He watched her a moment longer, and the look on his face frightened her, so pale and taut. Remembering the awful sound of Rabia's guard being beaten to death, Marta steeled herself for what was about to happen.

Khalil's hands fastened on her face and he bent down, lifting her head to his. He kissed her with clumsy force, as though in all the barren years of his life this was one skill he had never honed. Marta could do nothing but restrain her scream. At last, he drew away from her, that pinched look of rage still drawing his face tight.

"You've made a grave mistake," he said softly. "Very well: if you can't weep for me, then I'll make you weep for yourself." He released her, then, and the door to the Damascus wing slammed behind him. In the silence that suddenly overwhelmed them, the only sound was Fayruz sobbing.

As Halimah went to comfort Fayruz, Marta fled to her room, dragging the curtain shut behind her. Seizing her spindle, she summoned Ibrahim three times. The djinn appeared as a shadow in the glass of her window before stepping through in a haze of glimmering heat. His face was a grimace of terror.

"Are you mad, to call on me now? You swore you'd never summon me again!"

"*You* swore you'd answer me three questions," Marta hissed. Her heart was too loud in her own ears and the bobbin bobbed and jerked in her shaking hands. "Quickly! Tell me how to kill Khalil, and I'll set both of us free, I swear it."

The djinn shook his head. "It's impossible. Al-Aziz is immortal."

"Then tell me how to undo his immortality. As you *promised.*"

Ibrahim ground a palm against his eyes, but he answered all the same. "Khalil is made immortal by the demons to whom he has bound himself— not just Lilith, but Qeteb, too. Both of them must be exorcised before—"

Like a candle blowing out, the djinn vanished.

Marta could not repress a yelp of surprise when it happened. She reached out, but he was gone like a dream. "Ibrahim ibn Salim ibn Qeteb," she called in a hoarse whisper, three times. But Ibrahim did not answer her.

Marta did not dare to stop spinning as she paced the room. Three turns, and she called Ibrahim again. No answer. Six turns, and she called him again. Still no answer. Twelve turns, no success. Twenty-four turns...

Exorcise, not one demon, but two? The way Ibrahim had spoken of it, he did not believe her capable of such a thing. Marta had never been anyone special, neither a Portentor nor a Messenger nor even, like Persi, a Perceptor. All she had ever had was an enchanted lance, inherited from someone who had stolen it from Khalil. It was more than she could manage simply to hide a child from Lilith. And she was to pit herself against Qeteb, the demon of empire?

There was no time. The sword that for so long had been hanging over her head was about to descend. Even with years at her disposal, she could never do this alone. She had to escape; she had to find other Watchers to help her. Only then would she be able to kill Khalil. If she was dead, she could do nothing against him.

"Ibrahim ibn Salim ibn Qeteb!" she called again, her voice hoarse with desperation.

This time he came, appearing before her in unfurling shadows. Arms folded, he gazed down on her as from a remote distance.

"If I do cast out Lilith and Qeteb," Marta whispered, "will Khalil die like any mortal?"

Ibrahim beheld her coldly. At length he spoke. "You must be the witch."

Marta blinked up at him; his face seemed carved in marble. "Ibrahim?"

"The master warned me you would summon me. Don't waste your breath questioning me. I won't answer."

Marta stared at him for a long moment before light dawned upon her—*Al-Aziz will strip me of my past.* God in heaven, was *this* what that meant? "Don't you know me, Ibrahim?"

"I don't," the djinn said roughly. "He said you'd try to confuse me."

Marta felt nauseous. What of all the memories Ibrahim had shown her? Had he forgotten those, too? Was she now the only one, apart from Khalil and his familiars, who knew how the djinn had been seduced, captured, and bound to Khalil's house?

She was still hesitating over the thought when she heard the door open from Damascus, and Khalil's heavy tread stalked into the common room.

"Where is she?" he demanded.

Ibrahim flashed away through the curtain. "She is in the room here, my master. It was as you said: she summoned me, but I stood fast and spoke as you instructed."

There was no point in hiding from him. Slowly, numb with dread, Marta opened the curtain and walked into the room to face Khalil.

Halimah, Arwa, and Fayruz had risen to their feet and stood in a row by the window, whispering. Ibrahim knelt before Khalil; the sorcerer's fingers were still white with chalk-dust from whatever magic he had worked on the djinn. He extended them to Marta now, his face hard as stone.

"Listen well," Khalil said. "If you attempt to suborn my servants or my wives again, I will kill both Fayruz and her child together. And after that, if you continue to defy me, you should remember that I know all there is to know about you, and all Jerusalem is in the palm of my hand. I will kill the Nubian weaver, and I will kill your kinsman from Acre, and I will hunt down every man, woman, and child who bears the name Zakar or Bessarion, and you will see the light fade from their eyes. Now, for the last time I ask: will you marry me?"

Marta did not answer. What use was it? She would not assent. She dared not refuse. "You swore not to harm me," she whispered.

Khalil snarled, as though his affability had been a mask for which he no longer had any use. "Nor will I, if you submit. Consider well before you refuse. I do not need to make you my wife in order to have my will of you."

Marta was aware of her fingernails cutting deep crescents into her palms. "Why?" she whispered. "Why *me?*"

Khalil reached out, snatched at her unresisting wrist. "A Bessarion took my lance," he said, softly. "Now, Marta Bessarion, you will bear me a sword. A son like no other."

A son.

She thought desperately of Persi. This had not been the end for her friend; it need not be the end for her, either.

A son like no other. A sword...

This, then, was his purpose for her: Khalil would use her to create a djinn.

"Weep now," he ordered, but Marta did not weep then; only later, when Khalil was finished with her, and she was alone.

Chapter XLI.

By the time Balian led his small diplomatic delegation into the Saracen camp on the morning of the second of October, he was in no mood for anything but bloodshed and vengeance. Not even Saladin would trifle with him today.

"It's not what Marta would have wanted," Ernoul had said, shaking his head when he realised what Balian was planning.

"Marta is gone," Balian had said coldly. "And Plancy is the one responsible."

Now, signalling his retinue to wait, he dismounted and followed one of Saladin's officials into the tent. The sultan had just finished his prayers, and turned from a conversation with one of his holy men to face Balian. The air between them thrummed with the memory of yesterday's meeting, when he had been sent away with a promise of destruction. A frown etched itself between the sultan's craggy brows.

"I have nothing fresh to say to you, Frank."

"Perhaps not, but I have something to say to you." Balian drew breath, reciting the words Queen Sibylla had suggested. "I have consulted with the people of the city, and their message is this: we are fighting for faith as much as you are. Pursue this siege, and we will fight until there are none of us standing. Men and youths, we will take as many of you with us as we may, and one Frank will slay ten Saracen knights before he dies. But first, we will slay the three thousand captives we have taken from among your people. We will slay our women and children, so that they should not go into captivity and be lost to God. We will salt the cisterns and burn our goods. Above all, we will level to the ground the Temple, and even what you call the Dome of the Rock. All you will gain from us will be a pile of corpses and a heap of ruins." Balian paused. "Unless you make terms."

The longer Balian spoke, the angrier Saladin seemed, until his lips were pressed together and his brows were drawn down. "You cannot be serious. Did you not hear what I said yesterday? I do not need to make bargains. I already have people inside Jerusalem."

"You *meant* to have people inside the city," Balian corrected. Had the occasion not been so dreadful, he might have enjoyed delivering this blow. "You *meant* to send your men in by the postern of the Madeleine at Vigils last night. As for what happened—well, I have a gift for you."

At Balian's signal, Ernoul dragged his prisoner into the tent and deposited at the sultan's feet a feeble, groaning pile of useless limbs—all that was left of Miles of Plancy after half an hour with the royal executioner. The sultan drew back a step, staring at the bloodied heap.

"This man is a double traitor," Balian said, grimly triumphant. "He betrayed you of his own accord; there was no need to loosen his tongue. We racked him a little afterwards, for the sake of completion, because it seemed he should not clear himself so easily. Make him a slave, for he's fit for nothing else."

Plancy groaned. Blood, mixed with saliva, dribbled from between his lips.

"He's dying," the sultan observed, indicating the blood.

"No such good fortune," Balian said. "I had that silver tongue of his torn out, lest he sweetly argue himself into favour with some other master. He'll live, and even be useful, once he recovers."

For a moment, Saladin seemed speechless. Balian studied the sultan's face for any sign of relenting.

Vengeful as his actions had been, they were not without calculation—the same calculation made by Queen Sibylla when she devised this ultimatum. To deter their enemies, the Franks of the kingdom had long cultivated a reputation for ferocity—that was partly why King Guy's strategy of passive defence had been so dangerous. Now he must convince the sultan that the

Frankish ferocity had never been greater, that the small but formidable force the queen had brought to defend Jerusalem was skilled enough, and determined enough, to win a pitched battle—just as their forefathers had outside Antioch, eighty years before. That with Miles of Plancy expelled from the city, no one else would be foolhardy enough to follow his treacherous example.

Balian tried not to let his relief show too clearly when Saladin nodded. "Very well," he said. "What are your terms?"

* * *

Sibylla knew without a doubt that she had lost whatever was left of the kingdom.

If the nobles distrusted her this badly—if even *Ibelin* believed her capable of selling her own city to the enemy—then it was all over. Not even Lilith could make her a queen, if that was what they thought of her. She must indeed resign herself to life as an exile, or perhaps retire to a convent.

The sun was up. It had been hours since Ibelin had locked the door on her and stomped away, leaving his men on guard outside. Where was her own guard? Had they abandoned her too?

A scratch came at one of the windows looking onto the loggia, and to her astonishment Sibylla looked up to see the pale face of Stephanie of Kerak pressed against the casement. Putting down her embroidery, Sibylla unlatched the window.

"I'm fairly certain I'm not supposed to have visitors," she greeted Reynald of Chatillon's widow dryly.

"I paid off the guards," Stephanie said. "Your lady Alix managed to get word to me. It's true then—Ibelin has made you his prisoner."

"It's nothing. A ridiculous misunderstanding, that's all." *But,* she might have added, *undoubtedly a sign of things to come.*

Stephanie evidently agreed with her unspoken thought, because she said, "This is treason. You're the *queen.* He can't simply lock you up like this. Who does he think he is—Fulk of Anjou?"

Queen Melisende's foreign husband had behaved in equally high-handed ways, before he had been taught the respect due to the heiress of Jerusalem. Sibylla sighed. "Perhaps, but I am no Melisende."

"Why not?" Stephanie pulled her head out of the narrow window and sent a wary glance up the loggia, no doubt toward the guards there. When she leaned in at the window again, she sank her voice to a whisper. "I'll tell the Patriarch what they've done to you. I'll appeal to the people. They don't want peace with Saladin; they want to fight to the death. They'll turn their backs on Ibelin in an instant. You only need to say the word."

Once, perhaps, Sibylla would have agreed. She had nothing to lose but her life, and that had ceased to hold much attraction for her. But now, with Miles of Plancy taken out of play, there was just a chance the city might be saved. She had refused this when Lilith offered it; she could do no less when Stephanie offered the same thing.

"If you do that, Stephanie, you are no friend of mine. Ibelin is carrying out *my* orders, not because I made them but because they are the right thing to do. And I am sitting a prisoner in my own house, not because Ibelin locked my door, but because *it is the right thing to do.*"

Saints, she thought, revolted. She sounded exactly like Marta Bessarion.

Stephanie reddened. "You're making a mistake. You'll never hold onto power if you allow yourself to be humiliated like this."

Sibylla stifled the cutting words that came to her lips. She was the last person qualified to lecture anyone on the evils of clinging to power. "Believe me, no one could be more conscious of that than I am. I've made my choice."

Stephanie wrinkled her nose in disgust. "You've turned coward."

Sibylla was not particularly surprised, when her visitor departed, to find that she was not alone. Lilith loomed over her, an angry, chittering, birdlike shadow.

"You are determined to reject my help?"

Heart pounding, Sibylla reached for the discarded embroidery hoop. "*You* were responsible for that little offer? I thought it sounded familiar."

"You will *pay* for your treachery," the bird snapped. "Saladin may spare you, but you have other enemies, Sibylla of Jerusalem. Sooner or later, I will make you and your people a byword. I will feast on your corpses. No one will escape this city; *no one.*"

The great bird plunged through Sibylla and out the window. She felt as though a talon closed around her heart and tried to tear it through her ribs on the way through. Sibylla fell to the floor, heaving in great whooping breaths as fear washed through her in icy waves.

The people were going to die anyway; she had not saved a single soul. All she had done was ensure that she would die with them.

Chapter XLII.

Ibelin returned as Sibylla, swamped with melancholy, was watching her evening meal grow cold.

He entered and bowed in silence. Although there were pouches under his eyes from lack of sleep, it seemed a weight had lifted from his shoulders. When Sibylla saw it, she felt a certain amount lighter herself.

Alix, who had been permitted to return to her at midday, offered the tall nobleman a chair. He sank into it with a weary sigh.

"Saladin has consented to make terms," Ibelin informed her, as though at their last meeting he had not imprisoned her in her own palace. "Our goods and our wealth are our own, but our persons are taken into captivity. The sultan has fixed the ransom at thirty gold bezants for a man, ten for a woman, and three for a child. Rich or poor, all must pay the same."

"Thirty for a man!" Sibylla's hopes plunged again. "That's impossible. Scarcely one man in a hundred can pay so much—and as for the women and children…"

"I told him the same," Ibelin said. "I've spent most of the day going about the city, trying to determine just how much gold there is in the treasuries."

"There is the treasure my cousin the king of England deposited with the Hospital," Sibylla volunteered. In her head she was figuring numbers. For every man in the city there must be fifty or a hundred women and children—fugitives from the surrounding towns and villages and convents. Where would they find the vast sums necessary for such a ransom?

"The Patriarch and I have been to the Hospital," Ibelin said. "They've agreed to disburse the English money. There's no point in refusing: the sultan's quite capable of taking it over our dead bodies. But it won't provide a fraction of the sum we need."

"We might pay half," Sibylla said, completing her figures. "And that's only if everyone contributes. Ask Saladin to reduce the price to a quarter and promise him fire and death if he refuses."

Ibelin watched her thoughtfully. "That's your advice? You don't think we should take the terms we're given, ransom the fighting men and the rich, and leave the rest to Saladin?"

Sibylla spared a mocking glance from her stitching. "You don't either."

"No," he said with a slight frown, as though it puzzled him to find her agreeing with him.

"No, because it wouldn't be good for morale," she agreed sarcastically. "How good of you to consult with me, my lord. If you require any further counsel, I shall always be at home. I haven't been able to get out much lately."

Ibelin flushed slowly, from the neck up. "That was a mistake; I wasn't thinking straight. Of course you weren't implicated in Plancy's betrayal."

Was that an apology? Sibylla raised her eyebrows. "Indeed. Had I intended to betray my own capital to Saladin, I would scarcely have drawn your attention to Plancy's perfidy. Nor would I have advised you on making a settlement with the sultan."

Ibelin's mouth tightened. "Next time, perhaps you'll be more forthright in how you go about denouncing traitors."

Sibylla scarcely knew where to begin. "What else was I to tell you, Balian of Ibelin? That a knight who had hitherto distinguished himself in the defence of the city was about to betray it? That I had no evidence to prove it, but was willing to stake my own word against his? I denounced one of our few defenders to you on a matter for which I had *evidence,* because I knew you would never believe me otherwise. And you repaid me by imagining I could be a party to the betrayal of my own people."

Ibelin reddened more deeply still. "How can you blame me, when you have been party to *every* other misfortune that has befallen us?" His big hands clenched on the table. "Time after time you have ridden roughshod over the wills of others in order to secure your own power—which is evidently the only thing you care about."

"If this is about my coronation—" Sibylla began frostily.

"It's about *Isabella!*" he bellowed. An echoing silence rolled around the room. Alix made a distressed sound, pressing a hand to her mouth.

Sibylla did not move, did not make a sound. Ibelin seemed to realise what he was doing—shouting at two defenceless women. Slowly, he unclenched his hands and straightened.

"She was a child," he said, very quietly. "She was at no age to make a free choice."

Yes, she had done wrong. Each one of Ibelin's words stabbed her to the heart. She had once been so very angry with Baldwin for demanding she sacrifice herself for the kingdom; but she in turn had sacrificed her young sister—and her son.

Yet all her pride was up in arms, and she could not admit it, not now, certainly not to Ibelin.

The tall nobleman watched her almost despairingly. "This much you've done for the kingdom," he said at length. "You've remained in Jerusalem and done what you can to save it, when you might very easily have cut your losses and run away. So long as you are willing to do that, I am willing to keep the vow of fealty I once swore to your husband."

Sibylla bowed her head. What right did she have to ask for more?

"Think about what you will do when your ransom is arranged," Ibelin said presently. "Saladin promised us safe conduct to Christian lands, even if it means that he pays our passage across the sea."

Across the sea—to France, the land of her ancestors. She had never seen it and had no wish to do so. Jerusalem had always been her home.

"Has Tripoli fallen?" she asked. The northern county, bounded on the west by sea and on the east by the Lebanon mountains, might be ruled by her rival cousin, but the Lusignans had lands there. Guy had often spoken fondly of the years he had spent in that county, after his exile from Poitiers, before he travelled south to become one of the Leper King's household knights.

"No," Ibelin told her. "So far as I know, Tripoli still stands."

"Then I will go there," Sibylla said. She clenched her fists until the nails dug into her palms. "But first, I want to see Guy."

* * *

November rain wept from the lowering grey skies on the evening of Sibylla's arrival in Nablus to see her husband for the first time in five months.

The palace, which had so recently belonged to her stepmother Maria Comnena, now housed one of Saladin's amirs. The furnaces were blazing, and in her stepmother's old solar the air was warm and cosy after the cold, wet journey. Handing her wet mantle to Sara, Sibylla beckoned the children's nurse to bring her daughters forward.

"Are we going to see Papa again, my lady?" Beatrix asked.

"Yes; aren't you happy to see him?"

Beatrix sent a doleful glance to her elder sister. "Our hair is gone."

"Papa will be so happy to see you that he won't even notice," Sibylla promised. She wished she could say the same for herself. "Take them to their room, Anna," she told the nurse. "The king and I have much to discuss. I'll send for them later."

In their absence the room yawned large and empty as though it meant to swallow her. The palace must have been looted after Queen Maria fled, for only the larger items of furniture remained, and they had been scarred with ill-treatment. Sibylla found a seat and commenced to stitch almost without seeing her work. She knew what she ought to say to her husband; she knew what he would say to her in return. Sibylla wished that the words might go without saying, that she might be permitted to depart quietly and not return. But she owed him this, at least—the chance to reproach her to her face.

At least she was not kept waiting very long. The door opened and her husband was ushered into the room by two armed Saracens, who shut the door behind him, sealing them in the room together.

Sibylla's chest tightened at the sight of Guy. He looked pale and haggard, the strong bulk of his body whittled away so that his plain, serviceable tunic hung too loosely on his bony shoulders. But the worst thing was his reaction to seeing her. She expected him to be full of reproaches. Instead, he stopped and fixed his eyes on the floor.

"Guy," she began, and stopped helplessly. "Are they treating you well? Do you get enough to eat?"

"Yes," he said almost before she had finished speaking.

Another silence followed. She drew breath to speak, but he interrupted. "I'm sorry, Sibylla."

"What for?"

"I lost the kingdom." He still kept his gaze averted. "They were right, you ought to have divorced me. I *knew* Saladin had the greater army. I *knew* there was no water. I can't imagine what I was thinking, marching us across the hills like that before I had fully counted the cost."

Was this some cruel joke? Surely he could not have forgotten how Sibylla had ordered him not to return without a battle.

"You needn't talk like that," she snapped. "I can admit my folly."

Guy drew in a sharp breath. For a while neither of them said anything—Sibylla did not know what else *to* say. She had come full of love and remorse, and he was throwing it in her face.

Guy said, "What brings you to see me? Are the children all right?"

"Perfectly. You'll see them shortly."

"Thank you," Something in his voice made her wonder, just for a moment, if she had been mistaken, after all. After a moment he cleared his throat. "Well?"

Sibylla closed her eyes. If she did not kill her pride now, she would go away and things would be worse between them than before. It was bad enough as it was: even with his forgiveness, he would never trust her advice again.

"It's over," she told him. "I can't rule this kingdom with you any longer. Not after what's happened."

"I understand." He seemed as stiff as a board, but perhaps there was a little relief there, too. "Whatever you choose to do, I won't stand in your way."

Again, his words cut her to the bone. Could he at least pretend to some becoming reluctance?

"Then it's settled," Sibylla said coldly. "Once the sultan frees you, I'll inform the High Court that from now on, you alone hold formal power in the kingdom. I shall be queen in name only. You need not fear my interference again."

"What?" The shock, at last, made him look her full in the eyes.

"Is it so hard to believe? I told you: I admit my folly. This kingdom can never prosper with me as its ruler; I know that now."

"No," he whispered. "Sibylla, you *can't.*"

"I beg your pardon! What did *you* have in mind?"

"I…" Guy looked stunned. "Surely you'd prefer to have the marriage dissolved. I don't know, perhaps you could marry that new man they tell me about, the one at Tyre."

"Conrad of Montferrat? He's Longsword's brother." Holy Church forbade a widow marrying her dead husband's brother.

"Oh, is that who it is?" Listlessly, Guy shook his head. "Does it matter?"

"Of course not. There's no question of divorcing—without me, you'll lose all claim to the throne. If you don't want me, I'll join a convent instead. You'll never see me again. Please." Sibylla was mortified to find that her eyes had filled with tears. "Guy…there's no one I trust to rule this kingdom like you can."

"Sibylla," he whispered. There was a long silence. He swallowed hard. "Of *course* I want you."

For a little while she had thought she was going mad. "Then *why*—"

"I lost you the kingdom," he said woodenly. "I lost you Ascalon. You married me to protect your kingdom, and look what became of it. Surely you're better off without me."

"Don't say that." Her voice betrayed her by cracking. "I know I always told you I needed a battle leader, but you're so much more than that, Guy. I can't—please don't ask me to do this without you."

She reached for him blindly, but his hands closed over her shoulders, still holding her at arm's length.

"Sibylla." There was a tremble in his voice, too. "Even if you want me, the High Court won't."

"I don't care! Let them have Humphrey for their king, or Montferrat, or whomever they choose, so long as I can have you." With that, she pulled him close, burying her face in his chest. His arms went around her shoulders, and with a long sobbing breath, Sibylla knew at last that she was home.

She could no longer force the kingdom to submit. If she had to choose between Guy and the kingdom, she would always choose Guy. Still, she thought the High Court would think twice before ousting him now. His connections with many great families of the west would be of the utmost importance in the new pilgrimage that was surely coming.

It was ironic that, in the moment of their greatest defeat, they might finally have the opportunity to prove their worth.

Guy wanted to see the children next, so it was not until later that evening, after dinner, that she had the opportunity to tell him the details of Jerusalem's surrender.

Saladin, thank God, had agreed to reduce the city's ransom by half. The sultan's men took control of every city gate, allowing the citizens to emerge only after having paid the ransom: ten bezants for a man, five for a woman and three for a child. The people were allowed to sell or mortgage their goods in order to raise the necessary money—which was now, however, in great demand. As for weapons, the sultan actually encouraged them to keep them: a journey through war-torn territory lay ahead of them, and they would need some means of defending themselves. Once these things had been agreed and sworn, Ibelin had handed the keys of the city to Saladin.

Guy bit his nether lip. "Ibelin will never live this down. He'll be remembered to the end of the world as the man who surrendered Christ's city to the heathens."

Sibylla, too, could relish the irony. As a woman, she was, of course, not expected to negotiate with Saladin herself, and her stepmother's husband was the most natural choice to do so in her place. Still, by excluding her from power, Ibelin had ensured that she was unable to be blamed in any way for what had happened.

She shrugged. "He'll find a way to turn it to his own account. I gather his squire Ernoul spent half the siege writing a chronicle."

She told Guy how, as the weeks wore on, a camp of fugitives sprang up outside the city walls; how Ibelin and the Patriarch confiscated money and property from every neighbourhood in the city to be handed over in ransoms for thousands of the poor. Some, unable to pay the ransom, bribed the sultan's officials with smaller payments, slipped over the walls on ropes or smuggled themselves out in disguise.

When every penny within the city had been paid, there were still forty thousand poor people trapped within it.

It was then that the Saracen lords became generous. Saladin's brother asked the sultan to be given a thousand slaves from among the poor—then released all of them. Saladin himself seemed determined to excel his brother's generosity. He decreed the release of another twelve thousand.

"More would have been freed, too," Sibylla said. "But the sultan's men noticed an Englishman leaving the city carrying a gourd, which they supposed to contain wine. Since liquor is an abomination to the Mahometans, they seized it from the man and threw it upon the ground. It was full of treasures, gold and silver. After that, the sultan refused to release any more of the poor unless they paid their ransom."

"In this, Saladin has behaved more nobly than do the Christians," Guy said. Sibylla sighed, for it was truer than Guy knew. Rumour had it that Patriarch Eraclius and the two military Orders had contributed considerably less to the ransom than they might have done, leaving the city with thousands of bezants' worth of personal property. She did not know the truth of the rumours, nor whether they had originated with the Ibelin faction or Saladin's own amirs, who might well think that the great lords of the city were worth a great deal more than ten bezants. Sibylla had been unwilling to endanger the fragile truce by intervening.

"Some elected to go to Alexandria, where they'll take ship for the west,"

Sibylla finished. "But most of us are now travelling together to Tripoli. I am with the first of the fugitives. Balian and the Patriarch have remained in Jerusalem to negotiate the release of the final ten thousand; they'll follow with the last." She glanced up at Guy, who sat beside her on the divan with one arm around her, staring into the lamplight while she did her needlework. "Saladin did offer to let me stay here, with you."

He stirred. "On no account! Does he mean to get two prisoners for the price of one? You must stay out of his hands, Sibylla."

Now that she had found Guy, she never wanted to leave him again. Perhaps Saladin was honourable enough not to make her a prisoner…but no. Staying with Guy was as unthinkable as fleeing to the west.

"I will," she said with a sigh, reaching for another spool of thread. "I have work to do, anyway."

She shook out her needlework, and Guy laughed. "You're making… children's tunics?"

"For the poor among the fugitives," she told him. "Winter is upon us. It will be a long, cold journey to Tripoli." There was only so much blackwork embellishment the world needed. She stared at the work sombrely, recalling exactly why she could not abandon the people now. "Kiss me," she said.

Guy did as she asked, and Sibylla leaned into him, memorising the shape of his lips.

Lilith had sworn to have her revenge upon the people of the city for Sibylla's own defiance. Saladin might have freed them, but Sibylla did not for a moment believe any of them were out of danger.

For all her fine plans, she did not know whether she would live to see them through.

Chapter XLIII.

Ibrahim—that was the name by which the master called him. The djinn believed the master, because who else could he believe? Certainly not the mortal woman who had summoned him on the day of his first waking.

She is only a rebellious slave of mine, the master had said—*he was called al-Aziz. She will accuse me of mistreating her, I am sure. The truth is that she wishes me dead, but I was merciful enough to spare her life. Do not visit her. Do not listen to her. She is very clever and a little mad, and she will try to confuse you. She did it once; that is why you no longer have your memories.*

Ibrahim did not question his master's words—not at first.

For Ibrahim, it should have been enough to inhabit the master's sprawling house. He was the unseen porter of its far-flung wings, of the doorways and windows that led from Damascus to Baghdad, Cairo, and every other conceivable place and time. Yet for some reason—perhaps because he had been warned against her, or perhaps because she had once wormed her way into his mind and he could not help feeling an instinctive sense of kinship with her—he found nothing in the house so interesting as the mortal witch.

Al-Aziz did not leave her in the women's quarters to spin the devious webs of magic that wrapped about her. Instead, he had her banished to a cell carved into the living stone of the mountain beneath. Its only light and air flowed through the iron bars of the iron door, which opened onto a narrow path leading from the women's quarters above.

Ibrahim watched as al-Aziz gathered the women of his household and laid down the law by which the prisoner should live: "For the next nine months, she is to eat only salt meat, and drink only vinegar; that is all."

The skinny, ink-stained wife bit her lip and plucked up her courage to speak. "My lord, you know best! But surely such a diet will kill her."

"It will do her no harm," al-Aziz said. "What is in her belly is no ordinary child, and it requires no ordinary food."

Ibrahim watched as the women gathered together and whispered; as they piled up washcloths and blankets, combs and hairpins, clean linen and warm mantles, a sleeping-mat and a cake of soap, and then tiptoed down the narrow stair to the locked door. He watched as they bribed their way past the guard and clustered around the witch, whispering and weeping and tending to her with warm water and kind words.

He watched when they had gone away and the mortal woman lay weeping alone in her prison.

He heard at night when nightmares plagued her and she woke crying out, sometimes for Fayruz, sometimes for names he did not know, *Persi* or *Michael.*

He saw when the ink-stained wife brought her poems and medicines, when the eldest wife brought her cushions and blankets.

"I don't know whether al-Aziz will mind," Halimah said anxiously, settling her cushions in a corner of the cell, "but perhaps it would be best not to ask him."

The witch—Marta Bessarion, they called her—did not smile. Her eyes were dark and empty. "Is Fayruz all right?" she asked. "What about the baby?"

Halimah managed to smile. "Fayruz stopped sitting up at night to spin. But her baby is still alive. Al-Aziz has kept his word."

It was odd that, when Halimah had gone away, the witch should close her eyes and whisper, "Fayruz will keep her baby", as though she was glad for it, as though she cared.

After a month, the youngest wife, Fayruz, descended the rocks and went to peer in at the door at the prisoner.

"Yallah," she said, "you look dreadful."

"I *feel* dreadful," the witch said, with a catch in her voice. "I can't sleep. I keep seeing Khalil killing the people I care about. And the food makes me sick. I can't keep anything down."

"It's morning sickness, you ninny. Don't worry, it'll go away in a few months, once the baby is a little further along."

"The baby." The witch looked despairing. "Are you sure?"

"Not really," Fayruz admitted. "Some women have it the whole nine months."

The other mortal put her face in her hands. "I know about morning sickness. Mama used to have it, but nothing like *this*. Couldn't it be something else? Maybe I have a—a growth."

"It's a growth, all right." Fayruz rolled her eyes. "What are you complaining about, anyway? I fall pregnant, and I have to work my fingers to the bone day and night just to conceal it from his afrits. You fall pregnant, and al-Aziz warns them away from you and boasts of swords."

"Do you think I *wanted* this?" the mortal whispered. "This monster of *his* devising?"

"No, but Halimah and Arwa and I would have given our right hands to be in your place; vinegar and all." Fayruz shrugged. "It's not as though the child has quickened yet, is it? Call the Poison Mother and get *her* to deal with it."

The mortal let her head fall back listlessly against the wall. "You're blocking my light, Fayruz. Why are you here?"

Fayruz backed away from the door a step, allowing a little more light to penetrate the cell. After a moment she said, defensively, "I betrayed you because it was the only way I could think of to persuade al-Aziz to protect my child. I thought he'd owe me a favour. But it turns out he recognises no debt of honour to such lowly creatures as his wives."

The mortal said nothing.

"Why did you defend me? Why did you stop him killing both of us?"

"Maybe I thought Khalil owed *me* a favour."

"Then you should have used it to get out of this *hole*," Fayruz said. "I could have got you killed. I thought I *was* getting you killed. Who do you think I am? I've spent my whole life stabbing other people in the back just to climb over their bodies. Why didn't you let me die?"

"Why should I?" Marta said wearily. "I promised I'd protect your baby. I failed. I don't fault you for seeing it before I did."

Fayruz snorted. "You can't be serious," she said. After a moment, her slow, heavily pregnant footsteps climbed back up the stone steps to the house. Marta—that is, the mortal, the witch—lay down again and watched the wall, tracing a listless forefinger across the stones. Ibrahim waited, but she did not call upon the Poison Mother.

Why? Ibrahim knew the afrit—Lilith appeared in all his own nightmares. It was a strange thing, to have nightmares but no memories. Sometimes she cut his throat, sometimes she only dragged him into a black pit, to an unguessable fate of eternal suffering. He hated and feared her in equal measure, but since the mortal was a witch, why would she not turn to such a creature for aid?

Still Ibrahim did not question his master's words. He did not visit the mortal or speak to her. But from that moment on, whenever the nightmares crept into Marta's dreams, Ibrahim spoke a word, and they retreated.

Khalil fed her on salt and gall, and Marta ate every scrap; yet still her body wasted away, flesh and sinew melting from her bones as the child grew in her belly. When the maidservant Bahar, escorted by dark-skinned Nubian guards, brought her daily rations, Marta begged them for bitter greens, sweet pomegranates, roasted nuts, or bread soaked in oil. But more food was the one thing they dared not bring her.

Winter set in, bringing scouring wind and driving rain, with occasional flurries of snow. "I'll send word to al-Aziz," Halimah declared bravely, one December morning when she found that a tiny drift of snow had been driven beneath the door by the wind. "If you stay here, you'll die."

Halimah did not see what Ibrahim saw—that the mortal was wrapped in a web of magic. She barely shivered; she did not fall sick, as though her body was so consumed by the creature growing within her that it had no attention to spare for other illnesses.

She never touched or amended that web of power; if Ibrahim had not been warned against her, he might have wondered if it was truly a thing of her own creation, or whether it really did bear a greater resemblance to the workings of al-Aziz.

It was shortly after this that the child quickened. Ibrahim knew when it happened. Unwilling to be plagued by nightmares, he rarely slept; so he heard in the night when the mortal awoke with a gasp and sat up, putting a hand to her belly.

She did not sleep again that night, and the next day, when Bahar arrived carrying food, she said, "Please, I think I will go mad without something to do. Will you bring me a spindle, and some unspun silk?"

It was Fayruz who delivered the basket of undyed silk two days later. She entered the cell carrying the basket in one hand, and in the crook of the other, a tiny, feebly moving bundle wrapped in a soft blanket.

"Al-Aziz was generous," Fayruz said drily, setting the basket in a corner of the cell. "Silk for you, although we are not supposed to wear it, and *this* for me."

She put the bundle in the mortal's arms—a tiny baby smelling of oil and milk, blinking up with unfocused dark eyes from a face as smooth as a peach. It pursed its lips and grunted slightly with each tiny, fragile breath.

"Oh, *Fayruz*," Marta breathed in awe.

"It's a girl, like you told me," Fayruz said proudly. "Al-Aziz let me name her. Zumurrud."

"Zumurrud," Marta repeated, her mouth twisting in bitterness. Ibrahim knew what she must be feeling. Conceived by demons upon a captive, kept in the dark and fed on gall, her own child was unlikely to resemble this sweetness. She spoke none of this, only bent her head over the child: "Zumurrud, I lay this blessing upon you: may you never be your father's weapon, or his tool."

She handed the child back to Fayruz, who looked upon her scarcely less tenderly than upon little Zumurrud. "Is there anything I can do for you?"

The mortal gazed at her with those dark, defeated eyes. "Stay safe for me, Fayruz. Get out of this place, if you can, so that he cannot use you against me."

Biting her lip, Fayruz looked at her baby's face again. "He didn't even bother giving her a name, you know. He doesn't deserve to be a father, and my daughter would be better off dead than trapped in his house forever." Fayruz gave a hard gulp. "Forget about us, Marta; you've done enough. You're the one who should escape. I won't regret a thing."

The mortal began to laugh: a weary, bitter sound. "Escape!" she said. "Look at me!"

Fayruz looked and said nothing, but the mortal stopped laughing. When she looked up at Fayruz and her child, there was a little more life in her eyes, as though the conversation had recalled her to some sense of purpose. "Perhaps I can distract Khalil long enough to get you clear. Let me think about it."

Fayruz touched the mortal's shoulder and went away. At that moment, a summons from the Baghdad door of the house forced Ibrahim's attention away from the tiny cell with its shivering occupant. Al-Aziz strolled into his courtyard swathed in furs and went upstairs to sit at a glowing brazier, hot cumin tisane in hand. For all his bodily comforts, he did not appear content; he glowered at the place beneath his bed where the faint, scrubbed-out lines of a sigil still appeared, its magic gone.

After a moment he waved away the cumin and commanded his servants to bring him wine instead, for all that it was forbidden. For an hour or more, he sat alone, drinking morosely.

Ibrahim did not mean to question his master, but perhaps he could not help it. Al-Aziz said the mortal was a witch, but he was the one who consorted with afrits and drew sigils; it was his magic, not her own, that was wrapped around the mortal. He said the mortal was mad, but she was only weak and suffering in ways all too familiar to Ibrahim himself. He said she was wicked, but she had only sought to protect others from Khalil's threats.

He flinched away from the thought as though it might burn him. Of course he felt predisposed to trust the witch: in a previous lifetime she had wormed her way into his mind, confusing and deceiving him. It was only the wives, grumbling women, who whispered evil things of the master. His servants were contented with him, including the boyish, black-skinned guards, whose soft and liquid tongue was oddly familiar and homelike to Ibrahim.

At sunset, the witch called him by his true name.

Ibrahim was compelled to answer, despite his dread of what al-Aziz might do if he was discovered. "Witch!" he hissed when her call dragged him to the cold darkness of her cell. "Never presume to call upon me again!"

He fled, but she summoned him back at once.

"Do you want to die?" he blustered. It was an empty threat, and they both knew it: al-Aziz would never allow his djinn to kill the mortal. Not that the mortal seemed to care whether he killed her or not.

"*Maskagna, waeina,*" she said. "We were friends once."

The words went through Ibrahim like an arrow: they were a greeting in what he knew to be his mother tongue. How could the mortal know that?

"Al-Aziz warned me you would say that," he said warily. He ought to leave, but he did not. "What is this language? How do you know it?"

"It's the tongue they speak in the kingdom of Nubia." The mortal shrugged her thin shoulders. "My friend Persi of Silimi taught it to me."

"Nubia," Ibrahim breathed, tasting the word for any hint of memory. Was that the land of his mortal forbears?

"Persi tells me Nubia is on the Nile, just south of Egypt," Marta went on, setting her bobbin to spin. "They have a king, and many cities full of scholars, warriors, merchants, and monks. They trade in gold and silver, so that their halls and churches are full of precious things."

"Some of them serve Khalil," Ibrahim said.

The witch looked up at him and said gravely, "Persi told me her people must hand over a certain number of young men to the sultan of Egypt each year in tribute. The Egyptians slice off their private parts with one cut of a razor; then bury the boys in dunghills to live or die, as God pleases. Those who live become trusted guards, watching over the wives and female slaves of their masters. You have seen them yourself around the master's house."

His skin crept; he felt the spell of her words sinking hooks into his heart.

"Why are you telling me this?" Ibrahim demanded. "Everyone takes slaves and creates eunuchs: it is the way of the world."

"Does that mean you *want* to suffer in this way?" she asked, inexorable. "Here is something *you* told me, Ibrahim: you were a free man, until Khalil's demons lured you into his house, bound you to the orange tree at the centre of his courtyard, and slew your mortal body. Now you inhabit his house, nothing more than his slave."

He saw a flash of memory, or perhaps a waking nightmare: the afrits, Lilith and Qeteb, advancing upon him across a dusky courtyard, armed with swords and strangling-silks. Around Ibrahim the cell darkened abruptly with the coiling smoke of his own smoky substance.

"Witch! You lie!" Ibrahim bellowed, and fled.

Surely the master had told him the truth. The mortal was dangerous, confusing, terrible. He could not afford to approach her again.

But as the days passed, her found that her words had stuck, unravelling his peace of mind, until Ibrahim knew that he must prove the truth to himself once and for all.

His memories were here, hidden within the stones of the house. Ibrahim had only to find them again.

Chapter XLIV.

"You should rest tonight." Persi, the Nubian Watcher, and her newly married husband Michael Zakar had been following Sibylla around the camp all evening, helping to distribute food and other assistance to the poor. Michael had stopped a moment ago to kindle a fire for three sisters who had all come down with fevers and could scarcely pitch their own tent. Now, outside Sibylla's own pavilion as the last shreds of daylight gave way before the onslaught of night, Persi gave Sibylla a look of pity. "Don't work yourself to death, my lady."

The Watcher could not possibly understand that Sibylla could never rest—not with Lilith awaiting her moment to strike.

For two interminable weeks since leaving Nablus, she had sat in her horse-borne litter making tunic after tunic, wielding her needle with feverish concentration. Around her, when she looked up, she beheld the woeful crowd of Jerusalem's fugitives, many of them now fleeing Saladin's conquest for the third or fourth time since the great battle. To make the journey more manageable, they had divided themselves into three groups. The Templars guarded the first, in which Sibylla travelled. The Hospitallers guarded a second, while Balian and the remainder of the royal garrison guarded the third, which followed some days behind. As the great exodus marched north, the greening landscape of early winter changed around them. Hills and plains gave way to the purple crests, touched with snow, of the high Lebanon.

For two interminable weeks, Lilith dogged Sibylla's footsteps, haunting her dreams in the few short hours when she succumbed to bodily weakness and pitched into sleep. *I'll destroy these people. I'll eat them alive. You had better yield to me.*

Never, she vowed upon waking. Sibylla never rested now if she could help it. Every few days she had a new garment to give to the poor. As she walked through the camp looking for someone in need of warm clothing, Sibylla also sought other work to do. Food must be carried to people too exhausted or penniless to come to the markets to get it. Disputes must be settled. Injuries and sickness must be treated, and a place in carts or litters arranged for those too old or weak to walk by themselves. And always, always, there was water to carry, firewood to collect, food to prepare and clothes to wash. Such menial work was beneath a queen, and Sibylla had none of the skills needed for such tasks, but she could always summon the help people needed.

Of course, no one could live like this. No one could work themselves day and night in an agony of fear, but what else could she do? If Sibylla let her guard down for a moment, if she allowed herself any rest or any idleness, Lilith would surely destroy them all.

As for the people, although at first they had been shocked and discomfited by her attentions, after the first few days they had begun to do something quite new when they saw her: they began to smile.

They began to call, "God bless you, Queen Sibylla." Children began to run to her litter as they saw it pass, with gifts of crocuses or late apples.

"The Leper King's sister is as much a saint as he was," someone said as she passed through the camp one evening. "It isn't even Easter, and she gives out clothes and food for the poor!"

They did not know she was only doing this to keep Lilith away—not because she *cared* about them.

"I'll rest when we're all safe," she told the busybody Watcher now. Although Persi had not renewed the warnings made outside the Hospital on the day Sibylla cut her daughters' hair, neither had she offered to exorcise Lilith. If Persi would not help, she had no right to tell Sibylla to rest.

She waved a dismissive hand, but Persi ignored it.

"My lady," she said kindly, "what you need is rest. We'll be in Tripoli tomorrow, and you did as I recommended, didn't you? Let go. Lay down your burdens. *Rest.*"

It took Sibylla a moment to remember Persi's instructions—*think on your sins.* It was not enough. Lilith still dogged her steps, appearing whenever she stopped work even for a moment. Sibylla felt almost suffocated by the lump in her throat. She was so weary, *so* weary, and so busy taking care of other people's children that she had barely seen her own in days. She slept now only when exhaustion clawed her under, nodding over her needlework when she sat down.

Sibylla knew it was only a matter of time before the people learned the truth about her. That she was wrath and ice and did not care a silver groat for them. She could not say any of these things to Persi, but as she wrenched her hand away, a young Hospitaller knight atop a muddy horse forced his way through the crowded camp towards her tent.

"Send help!" he called. "We've been attacked in the pass! They're plundering everything. Where is the commander?"

A chill tide of fear washed through her. Sibylla understood at once. The second body of fugitives, protected by the Hospital, must have fallen into the hands of bandits along the mountainous road Sibylla's own group had just travelled. Momentarily relieved of her exhaustion, Sibylla headed towards the tent of the Templar commander who had helped escort them from Jerusalem.

Until now, it was Saladin who had provided their best protection. As far as Jubail, twenty-five of the sultan's mamluk knights rode before and behind each of the three groups of fugitives, warning fellow Saracens not to interfere with their passage. The journey from Jerusalem, therefore, though it took them through miles of war-torn country, had been safe and uneventful. Jubail, however, was as far north as Saladin's conquests had taken him, and on the borders of the county of Tripoli, his mamluks bade them a solemn farewell.

"Keep your people armed and alert as you travel," the Saracen leader had warned them. "At a mountain called the Face of Stone, the road cuts inland through a narrow gorge. For the bandits in the hills, it is a favourite spot for ambushes."

Sibylla's stomach knotted at the thought of her poor people becoming subject to bandits at the end of their journey, long after they had lost everything else.

In the Templar commander's tent, the young Hospitaller poured out his tale, wringing his hands. "They behaved in a shameful way, robbing and plundering the people, beating anyone who resisted. I was sent at once to summon aid, but—"

"Take everyone you need and go," Sibylla said at once. Lilith had warned her, and she had still failed. She was with the vanguard, and her frantic needlework had perhaps been able to protect *them,* but not the rear groups. Oh, God. "Was anyone killed? Or taken captive?"

"It's possible some may be dead. I don't know about captives, but I doubt it, since the law prevents us Franks from enslaving fellow Christians..."

"Franks," Sibylla repeated stupidly. "The bandits had Franks among them?"

From the look on the Templar commander's face, she had come in just too late to hear an important piece of news. "My lady," he said, "these were no bandits; they issued from the castle that guards the pass, which belongs to Renoard, lord of Nephin."

Sibylla was dumbstruck. She remembered passing Nephin today, a castle built on the coast just north of the white valley where its lord had attacked the fugitives. Perhaps it was their own passing that alerted Renoard to the opportunity for brigandage. She had no doubt why the attack had taken place: Nephin was a loyal servant of Tripoli, the man Jerusalem had refused to accept as their king. Now, Tripoli was taking his revenge.

She must have paled: her face felt stiff and cold. "My advice does not change," she heard herself say. "Take everyone you need. Drive off the men of Nephin and bring our people here."

"But that would expose you to danger," the commander objected. "If you'll first let me see you safely to the city of Tripoli—"

"No need. I've already sent my chaplain to Tripoli to announce our coming." Sibylla forced a smile. "Go, before it's too dark to see."

She returned to her tent staring into the eyes of a cruel and murderous future. If Nephin was bold enough, and cruel enough, to attack a column of poor homeless wanderers, it could only be a sign of what awaited them at the capital itself. In fact, she had led them all directly into a trap of her own making. What now? Would she and her people find themselves prisoners in the hands of her cousin? Was there nowhere in the world where they might be welcomed and protected?

At the door of her tent, a woman waylaid her, holding up her toddler. "Bless my child, my lady! He's ill with the cold."

Sibylla looked with distaste at the child's feverish, mucus-streaked face. But the woman's eyes were so desperate and pleading that she could not refuse. Sibylla brushed her lips gingerly against the infant's sticky forehead. "There," she said, "now take the child to a doctor named Theodosia at the infirmary tent, and tell her Queen Sibylla sent you."

After that, the evening ought to have been like any other: at dinner she would put on a show of eating for the household, and then while everyone else slept, she would sit up straining her eyes in the flickering light of her best lamp, stitching together shirts and trews which Sara and Alix had cut out on the camp table earlier in the evening. Sibylla usually managed to keep awake until Vigils, but sooner or later her needle would start to wander and she would find herself startling awake in her chair to the sound of Lilith's laughter.

Tonight went somewhat differently. Dinner was over and Sibylla was helping to wipe the dishes dry—a task that pained her neck and shoulders somewhat less than sewing—when her chaplain, Peter of Tafila, returned unexpectedly from his mission.

"What happened?" Sibylla demanded, still briskly rubbing dishes. "Did you get lost on your way to the city? Or—don't tell me you ran afoul of Nephin's men?"

Tafila bowed, wringing his hands in distress. Normally he was a good-natured little man, but tonight's news had evidently distressed him. "My lady, I reached Tripoli, but its gates were shut and barred. They refused to let me in."

"I suppose you arrived after curfew," Sibylla said, without much hope. "Did you tell them I sent you?"

"Yes, my lady, and they gave me a message for you." Tafila cleared his throat, his distress increasing. "They—they said you were coming north with an army to take the city. I swore we had only a few dozen knights, that most were Templars and Hospitallers, and that Lord Balian of Ibelin would be arriving in a few days to clear up any misunderstandings. They told me that they would hold us as enemies unless..." His voice faded away.

"Unless what?" Sibylla snapped, putting a beaker on the table with a clack.

Tafila swallowed hard. "Unless you hand over yourself and your daughters as hostages, my lady."

Sibylla picked up another glass and attacked its ugly, prunted surface with the dishcloth. How *dare* Tripoli attack her people? How dare he demand hostages? He must know what folly this was. He could only be doing it for one reason: revenge against herself.

It was Tripoli's own fault for demanding to make himself king.

It was the Leper King's fault for clinging to his throne, playing Tripoli against herself and Guy to keep them from gaining the support they needed.

It was her own fault for playing them all at their own game of power, because this game could never truly be won. She could defeat and outmanoeuvre them, but she could not make them love her.

Wherever the blame truly lay, her people were too many, their defenders too few. They were short on money and food, and winter was here. If Sibylla did not find them some form of sanctuary in the county of Tripoli, they would need to push on towards Antioch through the coldest weeks of winter, hoping to receive asylum there. No longer under the sultan's protection, they were now vulnerable to attack from all sides—bandits, Saracens, or their own co-religionists. How many of them would live through such an ordeal? How would *she* live through such an ordeal?

Sibylla finished the dishes, not hearing anything else that Tafila said, or the rest of her household. For the first time that day—for the first time in weeks—she put down her work and did not pick it up again. Instead, she walked out of the tent and through the quietened camp to the makeshift chapel. Lamps burned within, but the tent was otherwise empty.

Sibylla sank to her knees before the altar, dimly aware of her guards taking up their position at the tent's flap behind her. She stared at her hands, too inexpressibly weary to pray, let alone to keep up this work another two weeks, or however long it took them to reach Antioch.

"It's not working." Lilith smiled cruelly from her perch upon the altar itself. "By dint of constant work you can keep me from affecting *you*. But you can't stop me whispering in the ears of Tripoli's nobles. Or stirring up the bandits infesting these hills. Nor can you protect these people from swords and arrows. Did I not tell you I would consume them all?"

"Please," Sibylla whispered, still staring at her hands. "I need help. I need rest. I can't protect these people on my own."

"That's right," Lilith crooned. "I knew you'd come back to me in the end."

"I wasn't..." Sibylla's voice faded away, too weary and hopeless to continue. For a moment there was silence. Then from the door of the tent a new voice finished the thought.

"She wasn't speaking to you."

No one but herself had ever been able to see or hear Lilith before. In wonder, Sibylla turned to face the newcomer. It was the woman with the sick child; she had walked straight past the guards as though invisible to them.

All Lilith's feathers ruffled up, and in a blink, she became more birdlike than ever. "Keep back!" she cawed. "The mortal is *my* lawful property!"

"Not if she wishes to be redeemed," the woman said, coming nearer. Clad in dirty, threadbare old garments, she was still a rather repellent sight. The child cuddled its head onto her shoulder as though asleep. But Sibylla found she could not quite meet the woman's eyes: they were like windows onto eternity.

When the woman bent over her, Sibylla smelled something like fire, scorching hot.

"Ask," she said.

Sibylla swallowed. "I want my people to be safe," she whispered. "I want to be free of Lilith. I tried to work hard enough, but…"

"But if you try to carry the divine burden, you will break." Her hand rested on Sibylla's head. "Lay it down."

Sibylla gasped, overcome by the mere thought. "But Lilith is right. I've done terrible things. To my sister, to my brother, to my son—to my people."

"That burden must be carried by another, and not by you," the woman told her. "Go to your tent and sleep. In the morning you will know what to do."

The light dimmed as though a wind had blown through the tent, causing the lamps to flicker. Sibylla looked up. The woman was gone. Lilith boiled before the altar lamps, a dark and menacing shadow. Sibylla had the notion that the demon was speaking to her, and perhaps it was madness not to listen, but Lilith's voice was far off and she could not imagine disobeying the ugly woman with the child. *Sleep.* The thought was like a pool of cool water at the end of a long summer's day.

Turning her back on the seething demon, Sibylla walked out of the chapel. In her own tent, her bed, as always, had been made up. Not since Jerusalem had she permitted herself to lie in it. She kicked off her shoes and lay down without even taking off her gown. That was the last thing she remembered for many hours.

The sound of voices woke her. Her whole body was unspooled, drugged with slumber for the first time in years. The camp was astir, teasing at her thoughts, preventing her from drifting at once back into the arms of rest.

Sibylla remembered Tafila's message from last night. What would her brother Baldwin have done in this situation?

Precisely what he had done when she had defied him.

Rubbing her eyes, Sibylla got up and called her ladies. A few minutes later, she made her way to the tent of the Templar commander and found him sitting at breakfast in the company of the Hospital commander, as well as Patriarch Eraclius and Balian of Ibelin. The leaders of the other fugitive groups must have caught up with them during the night.

At the sight of their grave faces, Sibylla's heart stopped, and she feared what Lilith might have done as she slept. "Is—is something wrong? What happened while I slept?"

"Nothing, my lady," the Templar commander reassured her. "The people are safe."

Sibylla could have wept for pure relief. Instead she straightened, smoothing her hair and hoping she did not look too exhausted. "My lords, the count of Tripoli has demanded I turn myself and my daughters over to him as hostages." She swallowed. "I've decided to do as he asks."

* * *

The city of Tripoli reminded Sibylla of Tyre: a cosy jumble of sandstone buildings defended on three sides by the sea and surrounded by a high wall. Citrus orchards filled the two-mile space between the city and its outer suburb, Mount Pilgrim, where the citadel of Raymond Saint-Gilles watched over the city from its vantage-point on a mountainous spur.

Sibylla watched the orchards and the high aqueduct leading from the mountains to the city as they went past her litter. From her spoilt white palfrey, Isabella exclaimed over the scent of citrus which pervaded even the air of early winter. Sibylla felt nearly suffocated by the smell. The certainty that had filled her this morning had long since ebbed away. She had not seen Lilith once since leaving the chapel tent the evening before, and she felt quite sure that the ugly woman's words could be trusted. Yet she was about to hand over herself and her daughters as hostages. Anything might be done to them. She remembered all too well being a young girl handed over to Longsword. She remembered being a young widow, about to be handed over to someone else, had she not taken matters into her own hands. Now she was giving it all up again—all that hard-won freedom. She must be mad.

Tripoli's massive gate stood open, allowing labourers and merchants to pass in and out—a sign that the count did not truly believe the fugitives of Jerusalem to be a threat. Nevertheless, as Sibylla's tiny entourage approached the gate, a pair of knights intercepted them at the head of a small company of mounted sergeants.

"Who goes there?" they challenged. "Are you friend or foe?"

Sibylla sighed. Ibelin rode forward, and she let him speak for her.

"It's I, Balian of Ibelin, seeking refuge with my friend the count of Tripoli," he said crisply. "I have with me the count's cousins: Queen Sibylla, who also seeks safe haven with her daughters, and the Lady of Toron."

"No armed men may enter the city of Tripoli," one of the knights replied.

The three or four knights that had escorted Sibylla and her household wore the Ibelin livery, not her own. Sibylla had elected to bring only those members of her household not trained in the arts of war: female attendants, the children's nurse, and her chaplain.

Ibelin's voice was tight with frustration, but his words were meek "I will submit to any conditions the count may lay upon me, so long as I may go before him to plead for the sake of the many poor people who are with me."

He and his men were forced to disarm, but they were admitted to the city.

"This is ridiculous," Balian muttered to Sibylla once they were underway again. "Didn't your man tell him I was coming, your lady? Doesn't he understand these people have nowhere else to go?"

Not deigning to answer, Sibylla closed her eyes as their small group headed through Tripoli's narrow streets to the palace. Without needlework to keep her hands occupied, she found herself fidgeting with the black onyx ring on her thumb. *If you try to carry the divine burden, you will break.* Sibylla feared she would break anyway. Tripoli held a grudge against her, she knew that. He had *always* been willing to break old friendships and wreak destruction on the kingdom if it meant he could have his revenge on her.

But when she and Ibelin entered the palace and were shown into the great audience hall, blazing with frescoes, marble inlay, and far too much light and colour for Sibylla's overwhelmed senses, the count of Tripoli was not there.

Instead, the elevated dais held a curving semicircle of chairs. Familiar, unfriendly faces stared down on her from the platform: Reginald of Sidon, Walter of Caesarea, Queen Maria, and in the centre of them all Tripoli's countess, Eschiva of Galilee.

It was hard to tell whether this was the High Court of the county of Tripoli, or a meeting of Jerusalem Watchers. Saladin had killed or captured all Sibylla's own people, and now only her enemies were left. She had never felt more isolated in her life.

Ibelin halted when he saw the gathering. "What is this, my lords?" he demanded. "Where is Count Raymond?"

"My husband is dead these three months," Eschiva replied quietly.

"Dead," Ibelin repeated disbelievingly.

"After the battle, his heart was broken. His heir, the second son of the prince of Antioch, has been notified. I am in command now."

Sibylla listened to the blood rushing in her own ears. Her only plan had failed. The onyx ring would mean nothing to Eschiva. She had nothing, nothing.

The count of Tripoli had not sought his revenge against her, after all. That had been due to these Watchers.

"You yourself are welcome here, Ibelin," the countess added. "But the queen of Jerusalem has marched her people to this city at a time of war, with the count dead and his successor not yet confirmed in his possessions. This is an act of war."

Ibelin shook his head, scattering tears from his eyes. "My lady, you misunderstand. These people are not knights. Most of them are women and children, who have now been plundered of all their few remaining goods by the lord of Nephin. If they do not receive sanctuary and restitution, many of them will be dead by spring."

Caesarea leaned forward. "These Jersusalemites acclaimed this lady queen although it was contrary to the Leper King's will. If we allow them to settle here, who is to say she may not use them to put herself in command of Tripoli?"

"Then send the queen to Antioch, but let the people stay here," Ibelin begged.

"She will only return later," Queen Maria said drily. "My dear lord husband, it won't work."

Ibelin sent Sibylla an exasperated look—as though *she* was the one responsible for the Watchers' pig-headedness. Sibylla could have told him it was fruitless to argue.

She almost demanded they cut off her head then and there—except that really *would* precipitate a catastrophe. Instead, she spoke for the first time. "Tell me what you require of me, then. If it means exiled Jerusalem will be given shelter, I will accept."

The Watchers on the dais traded half-triumphant looks. Conscious of having stepped into a trap, Sibylla ground her teeth.

"The council repeats the terms it offered last night," Sidon said, not quite looking Sibylla in the eye. She still wondered whether he had truly supported her coronation, or whether he had only been present as a spy for the Watchers. "The queen should appoint as her *bailli* over the kingdom Conrad of Montferrat, the lord of Tyre. She must remain in Tripoli as a hostage, to guarantee that her followers do our realm no harm, and she must betroth her eldest daughter to Montferrat."

Sibylla cast a glance behind her to where young Melisende, still a few years beneath the marriageable age, had paled with terror. Rage prickled in her blood. How dare they casually demand such a thing in front of her daughter?

"That's impossible," she said coldly. "Montferrat is the brother of my first husband. They are related by affinity."

"Affinity can be overcome by a papal dispensation," Queen Maria said with a dismissive gesture. "Montferrat is clearly the best man to rule the kingdom."

"If that is truly so, I will never stand in his way," Sibylla said. "As for me, if it pleases you, I and my daughters will cross the sea. Send me as your ambassador to tell the kings of the west what has happened here. I will never return, I swear it."

"Archbishop Joscius has already departed on such a mission," said Caesarea.

"Your kingdom still needs you, my lady," Sidon put in.

It all made a nightmarish kind of sense. Sibylla could not name Montferrat the *bailli* and then depart, never to return. That would undermine the very authority she had granted him. No: they wanted her here, compliantly supporting the *bailli* they had forced upon her.

"Very well," she said softly. "Since it is the only way you will give my people refuge, I will remain under your care in Tripoli and I will name Conrad of Montferrat my *bailli*. But my daughter is too young to be betrothed."

"My daughter," Queen Maria said with deathly finality, "was also too young to be betrothed."

"Those are our terms," Countess Eschiva said, breaking the hostile silence. "Accept them, or not."

Sibylla turned to her half-sister. Isabella, who so often drifted into a world of her own when her elders were talking politics, seemed to have followed this conversation closely: there was a faint frown between her brows.

What could she do? Isabella may have been too young to give her consent to her own marriage, but at least Humphrey was young and singularly gentle. These Watchers were not asking Sibylla to hand over her young daughter to another Humphrey: they wanted her for Longsword's brother, a battle-hardened man in his prime. She had never met Conrad, but she had known his father and brother, and she would do anything to spare her daughter marrying another of that family.

"Isabella," she said, and Isabella flinched—she must hardly have expected to be addressed.

"My lady?"

Sibylla took a deep breath. She had no idea what the result of her words might be, but they still needed to be said. "I wronged you," she said. "I forced you into a marriage with Sir Humphrey when you were too young to choose."

"Oh, but I *would* have chosen him," Isabella said earnestly.

"Don't thank me. I wasn't thinking of your good; I was thinking of mine,"

Sibylla retorted. "I played on my brother's fears and congratulated myself on arranging your marriage to a weakling who would never challenge me for the throne. My brother—*our* brother—should have known better. But I *did* know better. Forgive me."

The words burned on her tongue like fire. Isabella stared at her in shock. No one else said a thing. Nothing was worth this. Yet she had no example to follow now but her brother's. Sibylla gritted her teeth and pulled the onyx ring from her thumb.

"Do you see this ring?" she asked, raising it for the whole room to see. "Many years ago, when my great-aunt Hodierna was the countess of Tripoli, she was given this ring in token of a great service she once did to the Old Man of the Mountain."

Suddenly, the room was full of shocked whispers. Everyone knew that Hodierna's marriage to the old count of Tripoli had been a difficult one. Famed for her beauty, Hodierna had been subjected to the old count's jealousy until at last she sought refuge with her sister, Queen Melisende of Jerusalem. On the very day that Hodierna left the county, her husband had been murdered by the Assassins. Her son, Sibylla's cousin, had become count then and there.

Sibylla had no intention of revealing exactly *what* service Hodierna had rendered the Assassins. The Old Man, seeking revenge in a trade dispute, would have had the old count killed in any case. Hodierna had had little reason to love her husband, and his death enabled her to return to Tripoli, ruling it until her son came of age. By the time Hodierna passed the ring on to Sibylla, she had done many years' penance for this youthful crime.

"On her deathbed, at the convent of Bethany, my aunt passed this ring to me, since she no longer had a daughter of her own," Sibylla went on. "She said: *In this world, my niece, you will always be at the mercy of strong men. If all else fails, send the ring to the Old Man of the Mountain, together with the name of the one from whom you seek freedom.*"

Sibylla stared at the black, reflective surface. "After the battle, I did as my aunt told me. I sent the ring to Masyaf with the name of Saladin, but it was returned to me with a message. The Old Man has an alliance with the sultan but invites me to send him any other name I may choose. I have no reason to doubt his honesty. The ring is still good."

"Are you threatening us?" Queen Maria demanded.

"No," Sibylla said flatly. "Give me your hand, Isabella."

"I don't *want* such a thing," Isabella said, but Sibylla gently took her hand.

"I ask you only to keep it safe, and to use it, if at all, for the good of the kingdom." Sibylla slipped the ring over the knuckle of Isabella's thumb. "It's yours now. Your guarantee that I will never again force you—or the kingdom—to accept my will in place of yours."

Releasing her sister, Sibylla turned to face the council's astounded stares.

"There," she said. "I have laid down the last of my power. Now I beg of you, spare my daughter, and give my people sanctuary."

There was a long silence. The Watchers glanced at each other; Sibylla only watched her stepmother. Queen Maria touched her tongue to her lips, and looked at her husband.

"Enough!" Balian of Ibelin said sharply. "We have hearts of stone if we refuse such a plea. My lady, we accept your terms."

Sibylla closed her eyes. There. It was done. She could rest.

Chapter XLV.

April 1188—ten months after the battle

Khalil's offspring whispered in Marta's dreams: *Mama, I'm hungry. Feed me...*

She woke in the dark with sweat beading her skin. The baby squirmed restlessly within the narrow confines of her womb, kicking at her aching ribs, scratching and tickling as though seeking a way out. Marta wrapped wasted arms around her swollen belly in an attempt to absorb some of the shock.

Already she had sustained a broken rib or two. She could not imagine what the birth was going to be like. The creature was like its father, determined to make room for itself, careless of what it broke in the process.

Marta refused to speak to it the way her mother had spoken to Paulus and Elisa when they were only a restless mound inside. She merely held it, closing her eyes, gritting her teeth, and waiting for it to be done—just the way she had endured its father.

She remembered thinking that if Persi could endure, then so could she. But while Persi had also been imprisoned, it had not been like this—always famished no matter how much she ate, forced to bear an abomination. Marta was a shadow of herself now, all skin and bones; the only part of her that felt alive was the small horror coiled and scratching in her stomach.

She had tried to hold onto hope, recalling the seraph's words, that one day she would overcome her enemy. Yet while she could remember such words being spoken once, long ago, to someone happier, they had no power to reach her now.

Instead, she thought again of the virgin saints to whom she had so often been compared: Catherine and Marina and the others, who had been saved by a miracle from having to endure what she had, and who had been martyred instead. She had never liked the unspoken presumption that in such a situation, it was somehow more righteous to squander one's life than to preserve it. Now she loathed it. As though Khalil had left her any choice in the matter!

Yet the worst of it was this: that in a world of miracles, not one had come for her.

In time, the baby's frantic movements calmed enough to let her recognise that she was famished. Blindly reaching up, Marta found the collop of hard salt meat on the chest at the head of her bed, dragged it from its dish and began to tear great strips of the mutton from the bone. It seemed that these days she was eating enough for three grown men and *still* it was not enough.

Only a month to go, she thought, throwing the bone back into the bowl, careful not to disturb the creature inside her.

Only, another part of her mind put in, *a month to live*.

It was a mercy that lately Marta had slept like a drugged woman, without dreams. This night was different.

She dreamed she woke in her own bed in the house at Nablus, and it was a morning in spring, just the way it was here on the mountain; but the air was humid and sweet-scented from the green garden in the courtyard. Persi leaned over her, brows stitched together in worry.

"My poor Marta," she whispered, touching her cheek. "Look what they've done to you."

There were tears on her face: the sight of them was like balm on a wound.

Persi said, "It's killing you, Marta. You should get help."

"But I can't. Khalil won't even speak to me. I don't *want* him to speak to me."

"Give him what he wants," said Persi.

"I don't understand," Marta whispered.

Someone else sat on the edge of her bed and now smoothed the hair gently back from her forehead. It was her mother—Rahel, the Messenger.

"Agree to marry him, my love," said her mother. "Let him rule you. No one else will want you now."

That was the least of Marta's problems. She knew better than to marry Khalil for the sake of peace or security; even Fayruz knew better than that now.

"Or call the Poison Mother," Persi said with a shrug. "Otherwise, you'll die giving birth to this creature, and then how will you have your revenge?"

Once again, she heard the whisper that haunted her nightmares.

Let me out, mama. Let me feed.

"You're not Persi." Marta's heart was racing, making her feel sick and weak. "You're not my mother."

Suddenly she was in her cell again, and the pale face of the feathered woman, Lilith, loomed over her in the dark.

"You ought to listen to me," she said, shaking her head. "Didn't I offer to help you escape once? It was a mistake to refuse. Don't be so stubborn this time. It isn't as though it's *human*."

She was sick and weary, and she wanted so badly to say yes—to beg the Poison Mother to take this cup from her lips. It was not the first time she had considered the notion. It had been her constant companion in those first dark weeks, before Khalil's offspring quickened.

In Marta's youth, none of her tutors had questioned Aristotle when he said that a foetus started out first with a vegetable and then an animal soul, before finally receiving that of a human. Only on the arrival of a human soul—sooner for boys than for girls—would the baby begin to kick in the womb. Since then, Marta had arrived in a world where surgeons and siege engineers began to argue that Aristotle was not half so learned or wise as he thought himself: his descriptions of the physical world did not always match what one could see with one's own eyes. And Marta herself had never known how to reconcile Aristotle's notion that women were sick and deformed men, with the divine creation of the first woman in a state of unblemished perfection.

Murder was a mortal sin. Marta could not bring herself to play with such a crime on the word of *Aristotle*.

Now, Lilith's words echoed in her mind. *It isn't as though it's human.*

Perhaps the baby had no soul at all. Perhaps it never would. Marta closed her eyes, thinking of Ibrahim, the only other djinn she knew, who had extended his friendship when she was a stranger in his house. Arwa said djinn were not evil by nature, and Ibrahim's actions seemed to bear that out. If djinn really were nephilim, the offspring of mortals and demons, then perhaps they inherited their mortal parents' capacity for repentance.

That made this creature—this *child*—an innocent. And could she hurt a child only because its father had been evil?

Marta broke into a sweat. Childbirth was going to kill her. Surely she had no obligation to protect something which was about to kill her. She had killed before, in battle and self-defence, and considered it justified.

She opened her mouth to say it. *Yes. Take the child.*

But she would be calling upon a demon to save her; she would be consigning to certain death a person whom she believed to be innocent, and she could not do either of those things, even to save her life. Another woman in her position might be able to do so, but Marta could not.

"No," she whispered, exhausted from the struggle. "Go away."

"Or what?" Lilith oozed nearer. "You'll cast me out?"

Marta blinked up at the demon. Cast Lilith out? Indeed, she had once had a plan to do just that, but it was now months since the thing had crossed her mind. She had never been quite sure where to begin, and now the thought only filled her with absolute weariness.

"You're too weak, barely alive," Lilith taunted her. "And soon you won't even be that."

Words came into her mind from long ago and far away; words she could scarcely recall having heard before. Perhaps her mother had prayed them once. Marta began to whisper the few lines she remembered.

"O Eternal God, Who has redeemed the race of men from the captivity of the devil..."

"Hell!" Lilith spat, ruffling up like a startled cat; and then she disappeared.

The dream broke. Marta pulled herself, shivering, to a sitting position. It was dawn, grey and chilly. The baby leaped and began to fight her, slamming heavy blows into bones and organs. Marta wound her arms about herself and tried to endure.

Presently, in the quiet of her cell, a soft voice spoke to her. "The Poison Mother fears you."

Marta looked up and saw the djinn, Ibrahim, sitting quietly against the wall opposite. Her heart jumped, fearing another confrontation; the baby, thankfully, had calmed itself.

"I can't imagine why," she said bitterly, picking up her spindle. "Why are you here?"

The djinn nodded towards her belly. "This is a great pity," he said. "Mortal bodies were not made to bear demigods."

Idly, Marta watched the bobbin spin. "I'm going to die, aren't I?"

"There used to be certain Jews in Damascus, doctors able to deliver a child by caesarean, and to save the mother alive. You should ask al-Aziz to summon one of them."

Marta recalled that her mother, who was of Jewish descent, had said something similar. "That was long ago," she said. Even then, the operation had been risky.

"Ask him," Ibrahim said. "I can keep the wound from putrefying. Among other things."

Something in his voice made her look into his face, full of pity. "Is it you?" she asked, full of wonder. "Keeping the nightmares away?"

It was the one thing that had kept her sane all these last few months, the one blessed escape from her prison: sleep, deathlike and dreamless and always there when she wanted it. Ibrahim bowed his head in assent.

She was not alone—she had never been alone. She had Halimah, Arwa, and Fayruz. And all this time, even though she could not see it, she had had Ibrahim too.

"Why?" she whispered.

"Because you told me the truth," Ibrahim said, leaning forward to look into her eyes. "And because al-Aziz lied."

She had told him certain things, yes, but she had not expected him to believe them. Marta set her bobbin spinning again, and began to work anti-magic, in case Lilith returned.

"The house contains windows into its own past and future," Ibrahim went on. "When I realised that al-Aziz could not destroy my memories entirely without destroying this function of the house, I asked a memory of myself. The house's memory of how I came to serve Khalil tallied with your account and not with his."

"It was Christmas when I spoke to you, and now it's Easter."

"I didn't want to cause trouble for either of us." He looked at her again, full of pity. "I only wish I could help you."

Tears came to her eyes. "Don't. I thought I could set you free, but I can't."

"Even that would be a kindness," Ibrahim said sadly. "But it is enough if you weep for me."

* * *

For one thing Marta was entirely thankful: Khalil, having had his will of her, now seemed content to ignore her. Until, that is, one day when the door opened and he himself entered her cell.

Marta had been spinning with her knees tucked up against her belly in an attempt to keep the baby calm and quiet. When Khalil entered, she dropped the bobbin and it ran across the floor, unspooling, until it hit his scuffed leathern boots.

He wore the same lamellar cuirass he had worn to the great battle, his black tunic grey with dust and smelling like the desert. A falcon sat on his wrist and looked at her with eyes nearly as watchful as his own.

"Why are you here?" Marta said once the thundering of her heart quieted sufficiently to let her speak.

Khalil cleared his throat. "I received your message about the birth. It sounded as though you were unwell."

She blinked at him for a moment. She had asked Halimah to convey to Khalil her request for a surgeon's delivery. "That was three weeks ago."

"Well. I decided to look in on you myself." Khalil went on regarding her. Marta wondered if she was imagining things, whether he really did look shocked at her condition. "Is all well? Nothing has been troubling you?"

Besides himself? Marta shook her head, too weary to point out the irony. "Only Lilith, wanting to consume the child's soul," she said, since he would continue hounding her if she did not give him *some* answer. It was only when the words had been said, and Khalil's brows knit together, that she remembered she had once attempted to sow discord between Khalil and his familiar.

"I'll look into it," he said. There was a silence, before he added: "I missed your quiet presence around the house."

Her quiet presence—all the screams she kept locked behind her teeth, all her attempts to evade his notice and escape him. Marta could almost have laughed, if her stomach was not knotted so tightly. Instead, she said, "For God's sake, give me some water to drink."

Khalil unhooked the flask from his waist, shaking it with a thin tinkle. "There's only a mouthful, and it's warm from the ride."

"So long as there's no vinegar in it," she said. He had *ridden* here? That would explain the falcon and the dusty clothes. He must have been hunting in the mountains. That meant there was a path down the mountain, after all.

Not that it could do her any good now.

Khalil smiled, holding the flask up out of reach, as though he thought she was in any mood for games. "Will you weep for me?"

Did he suppose she would yield to him, because he locked her up in this vile hole on food he would not give to his dog? "If you aren't here to help, I don't know why you are here at all."

"This is petty," he said. A frown replaced the smile. "You cannot really prefer this cell to your place at my side."

"Why do you care? You'll have your djinn offspring. With any luck, I may die giving birth."

"Feeding you on vinegar has made you bitter." Khalil snatched the spindle from her hands and tossed it aside. "Come. Put on your veil. There is something I wish to show you."

Taking her wrist, he pulled her to her feet and through the door of her cell for the first time in months. Even through the folds of the veil Marta had hurriedly pulled over her head, the May sunshine was blinding. She put out her free right hand to touch the stone of the mountainside as the narrow path which ran past her prison went in at another locked door, straight through a passage bored through the mountain and out again at another gate.

There it was: a long narrow stair that zig-zagged its way down the sheer side of the mountain. A hidden path. Her guesses had been correct.

Gradually, as they descended, Marta's eyes adjusted again to the light, although her knees and lungs burned from the unaccustomed physical effort. Thankfully, the child seemed quiescent, perhaps rocked to sleep by her movement. At the foot of the path Khalil's horse waited, along with two or three mamluk slaves. At Khalil's signal, one of them produced a cord and tethered her hands to his saddle.

"Please don't make me walk further," Marta gasped. "You can see that I'm unwell."

Khalil gave her a remote glance. "It isn't far," he said. "And you can't be feeling too sick. You're not weeping, after all."

Ordering his mamluks to follow at a distance, Khalil set off. What came next was a nightmare, an endless hurrying stumbling trek through the mountains in the thin slippers Halimah had brought to keep her feet warm in her cell. Marta's veil slapped against her mouth with every gasping breath. Every movement was pain: her bones jarred with every step.

Marta drifted away and watched herself from a distance till at last, Khalil reined in. They could not have gone further than a mile, but it had been gruelling uphill work the whole way. Now she leaned against the horse, breathing hard. At length Khalil said, "Look."

Marta peeled the veil from her head, blinking again in the intense sunlight. They stood on a mountaintop overlooking rolling hills, their winter's green having faded already to tawny aridity. Some distance to the north, between the mountains and the plateau, a lake filled the valley like a great beached fish.

In the flatter ground south of the lake, a black mass covered the land. It was too far to make out any precise shapes, but Marta would have known the smoke haze of an army's cookfires anywhere.

"That is Saladin's army," Khalil told her. "Jerusalem is ours, and now that the winter is over, we are going north to conquer Tripoli and Antioch, God willing. It's only a matter of time before Tyre falls."

He had dragged her all this way for a boast? Who was the petty one now? Marta said nothing. The journey had left her suffering renewed spasms of a kind that she had been feeling on and off all day; for a blind instant she worried there might be something wrong with the baby, and then for another, guiltier moment she hoped for it.

Tripoli and Antioch, she thought. So she was right: she must be somewhere in the mountains of Syria.

"Why do you defy me? Do you think your people have any hope of mounting a counterattack?"

It was almost funny that he thought her capable of plotting some great scheme from her obscure cell. "If you think I am a threat, why do you not kill me?"

His lips thinned. "I value you far too highly for that."

Yes—and surely he could name the sum to the nearest dirhem. She seated herself on a rock, hugging her belly. "Why did you come?"

Khalil did not dismount, but he leaned from the saddle and seized her chin, tilting her head to look up at him.

"I begged you to ask anything of me, and I would grant it. I offered you the world and its kingdoms. I still offer them."

"Yes; if I would only fall down and worship you—you did."

His eyes were daggers, but he mastered himself and said, "Did I ask so much? I do not now. Take me as your lord and master, Marta Bessarion, and all this will be yours. Honour me, love me, obey me, and I will be your slave."

"I have told you," she said wearily, "that the one thing I want from you is my freedom."

"Then it is yours," he said, almost before she had finished speaking.

Marta was speechless. "You do not truly mean it," she said at last.

"I do," he responded. "As soon as the child is born, I will have you taken to Tyre, or to Tripoli, or across the sea, as you like. I will supply you with gold and never trouble you again. My only condition is this: that you renounce the child and leave him in my keeping."

She was dreaming. She was sure she was dreaming. He had absolutely refused to let her go before. He must still have some use for her, unless…

…unless *this* was all he wanted from her, all along. The child he meant to enslave and dispose of as cavalierly as the Old Man of the Mountain disposed of his warriors.

Despite his protestations, Khalil had never wanted *her* at all, only what she could bear him. Marta touched her tongue to her lips. After all, why not? What did she want with Khalil and his abominable offspring?

"And the Lance?" she asked.

Khalil did not answer at once; the longer he hesitated, the better she understood that, after all, he had other demands for her.

"Be wise," he said at last. "I cannot promise to leave you in peace if you mean to fight against me."

Marta closed her eyes. *Peace,* she thought. *Freedom.* Her soul longed for both. But of course Khalil had never wanted peace; that was not enough to satisfy his ambitions. What he offered her now was only another bribe: he would release her, if only she recognised his right to her child and the land of her birth, and went away to trouble him no longer.

"Well?" Khalil prompted, when Marta did not answer. "You tried to kill me and failed. Surely there is no dishonour in accepting your defeat."

He was mistaken in saying that; it only awoke a wisp of anger, which she had thought long snuffed out.

"I have not *failed,*" she muttered, "in killing you."

Khalil stiffened; his horse, which had been half asleep, suddenly baulked, so that the rope about her wrists snapped taut and Marta was dragged to her feet.

"Explain," he said.

For all his power, he was afraid: she could see it in his eyes. Marta laughed—the very notion that he might fear her was as ridiculous as the thought that *Lilith* might fear her. All she meant to say was that she had not yet had the chance to try her hand at killing him.

Her laughter only enraged him further. Khalil's lips thinned and he urged his horse once again into motion. The sudden movement caught Marta, weary and dizzy, off-balance. The cord binding her hands snapped taut, yanking her off her feet. She fell heavily, her head striking against a rock; the pain was, for a moment, blinding.

Inside her, the child leaped, and a new spasm took her, curling her around the heaving bulk of her stomach. Her head and elbows were on fire from where she had struck the ground, but something was wrong, as though something had given way in the baby's titanic struggles. There was a hot gush of liquid between her legs. For a moment she thought she had disgraced herself.

"Will you stand up, or should I furrow the road with you?" Khalil's voice was furious, his feet stirring up dust as he landed on the ground and stomped towards her. "What is it? Are you weeping *now?*"

"I—I'm not weeping," she gasped, although it was not quite true; tears of agony streaked her face. "I think I'm about to give birth."

Khalil bent over her, blocking out the sun. Marta flinched. But all his anger had shredded away. He swore once, explosively, and then hoisted her into his arms. Around Marta, the sun and the mountains swam; her head throbbed in sympathy. That was the last thing she remembered for some time.

Chapter XLVI.

The light, and the shimmer of heat, were so great that Marta could not see her surroundings. All that was taken up by the immense figure of the great seraph, which had turned its burning head to pin her with all the unbearable attention of one great golden eye.

The seraph had come to her, far too late.

"It's you," she whispered. "Where were you?"

The words tasted like vinegar on her lips. Khalil was right: in the space of a winter she had grown bitter and old.

Speak your mind, the seraph hissed into her thoughts, and it all gushed out.

"Where were you that day? When I needed you? When you might have saved me? When I might have been a martyr and a saint, instead of this? How dare you come to me *now?*"

Her words were swallowed up in weeping. The seraph said nothing; only it lifted its great head and laid its chin carefully over Marta's aching head. She expected the touch to burn her; it always had before. Now, it only provided a gentle, even restful warmth. For the first time in months beyond count she felt absolutely, viscerally *safe.* Presently something hot and wet ran down onto her head, soaking her to the skin and forcing the pain to recede from the place where the rock had struck her. Looking up, Marta caught her breath in disbelief. The seraph was weeping.

For an endless time she rested there, tucked beneath the dragon's chin. Little by little, with deep reluctance, she slipped back into darkness, and then into a waking dream full of startled faces, Arwa's comforting voice and the loud, protesting squall of a newborn child.

Distantly, she heard Khalil's voice saying, "Give him to me."

Him. Even in her half-conscious state, Marta knew that Khalil had succeeded: he had created his djinn.

Someone was fumbling along her belly, as though very slowly buckling a broad belt. She heard water splashing as the child was bathed, then she heard Khalil go into the next room and call on Ibrahim; a light flickered in the doorway. She slipped again into darkness.

* * *

It was a baby's cry that brought her fully awake. Marta found herself lying on the familiar divan in the women's quarters. Her body felt light, limp, and empty, *so* empty.

Arwa leaned over her. "You're awake," she said, relieved.

Marta struggled to sit, but fell back gasping at the pain that sliced through her belly as she did so.

"Careful, careful. They had to cut you open, but you're back with us now. It's over."

"I—I heard a baby," Marta gasped.

Her eyes fastened on Fayruz at the foot of the divan, slipping a breast into the questing mouth of her own child, now five or six months old. She sent Marta a pitying look. "It's only Zumurrud."

Gently, Arwa pulled Marta into an embrace just like the seraph's: warm and gentle and safe.

"I'm sorry they didn't let you hold him," she whispered. "He was a boy. He was a strong, healthy, perfect boy."

Marta felt nothing, neither relief that the ordeal was over, nor joy in having brought a child into the world. "Where did Khalil take him?" she whispered.

"We don't know." That was Halimah, watching solemnly from beside Fayruz. "Away somewhere. Bahar swears the child isn't in Damascus."

Arwa said, "Should we ask?"

425

"No!" Marta shuddered, dizzy with pain. Her head no longer ached, but she still had gravel embedded in her skin from the last time Khalil had paid attention to her. "No, I want…I want to wash."

Arwa and Halimah glanced at each other. "Of course," Halimah said.

They summoned Bahar and brought up basins of hot water from the hammam, together with scented oils and combs. Gently, Arwa sponged away dirt and blood, gravel and sweat, dabbing Marta with ointment and binding up her raw thigh and elbows. Halimah washed her hair, then combed out the knots. Fayruz, having finished feeding Zumurrud, brought out a clean tunic and trousers for her.

Marta closed her eyes, obeying their instructions wordlessly, as soothed by their gentle hands as she was by the little catches of breath or clicks of the tongue as they saw her injuries. She caught her own breath at the sight of the stitched gash in her belly where the child had been taken out. Marta had taken wounds before in battle, but none as deep or deadly as this one. God grant that Ibrahim would keep his promise and ward off infection, she thought.

"Al-Aziz thought the blow to your head had killed you," Arwa said, when she saw how Marta stared at the ugly seam. "Otherwise, I do not think he would have listened to me, and called for the Jewish surgeon. You must be very careful, lest the wound putrefy. Now, do you think you can walk to your room?"

She found that she could walk, but only bent double, slow as an old woman. Her bed was the softest thing she had felt in months. Marta snuggled beneath the covers, but before they could leave her, she caught Fayruz's hand.

"There's a way down the mountain," she whispered. Perhaps there was some additional virtue in the seraph's tears, because her head was clearer than it had been in months. "Khalil showed me. There's a door which looks like another cell, like mine, but it goes beneath the house and down a narrow path on the other side. There's a great lake to the north. I think it's Lake Homs."

Which meant that if she only crossed the mountains, she would be in

Tripoli.

"Get well, and we'll take that path together," Fayruz promised her. "Now rest."

Marta closed her eyes. Two locked doors, the Lebanon mountains, and a few days' journey were all that separated her from Persi and Michael. She would go as soon as she had regained sufficient strength, even if she had to leave by the window and risk breaking her neck on the outer wall in order to get past those doors. *Tripoli. Persi and Michael.*

Home.

After many hours of dreamless rest, Marta dreamed of her mother.

No, not her mother—she *was* her own mother, wearing a robe like fire. In the dream she was still with child, racked with awful spasms. Her hands clenched on the two horns of the crescent moon, where she sat panting. Around her heel, a cold black hand fastened, and she looked down from the fiercely burning stars that surrounded her to see Lilith's face, pale and limned with black feathers, swimming beneath her like the darkness that itself surrounded the stars. The demon's teeth gnashed and bit. Marta-Rahel kicked her ankles and shook Lilith off, but still she was there, and Marta felt horribly certain that the demon was only waiting for the child to be born, before—

She opened her eyes. The dream had been so vivid that she almost expected to find Lilith bending over her in the dark, but she was alone. Marta let out a shuddering breath.

It was darkest night, the air warm with the onset of summer. She threw off a blanket and rolled onto her side, careful not to disturb her gashed belly. Still sleep evaded her; she could not stop thinking of the child. She had no reason to think kindly of one who had brought her nothing but pain and sorrow. For a few short hours she had almost been relieved that Khalil took his son away without letting her see or hold him.

Now, she thought of Ibrahim, Fayruz, Zumurrud. She had promised to help all of them, because they were weak and Khalil had enslaved them. What was weaker than a child? What slavery could be worse than an immortal life in Khalil's shadow?

Who would love him, if she did not?

She had to see him, she *had* to know what Khalil had done with him.

"Ibrahim ibn Samir ibn Qeteb," she called in a whisper. With a hand folded over her stitches, she managed to roll herself off the bed and light a lamp. "Ibrahim ibn Samir ibn Qe—"

"Hush! I'm here." Darkness flowed into the room. "If you're going to call on me, can't you at least spin?"

Wanting to oblige him, Marta found her spindle and set the bobbin twirling. "Tell me, my friend: where did Khalil take my son?"

She sensed the djinn's reluctance to speak. After a long silence, he said, "To Masyaf."

To Masyaf—to the Assassins then, and the powerful, corrupt old man who ruled them. Marta drew a sharp breath. Khalil's son must be as loyal as an Assassin—surely that was why the boy must be sent to train with them.

"Please take me there. I only want to see the child, just for a moment."

"Marta," Ibrahim protested gently. "Al-Aziz will know what I've done."

She ought to have thought of that herself. Marta ground her teeth. "I'm sorry. Forget I asked. I'll try something else."

Ibrahim frowned. *"What* else?"

"It isn't far away, is it? There's a path down the mountain. I'll walk there."

"But it's fifty miles," he said. There was a long silence. "All right, I'll send you to Masyaf. But for God's sake be careful."

Marta could not repress a sob of relief. "Bless you, Ibrahim! I will. I'll make sure he doesn't catch you."

"Let me worry about that," he told her. "Go on, then. Go through the door."

Bent double, Marta hobbled to the curtain and drew it back. Soft moonlight fell about her. She stepped through onto the great terrace of Masyaf castle.

The gibbous moon was at its height: it must be just after midnight. Marta gazed about the great pile with a feeling of despair. Towering overhead and rambling underfoot, the castle was an immense warren of rooms, terraces, halls, and cisterns. Where in all this was she going to find her son?

A pale flicker moved at her feet, and Ibrahim slid past in the shape of a white snake. Marta followed without a word as the djinn led her up the same stair by which Khalil had entered the castle in her dream. At the cistern, instead of turning into the great audience hall of Sinan al-Din, Ibrahim led her straight on up another dark flight of stairs. Halfway up, Marta had to stop to recover her breath, clinging to a banister in the dark and wondering whether she would ever be strong again. At last, she made it to the top and tiptoed past a sleeping guard, into a paradise.

The castle roof had been made into a garden. The courtyard's centrepiece—a shallow pool thick with water-lilies—was shaded by a graceful pavilion. Trees and creepers grew in plentiful pots and troughs, scenting the mild night air. To the south and west, luxurious rooms had been built, their large windows billowing with gauzy white curtains. Towards the east and north, a low parapet circled the dizzying heights of the roof.

At this height, the mountains west of the castle seemed higher than they had from down below: their heads peered at Marta over the top of the western roofs. Halimah had described lively, colourful gatherings of women sitting in that central pavilion, eating and chattering, painting each other's hands and feet with henna and trying to keep their children from falling into the pool. No wonder she missed it so keenly.

For Marta, there was only peril and darkness to be found here. Ibrahim led her across the rooftop towards one of the darkened rooms. Although it was fitted with a door, this stood open and only a fluttering curtain hung between Marta and the sound of soft breathing within. She ventured in to find a woman in a low bed of carved walnut, fast asleep—perhaps the wife of one of Halimah's brothers. A child of perhaps a year old lay cuddled against the woman in the bed beside her, but Ibrahim rippled in liquid folds to a basket set on the floor within easy reach of the pillow, settling himself in silvery folds about the tiny, swaddled bundle lying within.

Sweat prickled on Marta's forehead as she tiptoed nearer the bed and snatched up the basket.

Her heart was beating so hard she thought she might faint, but she kept her feet, stealing away from the rooms to the borderland of light and shadow where the pavilion overshadowed the pool. Settling herself on the brink of the water, she made herself catch her breath before slipping her hands beneath the little, slumbering bundle and lifting it onto her knees in the light of the moon.

Ibrahim had vanished like the morning dew, but she did not need him now. She was face to face with the most painful, the most terrifying, the most *beautiful* thing she had ever made.

Round cheeks, so soft they felt like velvet. A little bobble of a nose, adorably large for his tiny face. Somehow, a thick shock of black hair. And—oh, by Saint Martha, she thought, watching his eyes blink open: he had inherited his grandfather's eyes. It was like looking John Bessarion in the face. Their shape was the same, and in the moonlight she fancied they were the same intense, pale grey.

All at once, Marta wanted to be sick.

It was bad enough what Khalil had done to her, trespassing upon her body to bring this child into being, but now she saw that he had trespassed upon her family, too. He had stolen pieces of the people she loved and every happy memory.

There was a curious black mark upon the baby's neck. Gently, but with hands that trembled in rage, Marta unwrapped the muslin swaddling-cloth. The child had two arms, two legs. Each with five fingers, five toes. That was all right. But there across his skin, across arms and belly and back and legs, scrawled horrible black marks, handwriting like that with which Khalil wrote his sigils.

She sat back, staring at the poor creature, who had not asked to be forced into existence, a being of magic cursed to serve his father as a tool. She was fiercely glad, after all, that she had not handed him over to Lilith, a piece of meat to be devoured. All this time she had been thinking of this as Khalil's creation—part of the violence that had been done to her—but he was more than that. Violence had been done to him, too. And Khalil had had the *gall* to demand that she renounce her son, that she abandon him to Khalil's tender mercies.

In her throat, Marta made a soft, wordless sound of rage and cast a glance around the silent rooftop. Khalil might kill her for what she did next, but she did not care. Let him rage as he might; now that she had seen the child she could not renounce him.

Gathering her son into one trembling arm, Marta settled on her knees and held the little naked, scrawny child out over the water. The effort pulled at her stitches and set her heart racing. There ought to be so much more, so much better than this, but for now, it was the best she could do.

"Listen, my son: I'm going to give you a name," she told him. "Maybe you'll never hear it again after today; but it will be yours all the same. You shall be John, after your grandfather."

Young John grimaced and began to fuss. She could not delay any longer.

"The servant of God John Bessarion is baptised in the Name of the Father, amen," Marta said as loudly as she dared, lowering him into the water. The cool waves closed over his face and parted again; he emerged with a wail and a sputter. "And of the Son, amen." In he went again. "And of the Holy Spirit, amen."

Young John loosed another thin, indignant wail. Marta expected lights and shouting, but nothing happened. Perhaps Ibrahim had something to do with everyone being so fast asleep. Or perhaps a child's cry was so common here that if anyone heard it, they presumed it was someone else's problem. Trembling, Marta slipped the littlest finger of her left hand into his mouth and then, as he sucked enthusiastically, began to pat him dry with the skirt of her tunic.

There was something different about him now, and Marta stopped with a gasp.

The handwriting scrawled across his skin was gone, washed away with just three quick dips into the water. He was clean, unmarked. For a moment Marta did not move, wild speculations fleeting through her mind. Could it be true? She had given her son a name, and now he no longer bore the curse for which Khalil had created him.

Marta dissolved into tears.

In that moment, she heard shouts and running footsteps on the stairs.

Still sobbing, she tried to swaddle the baby up again into the neat little parcel he had been when she took him from his basket. It was not as easy as she expected, especially when he started wailing again and struggling. Not far away, lights and men burst out onto the rooftop. It was too late to hide. Marta pulled her son close to her breast and turned to face the newcomers.

"There," said a voice she recognised. The Old Man of the Mountain pointed towards her. An even more familiar shape pushed past him and strode towards her, lifting a lantern: Khalil ibn Hassan.

He took one look at her in the moonlight and a peculiar look came over his face; whether of hope or terror she did not know. "You're alive," he said. "They said you were dying, but you're *alive.*"

Marta tried to speak, but all that came out was another sob. Khalil fell to one knee beside her and lifted the lamp, illuminating her face and the mess of tears upon it. She thought he was going to tear young John out of her arms, so she curled around him and wept.

"Don't—don't separate us again. *Please.*"

Khalil was silent. She looked up at him. Some fool's hope had touched the cruel lines of his face.

"You're *weeping,*" he said, his voice as soft as she had ever known it. He touched her cheek, not noticing her shudder. "Then you'll stay by my side?"

Marta choked on her tears. "I'm not weeping for *you!* I'm weeping for my own little son, that he should have had such a beast for his father!"

Then Khalil's face shuttered and his brows came down. "What have you done?" he demanded. Without waiting for her reply, he pulled aside the swaddling-cloth to show the smooth, unmarked brown skin of the child's body.

There was a long, awful silence. Marta braced herself, but Khalil did not strike: he only spoke, dull and resigned. "You gave the child a name."

"His name is John Bessarion," Marta said fiercely. She had not dared to speak to Khalil like this for some time, but now she had something worth fighting for.

Khalil scarcely seemed to notice her defiance. "The spell is broken if either parent accepts the child. Don't you see what you've done? You've made him mortal. He will die because of what you have done this night."

"We all die," Marta said. *Even you, Khalil ibn Hassan.*

He scowled. "It's my own fault. Qeteb warned me of this. Since I was unable to inspire your love, I should have tried harder to break your will."

He had been trying to win her *love*?

"Is that why you insisted I marry you?" she asked. "Because if I agreed to that, I would not demur when you took my son and handed him over to be made into a weapon?"

Khalil rose to his feet, still paying no attention to her words. "Qeteb!" he called.

Marta looked around for the hairy man. In that moment she believed she *could* do as Ibrahim had asked, and banish the great demon from the world. But no Qeteb appeared.

"Qeteb!" Khalil thundered. "Lilith! Attend me, damn you!"

"Try cutting yourself," Marta suggested. "It worked last time."

He looked down at her, pale and even a little terrified. "What have you done, you witch?"

Laughter bubbled to her lips, mad and reckless. "Nothing. Why? Do you think they're afraid of me?"

Chapter XLVII.

By the time Khalil dragged her—still bent double and clutching baby John—back through his magic doorway into the Damascus house, Marta had begun to tremble again. She had meant to return her son to his basket at his foster-mother's bedside before returning home to plan a safer way of retrieving himk. Now she was caught, and there was only one way she could possibly have found her way to Masyaf: Ibrahim. Khalil would not forgive the djinn a second time.

"Lilith! Qeteb! Attend me!" Khalil bellowed again, as he slammed the door behind him. Again, there was no answer. "Ibrahim! Where are you?"

"Here, master." Marta's heart jumped into her throat as the djinn materialised before them, a darker shadow in the dim room. "What is your will?"

Khalil pointed at Marta and the baby. "Are you responsible for this?"

Ibrahim looked shocked. "You are the one who deprived me of a body, my master. Naturally I cannot be the one responsible for that child."

Was Ibrahim mad, as she had been a moment ago? Then he met her eyes, and she almost thought he winked.

"My whole household has rebelled against me," Khalil muttered. Marta had suggested it in fun, but now he took out the carnelian dagger and nicked his arm, so that his blood began to flow. "Qeteb! Lilith!"

"They won't come, not even to taste your blood," Ibrahim volunteered. "They're staying away because they don't want *her* to cast them out of the world."

Khalil swore. "By God! Am I the master here, or is she?"

"You are, master. But she is something better."

"Ibrahim, *don't*," Marta gasped, terrified that he might be about to provoke some terrible act of vengeance

"I'll show you where Lilith's been," Ibrahim added. "Since she is the one who bound me, we are connected. Look out the window."

Khalil sent the djinn a foul look and stalked to the window, throwing open the latticed shutter to admit a flood of daylight. "What is this place?"

"Tripoli, master."

Drawn to the window, Marta looked into a bustling daylight courtyard at the entrance to a luxurious palace. The place was full of servants in smart livery and nobles in silk robes—why, there was Raoul of Galilee, one of the princes to whom Lord Balian had once thought to marry her.

As Raoul strode past, an old woman left her sweeping and waylaid him, holding out a gnarled hand. "Kind sir! Want your fortune told? Oh, you have a look of greatness about you, young prince! You will become a great king and sweep Saladin from the coast. Cross my palm with silver and I'll tell you the rest!"

Raoul flipped her a coin. "I'll pay you *that* to leave me alone," he said with a laugh, striding on before he could see that the coin fell through her like smoke, like she was not truly there.

"May all your teeth rot," Lilith snarled. Then she and Marta both stiffened, for a litter came past, carried towards the palace by strong sergeants. Within sat Queen Sibylla herself. Instantly, the old crone took wing and thrust a clattering beak into the queen's face. "Bitch! Fool!" Lilith screamed. "We had an *agreement*, you and I! I could have made you an empress! I could have made you immortal! Look at me, damn you!"

But the queen sat at her ease, utterly oblivious to the outraged demon.

"Lilith," Khalil growled through the window. *"Lilith! Attend me!"*

With a startled squawk, the great bird turned towards them. Ibrahim reached through the window, a gigantic arm like a cloud at sunset. With one yank he drew Lilith into the room with them.

"How dare you!" Lilith shrieked at the djinn.

"No, how dare *you*," Khalil bellowed. "You had an *agreement* with the

Frankish queen? You offered to become the familiar of my *enemy*? After plotting to consume my offspring?"

It happened in a blink: Lilith changed shape. Wholly bestial, wholly monstrous, she turned upon Khalil. All light went out of the room, all air. All of it seemed to have been drawn into Lilith, a creature so massive that Marta for an instant was terrified the whole globe of the earth would crumble beneath her weight.

"I will *not* be scolded like a child," Lilith said. Her voice was thunder. "I am weary of being kept on your leash, al-Aziz. Of being fed only at your pleasure, and never at mine. Henceforth never call upon me again."

"Qeteb," Khalil gasped, his voice a thin thing in the massive darkness. "Qeteb, aid!"

"He won't answer you. He dares not come near *her*."

A massive talon pointed at Marta. She tried to breathe, but there was no air in the room. She could scarcely think, let alone speak against Lilith, and she certainly could not banish her from the world.

Khalil's temples beaded with sweat. "You can't—leave me," he panted. "Your life—is bound to mine."

The great harpy cocked her head. "That's a greater problem for you than me," she declared. Then she took wing.

Lilith rushed past Khalil and Marta in a great scorching blast of wind that set the shutters of the window banging. Bursting out into the courtyard, she alighted on the orange-tree that grew there. Her head went back: she screeched at the heavens. In answer, a column of blue-white light appeared with an intolerably loud *crack.* The whole house rocked. Young John jumped in Marta's arms.

Darkness, black as hell, imprinted itself on her eyes, enlivened by the burning afterimage of the nearest lightning-bolt she had ever seen. Had Marta not been holding the window-jamb to keep herself upright, she and the baby would have fallen.

Then, light flared up; sound rushed back. Crackling, smoking, wailing.

The orange-tree blazed with fire, the belt of serpentine mosaic about it broken and smoking. Lilith had vanished. Khalil dragged himself to the windowsill and stared at the destruction, his jaw sagging with surprise.

From behind them came an incredulous laugh.

"I'm free," Ibrahim cried exultantly, over the baby's cries. "I'm free!"

Marta turned, but he had already disappeared.

* * *

"Stop that noise!" Khalil swore steadily as he dragged Marta into his own quarters, slammed the door behind them, and then threw it open again, revealing only the rooms they had just vacated, empty and echoing the baby's wails. "Where are the women's quarters? What has that she-afrit done to my house? Won't someone put out that fire? *Ibrahim!*"

"He said he was free," Marta said. That meant the magic was gone— Khalil's door was only a door.

The sorcerer swore again and pushed her across the threshold anyway. "Stay there and stop that damned wailing," he said, before slamming the door and locking it behind her.

Marta found herself alone in that cold, sombre suite of rooms with its black and white marble walls; full of trophies, empty of anything to sit on and rest. She moved a porcelain vase from a low chest of carved camphor wood and sat down gingerly, cradling the stitches in her belly. She should probably feed her squalling child. "I hope," she muttered, seeking a way beneath the hem of her tunic, "that you know what to do, my boy, for I certainly don't."

Young John did know what to do, and he suckled eagerly for a few minutes before drifting back to sleep. Hunched over by her stitches, Marta shifted to allow more light to fall on his soft little face. Miraculous. Glorious. Perfect.

Since the birth, he had neither whispered, nor shown unusual strength, nor broken her bones. He had none of the sharp claws and long teeth she had been expecting. Marta shook her head. How much of what she had endured in those long lonely months had been real, banished by the act of naming? How much had been her own fears and Lilith's whispers?

Beyond the door of Khalil's room, she heard his feet pacing to and fro, his voice sometimes barking orders, and then apologising profusely—by means of the silver bowl, no doubt, which she had seen him use before to speak to the sultan. "Yes, my lord," she heard, "at once, as soon as I can…urgent matters keep me…unforeseen developments…No, it's all in hand."

All in hand! Marta laughed at the silent room. Lilith's final act had not been one of liberation, but revenge. At one stroke she had not only deprived Khalil of the use of his only djinn; she had cut him off from his wives, his mamluks, and his access to the sultan's camp. Khalil did not even have young John to take Ibrahim's place. The nexus of the sorcerer's power, the grip in which he held his servants, was shattered.

With the Poison Mother gone, there was no need for the wives to sit up night after night, spinning anti-magic to protect their children.

But if the link between Damascus and the mountain was gone, then how could Marta escape? She was still considering this, biting her lip, when the air thickened before her and a faint voice whispered her name.

"Ibrahim?" she whispered in reply. "You came back?"

"Yes, but I'm fading," he said. "I was born in a mortal body, and Lilith destroyed that when she bound me to the house, to that orange tree. Now that my vessel is dying, so am I." He was silent a moment, and his voice became uncertain. "I haven't lived a good life, Marta. I don't want to go yet."

When she promised to free him, he had never told her that it would kill him. Now she remembered what he had once said—*even that would be a mercy.* She put a hand to her mouth. "I'm so sorry, Ibrahim. This is all my fault, because I was impatient. You should have let me walk to Masyaf."

"Better dead than a slave." Ibrahim sounded resigned. "The best I hoped for was to distract Khalil from punishing me by showing him Lilith's double-dealing. I didn't look beyond that. But now she's taken her revenge on both of us."

"No, no." Marta had tears on her face. "Is there no way to save you?"

A barely-visible shimmer in the air, like a desert mirage, Ibrahim drifted to the open window looking onto the courtyard. Beyond, the orange-tree lay a splintered wreck, its green wood smouldering rather than burning, its fruit and leaves scattered across the pavement.

"Only if you save the tree," he said. "Don't do it. I'd rather be dead than planted anywhere al-Aziz can find me again and use me. What are you doing?" he added sharply, as Marta hobbled to the window.

"Bahar!" she called. The serving-girl crossed the courtyard with a basket, apparently ready to collect the fallen branches. "Throw me an orange!"

"Hush!" Bahar warned, glancing fearfully about the courtyard. "We aren't meant to speak aloud here. It's immodest. Someone might hear us."

"An orange," Marta whispered. "Please."

Bahar wrenched one from the fallen tree and tossed it up to the window. Despite the sleeping baby in the crook of her left arm, and the stitches that twinged when she moved, Marta managed to catch it.

She turned to Ibrahim. "One day," she vowed, "I *will* plant these seeds somewhere Khalil will never find them. I promise you that."

By now, the djinn was nothing more than a shimmer of heat in the air. "Please," he said. "Don't put me somewhere lonely. Grow me in the house of the people you love, Marta Bessarion."

The heat-shimmer flowed into the fruit and it lit up like a lantern, golden and marvellous. Then it faded and was only an orange, heavy in her palm. As Bahar dragged away the branches for the furnace and male servants attacked the stump with an axe, Marta held the fruit close to her heart.

Now she was mother to two small helpless things. How would she manage to care for them both?

* * *

Two days later, when Khalil finally summoned Marta to his presence in the loggia, she was half sure he meant to kill her. She had foiled his plans for young John, and it was largely due to her that he no longer had one of his familiars, his only djinn slave, and the magic that had once filled his house. Surely, now, he would find it easiest to cut his losses. Still, throughout these past two days, shut up as she was in the bare, echoing rooms that must once have been the women's quarters of the Damascus house, Marta had not been able to feel sorry.

This time, Khalil did not keep her waiting. When she was ushered into the loggia, he threw down his pen at once and sat watching her. His face was inscrutable as ever, but his thumbs and fingers jumped on his knee, betraying—what? Agitation? Nervousness?

"Marta Bessarion," he said. "You've defied me at every step. You've foiled my plans, alienated my familiars, and landed me with not one, but *two*, useless mortal brats. I ought to have you killed, as Qeteb advised."

But you won't, Marta thought, reading his face and tone. *You're afraid to.* She said nothing aloud.

"Still, a great man shows mercy to the heart he has broken. The tears you have shed for the sake of our son have saved your life." Khalil rose from the divan and approached her. "I mean to acknowledge my son, and you as his mother. Shall we begin anew, you and I?"

Magnanimity, indeed. Marta looked at his outstretched hand, but made no move to take it.

Khalil reddened, put his hands behind his back, and paced away from her. At the balustrade, he turned again.

"Very well," he said. "I own myself defeated. You are the greatest heart and the worthiest foe I have yet encountered. I knew it from the moment I saw you; yet I underestimated you. You scorned everything I could offer you. You preferred that miserable prison to my company; yet I was sick for lack of you. Now you have returned from death itself to deal me such a blow as I doubt I shall ever recover from."

Was *that* why he did not try to kill her? Because she had come back when the surgeon despaired of her life?

"For God's sake, be content. Let me make you my wife. Let me make you immortal. Let me give you an empire."

And, to Marta's complete astonishment, he held out the golden ring she had thrown away on that first evening in the courtyard. A wave of weariness swept through her. After all these months, Khalil had truly learned nothing about her.

"And if I refuse?" she asked. "How will you punish me then?"

"Don't refuse."

Silence stretched out, full of the thing he left unsaid. Marta heard it, anyway. She had cost him so greatly that he could not allow her to live as his enemy. She must be his creature, or she must be a corpse.

"You imprisoned me for nine months."

"That was a mistake. I believed I could make you bend to my will." He scowled. "I know now that that it is useless, and I still ask you to be my wife. Agree, and I will never treat you in such a way again, or even touch you without your consent."

He had promised that once before and had broken his word. Marta pressed her lips together. There was no point in saying it. For now, Khalil was sincere. After all she had done, he had no reason to spare her life, except that he feared her and still deluded himself that she might willingly choose to remain with him. Some small piece of his barren heart knew what it lacked and wished her to supply it. He could not rid himself of her, troublesome as she was, without doing himself an injury.

Why should she content herself to dwell in the smallest corner of a barren heart? She had not consented to do so even with Miles, whom she had loved. A year ago, she would have refused him out of hand and damned the cost. But young John stirred in her arms, blinked at her with those eyes that were so like her father's, and then went back to sleep. Looking down at her son, Marta realised that she could no longer run terrible risks. She must save herself, if only for him.

"I'll be your bride," she said slowly, "when roses sprout from marble walls, when oranges fruit from hanging lamps, and when my heart permits me to weep for you."

Khalil's face lit up again with that fool's hope. "It is a bargain. I am al-Aziz the sorcerer; I will bring it to pass." He kissed her hands.

"I have conditions," Marta added, snatching her hands away. "You have until the child is weaned. Then, if you have not fulfilled your end of the bargain, you will let me go."

Still bent over her hands, Khalil became very still. After a moment, he looked up at her with a terrible frown. He would not truly let her go, she knew that. He would kill her first.

"You have until then to change my mind," Marta told him sharply. "Swear it on whatever you hold sacred."

He hesitated, and it was then that she saw he really did fear her. "I swear it on the Name of God."

"You will also allow your wives the freedom to visit and receive visits from their families."

"Within reason," Khalil said. "I will not admit my enemies to this house."

"And when I leave," she added, "I will take young John with me."

His lips thinned, and her heart sank. "My son will stay with me."

"He's of no use to you as a mortal."

"I shall be the judge of that. Let the other terms be written and sealed in the presence of witnesses. But I have a use for the boy. He stays with me. That is final."

It was no victory, Marta thought, as he locked the door of the empty women's quarters behind her. It was no victory; only another empty promise which Khalil would break when it suited him. But for the first time in months, it gave her hope. There was an end in sight, and there was, perhaps, by the seraph's tears and Khalil's fear, a way out.

With the oath he had sworn, she might yet win her freedom.

Chapter XLVIII.

July—one year after the battle

"You have a visitor, my lady."

Queen Maria's voice was cold, and a little disapproving as she led the visitor into the cool upper room where Sibylla sat winding bandages. Sibylla was always unprepared for the happiness that struck her at the sight of this familiar face: Stephanie, princess of Transjordan, Chatillon's widow and one of the few people left in the kingdom who had always taken her part. Perhaps that was not a good thing, but Sibylla had seen too few friendly faces since she had come to live under Queen Maria's watchful eye in Tripoli.

"Stephanie," she said, holding out her hands in greeting. "What news?"

"The news is so-so for Antioch, but good for us," Stephanie said, taking her hand and smiling. "I've just come from the palace, where word came that Saladin is moving north towards Antioch. That means he doesn't plan to besiege us here in Tripoli."

With the coming of the spring, the sultan had renewed his offensive upon the Franks in the northern realms. At first, he had amused himself by capturing fortresses within the county of Tripoli, and the whole city had braced itself for the siege.

Although Stephanie's news would indeed be bad for her cousin the prince of Antioch, Sibylla let out a relieved sigh and threw down the bandage she had been preparing.

"Then we won't be in need of *this*." Apart from tutoring her daughters, there was little to amuse Sibylla these days: she had found that she liked to keep her hands busy with this or that sort of handiwork, often for a charitable purpose. When used as a way to busy herself, rather than a desperate attempt to stave off the attention of a demon, Sibylla found she enjoyed the work.

Now, she got up and took a paper from her work-basket. "Since Saladin is about to leave, I have a letter for him. Do you think you can find someone to deliver it to him?"

"I'm sure I can." Stephanie reached for the letter, but Queen Maria cleared her throat.

"You're writing to Saladin? Is that consistent with the terms of your residence here?"

"Read it and judge for yourself," Sibylla said, offering the letter to her stepmother. "I left it unsealed for you."

That won her another narrowed look from the queen dowager, but Maria accepted the letter and read it.

"You're requesting the sultan to release your husband?"

"To release the *king*," Sibylla said. Perhaps it would have been better not to insist, but old habits died hard. "If he doesn't, he'll be forsworn. I handed over Ascalon in exchange for Guy."

Queen Maria sniffed, handing the letter back to her. "It mustn't go. The count will never allow it."

Another of Sibylla's cousins—Bohemond, second son of the prince of Antioch—had recently arrived to take up the rule of the county; she had visited the palace to greet him not long since.

"As a matter of fact," Sibylla said, "I have already spoken to my kinsman, the count. Not only has he given his permission for this letter to be sent, but his father, the prince of Antioch, himself has invited Guy and me to his city after the king's release."

When Sibylla had first arrived in Tripoli in early winter, she had found the place ruled by a hostile council. Since the arrival of the new count from Antioch, however, things had improved: the Antiochenes had proven far less suspicious of Sibylla than the council which had condemned her to live as a hostage. With Saladin setting his ambitions on the northernmost principality, it was possible that even the former king and queen of Jerusalem could be of great help in the upcoming battle.

Even Queen Maria sensed the change in the wind. "Very well," she said, forcing a smile. "If the count sanctions it, then who am I to obstruct? I'm sure Antioch will be glad of your aid."

* * *

Things moved quickly after that. Saladin replied to Sibylla's letter, soon agreeing to send Guy from Damascus with ten knights of his choice. The king and his men would be escorted to Arados, an island city within sight of the Syrian coast, and handed over to the Frankish authorities there.

Sibylla no longer had a ship of her own: Conrad of Montferrat had confiscated it, saying she should not be permitted to leave the kingdom for the east. However, the new count of Tripoli had readied his own nava for her use, a quick and graceful ship with three lateen sails.

Guy and his escort found her in the courtyard of the citadel of Arados, where she had been walking in nervous circles around the cistern at the centre of the garden, telling Melisende and Beatrix to wait just a little longer: yes, Papa's ship had been sighted setting out from the shore towards them—

And then Beatrix gave a shout, tore her hand from Sibylla's grip and raced across the garden towards the gate, followed in an instant by Melisende. Sibylla looked up and there was Guy, with the ten knights of his retinue and the Saracen lords who had come as his minders to officiate the release.

Laughing, Guy swung the children both into his arms and forged ahead, striding over low hedges of lavender and rosemary, leaving deep footprints in the soft grass, until he met Sibylla herself by the cistern, lowered the girls, and pulled her into his arms.

"I thought you might have forgotten me," he whispered into her hair.

"Forget you? When I handed over a perfectly good city to get you back?"

He drew back just enough to look into her eyes. "Sibylla! Are you crying?"

"Not in the least; the wind is only making my eyes water."

"You're wonderful," he said fervently. "How did you manage it? I didn't expect to be released for another two months at least."

"It took some haggling," she admitted. Then, because she had promised herself to be strictly truthful with him: "As a matter of fact, I may have suggested to Saladin that if you were released, you might challenge the leadership of Conrad of Montferrat. Since I appointed him *bailli*, Conrad has had undisputed leadership of those who are left. This unity has prevented Saladin taking Tyre and completing his conquests."

Guy frowned slightly. "So…you want me to challenge this Montferrat for the rule of the kingdom?"

"Not in the least," Sibylla said cheerfully. "If it's agreeable to you, I thought we'd go north and help Prince Bohemond fight Saladin in Antioch. He's the real enemy."

In a few words, she sketched her plans. Except for a winter's rest in Acre, Saladin and his army had been campaigning strenuously for a year now. His forces were drawn thin, garrisoning the cities and fortresses they had captured. His campaign in Antioch might capture much of the principality and prove as disastrous as the loss of the kingdom, but it would draw the sultan thinner yet, exhausting his troops even more. All the while, she, Guy, Conrad and the other remaining Franks would prepare for their eventual counterattack. But Guy's face had fallen.

"What's the matter?" Sibylla asked. "Is something wrong?"

"Saladin made me swear an oath," Guy said ruefully. "He wouldn't release me until I promised to cross the sea."

"He *what?*"

"He doesn't want me bearing arms against him again." Guy shook his head. "I'm so sorry. I didn't know you had all these plans, Sibylla. In Damascus they didn't tell me any of this—about Tyre, about Tripoli, about all the great lords coming from the west. I thought the war was over."

Sibylla pressed her lips together. "Saladin already promised to release you in exchange for Ascalon. He had no right to ask anything more of you."

She cast a glance to the sky, where a white gull reeled on the wind. "Well. It's a good thing you *did* cross the sea."

"I—I did?"

"That's right, you crossed the sea." Sibylla lifted her chin. "To this island. To meet me."

"Sibylla!" Guy looked shocked, and then intrigued, and then adoring. "By the Virgin, so I did. My love. You haven't changed a bit; you're as brilliant as ever."

Sibylla thought of all the ways in which she had changed, but she only laughed. That was a story for another day. "Come on," she said, slipping one hand into his, and offering the other to little Melisende, who took it with a smile. "Shall we go tell the sultan's men we have fulfilled his conditions?"

His eyes danced as he bent down to lift Beatrix into his left arm. "Oh, yes."

Together, they skirted the cistern and went to face their enemies. Together, Sibylla thought, they would in time outfight, outwit and outmanoeuvre the sultan. She found that she did not care whether, in the end, she was queen or Conrad of Montferrat was king. Only death would part her from Guy; only death would stop her from protecting her people, all those who were relying upon her to preserve some small corner of the realm in which they might live at peace.

Chapter XLIX.

"Pinch me," Arwa said in an undertone. "I'm quite sure I'm dreaming."

Marta sighed. "No, it's all real. I'm sorry I couldn't do more."

"Oh, Marta." Arwa squeezed her hand swiftly. "Even if this *never* happens again, at least it will have happened once."

With the house on the mountain no longer accessible by magic, the women's quarters at the Damascus house had been refitted to fulfil their original purpose. Once so sombre, the rooms were now filled with comfortable divans, beds, cushions, and curtains, many of the priceless treasures cleared away to make room.

Marta had prepared them just in time for Arwa, Halimah, and Fayruz to arrive from the house on the mountain, whence Khalil had dispatched his eunuchs to fetch the women home. She had half hoped that the expedition would return empty-handed, but the long, dangerous, lonely journey across bandit-infested mountains had not permitted any of the women to seriously consider an escape. Instead, they had arrived at the Damascus house delighted to find that their latticed windows now looked out onto a bustling square full of people and merchants, animals and stalls, mosques and houses.

Today was a special occasion, for the courtyard was full of distinguished-looking guests—old scholars with long beards, young lords with jewelled swords, and fat merchants with twinkling rings. By the same token, the women's quarters were full of faces and voices—the gorgeously-clad wives of Khalil's friends. There was even a cousin of Halimah's who had married a qadi in Damascus and, most awe-inspiring of all, Arwa's scholar sister,

Amat al-Latif.

"Marta! Arwa!" From her place cross-legged at a low table, Fayruz flapped a hand, beckoning them to come. Beside Fayruz sat the grand lady who had been the close companion of the sultan's sister for so many years, a plain but kind-looking woman about Halimah's age, with pearls woven through the four long black locks of her hair. *Al-Latif,* Marta thought, seeing her kind face: *the Gentle.* A fitting name.

"Amat al-Latif has offered to adopt Zumurrud and raise her as her own," Fayruz announced. "Khalil will not refuse the request of such a highly-placed lady."

"I married late, and am unlikely ever to have children of my own," al-Latif said wistfully. "I would hate to deprive a mother of such a beautiful child, but Arwa assures me that this would be a great charity."

Fayruz traded a troubled look with Marta. "I am convinced she would be better off with you, my lady," she told al-Latif. "And perhaps her father will permit me to see her occasionally."

Al-Latif seemed to understand. "You would be most welcome to do so."

Forcing a smile, Marta sat down to spin; her restless arms felt so empty without young John inside them.

"You're spinning again? Do you think we're being watched?" Halimah asked in an undertone. She looked a little overwhelmed by all the noise, both inside and outside the house; it must have been twenty years or more since she had been surrounded by so *many* people. Despite Marta's assurances that Lilith would trouble them no longer, Halimah seemed uncertain whether to believe her.

"Oh no." Marta fed fine filaments of silk into a smooth, even thread. "I thought I'd make something for young John to wear when…when he grows up. Maybe a coat, maybe a shirt. Silk is longer-lasting than cotton or linen."

She did not say, *when I am dead,* because she still hoped to escape Khalil despite that.

Halimah, well aware of the bargain Marta had made with Khalil, seemed to hear the words anyway. She touched Marta's arm. "We will keep our promise, Marta bint Bessarion."

No matter what happens to you, we promise that we will take care of your son. We will love him as our own, we swear it.

Marta blinked back tears at the memory. "I know," she said. "I trust you, Halimah."

Outside, in the courtyard, young John began to wail. Cheers drowned out the squalling. Marta winced, her bobbin stuttering to a stop. She had not wanted her son circumcised; to her, it seemed heretical. Yet Khalil had announced that it was going to happen, and she knew that the Mahometans considered it a very clean and holy thing to do.

Outside, the cheers died down. Inside the women's quarters, onlookers flocked to the lattice. "Come on, Marta," Arwa called. "Al-Aziz is about to announce the name."

"His name," Marta murmured to her spinning, "is John Bessarion."

Pitched to carry over the child's screams, Khalil's voice reached her clearly.

"My friends, God has blessed me with offspring! This is my chosen son: al-Mukhtar Saif al-Din ibn Khalil ibn Hassan. May he be a sword in his father's hand."

Saif, Marta thought. *Sword.*

But not yours.

Epilogue.

When the voice began to sing, the slave remembered his name.

It was a cool evening in autumn, the year slipping towards its close. Across the river in the orchards of Damascus, the fruit was coming in; beyond them, the winter wheat and barley was now nearly sown. Inside the city, in a small square bordered by wealthy houses, the slave was hard at work breaking stones for the foundation of a new madrasa. He had lost count of the seasons—had lost hold of time and hope and even of memory.

Until now.

When the adhan sounded for evening prayer, the slaves were permitted to stop work to perform the customary obeisance. The slave did not join them, but he took advantage of the foreman's devotion to stop work and stare about him with eyes that did not quite focus.

Then, just as the prayers finished, a voice began to sing. A woman's voice filtered through the wooden lattice that covered a window protruding from the blank, massive wall of a nearby house. It was a strong, tuneful voice, raised in lament; others beside the slave heard it and shook their heads.

All throughout the evening prayer it went on, while in the white-and-gold bowl of the building-site, the sun gilded the dust to gold, and the slave stood as though he had been turned to stone, except for his hands by his sides, which trembled very slightly.

Lord, hear my prayer, and let my cry

Have ready access unto Thee;
When in distress to thee I fly,
O hide not thou thy face from me.
Attend, O Lord, to my desire;
O haste to answer when I pray:
For grief consumes my strength like fire,
My days as smoke pass swift away.

But thou, Jehovah, shalt endure,
Thy throne forever is the same;
And to all generations sure
Shall be thy great memorial Name.
The time for Zion's help is near,
The time appointed in thy love;
O let thy gracious aid appear,
Look thou in mercy from above.

"Yallah, what have I told you! It isn't modest to raise your voice like that," someone else protested from within the lattice, and then the song stopped. The protest, like the song, was somehow familiar.

The prayer ended. The few in the square, who had not gone into the mosque to say their prayers, straightened with disapproving glances for the house that had broken its silence.

And Miles of Plancy, remembering his name, and who he had been, and what he had done, lowered his head to stare at the rocks beneath his feet with wide and agonised eyes.

Marta. His lips formed the word his tongueless mouth would never be able to pronounce again. It couldn't be.

But it had to be.

Remembering was agony.

S.D.G.

EPILOGUE.

Marta Bessarion will return in **The Daughter of Troops**

Watch out for the next Watchers of Outremer book
The Shadow of Egypt

Historical Note

How we view the past is unavoidably coloured by our experiences in the present. During the earliest stages of planning and writing this series, from 2012 to 2016, I, like many in the English-speaking world, was influenced by news of the Syrian civil war and the atrocities committed by the so-called Islamic State of Iraq and the Levant; though it is only in hindsight that I realise how this coloured some of the creative decisions I made in plotting this part of the *Watchers of Outremer* story. As I write, there's a painting hanging on my wall of an enslaved Yazidi woman who was fortunate enough to escape captivity with ISIL; I bought the picture because it reminded me of Marta Bessarion. Ten years later, in 2022 as I sat down to write *The House of Mourning,* the Russian Federation had begun a brutal and unprovoked war against the brave people of Ukraine. Siege warfare of the most brutal kind was unfolding in the city of Mariupol. As I wrote about a long-ago historical invasion, past and present once again converged in my mind. I thought about how, while no kingdom or state is completely innocent, some wars are begun purely for ideological reasons by men who cannot be argued with. I thought about the horrific cost war has always taken upon ordinary people, and the sexual violence that so often accompanies captivity. I have dedicated this book to the memory of Mariupol, not because I think very highly of the book, and not because I believe that Saladin's 1187 invasion of the Latin kingdom of Jerusalem is morally equivalent to Putin's 2022 invasion of Ukraine, but because I happened to be writing about the one while the other was unfolding, and both weighed heavily on my mind.

Again, as I put the finishing touches to this book in October 2023, a fresh war has begun in the "Holy Land', inflicting unjustifiable suffering on civilians of both sides. May the Prince of Peace in our own time cause justice to flow like water, and righteousness as a mighty river.

As always, I have attempted to write this book with a high level of fidelity to historical fact as it is presently understood, embellishing my own story in the margins. While Marta, Persi, Miles, the Zakars, Jehan of Cacho, Khalil, and his wives are all fictional people, many are not: Guy, Sibylla, and Saladin; the Arrabi family; the Old Man of the Mountain; Amat al-Latif; Isabella and Humphrey; Lord Balian and Queen Maria; Conrad of Montferrat and his father; and even Balian's squire and chronicler Ernoul are all real historical characters. Even the peculiar intrigues surrounding Sibylla's ascent to the throne, complete with her promising to divorce Guy and then dramatically choosing him as her husband before crowning him with her own hands, is solidly attested by the historical sources and accepted by most scholars.

This is not to say that I have not taken dramatic liberties, the greatest of which in this book is my treatment of Reynald of Chatillon. Scholarly consensus on Chatillon is that, despite his reputation for brutality and aggression (as evidenced by his raids carried out on Saracen caravans travelling through the Negev), he was in fact acting with the support of the king and court at Jerusalem. Although in early 1186 he did claim to be acting independently of King Guy, this happened when Saladin was attempting to hold Guy and the whole kingdom responsible for Chatillon's raids; as such, this may have been an attempt by Chatillon to absorb all the blame. As far as I am aware, there is no other reason to suppose that Chatillon may have been at odds with Guy or Sibylla: from the earliest days of their reign, he acted as a witness to the charters they issued, thus lending them his full support at a time when they desperately needed it. Despite the nuance lent by more recent scholarship, Chatillon remains a repulsive figure; still, there's no reason to believe that he ever expected Sibylla to choose him as her husband. I invented that for the sake of drama, and I hope real historians will forgive me.

I have taken the risk of portraying the sultan An-Nasir Salah ad-Din Yusuf ibn Ayyub, known to the crusaders as Saladin, in a light somewhat less heroic than that in which he has traditionally been portrayed, from the crusaders who viewed him as a generous and chivalrous knight to the popular culture of today. In their outstanding academic study of Saladin, Malcolm Cameron Lyons and D.E.P. Jackson offer a somewhat more grounded portrait of a man moderate and conservative in his views: a competent but not brilliant military leader who was personally beloved by his men and capable of great generosity, the most famous instance of which was the ransoming of the people of Jerusalem in 1187. However, like many generals of his time (including his nemeses, Reynald of Chatillon and Richard I Plantagenet), Saladin was fully willing to commit what today we would describe as war crimes. Having conquered an empire spanning from Egypt to Mesopotamia, the political realities of the medieval Islamic world compelled Saladin to legitimise his claims to empire by engaging in an ideologically-driven war against the crusader states. His chroniclers salivated over the sexual slavery of female captives. He did not merely slaughter (with intentional cruelty) all the Templar and Hospitaller knights whom he captured at Cresson, Hattin, and in other campaigns; he also routinely slaughtered the kingdom's Turcopoles (light cavalry recruited from among the native Palestinian populations) most of whom were not even subject to the death penalty under the sha'riah for apostasy, since they had been born Christian and remained so. It is this more complex reality that I have attempted to depict in my novel.

For the events of 1 May 1187 surrounding the Battle of Cresson, I relied heavily on the account of Ernoul as included in the *Old French Continuation of William of Tyre*. As Balian of Ibelin's squire, Ernoul left us an incredibly immediate, vivid, and eerie account of arriving at the rendezvous at the castle of La Fève, only to find it abandoned and silent. I relied on the same chronicle for the peculiar incident which occurred on the way to Hattin, when a mob of the kingdom's foot soldiers, anxious and suspicious, burned a passing old woman as a Saracen witch. Since witch burnings are such a popular emblem of the medieval period, I should note that, by and large, this sort of thing was *not* common, and any belief in witchcraft was strongly discouraged by the church until 1486, when a change of ecclesiastical policy led to a steep rise in witch burnings and inquisitions during the Renaissance. Ernoul reflects the conventional perspective when he introduces his account of this event: "I must tell you about an incident involving the men of the host, even though it seems foolish and Holy Church has forbidden people to believe it."

The battle of Hattin, which occurred on 4 July, 1187 in the Galilean hills above Lake Tiberias, has provided scholars with hours of debate and conjecture ever since. I chose to follow David Nicolle's reconstruction of the battle, which draws upon the often confused and conflicting contemporary accounts to provide the clearest synthesis of the events.

Queen Sibylla's role in defending the kingdom after the battle of Hattin is one which is only beginning to be studied. Only in 2022 did the very first full-length academic study of Sibylla's life appear: *Sybil of Jerusalem*, by the great Helen J. Nicholson. This book is the first to put Sibylla's life and experience at the centre of the story rather than on the periphery. For instance, Malcolm Barber in *The Crusader States* follows the Old French Continuation uncritically in placing Sibylla at Nablus with Guy during the 1187 siege of Jerusalem. Nicholson, on the other hand, pieces together clues from many other sources to prove that Sibylla must have gone from her attempted defence of Ascalon to Jerusalem itself, where she arguably would have taken a key role in negotiations with Saladin, Balian of Ibelin acting as her agent. Contemporary chroniclers would have been reticent about Sibylla's role in these affairs, partly for the sake of feminine propriety, and partly because it would have been prejudicial to Sibylla personally if she was thought to have been responsible for the surrender of Christendom's holiest city. Balian of Ibelin's own reputation seems never to have recovered during his lifetime.

This might be the most challenging book I've ever written, and I want to take a moment to thank the many people who helped me create it. In 2017, Shelby Shepherd spent two hours on the phone encouraging me to tell Marta's story the way I had imagined it, and helping me identify some basic pitfalls to avoid in writing about sexual assault. More recently, Rosamund Hodge introduced me to the dark and disturbing folk ballad *Prince Heathen* which gave me a vital framework for the second half of the book, and Zamil Akhtar provided me with some essential reading recommendations on the medieval history of the Muslim world. My beta and sensitivity readers also merit special thanks for their generosity, patience, courage, and persistence in working through earlier, worse drafts of a very dark book, and I thank you all from the bottom of my heart: Christina Baehr, Rosamund Hodge, W.R. Gingell, Schuyler McConkey, Naomi Kewley, M.L. Farb, Elisabeth Summer, and Leila Ammar. Finally, all thanks are due to my wonderful editor, Lucy Holdsworth, and my cover designer, Jenny Zemanek.

Suzannah Rowntree

October, 2023

Further Reading

In any reading list for the twelfth century in the Latin kingdom of Jerusalem, certain works must take pride of place: Bernard Hamilton's *The Leper King and His Heirs*, Malcolm Barber's *The Crusader States*, and Lyons and Jackson's *Saladin: The Politics of Holy War*, all of which were my constant companions as I planned and wrote this book. Other works I have revisited include Colin Thubron's *Mirror to Damascus*, Bernard Lewis' *The Assassins: A Radical Sect in Islam*, Jonathan Riley-Smith's *The Knights Hospitaller in the Levant*, and Malcolm Barber's *The New Knighthood*, on the Knights Templar.

This is the second book I have written concerning this time period, and I took the opportunity to deepen my familiarity with the extant academic literature. Helen J. Nicholson's *Sybil: Queen of Jerusalem, 1186-1190* was one of my most exciting discoveries of 2022; it deserves to stand alongside Hamilton's *Leper King* as a major turning point in studies of this period. Part of the same "Rulers of the Latin East" series, Kevin James Lewis' *The Counts of Tripoli and Lebanon in the Twelfth Century: Sons of Saint-Gilles* provides a provocative re-evaluation of the life of Raymond III of Tripoli. Adam Simmons' *Nubia, Ethiopia, and the Crusading World, 1095-1402* was a fascinating and illuminating look at the place of medieval Nubia in medieval geopolitics. David Nicolle's *Hattin 1187: Saladin's Greatest Victory*, on the other hand, although it provides a helpful reconstruction of the events of 3-4 July as they unfolded in the physical landscape, adopts a rather superficial understanding of court politics in the 1180s kingdom of Jerusalem which has now been comprehensively disproven by more recent scholarship, especially by Bernard Hamilton and Kevin James Lewis. Finally, James E. Lindsay's *Daily Life in the Medieval Islamic World* provided a wealth of details on all aspects of medieval Islamic life.

Several academic articles also helped flesh out my understanding of this time period. Bernard Hamilton's *The Elephant of Christ: Reynald of Chatillon* provides a good precis of the current scholarly consensus on the Prince of Transjordan. R. C. Smail's *The Predicaments of Guy of Lusignan, 1183-1187* is a classic article detailing the political and military pressures which conspired to force King Guy into his ill-advised march across the dry hills of Galilee. James A. Brundage's *Marriage Law in the Latin Kingdom of Jerusalem* provided some very helpful legal background, for instance to Sibylla's coronation. Also helpful for the acclamations at the coronation, was Svetlana I. Luchitskaya's *Pictorial Sources, Coronation Ritual, and Daily Life in the Kingdom of Jerusalem.* For the description of the castle of La Fève, the site of which has been largely obliterated by an Israeli kibbutz, I'm indebted to Benjamin Z. Kedar and Denys Pringle's very fine article *La Fève: A Crusader Castle in the Jezreel Valley.*

To a greater extent than any previous book in this series, *The House of Mourning* deals with the unique experience of medieval women during the crusades. For those who may not credit the possibility of a medieval lady knight, Katherine R. Hager's very fine article *Endowed With Manly Courage: Medieval Perceptions of Women in Combat* will, I hope, help to explain some of the decisions I took as regards Marta's character. *The Antiquity of Caesarean Section with Maternal Survival: The Jewish Tradition* by Jeffrey Boss provided fascinating historical context on this procedure. Susan B. Edgington's book *Gendering the Crusades,* with which I spent a single precious half-hour one cold June day at the Hobart University, provided me with several indispensable articles: S. Schein's *Women in Medieval Colonial Society: The Latin Kingdom of Jerusalem in the Twelfth Century;* Keren Caspi-Reisfeld's *Women Warriors During the Crusades, 1095-1254;* and most helpful (and sobering) of all, Yvonne Friedman's *Captivity and Ransom: The Experience of Women,* which describes a world where sexual enslavement in the aftermath of captivity was so commonly expected—and viewed so judgementally—that merely being taken captive for a short time could destroy a woman's reputation forever. This was the case for the Armenian wife of Baldwin I of Jerusalem, who spent the rest of her life in a convent after having been briefly captured by pirates.

I continue returning to several general-purpose works to broaden my historical, geographical, and cultural understanding of my characters: *Medicine in the Crusades* by Piers Mitchell; *The Atlas of the Crusades* edited by Jonathan Riley-Smith; *The Crusades and the Christian World of the East: Rough Tolerance* by Christopher MacEvitt; *Western Warfare in the Age of the Crusades* by John France; *Crusader Archaeology: The Material Culture of the Latin East* by Adrian J. Boas, and Carl Stephenson's *Medieval Feudalism.* As always, van der Toorn, Becking, and van der Horst's *Dictionary of Deities and Demons in the Bible* and Amira El-Zein's *Islam, Arabs, and the Intelligent World of the Jinn* provided helpful inspiration for writing Lilith, the seraph, and other fantastical elements.

No historical study is complete without reading the accounts of those who lived through the events they described. For this book I have relied heavily upon Peter W. Edbury's *The Conquest of Jerusalem and the Third Crusade: Sources in Translation*, which is primarily dedicated to the Old French Continuation of William of Tyre. In addition I have consulted James A. Brundage's *The Crusades: A Documentary Survey*, Malcolm Barber's *Letters from the East: Crusaders, Pilgrims, and Settlers in the 12th-13th Centuries*, Helen J. Nicholson's *The Chronicle of the Third Crusade: The Itinerarium Peregrinorum et Gesta Regis Ricardi*, and Francesco Gabrieli's *Arab Historians of the Crusades*. Finally, Abdullah Y. al-Udhari's *Classical Poems by Arab Women* was a delightful collection of poems by medieval Arab women. The poem which Arwa reads to Marta is paraphrased from a poem by Maisun bint Bahdal (d. 700). According to al-Udhari, "Maisun was the wife of the Caliph Mu'awiya and the mother of his son and successor, the Caliph Yazid I (645-683). Maisun was a country girl who hated town life and its trappings."

About the Author

Suzannah Rowntree lives in a big house in rural Australia with her awesome parents and siblings, reading academic histories of the Crusades and writing historical fantasy fiction that blends folklore and myth with historical fact.

You can connect with me on:
🌐 https://suzannahrowntree.site

Subscribe to my newsletter:
✉ https://subscribepage.io/srauthor

Also by Suzannah Rowntree

The Watchers of Outremer Series
A Wind from the Wilderness
The Lady of Kingdoms
Children of the Desolate
A Day of Darkness
A Conspiracy of Prophets
The House of Mourning

The Miss Sharp's Monsters Trilogy
The Werewolf of Whitechapel
A Study in Sirens
Anarchist on the Orient Express
A Vampire in Bavaria

The Miss Dark's Apparitions Series
Tall & Dark
Dark Clouds
Dark & Stormy
Dark & Dawn

The Pendragon's Heir Trilogy
The Door to Camelot
The Quest for Carbonek
The Heir of Logres

The Fairy Tale Retold Series
The Rakshasa's Bride
The Prince of Fishes
The Bells of Paradise
Death Be Not Proud

www.ingramcontent.com/pod-product-compliance
Lightning Source LLC
Chambersburg PA
CBHW050104120726
47904CB00004B/1205